GREAT BIG SMILE

A NOVEL

JEREMY DORFMAN

Published in the United States, 2022.

Copyright 2020 © Jeremy Dorfman.

All rights reserved.

ISBN: 979-8-9855791-1-6

This is a work of fiction. All the names, characters, businesses, places, events, and incidents in this book are either the product of the author's imagination or are used in a fictitious manner. Any resemblance to actual persons, living or dead, or actual events is purely coincidental.

Front and back cover images were purchased from Adobe Stock. Cover design by Jeremy Dorfman.

Special thanks to Jill Dorfman and Olivia Bonin for helping to edit the book.

TABLE OF CONTENTS

I. BLAKE — 1

II. ME — 7

III. LINDA & ED — 21

1. A Simple Prayer — 23
2. Another Lull in the Conversation — 37
3. A Little Respect — 48
4. Something He Would Probably Never Do — 56
5. Let it Go — 71
6. I Really Need a Friend Right Now — 86
7. Christmas Party (Or: A Well-Earned Nap) — 99

IV. DANA & ETHAN — 105

1. The Last Thing on Her Mind — 107
2. How Little He Cared — 117
3. The Familiar Fire of Resistance — 133
4. Who Doesn't Like Bacon? — 146
5. Some Sort of Lazy, Purposeless Waste of Space — 163
6. A Normal Twenty-Year-Old for the Night — 176
7. A Second Kind of Happiness — 188
8. The Exposed, Genuine Artifact — 202
9. Honesty — 212
10. The Ceaseless Flow of Children's Bladders — 225
11. Exactly the Opposite — 231
12. Something New — 236

V. ME & JOSIE — 241

1. At a Crossroads — 243
2. A Real Photographer — 246
3. The Supposedly Unbreakable Mathematical Laws of The Universe — 260
4. Pure Moments to be Found Amidst the Superficiality (Or: Those Photos are Weeeeird) — 278
5. Eventually, Things Turn Out All Right — 300
6. An All-Encompassing Question — 315
7. The Public and Private Lives of Those Around Us — 335
8. Uncharted Territory — 359
9. Sunday, Monday, Tuesday — 372
10. The Middle — 398

VI. BLAKE (CONTINUED) — 407

I.
BLAKE

AS THE BRIGHT FLASH pierces the eyes of Amelia Zwybeski, the final child in the line of alphabetically arranged fourth graders, Blake begins to cry.

Blake and Amelia close their eyes simultaneously. She, to protect them from the stinging rush of light. He, to prevent open weeping in front of a child.

Blake is in the gym of Upper Wissahocken Elementary School. The canary yellow walls of the phys-ed classroom are covered with an eclectic mix of laminated posters. Here, a 1990s-era image of Michael Jordan with a milk mustache, asking the age-old question – "Got Milk?" There, a diagram of the long-outdated food pyramid taped next to a graphic of the longer-outdated four food groups. Nearest to Blake is a parody of a speed limit sign that reads "Excuses Limit – Zero." In here, the children have no excuse for their failures. It's an inspiring message.

In the pack of already photographed students beyond Blake's camera station, twenty-eight pairs of sneakers squeak as they shuffle against the maple wood floor. It's picture day and the ten-year-old children buzz with their temporary freedom from the classroom. A trio of boys hover just beyond the blue-screen background, staring directly into Blake's main flash. When the light pops, they scream in agony and pleasure at their temporary blindness, enthralled by this masochistic game. Normally, these screams grate on Blake's nerves, but right now he is too focused on his imploding emotions to notice.

Blake looks at the digital image of the pupil sitting before him and wipes his own pupils, desperately trying to hold back the waterworks.

In the photo, Amelia's eyes are closed, scared of the light.

"Your eyes are closed," he says, his voice shaky. "Just once more."

Amelia, now frightened both of the flash and of her photographer's inexplicably sorrowful tone, cautiously repositions herself.

"Head a little this way," Blake instructs as he points to his right, positioning Amelia once again into the exact pose demanded by his bosses at SmilePosts, the nation's number one purveyor of school picture days.

"Great big smile," he instructs her, wavering far from his typical enthusiasm, trying as he is to fight the tears.

The girl smiles cautiously. She fights with her anxiety about the flash and forces her eyelids wide open. The result is a rather unflattering photograph of poor Amelia, looking like a French Bulldog, her eyes bulging nearly halfway out of her skull, an uneasy smile on her face that conveys, *I am trapped – please help.*

Normally Blake would give it a third try, determined to take a photo where Amelia looks like a normal human. But there is no time. In a few more seconds he'll erupt in a fit of weeping in front of three classes of fourth-grade students, five teachers, and two co-workers from SmilePosts.

He says, "great, thanks, you're all done," to Amelia, who will surely be back for retake day once her parents get a look at her petrified portrait. He mumbles, "going to the bathroom," to his co-workers at their camera stations, as he turns his back to them. He runs to the boys' room across the hall with a frantic skip.

The boys' restroom has been designed specifically for children ten and under. The urinals are a third the size of the adult variety and their bases practically sit on the floor. Despite the diminutive toilet design, the kids' aim has been poor. There are flecks and pools of urine all over the ground, as well as splatches of pee on the walls. Heaps of wet toilet paper are clumped and strewn everywhere. In his current emotional state, Blake takes no time for his usual confusion as to how and why the toilet paper has spread in such a chaotic arrangement. Instead, he makes a beeline for one of the extra-thin stalls, locks the door behind him, and sits on the miniature toilet seat, which rests nine inches above the ground.

The door locked shut, safely hidden, Blake lets the tears flow.

It has been nearly three years since he last cried. As sad as he often seems to be, waterworks are rare. This morning a grief pipe has burst within him and there is no stopping the tide.

As the rush of memories bombards him – all the failures, all the rejections, all the disappointments – he cries violently, tears expelled like an incurable disease he is trying desperately to purge from his body.

He knows his break time is short and he will have to return to the camera at any moment, but he can't get a hold of himself. The tears will not slow.

"I deserve her," he whispers to himself. "I deserve this. It's not fair."

His heaves of misery are interrupted by the sound of the bathroom door opening. Little footsteps shuffle into the restroom and then stop.

Blake takes several deep breaths, attempting to quiet his sobs.

There is an ominous pause.

And then...

"Hey!" says a little voice.

Blake waits. He says nothing.

"Hey!" repeats the little voice. "Are you pooping in there?"

Blake sits still. He continues to cry, unable to stop despite his best efforts.

"Are you pooping in there?!" repeats the little boy, louder and more aggressively. He is a detective interrogating an accused criminal.

Blake doesn't know what to say.

He sits on that tiny toilet, wiping away tears, wondering how his life has led him to this hilarious, miserable moment, and where things could possibly go from here.

II.
ME

THERE WAS A TIME when the scent of a flower or the gleam of the sun or the echo of unseen birds giddily greeting the day was enough to make me nearly immobile with a sense of rightness about the world. Cliché, Hallmark, bastardized concepts of beauty for sure, but still immensely powerful in their genuine unfiltered appearance. The long cold stretches of winter could be harrowing. The short days and long nights with temperatures below freezing and instant icicles of snot hanging from my nostrils the second I stepped outdoors were enough to make me lock myself inside and fuel on syndicated sitcom marathons and not talk to anyone for weeks, wrapped in a dark blur of unforgiving emptiness and laugh tracks. But when spring rolled around and green became a color again, I received some much-needed happiness Viagra and my spirit rose for sustained periods of longer than four hours.

I'm not sure when exactly the darker globs of my disposition leaked into my everyday routine. I'm also not sure what precisely caused the crack. The stain is there now though – grim, pessimistic, and stubbornly resistant to all manner of philosophical cleaning products. It colors my inner movies of the possible future. The imagined glimpses are painted in black and white, and not the cool black and white of classic films and pretentious Instagram filters, but the devoid colorlessness left when hope steps out for a cigarette and never comes back.

As my twenties near their end and the 2020s near their beginning, I look to the future and I see restlessness, poverty, and such an over-abundance of online streaming services that I can't possibly keep up with every buzzed-about new show, perpetually out of the loop. I see solitude, the ranks of friends lost to marriage and children, and older family members lost to death. I see myself lost in the soft but unyielding grip of reality, all of my childhood dreams evaporated under the heat lamps of the actual. It's a burden to search for the truth and find it in all its unromantic bland nakedness. The truth is like a naked body without any nipples or holes. A soft, innocent but horrific, genital-less human worm.

Josie rejected me yesterday.

It was embarrassing and not because my pride felt gutted, which it did, but because my whole romantic speech, painted as the culmination of destiny's one lane highway, felt punctured and deflated even as I rousingly recited it. It was forced. I went back to longing for Hailey seconds after the rejection – no, *during* the rejection. And now a friendship is ruined because I mistook reality for a story and used my sloppy ungraceful hands to sculpt something meaningful out of life's unmoldable clay, deluding myself into thinking I saw signs that were never really there.

But what else is new?

For five years now I've been an employee of SmilePosts, the school portrait behemoth of America. For seven out of twelve months a year I venture into educational institutions in Southeastern Pennsylvania and photograph a highly structured, highly traditional glimpse of passing youth. I photograph adorable squirming kindergartners who couldn't stay in place if they were held solid by an Arctic iceberg, obnoxious acne-covered middle schoolers desperate to make their friends laugh with jokes so terrible they could single-handedly sink a presidential candidate's campaign, and moody high schoolers who would rather be publicly caned in a fourth world nation than smile in their yearbook photos.

It's hard to believe I've known Josie and Hailey for five years now. Them and the rest of my SmilePosts co-workers. Them and the perpetual influx of new hires, ever-younger faces, each continually siphoning away from the precious sense that my job is a temporary pit-stop on the way to bigger things. These recent graduates, hired in bulk year after year, their very presence dilutes my confidence that it's early enough in my narrative timeline for this to be what I'm *doing* and not what I *do*.

"You're still young," people have begun to say to me, offering an unsolicited reassurance when I haven't openly expressed any dissatisfaction. Apparently, the very facts of my circumstances speak for themselves without any input from my mouth necessary. At least these well-wishers seem genuine. These people – parents' friends, old teachers, second cousins with newborn children – say I'm young and have time and they honestly believe it. They think I am still low enough on the ladder of age to make something significant happen on the rungs above. But I'm beginning to grapple with the gnawing reality that there's nothing up there worth climbing toward.

Five years ago, I tossed my unflattering square hat into the air and whelped and cheered with my classmates, celebrating the fact that after sixteen long years, school was finally over. No more teachers. No more books. No more lengthy lectures whose lessons vanished from my memory the second I handed in the test paper. The future looked bright, or at least, illuminated enough for me to see a clear path. Following my dreams, supported by my loving, if somewhat skeptical, parents, I had attended a well-regarded film and television program at a private university about two hours north of my hometown. (Feels odd to use the word "hometown," though it's technically correct. Growing up in the residential, admittedly suburban-looking, Northeast corridor of Philadelphia was hardly similar to the quaint main street imagery that the term hometown elicits.)

I had already fallen in love with the greatest hits of cinema while in high school, but in college I was introduced to the deep cuts and hidden tracks – films that might never appear on an average greatest-of-all-time list, but which experimented with narrative in fascinating ways. Every time I was sucked into the world of a terrific motion picture, the fire of my desire to join the pantheon of great filmmakers was stoked until the smoke of ambition filled my lungs and I descended into a fit of coughing.

On graduation day, my hopes were high. I would write a great screenplay. I would win a major contest. Toasted in Hollywood as a new genius, I would move out west and my career would soar, capping in Academy Award wins for writing and directing less than a decade after I threw that stupid hat into the air.

Before I could do any of that, I needed to move back home, get a job, and live with my parents to save money, because attending a university had left me (and my entire generation) with massive, almost inconceivable student loan debt.

The Craigslist ad for SmilePosts appealed to me. The work was seasonal so I would have a period of the year off to focus on my screenwriting. Still feeling rather unmoored after my ejection from the education system, the idea of returning to school (albeit in a different capacity) sounded comforting. Plus, I liked photography, having studied framing and color techniques for film in college.

I was hired less than ten minutes into my initial interview, which I originally took to reflect my obvious value. It later became clear that SmilePosts hired any fall applicant who didn't seem like an immediate physical threat to children.

In mid-August, I attended my first day of training. I stuck the "My name is…. BLAKE" sticker to my shirt and joined the thirty other fresh employees, all hired for the yearly surge of fall pictures. The company went all-hands-on-deck each year from September through Thanksgiving when the vast majority of picture days took place. Most of the annual new employees were either too smart or too dumb to stick around post-Christmas, fleeing with the good sense that such intermittent work was not financially viable or laid off because they lacked the basic competence to screw in a light bulb. (I mean this quite literally – our photography equipment contained a great number of light bulbs.)

We met in the local SmilePosts territory office in central

GREAT BIG SMILE

Montgomery County. The office is divided into two distinct floors. Upstairs is the bright and colorful main office populated by full-time middle-aged women (full-time employees that is, not full-time middle-aged women – though I suppose they are that as well) who handle customer service, finance, and all of the other nuts and bolts that keep the train moving. They work in grey cubicles among bright yellow walls decorated with past award-winning student portraits and framed inspirational quotes. Downstairs is the photographer lair – a water-stained, musty basement office furnished with folding tables and hard metal chairs. Next to the office is the always locked equipment room, where forty-two units of portable photography sets are housed, along with any insect attracted to moisture. Our training took place in the photographer office, where we would spend all of our time.

Once all of the new employees had arrived on that first day of training, we were greeted by the territory manager, an astoundingly enthusiastic, slick haired and goateed man named George, whose sentences moved at the speed of certain predatory African cats. He told us of the important work we would be doing, "capturing memories" and "touching children's lives." A collective hush of horror cascaded through the room at the start of that phrase, "touching children's..." and there was a sigh of relief as the word "lives" acted as a caboose to that treacherous sentence. We all eyed each other with snickering disbelief that a man in a position of leadership such as George would be naïve or foolish enough to use the word "touch" in such close proximity to the word "children." Surely this was a faux pas, if not a criminal offense in this day and age. Must have been a mistake, we figured, a slip of his rapidly moving tongue. He was, after all, throwing out words in Olympic record time. But no, it was not a mistake at all. Rather, it was a central tenet of his speech. He went on to insist that we would not just take children's pictures but instead "touch children's lives" about seven to nine more times. At which point all but the most oblivious among us were struggling to hold in our laughter at the child molester vibe our innocent manager was unknowably projecting.

After the uncomfortable opening lecture, we were split into teams of five. Each group was led by a SmilePosts "veteran" photographer, one of those rare individuals who remained employed by the company despite the part-time work in December through May and the nonexistent work in June and July. These veterans were either content to collect the state unemployment that the seasonal work allowed or simply could not find anything better.

That's when I met Josie.

Neon green sunglasses rested on the top of her head and she wore a small pin, representing an indie rock band I'd never heard of. I soon learned that pins were her signature method of spicing up the uniform: a collared navy-blue shirt with the SmilePosts logo embroidered on the left pec and khaki pants you had to purchase yourself.

Josie was my training group leader. I laughed a little at the caustic humor barely hiding beneath the surface of Josie's benevolent teaching. She was ever-skilled at mocking the unintelligent without their knowing it. I listened to her unenthusiastic instructions, wanting to be a competent employee. But I was also distracted by the freckly redhead on the other side of the office. She had a smile that completely magnetized me, instantly becoming the symbol of my romantic longing.

That was Hailey.

We trained for two weeks, learning to properly assemble and use the photography equipment, learning how to properly pose a child to meet SmilePosts's standards. Then we were sent off into battle. We invaded schools large and small, urban and suburban, in expensive modern buildings with open glass walls and in dreary stone prisons from the early 1900s. We journeyed into the crowded city streets of Philadelphia and out into the open farmland of Berks County.

We set up on dusty, dark auditorium stages or in sweat-stinking gyms or in underused libraries filled with moldy yellowed children's books. Occasionally we set up in the classroom of an art or music teacher who had not been warned that their home-base had been donated to our cause. We were then screamed at by these teachers for ten minutes until the principal confirmed that we had, in fact, set ourselves up in the right place and the teachers would have to deal with our interloping presence. All day these teachers would seethe at us from behind their desks as we tried to ignore their glare of hatred.

We woke up at exceedingly early times each day, traversing the multitude of highways in five A.M. autumn darkness. We were let into the schools by custodians who were the only ones present at that pre-dawn hour. We arrived early to have a full hour of set up time for our complicated photography station. We needed to be ready to photograph the earliest arriving staff members. But some staff always arrived earlier than our scheduled start time. They inexplicably asked us whether we were ready for them as we mired our way through collapsed metal stands and a snake's pit of unplugged wires. "We're not ready just yet," we said, our eyes darting around at the clear visual evidence of our unreadiness, worrying for the state of our youth in the hands of such oblivious individuals.

Each day we were split into different configurations of co-workers, sometimes working all by ourselves, sometimes in groups as large as ten employees, depending on the enrollment size of the school. On the rare lucky days that the scheduling gods were in my favor, I worked with Hailey.

During that first fall, on those precious mornings when we were at the same school, she received me with the bitter scowl of the unhappily awoken. But as the years passed, her demeanor melted as we became friendly and she greeted me with a smile no matter how absurdly early it might be.

There is no greater satisfaction in life than the sight of a person you are genuinely glad to see, showing no constraint in how glad they are to see you.

I think about her.

Her not being one, but several. The real-life girls who've netted my affections, unknowingly mostly. The imaginary notions of who I might be waiting for, eternally unformed, eternal potential. The females who provided a road map for my longing, a direct filter of my yearning for the archetypal salvation of love. This gallery of the pretty and sweet and spunky, a small but powerful lineup of faces and bodies and skin tones I've wished to fall into like the world's softest pillow, billowing all around. Dreams, reality, all crossed together so that it's hard to know which came first. The spinning wheel of romantic desire typically lands on one for an extended period of time. A real-life person is transformed through want and dream, both waking and not, into an omnipresent cerebral overcoat, never far off from any thought stream, ready to ride the waters, to be the waters, a beautifully distorted version similar and not to the real living and breathing human I could never know even if my desire was fulfilled. They rarely ever know that they're the only show in town. The flame that sets the machinery in motion.

Hailey might know.

Josie certainly didn't. But that's probably because I never had romantic feelings for her – I only convinced myself that I did.

Though at a certain point, what's the difference?

Scientists say that every time we recall a memory it changes a little, reconstructed by the galaxy of neurons firing within our brains. Over time, our favorite, most frequently revisited recollections become the most untrue, our every remembrance an unstable game of whisper down the lane. What's really left of the time that's gone? Only a few shards of a few mis-remembered moments, standing in for the larger lost whole.

What am I supposed to do with this knowledge? How am I to comprehend a life that is constantly shifting right beneath my feet?

GREAT BIG SMILE 17

"Capturing Memories." That's what our promotional pamphlet says is SmilePosts's primary company task. The word photography first appears way down at the bottom of the front flap, as if it's a secondary chore, a bit of practical toil which we perform only in service of this larger ethereal goal of "capturing memories." As if memories were beautiful fireflies in the summer twilight and we were eternal youths running around with nets and mason jars. The phrase implies that our photos are some sort of direct transfusion of a real moment onto an assortment of 8x10, 5x7, and wallet size glossy prints. But this is misleading.

For one, not a single person in the normal context of their life has ever sat with their body angled forty-five degrees and their head tilted twenty-degrees to the left in front of a pastel-colored background. Hard to believe I know, but this is a highly structured, photographer-invented creation, albeit one that looks good hanging on a staircase wall. Second, and perhaps more important, I have instructed every single student and teacher I have ever photographed to smile. It's a part of my basic speech routine as I try to get each new subject in and out of my camera station in thirty seconds or less, ensuring that I'll get through the hundreds of students on the docket and make my day.

"Have a seat, turn your body, tilt your head, look right here... great big smile!" I say. FLASH. "Great, thanks, you're all done." I move on to the next person in line.

Of course, some people refuse to smile. And some are biologically incapable, struggling to lift the corners of their mouths in any natural manner. Outliers aside, the majority do as I've asked. They smile for the camera, accomplices in the photographic evidence documenting another contented year of their life. Perhaps some of these kids and staff members feel genuinely happy at the moment the bulbs flash blindingly into their eyes. It's a futile enough task for me to try to grasp the internal life of my closest friends and family members. I don't claim to ever understand the true mental world of someone with whom I interact for less than thirty seconds. But recognizing the real or false happiness of my subjects is beside the point of my job, promotional pamphlet be damned. I don't "capture memories." I'm not some sort of scientific preservationist trying to ensnare a student's real experience in amber. No. What I am is a storyteller.

At work, day in and day out, I go to schools and I tell a simple story over and over again. A story of a joyously unfolding childhood. The kids get bigger and more pimply from year to year, but the story of happiness never changes.

Is this a bad thing? I honestly don't know. Should photography exist only to reflect some essential truth? Is it damaging to force children into an image of themselves that may not represent their reality? Would it be best if all acts of creation were only a mirror reflected on life as it actually is? Probably not. We need our stories. We need our creations. It would be a burden to get through life without them.

I am a storyteller. We all are to a degree. Not everyone spends their time writing one-hundred-and-forty page screenplays that are thinly veiled modern retellings of second tier Greek myths, which you read again four years after completion and cringe at how you ever could've thought that what you wrote was any good, and wonder whether you're wasting your time and what the hell you're ever going to do with your life, (okay getting off track...) but we all, to some extent, see our own life in narrative terms and organize our memories and hopes in a structure that gives them meaning.

I will say this. There is one facet of truth that the school portraits can never hide.

The passage of time.

Year to year the kids grow and change, inevitably and unceasingly. The successive photos represent this unstoppable motion of reality with an undeniable purity. I've known many who seem fixed in their ways, and yet when I look at old photos of them, I'm reminded that really, we're nothing but change. We look for our place in the world and all the while, time keeps marching on.

Five years. Five years I've been photographing these tykes now.

The days quickly turned into weeks and the weeks turned to years and here I am, feeling stuck amidst reality's forward arrow.

For years I've watched co-workers come and go from this job. I've made a few true friends and I've made split-second acquaintances who are out the door before I get a chance to remember their names. I see the yearly influx of new employees and I watch the stories of all these people unfold. I look around and I see stories everywhere. I see stories that are hidden and stories that are revealed.

I see stories of passion, yearning, and attempts to seize the impossible. I see stories of despair, longing, and the mind-spinning absurdity of day-to-day modern existence.

I see stories worth telling.

III.
LINDA & ED

ONE
A SIMPLE PRAYER

FIVE YEARS AGO, on the same late August day when I met Josie and kickstarted my photography career, Linda Gogol, a fellow trainee, listened hazily to her own veteran trainer's instructions at the other end of the office and wondered how her life had sputtered so irreparably off track.

Linda had remained quiet and impassive throughout George's infamous opening speech about the proper methods of touching a child's life. She missed most of the conspicuous pedophilic innuendo that sent the rest of us into stifled fits of laughter because she was too lost in her own thoughts. She was compliant but mostly mute as she was placed in her training group along with a group of people all born in the nineties, instructed by Gabby, a returning SmilePosts photographer in her second year who was also born in the nineties.

Linda, eighties born, was thirty-three, but that afternoon she felt twice her age, so crucially separated from the millennials glued to their phone screens, completely ignoring sweet Gabby's attempts to corral them. (At least when Gabby wasn't glancing at her own phone screen, because c'mon, it's not like she was going to leave that text waiting.)

Linda wondered if she was considered a millennial herself. She wasn't sure of the precise cutoffs or boundaries that separated one generation from another. She did know that she felt disconnected from the laughing, joking, seemingly unburdened youths surrounding her.

She was thirty-three and an irritating fourteen pounds heavier than she had been ten years earlier. A stubborn squatter were those fourteen pounds. They made their home in her formerly svelte frame, filled in her cheekbones, and refused to be evicted no matter how many times she went to the gym, which was admittedly not that often, or how much she cut back on sweets, which lately was not at all. A permanent resident now were those fourteen pounds, so enduring that they ought to pay property tax. She was terrified that further weight would ignore her "no vacancy" sign and take up residence in her already overcrowded body.

Feeling embarrassed for no specific reason and plagued by the simultaneous, contradictory fears that everyone in her group was judging her and that everyone was ignoring her completely, Linda looked around the office in search of comfort she didn't expect to find. As she peered from group to group, she spotted at least three fellow trainees who were definitely older than she was. One, a tall, mildly handsome man with a beer gut, was probably in his mid-to-late-forties. The other two, a scraggly gray-haired man with bony elbows and a petite woman with fishbowl glasses and arthritic finger joints, stood out like historical relics. They must have been in their early sixties. It was hard to believe they would be capable of performing what seemed to be such a physically demanding job. Perhaps there was some sort of equal opportunity, anti-ageism law on the books that made SmilePosts employ a certain number of individuals eligible for AARP membership. They probably had to hire these older folks to prove that the company didn't discriminate. Let it be the geriatric's own choice to quit when the demands proved too taxing. For a moment Linda felt better about herself. After all, she wasn't nearly as pathetic as this Social Security pair. But then another worry struck her. Shit, she thought, do these twenty-somethings think that I'm more similar to the elderly people than I am to them? Her name, written in red permanent marker on the "Hello my name is..." tag didn't help. Linda. It was your mom's name. Or your mom's friend's name. They probably saw her old lady's name and assumed that she read Good Housekeeping and emailed people in all caps.

Linda watched the others chatting in her group. They all took the conversational lead from a charming trainee named Ethan with nice hair and a permanent smirk plastered across his face. Her second fear enflamed. Maybe these people didn't think of her as old, but only because they didn't think about her at all. They saw her as a non-entity, hardly worth paying any attention. That was the most depressing notion of all.

Dismayed, glancing once more around the room, she caught unexpected eye contact. The mildly handsome forty-something with the beer gut was looking right at her. His nametag said his name was Ed. He smiled at her with an acknowledgment of their shared odd place in this mostly twenty-two-year-old crowd. Linda quickly and reflexively looked away. She always looked away as soon as someone new made eye contact. It was instinctual and unpreventable. She had done the same thing the first time she saw Jeff at that intolerable Center City yuppie bar in Philly. He had approached anyway, not dissuaded by her shyness. She was still embarrassed that she had met her husband at a bar where people paid a ten-dollar cover to vomit on the floor.

Returning to herself, she felt bad for averting her eyes so quickly. Perhaps Ed was only trying to be friendly, desperate to find an ally amongst this crowd of toddlers. She looked back over towards him, but his attention had returned to his own trainer's instructions on how to use their photography station's touchscreen monitor. Those same instructions were being doled out by Gabby at that moment and Linda realized she should really be paying attention.

For a few minutes, Linda forced herself to focus on the instruction. But then Jeff's self-righteous grin barreled into her mind like a screeching freight train and she imagined what he would say if he saw her there.

Really? He'd say with that putrid laugh that contained no actual humor. Linda, why are you lowering yourself to this level? As if he had ever given her a chance to rise to anything higher.

"I liked your old haircut." That was the last thing he said to her as she moved out of their house. He stayed in the house, of course, because he was the one who paid for it. He always liked to remind her of this, despite the fact that he had actively discouraged her from ever working, and thus, contributing any income. He made the comment about her dark brown hair like it was a compliment to the past version of her who he had loved, rather than an insult to her current self. He seemed to think she had changed and he felt betrayed by her evolution. If she had stayed the sweet, submissive, potentially child-bearing person he had imagined her to be, this would have all worked out fine. That's what he implied with his five-word sentence about her old haircut, a wavy shoulder-length style that was barely varied from the current look. He couldn't or didn't want to grasp the concept that maybe who she was now was the same person she had been all along, and he hadn't seen her correctly. No. She had changed, he insisted. She had been one thing and now she was another, while he had remained the same steady rock of a man and that's why their marriage was over.

It was hard to imagine now how she had been so exuberantly in love with him. How had she spent every waking moment and most dreaming ones imagining his arms wrapped around her, his whisper in her ear telling her everything was all right and always would be? This man, who she now wanted to strangle with the necktie he always wore, even when they were just out shopping at Target, pompously needing to project an image of business acumen and corporate importance to strangers at all times – how had he been her sun and moon and stars and, through his very presence in her life, made her willingly abandon everything else?

He had been so charming. She couldn't see past the shiny veneer. Although that made sense because really there wasn't anything beneath the shiny veneer. He was all veneer!

She met Jeff at that awful bar with its too loud music and its pompous fraternity décor and he charmed the pants off her, literally, and she fell helplessly for the veneer, which was admittedly a great veneer, one of the best veneers, and it wasn't long before she was spending all her time at his apartment and ignoring her studies completely. She was a senior in college at the time. She was a sociology major. She had no idea what she was going to do with a sociology degree, but she loved the subject. She found the studies of social structure and the way people relate within different cultures to be absolutely fascinating. Though she felt second tier to the students around her who constantly contributed during lectures with fascinating insights that never occurred to her. Jeff was out of college for three years and he was making ninety grand a year as a "consultant." His job description Linda could never, at any point, completely comprehend, but it involved a lot of Excel spreadsheets and crunching data to help investment banks lay off employees who brought in less money than they were costing the company to keep. He was one of those people who voted both Democratic and Republican, depending on the election cycle. He was the rare swing voter the politicians so coveted, whose vote could be swayed by personality and the potential impact on his wallet. Linda, liberally minded herself, found this admirable at first. She thought he was open-minded in a way most males weren't. Later, his political indecisiveness became another indication of his emptiness. He had no real principles through which he lived his life – only a glistening image of success which he strived every moment to create.

Or... maybe she was being too hard on him. He wasn't some robot. He had feelings, she guessed. But he was also an asshole.

Within nine months of dating, Jeff had asked her to marry him. He was so sure that she checked all the boxes that he was looking for in a wife. She completed his paint-by-numbers picture of the fulfilled American adulthood. He demanded – okay, requested, but it was clear he would only accept one answer – that she drop out of school ("because what could you possibly do with a sociology degree anyway?") and let him do the work and provide for the family that they would invariably start. In retrospect she wasn't sure if she should feel complimented or insulted by his fawning initial impression of her. At the time it was extremely flattering and glorious to be treated with such reverence, but later he made her feel that she had fooled him with some false projection of a personality she didn't know she was putting on. Is it complimentary when someone loves you for something you're not? She didn't know. All she did know, with complete confidence, was that within five years everything had gone to shit, and they stayed married for another three years after that only because Jeff hated losing, in any capacity.

Jeff wanted a child. He wanted to start a family. In retrospect, she wasn't certain whether his intense desire for offspring was a pure wish for fatherhood or just another essential signpost he felt he had to hit on the success map to being a worthwhile member of society. (She had paid attention in her sociology courses.) Not wanting to become entirely cynical about a man who, at one point, she had loved, or imagined she had loved – two conditions that were ultimately indistinguishable – she gave him the benefit of the doubt that it was a little of both. Sure, he was fulfilling cultural archetypes, but he also was really excited about being a dad. He was good, if not exceptional, with kids. He was enough of a narcissist to be one of those people who would swoon over his own child, even if he didn't go all gooey for any average baby, for the simple fact that his child would be a fifty percent reproduction of himself. He wanted his own offspring to love and provide for. The joy in seeing all his impressive genetics reproduced in a fresh human being would have been overcoming for him... if they had ever managed to conceive.

Her infertility was a long and arduous drama, which drained Linda in a permanent way. For a long period of time, she felt more distraught about disappointing Jeff than sad for her own personal loss. She hated the fact that his palpitating anger over the situation had superseded her own personal pain. She had dreamed of having a child since she was a child herself. She was angry and disappointed that she had let him hijack her emotions. She was entitled to her own pain. She had let him convince her that he wanted a child more than she did and that was bullshit. She just didn't want to be reminded of disappointment and pain every moment of every day, while he seemed to revel in it.

They tried and tried and tried. Two years and no results. Then she finally got pregnant, but had a miscarriage. And Jeff screamed at her at the top of his lungs as if she had intentionally done something wrong. As if she didn't want the child. As if she wasn't completely devastated to the point of incapacitation by losing it. He apologized later, saying he was caught up in the moment. She forgave him but his anger only flared again with each additional failed attempt and each additional miscarriage. Eventually they went through all the medical checkups and all the proper procedures and, as fate would cruelly have it, they determined that he was functioning fine and the problem lay with her.

And then they paid twelve thousand dollars for in vitro fertilization that didn't take and he was immediately ready to open up his wallet and pay once more but she didn't feel like she could put herself through the whole thing again yet, physically or emotionally. She needed some time. She told him this as caringly and cautiously as she could. He broke a plate.

"Linda. Are you listening?"

It was Gabby speaking. Linda's youthful training group were all staring at her.

"What?" said Linda.

Ethan, the instant ringleader of the group, laughed at Linda's disappearance into daydream and the others followed his lead. Linda blushed a deep shade of crimson. The ten years she had over these others only compounded the embarrassment. She should be the mature intelligent one and instead she was a mess.

"Did you understand the process?" said Gabby.

"Umm... could you say it one more time?" said Linda, mortified as the others stared at her.

"Sure," said Gabby, who clearly thought that Linda was a dud of a worker who would only make her days at schools a miserable burden.

Linda forced herself to pay attention as Gabby pointed out the various buttons and categories available on the touchscreen computer that powered the photography station. She showed her how to adjust the settings of each of the three lights. The main light, key light, and backlight, respectively. She showed her how to calibrate the camera for the day, such that the aperture settings would be automatic.

After running through a number of other technical details, Gabby pivoted the instruction to the portraits themselves.

If you've ever seen a school portrait in your life you know that these photos have had a very specific look since basically the invention of photography. The camera is cropped from a few inches above the head on the top of the frame to below the upper pec on the bottom. Face and body are turned to a modified profile in order to present a more flattering angle of the human shape. The head is given a slight complementary tilt, which has the intentional effect of balancing out the turn of the body and the unintentional effect of infuriating parents everywhere when the tilt is inevitably overdone and their child looks like their neck has been severed. This is the photo we all know and love, which we've seen on the staircase walls of happy homes and tragic televised evening news reports for more than a century.

Gabby asked for a volunteer to help teach proper posing technique. Ethan, never shy, stepped forward. Linda naturally shifted to the back of the crowd, always one to avoid a confrontation even when there was none.

Gabby told Ethan to stand on a pair of red feet painted on the floor mat. She mentioned that obnoxious middle school kids (and some teachers) would joke exasperatingly about how their feet were so much bigger than the feet on the mat. (She would not be wrong.) She told Ethan to turn his body a bit to the right, mirroring him with her own body for instructional ease. Many of the trainees would not pick up on this visual trick of mirroring, which was the most effective way to get the kids to move the proper amount. Instead, they would say "turn to the left," to which the child would turn to their right. One pompous overconfident newbie named Otto liked to tell the children to "rotate your body forty-five degrees," a directive which he seemed irrationally determined to keep issuing though he was only ever met with a blank stare in response. Gabby told Ethan to tip his head slightly to the left, to which Ethan, of course, responded like most of the annoying children would, and dropped his neck all the way over, like he was the headless horseman chasing after poor Ichabod Crane, to which the others (excluding Linda and Gabby), laughed hysterically, acting like it was one of the funniest things they had ever seen. It was a reaction they would deeply regret when they later had to face child after child who replied to their request for a slight head tip with the same exaggerated head careen.

When Gabby got Ethan to hold his body in the ideal position, she showed the others the proper way to frame the camera, resulting in the ideal portrait on the screen.

They then spent the next hour and a half taking practice portraits, rotating in individual turns as the photographer at the camera and as the subject being posed. They got used to moving the camera around and attempted to capture amazing photographs of their new compatriots. It was a process that was only interesting or beneficial for the first half hour or so, then became tedious and dreary for the next half hour, and finally became a recipe for goofball behavior and intentional absurdity in the final half hour as Ethan and the others posed in increasingly juvenile and borderline inappropriate ways and seemed to completely forget that they were in a workplace, on their first day of a new job.

As the training devolved into nonsense, Linda's labored attempts to remain focused slowly withered. She slipped back into thoughts of her failed marriage (and, by extension, her failed life).

Towards the end, screaming matches were a regular occurrence. They increased exponentially once Linda decided she didn't want to be yelled at without returning the favor. This practice, not unexpectedly, only increased Jeff's anger and volume. In comparison, the moment when Linda knew that things with Jeff were officially over was relatively subdued. It was a mild January Thursday evening. She brought him a plate of her always disappointing cooking and he replied with a mumbled "chicken again, huh?" He stuffed the chicken in his mouth and continued to watch CNBC on the television, all without making any eye contact whatsoever. And just like that, something within her snapped and the wasted years poured down, drenching her with the frustration of misspent time that she could never get back. And she knew then that there was nothing salvageable in their union and that she would have to scavenge the pieces of her shattered life. She prayed that she could at least locate a crucial shard or two of her old self, which she could clean and use to start over, because there was no longer any question – life with Jeff was a dead end. She ran upstairs to their bedroom, unnoticed by Jeff, and she cried and cried. She cried for the children she could not have and for the youth which had been squandered. She cried thinking of the dead end she had arrived at, which she could only hammer at slowly and uncertainly, unsure if she could ever chip the wall away enough to reveal an open path beyond.

Packing up her things was an excruciating process in which Jeff insisted on watching her at every moment, ensuring that she didn't secretly snag any of his precious material goods. He went so far as to insist she leave behind a DVD copy of *The Breakfast Club*, which he had once gifted to her on a random Tuesday in one of the few moments of unexpected, genuine kindness throughout their marriage. He had bought the DVD he said, so he would keep it. The son of a bitch didn't even like *The Breakfast Club*.

After leaving him, Linda moved back in with her parents. Her dad, the lovable schlub, was kind enough to her about the whole thing, but her mom couldn't (and didn't try to) hide her distaste for each and every one of her daughter's decisions. She criticized Linda both backhandedly and directly over her decade-old choice to abandon her college education and her more recent decision to abandon her marriage. The contradiction in criticizing Linda both for marrying Jeff and for leaving him didn't seem to be one Linda's mom had much interest in exploring.

Career-wise, Linda was completely uncertain of which way to turn. She briefly entertained the notion of returning to school and finally acquiring her degree, but there were too many roadblocks to overcome. The embarrassment of being a thirty-something in a class of twenty-somethings seemed too much to bear. (Though she was stepping right into the shame of this same age dynamic at SmilePosts.) A decade removed from her youthful naiveite, her sociology major seemed a road to nowhere, which meant that she would have to start completely over if she wanted a degree in anything useful. Four full years of college at this stage in life seemed overwhelming. Plus, there was the absurd cost and the loans she would have to take out, any payment of which would be further delayed because she couldn't earn much money while she was in school. She didn't even know what she would study if she did go back. She was hopelessly undecided on what she might be interested in doing.

Desperate for her own income now that she was removed from Jeff's (because, of course, his lawyer had asked her to sign a prenup when they got married and of course she had gladly agreed, not bothering to consult her parents or anyone else with knowledge of what the document actually implied), she took the first job she could find that seemed like it would be mildly pleasant. It was a minimum wage position at a chain pet store. She took the job despite the disapproval of her mother, who declared in an impressively multi-angled insult that she was "wasting what little she had to offer the world." Linda thought it might be nice to be among cuddly creatures and the excited children who bought them. What could be more heartwarming than a daily affirmation of sweet-tempered five-year-olds falling in love with baby animals? But the touching side of the position was quickly overshadowed by the mountain of different species' feces, which piled up unendingly and which it was her job to clean. The fish tanks were surprisingly foul, caked with layers of unidentifiable grime. The puppies, adorable as they might be, liked to vomit and shit with the persistence of trained soldiers attempting to vanquish an unseen enemy. The parakeets and finches flew through slivers of opened caged doors at every chance of escape and Linda would run frantically around the room, jumping on and off stepladders, trying to wrangle their flapping wings into her hands, all while they dropped poop morsels in all the hardest-to-reach places. That wasn't to mention the dedicated regimen of shitting by the ferrets, the hamsters, the mice, and all variety of reptiles, the latter of which you wouldn't expect to have particularly smelly feces, perhaps because they were cold blooded, but whose poop was extra pungent. A few months in, this literal shitstorm proved quite enough for Linda and she spent her evenings searching the Craigslist classifieds for something better.

She spotted an ad for a photographer job at SmilePosts in early August. "No photography experience necessary," it said. Linda had never considered learning about photography, but she liked the idea of working with children, so she sent in her pathetically barren resume.

Now here she was, at another job that her mother said was "meant for those who are even less capable of contributing to society than you are."

"But you still have my school pictures hanging in the hall," Linda had pointed out to her mom. "That shows that this job has some lasting importance."

"I save those pictures because they remind me of what's gone," her mother said.

Linda shuddered.

"Cold?" said Ethan, at training. He stood on the two red feet, waiting for Linda's instruction.

"What... no I'm fine..." said Linda, forcing herself back into the present moment. She was at training for a job, at which she needed to succeed. They were practicing poses and giving instructions to their fellow trainees.

"Okay," she said, "turn your body a little bit this way." She pointed to the right.

Ethan rotated his body way too far.

"No," she said, "not that much."

He spun his body all the way back in the other direction.

"No," she said, getting annoyed to his apparently great pleasure, "just a little bit this way."

He turned completely around until his back was facing her. The others in the group laughed. Linda looked over at Gabby, who this time laughed right along with everybody else.

Perhaps it was all the reminiscence about Jeff, but Linda was suddenly overcome with a swell of fury. She marched over to Ethan, grabbed his arms, and physically forced him into the proper position.

"Whoa," he said, still casual and smiling. "That's aggressive."

"No touching the children," said Gabby in monotone.

(A quick aside here. We were all told at training that it was strict company policy that we were never allowed to touch the children. Surely a sensible directive in these modern times, but an immediately and obviously impractical one once you got on the job and realized how futile it was to try to explain to a five-year-old how to pose with words only. The same veteran photographers who repeatedly reiterated this no touching policy during training, dove right in, adjusting the body frames and head positions of every single child in kindergarten through second grade the moment we entered the trenches of an actual day at a school. In later years, when I became a veteran trainer myself, I was told by the bosses to repeat this same lie, which was official company policy, dictated from the lawyers on high. "But we do touch them. We have to touch them if you want a decent photo," I said. "I know, but officially, we never touch them," I was told back by Dee, a veteran photographer a little older than Linda who functioned as our assistant photo manager, but without the title or pay to go along with it. Dee and I then both became too uncomfortable with the word "touch" floating around like a soap bubble we knew would burst and I went to the vending machine to escape the conversation, even though I didn't have any change on me and had packed my own snacks.)

Linda removed her hands from Ethan's arms and her anger quickly morphed back into defeat.

Ethan noticed her slump.

"Hey, are you okay?" he asked, somewhat genuinely.

She noticed him noticing her, the real her, and she feigned the return of her anger.

"I'd be okay if you would cooperate," she said, without the true level of oomph that such a statement needed.

He was skeptical, but he didn't care enough to pursue.

"Whatever," he said.

Blushing a deep shade of red that she turned to conceal, Linda shuffled back to the camera.

She turned her face away from the others for what was definitely a moment too long, bringing attention her way instead of concealing it. Or at least that's how she perceived the moment. In reality, none of the others paid her any attention at all.

Linda briefly and unexpectedly found herself praying to God. She was halfway through her prayer when she realized what she was doing. It had been some time since she had spoken to the Lord almighty.

It was a simple prayer, unrefined in its intentions.

She asked only that everything would be okay.

TWO
ANOTHER LULL IN THE CONVERSATION

AT TRAINING, distracted as she had been by her flood of regretful memories, Linda had seemed scatterbrained to the veteran photographers. So, it was a pleasant surprise when she proved most capable. Amidst the mounting evidence of incurable incompetence among many of the newbies, Linda proved time and again to be a valuable asset. She maintained the knowledge imparted to her and what's more, she took good pictures of the kids.

George, our motormouthed manager, was particularly pleased with Linda's results.

One afternoon while reviewing her photos, he told her, "These are really good pictures, they're sitting up straight, they've got big smiles, their eyes are open, their heads are tipped the proper amount, I really like what you're doing, I really think you're doing good here, everybody says you're doing a good job, you're going through classes at a good speed, you're good with the kids, I like the smiles, I like the eyes, this one could use a little work, yeah you can't do them all perfect but overall good, really good, really really good Linda..." And so on.

Linda was proud of her photographs. She wanted to take great photos of the kids to repay them for being the wonderful mini-humans that they were.

Spending all day around children was a tremendous joy for Linda. The kindergartners were predictably precious. She loved the way they would spout out a completely out-of-context thought within milliseconds of meeting her.

"My mom's car is blue," one might say.

Or...

"I have a cat named Howdy."

Or...

"How old are you? Eighty-seven?" which managed to be ninety percent adorable and only ten percent insulting.

She even loved the way the young ones squirmed and shifted as she tried to pose them, jittery gelatin creatures, all incredibly hyperactive, but endearingly so. Many of her co-workers were frustrated by the often-fruitless task of pinning a five-year-old in position for fifteen seconds. To Linda, these little humans were so wonderful it only added to their appeal. When she told them to look at her, they whipped their heads like a snapped rubber band. When she asked them to smile, they responded with an awkward display of all their teeth as if submitting to a dental examination. It was endlessly charming.

"Freeze like a statue!" Linda would say in her fun kiddie voice – a rather effective trick in getting them to stay still, which she had picked up from Josie when they worked together.

"Now say money!" she'd say, a trick stolen from a spunky tattooed veteran named Rita.

"MONEY!!!!" the kindergartners would declare, delighted, allowing Linda to capture their smiles at just the right long-E moment.

Linda knew she would enjoy time spent around the cute, young kids. What surprised her was how much she liked the older children as well. Yes, they were awkward and crushingly self-conscious. Yes, they liked to annoyingly play with the small plastic combs that Linda was required to offer every child to fix their hair; they messed up the coifs that their parents had carefully brushed and then held the comb teeth against upper lips, pretending to have mustaches. Yes, they were way too concerned with trying to impress their peers and terribly oblivious to the fact that their lame jokes and military-issued sneers did little to achieve their aims.

And yes, many of them really needed to be told about deodorant. But beneath all of these layers of negativity, she observed, for the most part, fundamentally sweet people caught up in the difficult aging process, possessing an admirably high expectation for the future. Some adults would spot this misguided hope and want to deflate it with the pinprick of reality's indifference. Not Linda. She loved seeing the hope preserved, like an archeological treasure.

Still, she couldn't deny that the experience of being around children had a bittersweet underbelly. Each smiling face was a visceral reminder that she would never have a child of her own. Each awkward growing body was a slap in the face, whispering in her ear that the one thing she most wanted was a lost cause and this vicarious fifteen-second mothering was the closest she would ever get. The quick stabs of pain, which pierced her mindset several times a day, were unpreventable. They were an unpleasant side effect to the medicine of spending her time with children. It was a side effect she was willing to bare. She so preferred interacting with children to adults. Adults, she had no idea how to deal with.

The increasing respect Linda's SmilePosts co-workers had for her as an able photographer didn't make her any less awkward at attempts to talk with them. While her interactions with the children felt natural and life-giving, her attempts at speaking with her co-workers were about as smooth as a spoon caught in a garbage disposal.

Each morning, during the hour-long equipment set-up, and each afternoon, during the hour-long equipment breakdown, and most days, during the occasional breaks or the lunch slot that less torturous schools provided, the SmilePosts employees, old and new, engaged in conversations to which Linda found it vexingly hard to contribute. It wasn't as if the talk plumbed any depths or broached any topics to which Linda couldn't have added her two cents. They talked about popular TV shows or funny things their friends had said in a text or how the Eagles were playing this season. Basic stuff. And it wasn't as if they intentionally excluded her. When she spoke up, they listened and responded nicely enough. But Linda rarely found a thought jingling around in her mind that she felt was worth adding to the mix of voices. Then, because she so rarely spoke up, it felt as if there was a special awareness given to her whenever she did, like the chatter of a classroom silenced by a scratchy loudspeaker announcement. The anomalous attention her interjections elicited made her uncomfortable. Since she was unable to convince herself to speak up more, so that her sentences wouldn't garner the special attention given to the unexpected, she instead spoke less and less. Until, under a month into her new profession, she didn't contribute to the conversations at all.

The awkwardness of failing to converse with her co-workers was not the only hardship of working for SmilePosts.

The early morning hours were brutal. Linda would pick up the paperwork for the next day's school, and see the arrival time scheduled for a soul-crushing six-forty-five A.M. When her four-thirty A.M. alarm went off, her body went into total rebellion, refusing to budge an inch from her bed. She had to peel her skin from the sheets like a moth flapping itself away from a sticky sandpaper trap, shedding off its wings in the process. Each morning Linda would chug a cup of coffee from her parents' K-cup machine and each morning she reprimanded herself for forgetting to order a portable coffee thermos from Amazon that she could take on the go. With a portable coffee cup, she wouldn't have to burn her tongue while gulping down the crucial caffeine influx before rushing out the door. She was always so busy the rest of the day that she forgot about wanting to order a thermos until the next way-too-early rushed morning. And the cycle continued.

The equipment was another burden.

Throughout the season, every photographer hauled around a traveling photography studio made up of an assortment of nine hefty cases and one thin, but problematically long, background bag. Contained within the bulk were expensive flashing lights, metal stands to hold the lights, a sturdy rolling monopod which connected to our expensive Nikon camera, and a set of thick cables to connect it all to a central power grid. The aforementioned background was a big rectangular bluescreen, allowing for the background image chosen by the kids (or more accurately, by their parents) to be inserted digitally. This was in replacement of the physical backgrounds of my own elementary school picture days, when everybody in my class wanted the laser backdrop that looked like you were being sucked into some 8-bit computer's poorly conceived galaxy vacuum.

Every morning, Linda would lug all the cases into the school and assemble the photography station. Every afternoon she would disassemble all the equipment and stuff it back in her car.

And the cases were damn heavy.

Each time Linda heaved the light bags in and out of her beaten up 2002 Toyota Corolla, she could feel the vertebrae of her spine subtly compounding, cracking, and preparing for a lifetime of arthritic back pain. She had been provided with a small, wheeled cart, on which she could attempt to stuff the cases, including the long, cylindrical background bag, which was unwieldly in any position. But several of the schools, particularly the old stone buildings in the heart of Philadelphia, did not have ramps or elevators and when Linda was told to set up in the third-floor library, it meant carrying each back-breaking case up multiple flights of stairs. She would wake up the next day sore in unexpected places, having used muscles she had, quite possibly, never used before in her entire life.

The school staff always seemed surprised by the amount of equipment. "Why do you have so much stuff?" they asked, in an almost insulted tone, expecting Linda to waltz in with no more than a camera, a background, and a single stool.

"This is what we have," she answered, unable to think of any better response and then feeling like an idiot as the staff members watched her unload her cases, her armpits already covered with sweat at seven A.M.

When the day's end came, Linda was forced to figure out anew exactly how to fit all nine cases, plus the oblong background tube, into the Corolla. It was like the world's worst game of Tetris. At first, Linda could never remember the exact winning pattern that had miraculously stuffed it all in her car. Each day, after much struggle, she would think she had figured out a successful arrangement after haphazardly twisting and turning various cases until she could finally slam her trunk closed. And every day, she would then realize that she had forgotten about the fucking background bag, the scourge of her existence, which had to sit diagonally across the entire length of the car, completely blocking the slim remaining view of her rear-view window. She would fight with the background tube as she squeezed above the cases in the backseat, banging her hip against the door, painfully contracting her chest against the handles of cases crammed between the seats, trying to force the background into place. At which point her body was completely wedged in and the only way she could remove herself from the car was to start moving around cases. This, of course, messed up the whole system, and by the time she was outside the dirty rusted doors once again, she would have to rearrange the whole puzzle of equipment, nearly ready to cry from exasperation.

At these tough moments, she would remind herself of the things she liked about the job. She would remind herself that she needed the money and that it was so much nicer taking photographs of cute kids than cleaning up reptile shit in aisle nine.

She would take a deep breath, rearrange the cases once more, and think of the children.

"Can I ask you something?" said a male voice.

Linda looked up from the romance novel she was reading. She quickly and instinctively turned the front cover towards her lap, embarrassed by the image of the shirtless, muscular Count and his sexy maid. She had taken to quietly reading during break times while her co-workers chatted. She found that trashy romance novels were the only thing she could concentrate on in such protracted segments. Their fantasy world of pure magnetic attraction and clothes waiting to be ripped off was the kind of uncomplicated escape she needed during this uncertain period of her life.

Linda was on the auditorium stage of Weddington Middle School in the suburb of Upper Perkiomen in Montgomery County. She was set up in front of the freshly painted flats of Narnia, soon to be used for a school production of *The Lion, The Witch, and the Wardrobe*. Periodically she felt a little lightheaded from inhaling the fumes.

It was Ed who had approached her. Ed, the mildly handsome forty-something with a beer gut, who she had spotted looking at her during training. The other gray-haired pair that she had noticed had vanished from the SmilePosts office within the first week of work. Shirley, the older woman, had quit within seconds of being asked to lift the heavy camera case, falsely presuming that there would be "strong young boys" hired to do the heavy lifting for her and completely indignant when she was told she would have to move the equipment herself. Garrison, the older man, was fired after taking an unapproved hour and a half lunch break away from the school during the middle of a busy schedule, apparently assuming that such a lunch break was the unspoken right of any worker in any job. Upon being fired, he descended into a twelve-minute rant about unionization in the 1960s, which included an unnecessarily graphic tangent about the sexual revolution, thoroughly grossing out everyone in the office.

So, Ed and Linda were the only "elders" who remained from the training group.

"What's that?" said Linda after properly disguising her book. I should really get some sort of book covering, she thought. But then will people wonder why I'm disguising the real book cover? Maybe hiding it will make it worse...

"What's ratchet mean?" asked Ed.

"Huh? Like the tool?" said Linda.

"I don't think so."

Linda looked at Ed with a confused glare.

"A girl just said it," he clarified. "She asked if she could see her picture, like they all do. And I told her no, like we always do. And she groaned and said she better not be ratchet. Or something like that. I didn't think she was worried about looking like a socket wrench."

"Probably not," agreed Linda.

"So you don't know what it means?"

"I don't."

"Huh."

"Why don't you ask Mackenzie over there? I bet she would know," said Linda. She pointed across the stage where they were set up towards a twenty-one-year-old co-worker buried in her phone.

"I have a crippling fear of eye rolls," he responded.

She laughed.

"Besides," said Ed. "I don't know how to interact with these younger people."

Linda took a quick moment to feel terrible about the fact that this guy, who had at least a decade on her, didn't consider her to fit into the category of 'younger people.'

A moment of silence passed between them.

"We could look it up," she said. "The word. Ratchet."

"I suppose we could," said Ed.

Linda pulled out her phone and Ed followed suit, taking out his own device.

"It says on Wikipedia it's a hip-hop term referring to an 'uncouth' woman," said Ed. "I doubt these kids would know the term uncouth."

"I'm on Urban Dictionary," said Linda. "Here it says it's a slang twist on the word wretched. Oh, there's an example of it used in a sentence." She paused. The example sentence would be considered a straight path to hell in most churches. "Don't think I wanna read that one out loud though," she said.

"Can I see?"

She passed him her phone. He read the words on the screen.

"Yep... That is not a great thing for a twelve-year-old girl to be saying in a school," he said. "Generally, any term that finds itself in the same sentence as the phrase 'hoochie-ass' is not the most appropriate."

He gave her the phone back. She laughed.

"Well at least we've learned something new," she said.

"That is true."

Linda searched her mind for something else to say and came up blank. The conversation appeared to have reached its natural endpoint. But Ed stayed.

"What're you reading?" he asked.

Linda panicked. She didn't want to reveal her embarrassing reading selection.

"Oh... it's nothing. Some book," she said, shielding the cover tighter.

He smiled with a mixture of confusion and mischievousness.

"I figured it was a book."

He left it at that and continued to smile at her, waiting to see who would break first.

"It's just a stupid romance novel," she said, mortified, wondering what the hell she was thinking in bringing such a book to work in the first place.

"Hey, no judgment here," he said. "The only things I read are photography manuals and the sports pages."

She said nothing, still flushed, still hiding the book even after admitting its content.

"What's it about?" he asked.

"It's stupid."

"That's okay."

He looked at her expectantly.

"It's like about this Danish Count and this young ingénue maid working in his mansion... and you know..." she said.

"Sounds like a good read."

"Yeah, it's fine."

She desperately wanted to move on from the subject. There was another lull in the conversation and still he didn't return to his station.

"So how do you like the job so far?" he eventually offered.

It suddenly occurred to Linda to wonder whether Ed was flirting with her. Nothing he had said was overtly flirtatious, but one could never trust male intentions. And how old did he imagine her to be? Maybe, she thought, she should point out her age to be clear how much younger than him she really was. Though age difference usually encouraged older men rather than dissuading them.

Her anxious thought stream, wondering whether she should feel threatened or uncomfortable, slowed significantly as she glanced at his meaty hand and spotted a wedding ring. That didn't guarantee good intentions, but it mildly tempered her worries.

"I like it. I like being around kids," she answered. "How about you?" she added after slightly-too-long a pause.

"Yeah, it's pretty good," he said. "I think I'm getting the hang of it. The early hours are a bit rough."

"Yeah," she agreed. "Six A.M. arrival today was tough."

"I got up at four," he said.

"Three thirty," she retorted.

"Shit," he said. "Oh sorry – shouldn't curse in the school."

"Probably not."

"I try not to wake up the wife and kids. But at least I get home pretty early so I get to have dinner with them which is nice," he said, as if he was aware of her concerns and wanted to address them directly by mentioning his marriage. "Then I go to bed at like eight P.M."

Feeling eased now that he brought up his family, with affection no less, Linda laughed. "Yeah, I know. I feel like an old woman."

"Nah, you're plenty young," he said.

Linda felt most of her remaining battlements drop with the

complimentary acknowledgement that she was fairly young after all. But then the next classes entered the gym, interrupting the conversation. Ed and Linda stared at the coming front. Sixth grade classes on the march. It was that awkward age group where the kids were wildly varied in size, as some waited impatiently for puberty and some had already undergone that mystical transformation. Most were primped and well-dressed and ready for their yearly photos, except for the few uncaring boys in mesh shorts, who messed up their hair intentionally in a feeble act of rebellion.

"Back to work," said Ed, somewhat regretfully.

"Yep," said Linda.

She carefully tucked away her book and returned to the camera station.

THREE
A LITTLE RESPECT

THE FIRST FALLEN leaves of autumn crunched under Ed's shoes as he crossed his front lawn. He was practically ready for bed at only five-thirty P.M.

His two shaggy haired boys, Mason and Caleb, played basketball ineptly in the driveway. Future LeBrons they were not. *I really ought to lower that net*, he thought.

"Hey boys," he said.

Mason gave him a head nod of hello. Caleb grunted. At eleven and thirteen years old they were not the most communicative.

Mason tossed a layup that missed the backboard entirely.

At least they don't give up easily, thought Ed. He figured that had to count for something in this world.

"How were your days?" he asked.

"Fine," the boys repeated in unison, not sparing any eye contact for their dad.

"That's good," said Ed.

Ed made his way to the front door, chilled by a cool breeze. It was time to start wearing a light jacket to work. Summer had officially flown the coop.

He opened the front door to the quiet house. He had arrived home before his wife, a newly regular occurrence.

He brought in the mail, dropped it on the kitchen counter, and scanned through the pile of bills. Lately, he had contributed far less of the payment than he would have liked. His wife's income covered the bulk of the balance.

He put on the evening news as he turned on the oven and took the pre-cooked pork chops out of the refrigerator. He watched the stories about murder and arson and general misery and reminded himself to feel good about his own life, despite the recent setbacks.

A little while later, he heard the front door open. His wife Carrie walked in.

He gave her a chaste kiss of greeting.

"Hi," he said.

"Hi," she said.

"How was your day?"

"Good. How about yours?"

"Good."

"That's good."

"Yeah."

"Did you put the pork chops in the oven?" she asked.

"I did."

"And the green beans?"

"I have them ready."

"Thanks."

"You're welcome."

"I'm going to go change."

"Okay."

They had more or less this same modest interaction every single day and Ed didn't mind the simplicity of their conversation too much. There was something pleasing about routine and, really, what more was there to say after eighteen years of marriage?

Twenty minutes later, Ed called in the boys and they all sat down for dinner. Ed struggled to keep his eyelids open. Four A.M. wakeups were brutal, though the SmilePosts veterans assured him that as the season progressed and they went to more elementary schools than middle schools, the start times would get a little later.

The boys shuffled in, tracking dirt on the carpet, smelling like a zoo. They took their assigned seats at the dinner table, grunting like hogs, and immediately shoveled food into their faces. They chewed with their mouths open despite regular requests from their parents to keep their food-filled lips sealed.

"Are you asleep Dad?" mumbled Caleb through a chortle of pork particles.

Ed flicked his eyes open.

"What? No. Just a little tired."

The boys laughed. They emptied the mashed potato bowl.

"You do look like you're falling asleep," said Carrie.

"I'm fine," said Ed, growing annoyed for no reason he could discern. After all, they were correct. He was quite tired.

"How *is* the new job going?" said Carrie, curiously, as if her other inquiries about his day had been practice swings and now she was ready for her first inning at-bat.

"Good," said Ed, not quite ready to violate the tacitly agreed-upon response to such a question. "Good," was always the answer, no matter how awful a day at work may have been. They left their work burdens at work.

"Do you like it?" she asked.

Ed paused.

For some reason, he felt that no answer to Carrie's question would be the right one. Either way his family would judge him.

If he said he didn't like the job, they would pity him. Eighteen years he had worked for Renbeck, overseeing floor safety. Apparently, safety was no longer at a premium or, at the very least, wasn't worth his salary, and they laid him off. "The economy is in the toilet," his boss had said as he let him go, though on the news lately they had said the economy was much improved. Ed spent six months looking for a similar job but there were a shortage of floors to monitor safety on in the local area, manufacturing having moved overseas to the degree that it had, and eventually he became desperate for work of any kind.

If he told his family that he didn't like SmilePosts, they would see him as a pathetic victim of circumstance, forced into a job that was unsuitable for his qualifications and with no clear future ahead of him. They would see him as societal roadkill, unable to peel his smeared form from the asphalt.

But if he said he liked SmilePosts, then they might pity him even more. They might feel he had debased himself by settling contentedly into such a meager, silly profession. They would see him as a poor representation of the American male patriarch, who was supposed to take charge and scale the corporate jungle gym until he lorded over all of the other toddlers in the workplace playground. Instead, Ed lingered in the sandbox, sifting for turds. Or so his family would see it.

"It's fine," he answered as a compromise. "It'll do," he said, not speaking the implied next phrase – "for now" – as in, it'll do for now, because something better is bound to come up and you'll all be proud of me again.

"It's nice to get paid for photography," he added. He tested the waters with this one. He waited to see if anyone would acknowledge the sentiment.

The boys continued to eat as if the food would self-destruct if they didn't consume it in three minutes or less. Carrie said nothing.

The reason the SmilePosts ad had caught his eye in the first place was because Ed had recently taken up a fairly serious photography hobby. A little over a year earlier, he had bought himself an expensive SLR camera and an expensive set of lenses and other expensive odds and ends, all of which the lady at the store had assured him were essential for a photographer. The purchase was completely on a whim. He had passed the photography store on the way home from work and went in without quite knowing why, leaving with a seventeen-hundred-dollar tab. Carrie had been furious with him over this un-consulted money dump for a hobby that he surely wouldn't stick to, and this was before he had lost his job, cutting off half their cash flow at the source.

The irony was that if he hadn't been fired, she might have been right.

It might have been a passing interest he would have never found the time for. The equipment would have been another box of crap in the garage that everyone forgot was there. Instead, he found himself with more time to kill than he'd had since he was a teenager and when he wasn't searching for a new job, he learned how to use his camera and all the accessories that came with it. He learned about aperture and shutter speeds. He learned about depth of field and the best ways to reflect light. He attempted to photograph Mason and Caleb, but they were resistant and refused to sit still for even a moment. Thus, the photos of the boys were mere blurs of unbrushed hair and skin in need of moisturizer. He didn't bother trying to photograph Carrie, who treated any camera like a nightmare machine intent on vaporizing the last of her youth, and who snarled with extra revulsion every time she saw Ed's new camera, linked as it was in her mind with the anxious instability of their bank account. So instead, Ed focused on his mother Millie, who happily let him take her picture because it led to more visits from her son, and on his dog Chowder, who was a willing, if easily distracted, subject, and on the neighborhood trees, which never complained in the slightest and all stayed perfectly still while he figured out the correct ISO.

Several months in, Ed thought that he had become quite skilled. (Not that he had anyone else to confirm his opinion, other than his mother who irrationally praised his every word and action as if he put Einstein and DaVinci to shame.)

Shortly before he came across the position at SmilePosts, Ed began to wonder if there was a way that he could make a living through photography. He believed that he could be an excellent wedding photographer. It was just a matter of being given an initial opportunity to prove himself.

Tentative, he broached the idea with Carrie one night as they got ready for bed. He had printed some glossy 8x10s of his work at the nearby CVS and he presented them to her in a manila envelope, hoping that his wife would confirm the belief in his talent.

"They're very nice honey," she said in a diplomatic voice, through which it was impossible to sense how she might really feel.

She slid the photos back into the envelope. She turned off the light on her side of the bed. He decided against pressing her for a more detailed opinion.

"I said it's nice to make a living as a photographer," Ed repeated at the present dinner table, feeling an itching annoyance at the silence he was met with the first time he said it.

"That's nice," said Carrie, pleasantly enough, not looking at him.

Mason scarfed down a last bit of pork and slammed his fork down on the table.

"Done!" he said in Caleb's face, splattering green bean shards in his brother's eyes.

"Shit," said Caleb, realizing he had lost the inferred competition.

"Hey," said Carrie. "Language."

Ed looked back and forth between the three of them and felt a sudden ache of solitude.

Much as he tried to ignore being ignored, it was clear that his family did not take his photography skills seriously. The lack of respect was somewhat galling. Wasn't he entitled to do something he liked for once?

Ed knew there had been an invisible veil of embarrassment around him ever since he had lost his job. He couldn't challenge his family out loud on this point because they hadn't actually *said* anything negative – Carrie, at least on the surface, was completely supportive – but he still felt they were all off base for thinking what he was pretty sure they were thinking.

There was this unspoken sense in the household that Ed losing his job had been a great tragedy, so obvious in its shame that it didn't need be acknowledged out loud. But it wasn't as if he ever particularly liked his job at Renbeck all that much or that it was all that prestigious of a position. Could a job only be considered respectable if any description of its daily tasks caused the listeners to yawn and drift away, the most focused of people unable to grasp onto the mundane details? Was it a "real job" because no one wanted to hear about it? Sure, his old employment had paid a lot more than his pitiful $12.50 per hour starting salary at SmilePosts. It was a better job in that regard, but that regard alone. Photographing at SmilePosts was infinitely more engaging than mulling around, watching an endlessly repetitive assembly of products, actively ensuring that nothing went wrong or deviated in this monotonous assembly. Ed had sometimes secretly, shamefully hoped that an accident *would* happen just so he would have something different to do.

And yet his family didn't see the good in the transition. He was sure they didn't. He could feel the respect for him withering away. They kept up their normal manner with him and there was no tangible evidence he could point to, but he *felt* their embarrassment. They were embarrassed that he was laid off and they were embarrassed by his photography. He felt their lack of respect and it was unfair of them. He had done nothing to deserve being fired. It wasn't his fault. And his photography was good – he knew it was. They just didn't have the right eye to see it. They didn't want to acknowledge that he was skilled. For some reason they wanted him to be bad. His family wanted him to fail at his art. It was incredibly frustrating, this lack of respect. Ed had always been good at shrugging off life's little annoyances and setbacks, but goddammit, he deserved a little respect, *didn't he?*

"Are you okay?" said Carrie at the dinner table.

Ed realized he was grimacing – a constipated look caused by his stream of thoughts.

"Can we be excused?" said Caleb, inhaling the final crumbs of his dinner.

"No!" Ed shouted.

The others froze. There was no precedent for Ed's outburst. He never raised his voice.

"Honey?" said Carrie, more confused than anything else.

Around the table his wife and his two sons stared at him like he was off his rocker.

He looked at them and he looked at his homecooked meal and he looked around at his pretty nice house and he suddenly felt silly. He was getting all worked up over nothing. He loved his wife. He loved his Neanderthal sons. It was a good life he had made, if not an overly unique one. Maybe they didn't view him with as much disregard as he imagined. He was exceedingly tired, which didn't help. Four A.M. wake ups were brutal.

Besides, he could prove himself to them. He would keep getting better at photography and he would work for the right opportunity. His family would be impressed with him once outsiders had told them how good his pictures were.

There was time for that.

Right now, he really needed to go to sleep.

FOUR
SOMETHING HE WOULD PROBABLY NEVER DO

WEDNESDAY OCTOBER 31ST. Halloween. Most schools had a strict NO COSTUME policy.

Many elementary principals had attempted to combat the descent into masquerade anarchy by holding Halloween parades on the previous Friday afternoon – an attempt at organized chaos, permitting the kids to roam the building dressed as Iron Man and Elsa from Frozen to their heart's content on those waning weekday hours when the children's attention is already at its grainiest. They hoped that their permitted pageant would ebb the tide of unpermitted costumes on the Wednesday, a weekday specially designed for tedious uneventful lessons and quiet minutiae.

Middle schools offered no such outlet to their children. Their costume prevention strategy involved punishment rather than reward. Any student caught wearing a costume would be given a week's detention. (The specific parameters of what defined a costume were left foolishly unspecified. A number of children dressed in a mocking manner as their teachers, but claimed, when accused of costuming, that they weren't dressed up at all and sweater vests had simply come back in style.)

These schools were hopeful that the children would obey their guidelines, whether out of respect for the rules or out of fear for the consequences.

These schools were so very naïve.

That Halloween, Linda photographed at James K. Polk Elementary, a suburban school so named because, I guess, all the good presidents were taken. She was set up on the milk-stained floor of the bright green cafetorium. (A cafetorium is a combination cafeteria and auditorium, in case the word smash wasn't immediately clear to you.) At the beginning of the day, the principal, an intimidating, stout woman in a gray suit named Dr. Godrich, came down for her picture. When Linda asked Dr. Godrich to smile, the principal insisted, with not-insignificant annoyance, that she was already smiling, though she definitely wasn't. Dr. Godrich then looked at the photo and sneered, "*awful*," as if her unpleasant appearance was Linda's fault. She ordered Linda to decline taking the picture of any child wearing a costume. If any child refused to take off their costume for the picture, Dr. Godrich wanted Linda to keep their parents' money and tell the child they would receive nothing in return, and it would be entirely the child's fault.

"I can't take their money if I don't take their picture," said Linda, reasonably.

Dr. Godrich stared at her with a look that silently said Linda was weak and would never amount to anything in life, then said, out loud, "If I see one photograph in the yearbook of a child in a costume, our contract with SmilePosts will be over." She stomped off. Linda could have sworn the overhead lights dimmed beneath her as she passed.

During the second class of the day, Linda's photo station was visited by Liam Weller, a fourth-grade boy dressed as a zombie. He wore tattered clothes and impressively revolting makeup. Flaps of fake decayed skin hung from his cheeks. Rotting boils bristled across his forehead. Bloody entrails hung from his mouth. Linda took one look at him and her eyes shot desperately towards Liam's teacher, Miss Jenkins, for help, but the meek woman purposely avoided Linda's eye contact, pretending to study one of the many stains on the cafetorium floor. Linda was on her own.

"I'm sure your mom doesn't want a picture of you as a zombie," said Linda.

"No she does! She thinks it's hilarious!" said Liam, posed and ready to go.

Linda looked down at the envelope and, of course, Liam's mother had purchased two of the highest-priced "A" packages, plus extra wallets.

"Well... I don't really think I'm allowed to take your picture with you in a costume..." said Linda.

"It's fine," said Liam.

"Uh..."

"Don't worry about it," said Liam.

"You see, your principal said..."

"Here, she'll tell you it's okay," said Liam. With astonishing speed, he whipped out a cell phone (which were banned for students), dialed his mom, and handed the phone to Linda.

"Hello?" said Liam's mom on the phone.

"Uh yeah, hi," said Linda.

"Who is this?" said Liam's mom, angrily. "Where's Liam?"

"He's right here. I'm taking his picture."

"What? Who is this?"

"I'm the photographer! It's picture day!" Linda said, realizing how her statement may have sounded out of context.

"Oh right," said Liam's mom. "Well, what can I do for you? I'm very busy at work."

"It's just... Liam seems to be wearing a Halloween costume."

"I know – isn't it hilarious?"

"But the thing is... we do a yearbook here and the other kids aren't dressed up, so he'll be the only one in the group composite in a costume."

"Hilarious," said the mom. "I love it."

"Right... but," said Linda, "the principal told me that no one is allowed to wear a costume in their picture. So..."

"That bitch. I don't care what she says. I'm paying for this, aren't I?"

"Well yes...," said Linda. "But... um..."

"So what did you do?" asked Ed.

GREAT BIG SMILE   59

Linda was back at the office, waiting for the weekly Wednesday afternoon meeting as other photographers trickled in from their schools. She was recapping the Liam incident to Ed.

"I told her I couldn't take his picture unless he took off his makeup and she screamed at me and said a bunch of mean things and then I felt shitty for the rest of the day."

"Oh," said Ed. "Well that's not a very fun ending."

"No. But it's the real one," she said.

"Right."

"Part of me wanted to take one picture of him for the mom's photo order and then just have him take off the makeup and take a second picture for the yearbook."

"Yeah, you could've done that."

"I mean, normally that's what I would have done. It would've been the best compromise. That principal got into my head. I was scared she was going to like track me down and kill my cat or something."

"You have a cat?"

"No, but you know what I mean."

"Sure. You didn't want her to kill your imaginary cat. Perfectly understandable."

She looked at Ed and smiled. It was nice to have an ally.

In the weeks since their initial conversation, Ed and Linda had struck up a friendship. Linda supposed it was inevitable. It was natural for them to seek solace in each other, isolated already as the elderly people of the new-hire class. There were other older photographers at SmilePosts but they were all multiple-season veterans and there seemed to be an unspoken understanding that you weren't accepted into the exclusive veteran club until you made it through a complete fall season. Ed and Linda decided to form their own mini club.

Membership in their two-person group required adherence to the following rules: 1) Each afternoon, when they had both returned to the office from wherever they had been that day, they would take a moment to convene and recap any mysterious phrases, actions, and references that had been brought up by any young folks – students or co-workers. They would then conduct an internet search to attempt to understand this strange culture that surrounded them. 2) During that same post-day meeting, they would each allow the other person two minutes to describe all of the physical aches and pains that accumulated from lugging the heavy photography equipment up flights of stairs or down endless hallways. 3) They would sit next to each other at the weekly Wednesday afternoon meetings and do their darndest, in general, to ensure that the other person never felt too alone.

Of course, these rules were never spoken or recorded anywhere. They were agreed upon without the need of any conversation to establish them. Ed and Linda knew instinctively what they required from each other, islands that they were among the ocean of millennials.

But it wasn't only the mutual avoidance of loneliness that made them friends. The more that they talked, the more they got along.

"Do you want a cat?" said Ed.

Linda thought about it.

"I like the *idea* of having a cat," she said.

"BOO!" someone shouted, scaring the hell out of them.

The room of waiting photographers all jumped as their manager George rushed in the room, dressed in a disturbing crying-baby mask, an oversized cloth diaper, and a flesh-tone, skin-tight body suit.

"What the fuck?" said Ethan, which led to widespread laughter.

"Hey, watch your language," said George, who was absolutely impossible to take seriously while dressed as a wailing infant.

"Ethan, you can't talk that way in the office," said Dee, the veteran photographer who, as usual, was the real voice of authority in the office, despite not having the assistant manager title she deserved.

Ethan looked at Dee imploringly, as if to say "c'mon, look at him, he's literally dressed as a baby," but Dee's expression remained stern and Ethan said "sorry," in a barely audible voice.

George took off his mask.

"It's me!" he said, as if they weren't already aware. "I'm dressed as a baby," he added.

The room nodded their assent. There was no doubt he was dressed as a baby.

"Happy Halloween!" said George. "Trick or treat, smell my feet, bring me something good to eat!"

Mackenzie, who was mortified to be seated closest to George, took a rare break from looking at her phone to glance warily at George's feet, worried about how far he might take his performance.

"I've brought you all candy in the spirit of the holiday!" said George.

Dee went into the closet and carried plastic pumpkins filled with candy to each folding table.

"Please enjoy these sweets as we meet!" said George, giving himself a tremendous chuckle with his rhyme.

As the room sounded with the crinkle of unwrapped Snickers, Reese's, and Kit Kat Bars, George began the weekly meeting, diving into discussions of how they could improve their portraits, criticisms they had received from schools, and errors in paperwork that needed correcting.

"That was actually really nice. Him giving us candy," Linda whispered to Ed, as she chewed on a Milky Way. She tried to ignore George's skintight body suit and focus on the act of generosity. Ed nodded in agreement, but really, he couldn't get past the body suit.

After the meeting ended, Linda and Ed got in line to take a peek at the next day's schedule.

Each day, George and Dee (mostly Dee) sat down and solved the schedule puzzle, attempting to distribute the photographers on their roster in a sensible way among the schools slotted for the next day. It was a tricky task that involved various considerations including location (both of the school and the photographer's home) and photographer competence. Generally, the weakest photographers were paired with the best ones to balance out the skill levels. So, it was a rare gift when it worked out for two good employees to go to the same school.

"Look," said Linda, "We're scheduled together!"

And there they were. Linda and Ed, working together for the first time since their initial conversation. They would be going to Oakwind Academy Charter School in Northeast Philadelphia.

"So exciting," said Linda.

Linda felt her mood brighten. Here was a rare piece of good news to end her stressful day. Something to counterbalance the memory of the zombie's mother telling her she was a "pathetic failure." The insult kept rattling around in her head, feeling more on-point than she would have liked.

"Yeah, that'll be nice," said Ed, as he shifted aside to let the next person in line look at the schedule. "Well, I got to get home. Mason's going trick or treating."

"Oh right. Yeah, have fun!" said Linda.

Ed hurried off. For a moment, Linda felt that something strange had occurred. She detected some hard-to-pinpoint shift in Ed's mood.

She shrugged it off, supposing he was merely anxious to get home to the boys.

She glanced down at a nearby plastic pumpkin, which was still filled with plenty of candy. She froze.

You don't need it, she said to herself.

A long moment passed.

Linda grabbed just one more Reese's Cup and then hustled away from the pumpkin.

She considered it a victory.

Costumed children roamed the suburban streets like packs of wolves, carrying their candy kills. Their prize was acquired through stealth – a.k.a. knocking on neighbors' doors and politely saying "trick or treat."

Some parents, like Ed, tried to keep watch on their kids, but they were warned under threat of complete ostracization not to get too close. Ed stood fifteen yards away from Mason's eleven-year-old crew. Mason, dressed like Jon Snow from *Game of Thrones*, a show he was surely too young to watch but not-so-secretly viewed anyway, insisted he was old enough to roam the streets on his own and Ed agreed. After all, when Ed had been eleven, he used to stay out all evening prowling his neighborhood with his buddies and nothing bad ever happened to him. But Carrie insisted that the world was a different place now, or at least the news made it seem like it was. She watched the local anchors report one horrifying story after another and it made her want to lock the boys in their rooms and never let them out. Tonight, she and Ed had reached a compromise. Ed would follow Mason and his friends from a distance of an unnecessary-roughness penalty to make sure they didn't get abducted and Carrie would only text him once every ten minutes to make sure everything was okay. For his part, Ed was more concerned about Caleb, who at age thirteen had decided trick-or-treating was for babies. He was going to a party at some kid named Newt's house. Eighth grade was when Ed had first tried alcohol and he doubted that teenagers had become more responsible in the intervening thirty years.

In reality, though, Ed's mind was not particularly focused on either of his boys – not the one roaming around in his view-line, stuffing six fun-size Snickers bars in his mouth at once to prove a point to his doubting friends, nor the unseen one likely getting wasted on half a red cup of Keystone Light at Newt's house. Instead, Ed's mind kept circling back to Linda.

He felt excited about the next day in Northeast Philly when they would be working together. It was a rare treat to make a new friend in one's forties. It made him feel like a kid himself, when each new school year presented a fresh roster of new peers to bond with. He thought back to that aforementioned eighth-grade night when Mark Sterner first passed him a beer from Mr. Sterner's poorly hidden beer supply. They got drunk and all Ed could think about was Judy Grosso who sat behind him in Algebra. *But wait, no, that wasn't the same.* Ed had a crush on Judy. Linda was just a friend.

Linda is just a friend, he reiterated. Why did he feel the disconcerting need to keep telling himself that?

He felt an urge to text her. He wanted to let her know he was looking forward to working together.

But he shouldn't do that, *right?*

Ed suddenly felt very confused. *I don't have feelings for Linda*, he thought. The repeated denial itself was an unexpected violation that surely shouldn't have needed to be made.

Do I have feelings for her?

He took out his phone. He thought about what his text could say. He wanted it to be funny, but he couldn't seem to think of a joke.

As he stared at his phone, a new text from Carrie came through. Apparently, he had missed his ten-minute interval for letting her know that Mason wasn't being tortured in some neighbor's basement.

"Everything okay?" she said.

He wrote back swiftly. "Yep!"

"Thank you," she said.

He continued to stare at his phone as the chatter of little costumed kids and their parents swirled all around him. Finally, he shoved it back in his pocket, shaking his head at himself. He shrugged off his bizarre thoughts about Linda. It must have been Halloween and the nostalgia that came with it that mixed up his youthful memories with his current feelings.

He looked over at Mason, who had succeeded in the Snickers challenge and now triumphantly stuffed two Twizzlers in his nostrils to the roaring delight of his friends. Ed wished he had brought his camera with him. It was a good image.

Ed looked at his watch. It was approaching his new nine o'clock bedtime and he still needed to pay the electric bill and replace a light bulb in the den. He wanted to edit some photos he had taken over the weekend of a pretty roaming deer, but he doubted he would find the time.

The next morning Ed drove his Subaru Outback into the parking lot of Oakwind Academy Charter. He had arrived before Linda. He sat in his car, waiting for her, and looked out at the Northeast Philadelphia neighborhood, a steadily deteriorating residential community full of beige brick rowhouses and 1970s-era storefronts. The local shops were trying hard to look respectable and wholesome, but they couldn't disguise the rakish temperament hiding underneath. It was pure Philadelphia – the architectural equivalent of wearing a suit and tie for a job interview, only to tear the clothes off, chug a beer, and beat up a Dallas Cowboys fan as soon as you're out the door.

When Linda pulled up, eight minutes later, Ed felt a flutter in his chest. He made himself wait to look over at her. He felt the shameful need to pretend that he hadn't noticed her, that he wasn't anxious and eager to look over at her. After twenty-four seconds had passed (an exact amount he knew, because he was counting), he looked over casually, as if he was surprised to see her there. She waved hello and smiled. He waved back. He wanted to roll down his window to talk to her, but it was fifty-six degrees outside and opening his window to talk would seem weird and overeager. He reassured himself that he would have plenty of time to converse with her all day. Then he got annoyed with himself for desiring this reassurance.

The clock hit seven-forty-five, their scheduled arrival time, and Linda opened her car door, clutching the clear plastic bag that contained the day's paperwork. Ed opened his own door and stepped outside.

"Shall we?" she said.

They made their way through the front doors of Oakwind Academy Charter. The school, like many new charter schools, had been built inside a repurposed retail space. The parking lot and exterior design screamed Dollar Tree rather than academia. Inside, the flimsy walls which had once separated the various stores of a shopping center had been torn down, leaving behind an echoey openness. The classroom divisions had been built out of thinly erected new walls, none of which quite reached the high, exposed ceilings.

Linda and Ed said hello to the main office. They were instructed by the secretary to set up in the gym, which apparently used to be a Payless shoe store. They could tell this because of the discolored wall stain reading "Payless," that had been left where the store's signage had been removed.

The minute they were set up, the teachers showed up to have their pictures taken and declare their low self-esteem for all to hear.

If there's one thing you learn as a school picture day photographer, it's that adults, fairly universally, hate their own appearance. The staff photos, both that morning and almost every morning, went as follows:

A teacher walked in, reluctantly. If it were up to them, they would skip their photo, but the principal had insisted that every employee cooperate for yearbook and school IDs. The teacher looked at the photographer and said, "well I might as well get this over with," as if they were a death row inmate, finally accepting their execution. They approached the photographer. They figured they would lighten the mood by making an oft-repeated, but never-funny joke, such as the following: 1) Is this the camera that takes off ten pounds? 2) Is this the camera that takes off ten years? 3) Is this the camera that captures my soul and takes me away from this existence of darkness and suffering? (Admittedly, I only heard option three on one occasion and I sincerely hope that person got the help they needed.)

Once the photographer had pretended to laugh at the joke to the teacher's satisfaction, the teacher stood on the designated feet, continued their lousy comedy routine, saying, predictably "My feet are too big for these feet!" Then the photographer posed them and said, "great big smile," and the teacher either smiled for their picture or didn't, because who cares, they were going to look like shit anyway – where did youth go and why was time so cruel? Finally, the photographer called them over to the view screen to give approval or disapproval of their image, an exclusive privilege never afforded to the children, for which teachers were never remotely grateful. Upon seeing their photograph, most insisted on taking their picture again a minimum of three times. Each time the picture looked exactly the same and yet they kept hoping that somehow their face had changed in the intervening seconds. Finally, they scoffed at their own image and said cynically, "well... it's not gonna get any better than that" or simply, "horrible," and stormed off as if the photographer had insulted them in some deeply personal way.

Linda turned to Ed after the last teacher in a long line made their way out of the Payless – ahem – the gym. The room had once again become quiet. "Do you ever think it's weird that in this job, people think it's perfectly acceptable to insult our work?" she said. "We do our job, trying to take a nice picture and they just come in and say it looks horrible."

"It's not about the picture. It's about their own self-esteem," said Ed, reasonably.

"I know," said Linda. "But I still think it's kind of rude. It's not like I would go into a restaurant and order a meal and then openly say 'terrible,' right in the chef's face."

"That's true," said Ed. "People don't practice kindness nearly enough."

"Yes! That's what I'm saying," said Linda. "I don't know why everybody has to be so mean all the time. We're all trying our best."

"I think you're doing a great job," said Ed.

"Thank you," said Linda.

They sat down on the floor, leaning against the wall behind their photography stations.

"My ex-husband was pretty mean," said Linda.

Ed gave Linda's revelation of a former marriage a moment of respectful breathing room.

"I didn't know you were divorced. I'm sorry," he said.

"Thanks," she said.

"Do you want to talk about it?" he asked.

"Not really," she said, which was true. But she was glad to have brought it up. Her divorce always seemed like this insufferable weight. It was a secret she guarded tightly, though she didn't intend it to be a secret. With this simple revelation, it felt like Ed went from someone who didn't know her to someone who did –a door to her protected personality had been unlocked and now he could be a real friend.

"I'm better off without him," she said, wanting to believe it and coming close.

"I bet that's true," he said, wanting to be supportive.

For a moment Linda was annoyed at Ed's reassurance. After all, he hadn't known Jeff – did Ed think Linda wasn't capable of having a successful marriage? But she was overthinking it. He was only trying to be nice.

"What is a charter school anyway?" asked Ed, presuming that Linda wanted to change the subject or perhaps wishing to change it himself. Part of him didn't want to imagine Linda in a relationship.

"I don't know exactly," said Linda. "I think it's like a private school that the kids don't pay for. But there's a lottery involved? It's like a privately-run school for kids to apply to so they don't have to go to a public school?"

"How do they make a profit? Who pays for it?"

"I'm not sure."

"Huh," said Ed.

Quiet. They looked around the dusty walls of the converted gym and across the beige carpeted floor, which had been spray painted with yellow basketball court lines, although there was no basketball net in sight.

"What time does the first class come?" asked Ed.

Linda glanced at the schedule that the SmilePosts account rep had provided in their paperwork packet.

"Not until nine-twenty," she said.

Ed glanced at his watch. It was nine-twelve. Eight more minutes.

Eight more minutes of crucial conversation time and he couldn't think of anything interesting to say. But why did it matter if he could?

"It's pretty cold outside, huh?" he said.

"Yeah, it's a bit chilly," she said.

"Always seems like it's fall for maybe two weeks and then all of a sudden it's winter."

"That's true."

A rumble in the halls. Laughter of kids who should probably be in class. Their screeching humor was easily heard through the gap between the plywood wall and the ceiling. A bunch of "shits" and "fucks" and "damns" all grumbled together as if the word paste that mixed these swear words hardly mattered.

"I am looking forward to the first snow though," said Ed.

"Not me. The cold weather depresses me," said Linda.

"Oh no, I mean, I don't like the cold weather either. I just like snow because it leads to some nice photos."

"Sure. Yeah, I mean it is pretty."

A glance at the watch. Nine-sixteen. Four more minutes. Was that the sound of someone dribbling a basketball down the hall? There had to be a net somewhere.

"I took this really nice photo of a deer the other day," said Ed.

"Oh yeah?"

"Do you want to see it?"

"Yeah, of course."

Of course. The words warmed Ed's heart. Of course, she wanted to see it. Why would she not want to appreciate his photography. A wonderful contrast to his uninterested family.

He stood up and moved closer to her. He took out his phone and pulled open the edited photographs of the deer.

"Oh they're pretty!" she said.

"Thanks," he said. "I'm working with a new lens I really like."

"I barely know anything about photography," she admitted. "I feel like a real pretender around everyone at SmilePosts."

"Well maybe I can teach you some things," he said.

"Sure, I'd like that," she said.

The rumble of approaching madness. The door swung open and in marched a sixth-grade class, clawing at each other. The crowd was elastic, stretching and snapping back into its fizzy unfocused whole. The girl in the front of the line was fed up with someone or another. "Oh my god-dddddd, you need to stop it!" she said. Knowing kids, they probably did need to stop it, whatever it was.

Ed and Linda looked at each other and smiled. Linda turned to the class.

"I'll take the first person in line," she said.

Ed continued to watch Linda as she shifted into work mode – smiling brightly, encouraging the moody, uncooperative girl with kindness. He felt happier right now than he had felt in years. He felt like a schoolboy.

He also felt ashamed. Ashamed of something he hadn't yet done. Ashamed of something he would probably never do.

"Next person in line," he said.

FIVE
LET IT GO

ED WAS RIGHT about the quickly vanishing autumn. There were a couple of beautiful weeks of crisp fall weather when daytime temperatures were in the upper fifties. The leaves on the trees turned shades of orange, red, and yellow, before tumbling gracefully to the ground in crunchy picturesque piles. People walked around in that seldom-used garment, the light jacket, so fashionably beneficial yet so rarely appropriate for Pennsylvania temperatures, which swung from summer to winter with the speed of a pitcher's third strike eliminating the Phillies from playoff contention.

Then, it was winter. Barely even mid-November when we woke up to the first frost on the dead-leaf-covered ground and a sheet of ice on our windshields.

(Let me tell you, when you've been waking up at five-thirty A.M. to arrive at a school that's an hour away by seven, you certainly haven't been leaving any spare time in your tight morning schedule to warm up your car. You've been rushing outside after forcing some oatmeal in your mouth, never hungry at that early hour but determined to eat anyway, knowing you won't get a lunch break for another seven hours. Rushing into your car, you look at Google Maps and see that your estimated arrival time is 7:01. You need to be at the school by seven. You know that the traffic will only get worse as the morning progresses and you're determined to make up that pesky minute, because there's always the chance George or Dee will make an appearance at the school and mark you down as late. So, you certainly don't have time to warm up your car. You get in and turn the key and as soon as the ignition starts, you put your foot on the pedal and you get the fuck on the road. That's your morning routine. Except now, abruptly, it's winter, and there's a frost on your windshield and you haven't left any spare time. You put the defroster on high and you get to work with your scraper, chipping away at the ice. You struggle, using forearm muscles you never use to slide the cheap tool against the angled glass – muscles which are immediately sore when the driver's side is only halfway clear. You get fed up with the process when there's a reasonable sized hole in the ice to see through, even if the frost left on the glass could still be a dangerous hindrance to driving. You hope that the defroster will do its job eventually. You get in the car and look at Google Maps again, which now has an arrival time of 7:12 listed, which doesn't make any sense because that whole process only took seven minutes and yet the arrival time has been pushed back eleven minutes. You peer through the small, scraped hole in the windshield of ice, you put your foot on the gas pedal, and you get the fuck on the road.)

Winter descended quickly, but to Ed that November autumn seemed stretched into an epic era by personal significance.

It's amazing how time can expand and contract. Months and years may slink past, a blink of experience and then there you are, older. But a day or a week might take up acres of recollective real estate, if built upon crucial, formative life events.

That was the November when Ed texted everyday with Linda.

The orange and yellow trees were associated with the thrill of connection and the confusion of unwanted feelings. The sight of falling leaves and the feel of the plummeting temperature were linked to the invigorating tension of denial.

Ed felt a shiver of apprehension go down his spine when he sent her that first text. He thought he might be giving away the game, though he wasn't sure exactly what game he was giving away, since he insisted to himself (over and over) that he felt nothing for Linda but the deepest friendship.

The content of his text was innocuous enough.

ED: They made me set up my camera in a closet today

LINDA: What? Oh no!

ED: There's a mop in the corner. I don't think there's any ventilation.

LINDA: Where are you?

ED: Stark Elementary in Philly

LINDA: That stinks

ED: Literally. It smells bad in here

Later that day Ed was rewarded for his texting boldness when Linda initiated some small talk of her own.

LINDA: I think I'm going to have Mexican food tonight. I always think about having Mexican food and I never do.

ED: Yum. What are you going to eat?

LINDA: I don't know. Maybe a burrito?

ED: That sounds good. I go to Taco Bell sometimes.

LINDA: I want to go to a REAL Mexican place

ED: (...)

Linda watched her phone as Ed typed. On his end, he wrote and then deleted the sentence, "Maybe we could go together." He knew he couldn't get dinner with her, even from a practical standpoint. He had dinner with his family every night. How could he get out of that? What would he tell them? "I'm having dinner with a friend from work?... What friend you ask?... Oh, her name is Linda... That's right it's a her... No she's just a friend I swear..." When did Ed ever have a one-on-one dinner with a friend? Any friend? Never. He would watch the football game with Steve on Sundays and he'd get together with Al, Craig, and Paul sometimes for a beer, but he didn't go out for Mexican food with just Al. Of course, he didn't *have* to tell Carrie that he was having dinner with Linda. He could *say* he was going out with Al and Craig and Paul. But what if she called Al's wife? Or Craig's wife? Or Paul's wife? No, he couldn't very well lie to her. Why was he even *thinking* of lying to her? Linda was just a friend. Goddammit she was just a friend!

He texted back.

ED: Enjoy! Let me know what you get

[Later that night....]

LINDA: I got a burrito! Shrimp burrito!

ED: Sounds delicious!

LINDA: It is!

"Who are you texting with?" said Carrie at the dinner table.

Ed looked up from his phone.

"Uh, just a co-worker," he said, flushing with relief at responding honestly. "About the job tomorrow." *Now why did I feel the need to add that!?* he thought.

Ed and Linda's text conversation became a regular part of their routine. At first, they only wrote one another on weekdays and mostly spoke of work-related matters. But as the weather cooled, their conversations branched out and their texts spread into the weekend.

One Saturday morning they had the following exchange:

ED: Boy do I feel old

[Half hour gap before Linda's return message, during which Ed's heart palpitated and he walked the family dog, Max, at an atypical walk time because Ed couldn't sit still, much to the delight of Max].

LINDA: Why's that?

Ed exploded with relief at hearing his phone buzz.

ED: The pain in my knees

ED: Also the boys talk in rap music and I don't get it

ED: Does that sound racist?

LINDA: A little bit

ED: Oh

LINDA: My knees hurt too. They should be made better. Didn't cave people used to have to carry wildebeasts and stuff?

ED: Wild beasts?

LINDA: Wildebeasts. They're the animal that killed Mufasa in The Lion King.

ED: I thought Scar killed Mufasa
LINDA: You know your Disney. I'm surprised
ED: Oh yeah. Big Frozen fan
LINDA: Lol
ED: I sing Let it Go in the shower
LINDA: Stop it. Lol

Ed filled with warmth at the thought of Linda laughing out loud, although he suspected that people often wrote "lol" without literally laughing out loud. That was modern life for you.

ED: Let it go, let it goooooo
LINDA: You're too much

Ed smiled. Linda said he was too much, but what she really meant was that he was just right. That made him deeply happy.

He dropped his phone. *Why did Linda's words make him deeply happy? They shouldn't make him deeply happy.* He felt restless. He needed another walk. Where was Max?

During the half hour in which Ed had nervously waited for Linda's text response, she had been using her laptop in her house (which was also her parents' house, because that's where she *still* lived), looking at apartment listings.

She was desperate to get out from under the judgmental eye of her mother, whose every look conveyed a sense of profound irreversible disappointment. When she said something as simple as "pass the salt," she spoke in a tone suggesting no surprise if Linda's failures in life included an inability to hand her a saltshaker.

"Here mom, here's the salt!" Linda would say, forcing the shaker into her mother's hand far too aggressively. Her mom had gotten under her skin and stayed there. She was an exasperating itch, too deep to scratch.

Linda really needed to move the hell out of there.

The problem was that on her SmilePosts salary she couldn't find a reasonably priced one-bedroom in an area she felt comfortable living. It was hard to afford living alone. From a financial standpoint, the game was fixed for people in relationships. If you could share a one bedroom with a significant other, living in a nice apartment was immediately more feasible. Linda had no savings, no investments, and still had to pay college loans for an enrollment she never completed. She scrolled down the apartment listings and looked at the pictures of unaffordable residences. She cried a little bit. She cried most days when she thought about the future.

Linda closed her web browser, unable to torture herself any further with a life she couldn't afford.

She looked around the pink-walled bedroom she had lived in when she was a little girl and tried to figure out what do in the short term, since the long term was such an unforgiving black hole. It was Saturday morning. Later it would be Saturday night. She thought she should get out of the house, do something, see friends.

She rarely ever saw her friends anymore. She knew it was her own fault. When she met Jeff, she had become reclusive. She vanished rudely from her social circle, as if she couldn't possibly need friends once she had a man. She hadn't meant her disappearance to be mean-spirited, but in the early days of her marriage, when she felt so consumed with love, she had forgotten about most of the other people in her life, casting them in the shadows of her closet like a winter jacket on the first days of spring.

To their credit, her two closest friends weren't as pissed by her silence as they should have been. While the others faded from her life, Kate and Steph continued to reach out every few months. As Linda's marriage with Jeff deteriorated, Kate and Steph were there for her and she was glad to learn she hadn't lost them.

When her marriage officially crumbled, she became so depressed and ashamed that she once again avoided the company of others. She knew they would ask how she was. It was too painful to rehash the events of her days so the best solution was not to see them at all. She avoided their calls and texts.

She saw Kate and Steph again a few times after the divorce. Knowing she was in a bad emotional way, they increased the effort of their invitations. They asked her over to their respective houses, encouraging her to step out of her own fugue state and socialize.

These days there was a new painful impediment to her friendships. Kate and Steph were both happily married new mothers. This wasn't a problem for them. They seemed to rather enjoy their babies. For Linda, it was a painful experience to be around her peers and their children. It was tough to watch her friends having the thing that she most wanted in the world. Motherhood would always be denied to her.

It was Saturday and Linda was feeling lonely and restless. She wanted to do something with her weekend other than sitting in her childhood bedroom, bemoaning her life, and scrolling and scrolling through Netflix content options without ever settling on something to watch.

She reached for her phone, trying to decide who to text. That was when she saw Ed's message.

As they talked, Linda wondered whether she should ask Ed to hang out that evening rather than awkwardly reach out to her old friends. She liked talking to Ed because he felt separate from her real life. Kate and Steph knew about all her personal pain and anguish. They knew all the details of her miserable marriage and her barren womb. Yes, she had mentioned her divorce to Ed and yes, she was glad she had because it released the pressure of feeling like she was hiding something. Plus, she didn't want him to think she was a pathetic, unmarried thirty-three-year-old. Sharing that she had been married before somehow justified her single status. It wasn't that no one wanted her. Someone had wanted her, but it didn't work out. Nonetheless, Ed didn't need to know everything about her fucked up life. To him, she was a normally functioning human being. She liked being perceived that way instead of as a disappointing wreck that needed to be salvaged, which was surely how her friends saw her. It sucked when people you cared about thought you were a disaster, even if they were right.

After Ed texted "Let it go, let it goooooo," Linda typed "Hey, what are you up to tonight?" into the message bar on her phone, hovered her thumb over the send button, then stared at the words and realized how weird it would be to ask a married man to hang on a Saturday night. She quickly deleted the question. Instead, she wrote, "you're too much," as previously documented. She was grateful for her friendship with Ed. She didn't want to risk the chance that he would misread her hangout request as something it wasn't. He was happily married. He would be uncomfortable if he suspected that Linda felt something romantic, even if he would be misjudging her intentions.

When she stopped texting with Ed, Linda was left with the same restless craving for a Saturday night activity that she had felt since shutting her laptop screen on those unobtainable apartments. Her phone still in her hand, she scrolled through her contacts without thinking and then, against all current fashion, actually *called* Kate (who she chose over Steph simply because her name appeared first in the alphabet). She called because at that moment she couldn't stand the anxious uncertainty of sending a text and waiting for a reply.

"Linda?" said Kate, answering with concern.

"Hey Kate."

"Is everything alright?" asked Kate, surely assuming that an actual phone call meant something tragic had happened.

"Yeah, I'm good, I'm good. I just wanted to reach out. How are you?"

"I'm great. It's good to hear from you."

"Yeah, I felt like it had been too long."

"For sure."

"Ummm... so I was wondering, are you up to anything tonight?" said Linda.

Kate had no plans. She was watching Sophia, her baby. Her husband Brett was going out for a friend's bachelor party.

"He swears it's going to be a quiet evening of intellectual conversation but needless to say, I'll be watching his Instagram closely. He has a tendency to drink and post," said Kate.

"Oh," said Linda.

"But you should come over! Me and Sophia would love to have you. I was planning on ordering Chinese. Mu Shu Pork! My favorite!"

That night Linda went to Kate's. Her friend gave her a big hug on arrival.

"It's so good to see you!" she said and seemed to mean it.

Sophia was one and a half. In those eighteen months of parenthood Kate's house had transitioned from its pre-child state of immaculate organization to a haphazard play pen of tactile toys. There were soft, squeezable toddler books, ridged rattles, and magnetized puzzle pieces spread across the floor in every room.

"Sorry for the mess!" said Kate in a tone that conveyed she wasn't really sorry at all, because the mess was a direct result of her daughter, who was the love of her life.

They settled in. They exchanged small talk. They caught up. They ordered Chinese food and then waited an hour and fifteen minutes for it to arrive. Linda asked about Sophia, who was adorable, and Kate happily talked about all the cute little things her daughter did, gushing over every detail. Linda played with Sophia, who was nearing her bedtime. Sophia was at the age where she could understand a great deal of what Linda said but didn't have the ability to express herself in response. Linda got a kick out of asking the little girl to bring her various objects. Sophia would pass Linda her toys and smile, delighted by her own ability to share. Linda felt the usual mixture of love for her longtime friend's child and deeply bitter envy, accompanied by the guilt that such a pure little human could inspire any bad feelings. The experience was a lot to take. After playing with Sophia for a while, Linda excused herself to the bathroom. There she cried small tears at her own piteous rage. She wasn't sure exactly who she was angry at. God, she supposed. Jeff, for sure. Kate, for having what she wanted, though Linda thought it was unfair of herself to feel that way. She kept the sound of her crying quiet and wiped her face dry. *Stupid. So stupid*, she thought. She made herself calm down and turned to leave the bathroom when she awkwardly realized she had to pee. She debated ignoring her bladder since she had already been in the bathroom for an uncomfortably long period of time. But then, she figured it would be worse if her bladder started hurting so much that she had to run to the bathroom awkwardly again after ten minutes, so she stayed and peed, though she knew her friend would incorrectly assume she had been going number two from the amount of time she had been in there.

When she reemerged from the bathroom, Kate asked Linda how the new job was going. Linda told her about SmilePosts. She spoke about all of the quirks and joys of the job. She told Kate that she was surprisingly happy with her new profession.

"That's great," said Kate. "I'm glad to hear it."

Linda's phone buzzed. She glanced at it.

"Speaking of SmilePosts," she said.

It was Ed. He had just texted her: "Let it go is really stuck in my head now."

"It's my friend Ed," said Linda. "He's one of my co-workers."

"Ah. Tell me about Ed."

"He's a nice guy. Most of the people there are like right out of college, so we kind of bonded since we're a little older."

"I see," said Kate, in an openly curious tone. "New *friend*, huh?" She used the word "friend" to imply that Ed might be something more.

The phone buzzed again. A follow up text from Ed. "That's pretty embarrassing, I guess," he wrote.

"Yes, friend," said Linda. "It's not like that."

"Mmmmhmmmm," said Kate suggestively.

"No really," said Linda. "He's married."

"Oh. He's married," said Kate, now more concerned than intrigued. "But he's texting *you* on a Saturday night?"

"He's just following up on a conversation from this morning."

"He texted you this morning too?"

"Yeah, but we text a lot."

"And you don't think that's at all weird that a married man is texting his attractive female co-worker all the time?"

"I don't know that I'd say I'm attractive, and anyway—"

"Of course you are honey."

"—and we're friends."

"*We're* friends. We don't text all the time."

"It's different."

"Yeah, we've been best friends since seventh grade and this is a married man who probably wants to get in your pants. That's the difference."

"You don't know him," said Linda, getting angry.

Kate paused. She let the interaction breathe for a moment.

"Sorry. Look, obviously, I don't know the full situation. I'm only asking if you've considered the possibility that he might be interested in you as more than a friend."

"Well... yeah, the thought has crossed my mind."

"Okay then."

"But really. He loves his family. He talks about them very fondly."

"I'm just saying, you never know. He could love his family and also be hitting on you."

"I really don't think he thinks about me that way."

"Okay."

They were quiet. Sophia walked over with a doll and offered it to Linda.

"Thanks," said Linda. She held the doll. She looked at the lifeless baby in her arms and she was thrust into a swirl of confusing questions. Did Ed have feelings for her? And how could an inanimate doll make her feel so sad?

"Do you like him?" Kate asked tentatively.

"Just as a friend," said Linda. "He's like more than ten years older than me. It's nice to have a friend at work. Somebody to talk to."

"Okay, okay," said Kate, on the retreat.

Linda glanced down at her phone.

"You want to respond to him, don't you?" said Kate.

"Yeah, but now it's weird," said Linda.

Kate laughed. "It's fine, go ahead. I won't think anything of it."

Linda didn't believe Kate, but she unlocked her phone and sent Ed a quick response anyway. She didn't want to leave him hanging. "Hey, it's a good song," she wrote in response to his "Let it Go" fandom.

"Is it alright if I ask you a related follow up question?" said Kate.

"Umm, yeah," said Linda, not sure what to expect.

"Have you dated anyone since Jeff?"

The question caught Linda off guard, though she supposed it shouldn't have.

"Where's that Chinese food already?" Linda heard herself say.

"Okay," said Kate, resigned. "You don't have to answer if you don't want to."

"No, I'm just hungry."

"Yeah, me too, I don't know what's taking so long."

"I haven't dated anyone," said Linda.

"Like you haven't dated anyone, or you haven't been on *any* dates?"

"What's the difference?"

"A date is like a single date. Dating someone means you're like, going on dates with them on a regular basis."

"Maybe the delivery guy got into an accident," said Linda.

"What a horrible thing to say. God forbid," said Kate.

"I haven't been on any dates," said Linda.

"Haven't you wanted to get back out there?"

"It is kind of a rainy night."

"What?"

"For driving. The roads are slick. Those delivery guys sometimes speed around delivering all their orders. It wouldn't be a surprise if they were driving recklessly in the rain. Easy way to get into an accident."

"I'm only saying..." said Kate, trying to keep the conversation on track, "it's been how long exactly since you and Jeff got divorced? A year?"

Linda avoided eye contact. She looked down at the doll still in her hands. The plastic baby offered no support. "Like fifteen months."

"Aren't you feeling lonely?"

"Thanks Kate," said Linda bitterly.

"I'm sorry. That's not how I meant it. What I meant is that you're a great catch and just because your marriage didn't work out, I don't want you to give up on finding somebody."

"I know," said Linda, asserting agreement but not sounding convinced.

"So, you haven't been on a single date?"

"Maybe we should call the restaurant. Make sure the delivery guy is okay."

"Linda."

"No, I haven't. I haven't wanted to, okay?"

Kate looked at her friend with concern. Linda wished that she had stayed home.

"Okay," said Kate.

There was a long moment of quiet. Linda fought her feelings of depression and worthlessness. She wondered if they were worth expressing out loud. She wondered if it might help to share those profane simmering feelings that bubbled within her continuously like the destructive magma of an active volcano.

Linda braced herself. She took a big breath.

"The truth is I think Jeff kind of messed me up. He—"

Right then Sophia started wailing. She had tripped over a pile of blocks and banged her knee on the ground. Kate leaped into action.

"Oh honey," Kate said to Sophia. She picked up her baby and held her tight as she cried. "It's okay. It's okay. You're okay."

Linda watched and waited while Sophia slowly settled down, feeling frustrated by the interruption when she was ready to spill her guts.

"I'm sorry," said Kate, finally turning her attention back to Linda as Sophia stopped crying. "What were you saying?"

Linda took a deep breath. She began again.

"I was saying... the truth is that I think Jeff kind of messed me up. After all the things he said to me, I can't help feeling that I'm kind of deeply unworthy of—"

The doorbell rang. Several times in a row. One push of the button wasn't enough for the tardy deliver guy.

"I'm sorry," said Kate.

"No please get it, I'm starving," said Linda, exasperated.

Kate put Sophia down, but the toddler started crying again immediately so she picked her back up.

"I'm sorry," said Kate. "Could you get the food?"

"Yeah sure," said Linda.

The doorbell rang again.

"We're coming!" Linda shouted. She looked down at the doll still in her lap and tossed it aside like a discarded bill she needed to pay, but wouldn't.

Linda opened the door. The delivery man waited with the food. Linda wanted to say something biting and sarcastic like "took you long enough," but her non-confrontational instincts took over and she politely paid him with a full twenty percent tip. "Thanks," she said and brought the food inside.

"Yum. I'm starving," said Kate, who was still trying to calm down Sophia. "She's ready for bed. I need to tuck her in and read to her. I'm really sorry. Can you put the food out and press pause on what you were saying? I really want to hear it."

"Yeah of course, it's fine," said Linda.

Kate put Sophia to bed while Linda sat at her friend's dinner table and ate lo mein alone.

Linda looked at her phone. Ed had responded, saying, "Maybe I should sing it at karaoke some time."

Linda smiled and responded back. "I would love to witness that."

It was nice being friends with Ed. There wasn't any baggage or judgment. There was only kindness and companionship. Linda wouldn't let any of Kate's worries bother her. She needed Ed right now. She needed his friendship, no matter what Kate said. And despite Kate's encouragement, she had no desire to be romantically involved with anyone right now. It was too hard. She didn't want to face those pains again.

Eventually Kate emerged from Sophia's room and begged Linda to resume what she had been saying about Jeff. But Linda wasn't in the mood anymore and she repeatedly rebuked Kate's efforts until she finally gave up. They ate the Chinese food and they watched some TV. Linda excused herself early, claiming that her sleep schedule had been thrown off from all of the SmilePosts five A.M. wake up calls. This was true. But it was not the reason she wanted to leave.

SIX
I REALLY NEED A FRIEND RIGHT NOW

THANKSGIVING CAME AND WENT. In early December, the all-consuming work schedule shrunk into a smattering of small jobs. The hours were depleted to the point where Linda and Ed could barely be considered part time.

After Thanksgiving, most of the jobs were not full picture days, but retake days for students (or more accurately – their parents) who judged their original photographs to be unworthy and wanted a second go-round.

The majority of the retake jobs were assigned to the veteran photographers who George and Dee trusted. Only occasionally would they enlist the help of proven newbies like Ed and Linda, when a particular day's retake schedule was stacked.

With less days on the schedule, there were far fewer opportunities for Ed and Linda to see each other in person. This drove Ed into a mild panic. (*Even though he didn't have romantic feelings for her*, he swore, over and over to himself.)

Ed would glance at the schedule on George's desk and feel an ache as he saw the scattered assignment of his own name, never on the same day as Linda's.

His texting output increased tenfold.

When Linda was at home, shielding herself from the December chill, feeling like she should be looking at job listings to find something more permanent, but instead rewatching *The Office* on Netflix, she would get texts from Ed. He would be at a school, on a retake. He would tell her about the perfectly adequate picture that a middle school girl wanted redone because she "looked like a shitburger." Linda wrote back "LOL," in all caps, actually laughing out loud in a rare instance of the "LOL" acronym used truthfully, not that Ed had any way of verifying.

When Linda was at an eerily quiet fortress of a school in West Philadelphia, doing a retake, feeling lonely, isolated, and bored, she would get texts from Ed. Only nine-thirty A.M. and he would write her, while off work, to ask her how her retake was going. She told him it was boring because barely any kids had bought packages on the original day and only one person had arrived for a retake in the half hour she'd been set up. He sent her a cute video of a dancing monkey to make her feel less bored. It occurred to Linda that as much they joked about their advanced age and the cluelessness of millennial culture, Ed was acting like a millennial himself. Where did he even find that dancing monkey video? Linda wondered.

(For the record, Ed found the video by typing "entertaining video" on Google on his home laptop, then emailing himself a YouTube link, then frantically trying to figure out how to copy and paste a link onto a smart phone – which he had never done before. He had to go back to YouTube and watch an instructional video on how to copy and paste links on a phone in order to complete the task.)

Ed successfully kept his text sessions with Linda from his wife (though he insisted to himself that he didn't have anything to hide), but Carrie did notice the disappearance of his work hours.

One night, after dinner, as Ed washed the evening's dishes, Carrie approached him to discuss the subject.

"They don't seem to be giving you a lot of work right now," she said.

"Yeah, they said there's not a lot of full-day jobs after Thanksgiving. Mostly retakes. But apparently it picks back up in the spring."

"The spring?"

"Yeah."

"When exactly in the spring?"

"I don't know. March?"

"March?"

"Yes, that's what I said."

"I think that pan is clean by now," said Carrie.

Ed looked down. He had been intensely scrubbing a single pan in violent counterclockwise circles ever since Carrie had begun the conversation. He attacked the pan like he was scraping off a disease that could bring about human extinction.

"Oh," he said. "Yeah, I guess so."

He placed the pan in the drying rack and picked up the next plate in the sudsy sink.

"Have you thought about, maybe, seeing what else is out there?" said Carrie.

Ed froze, clumps of crusted marinara sauce still stuck to the plate in his hand.

"What else is out there?" he said.

Linda's smiling face flashed through his head. Could Carrie have seen the texts?

"Yeah," said Carrie. "Like, you know, take a look to see if there's anything interesting in the job listings. Try to find something a little more… full time?"

"Oh." Ed returned to the plate. He grabbed the steel wool to scrape off the marinara.

Carrie waited for a longer response. She was clearly trying to be patient, but the effort of her patience was too obvious and it pissed Ed off. She spoke to him in the same quiet condescending manner she used with the boys when they were misbehaving. He silently continued washing.

"We have kids to support," she said.

"I haven't forgotten about our kids."

"I'm not saying that you did."

"Good. Because I haven't. They're hard to miss."

An unidentified crash was heard from Mason's bedroom, as if to confirm Ed's point.

"Then what are you saying?" said Carrie. "I don't understand your reluctance to look for a real job. Explain it to me."

"SmilePosts is a real job."

"Well it's not a full-time job. Or a job with a decent salary."

"I like photography."

"No one is saying you can't have your hobby."

For a split-second Ed yanked the plate he was holding upwards as if he were about to smash it onto the counter in a hundred pieces. He composed himself before the act of destruction. He gently placed the plate back in the sink. He turned off the water and turned towards Carrie.

"You don't have to say it like that," he said.

"Say what like what?"

"A hobby."

"Is that not what it is?"

"You talk about my photography like I'm a boy collecting stamps."

"I don't think boys collect stamps anymore. This isn't the 1950s. Now boys play video games and watch porn when they think their parents aren't looking."

"That's not the point – wait, have the boys been watching porn?"

"Of course."

Another bang from Mason's room. What exactly was he doing up there?

"What—" This was getting off track. Ed would deal with the boys' puberty later.

"Photography is not a hobby," said Ed.

"Then what is it?"

"It's a profession. A career."

"You're making twelve dollars an hour and working fifteen hours a week," said Carrie.

"I was working fifty hours with overtime in October," said Ed.

"Yeah, that was October. This is now."

"That's not what you mean though is it?"

"What?"

"You don't believe in me. You don't think my photography is any good."

"I didn't say that."

"But you think it!"

"I don't. I think it's good. I just don't think it's easy to make a living taking pictures of trees and your mother."

"Obviously, I'm not selling *those* pictures," said Ed, increasingly annoyed and defensive. "Although I could. The nature ones anyway. I could go to some of those street fairs they have in the city in the spring."

"The spring again. I guess all our problems will be solved in the spring," said Carrie.

"A lot of people at work photograph weddings on the side. There's no reason I can't do that too."

"How easy do you think it is to get booked to photograph a wedding?"

"I don't know, but I won't know unless I try."

Ed's tone had abruptly shifted from irritable to discouraged. His wife thought his dreams were delusional and it stung. He was entitled to want something more from life than a boring, exhausting nine-to-five job.

Carrie saw his hurt expression. She decided to pump the brakes, but wanted to be certain that her point had been conveyed.

"Okay," she said. "We can talk more about this later. But if photographing weddings is what you want to do, maybe you should place some ads on Craigslist or something. You know, be active. And try not to forget the reality of what it takes to support a family."

She walked away, leaving him alone with the remaining dirty dishes.

He stared at the food stains, his hands wet with suds. From the window above the sink, he could feel the cold of early winter pushing through the glass.

GREAT BIG SMILE

The days became shorter and shorter. On a Wednesday in the second week in December, Linda left the SmilePosts office after an afternoon retake. Only 4:25 P.M. and it was already dark outside. Linda felt her soul shrivel up as she stepped outdoors. She took the local roads home, thinking that she might avoid the turnpike traffic, but unexpected suburban streets were backed up for miles and her car never got above twenty miles an hour. Sitting exasperated in residential traffic on a cold, dark night at five P.M., Linda ruminated on the future, her mind running in circles while the tires stayed still.

Do I want to get married again someday? She had been trying to ignore the question ever since Kate had raised it, but here it was, sneaking through unimpeded, with nothing to distract her from facing it. *Fine*, she thought, aggravated, *I'll think about this.*

I'm not sure whether I want to get married again. That was her initial answer. But it rang false. The real answer was disguised so poorly underneath her uncertainty that it was barely hidden at all. *Yes, of course, I do. Of course, I want to get married. Why wouldn't I?* Opposing thoughts fired back: *Because it went horribly the first time! That's why!* Counterpoint: *Like you're the only person who's ever had a lousy marriage. Get over yourself!*

Ugh, thought Linda, as the traffic slowed to a complete stop. She turned the radio up, hoping foolishly that the music could drown out her bickering thoughts. It did not.

Where am I going to meet somebody? / Online, stupid, that's how everybody does it now / I don't know – seems awkward / It is awkward but who cares / I care! / Get over yourself! / You already said that / Jesus this traffic is taking forever – I should've taken the highway / It would've taken just as long / I don't know / It would have / Who could love me? / Oh, shut up, you're as likeable as anybody else / That's not true – I'm boring / Stop it / I'm not bad looking / I used to be better looking / I look better than some / Not as good as others / Please stop it / Maybe I should get some better clothes / With what money?? / Oh god, can I keep this job? / I like this job / It doesn't pay enough / I know but I like it / Because of Ed? / Ed is a good friend / You think he sees you as a friend? / Yeah... / Are you sure about that? / I like the job for other reasons besides Ed! It's nice – being around kids, taking photos – I just like it / You could be around kids if you had one / Please shut up / You could have a kid / I can't go through that again... / The job doesn't pay enough / I know / You have no financial future / I know! / You're thirty-three, you need to be an adult / What does that even mean? / It means moving out of your parents' house! / Of course, I want to leave my parents' house! / Do you though? / Yes! / Oh my god, will this traffic PLEASE move!

And so on.

Eventually Linda got home. She took a hot shower for twenty-five minutes, then cuddled up in her childhood bedroom, turned adult bedroom, and watched some trashy reality TV about people trading spouses.

9:45 P.M. As she was lying in bed, already half asleep, Linda heard her phone bing.

She knew it was Ed without looking.

She lay in place, feeling reluctant to pick up her phone and not sure why. It wasn't because she was sleepy, although that was the easy excuse.

She stayed still. She looked over at her phone on the night table. It waited expectantly for her to check on it. A needy, never-aging infant was that stupid phone.

She looked at the clock. 9:47. Linda suddenly felt very sad. It was the particular mournfulness attached to the realization that a pleasant denial won't prevent approaching loss.

Without seeing his message, she knew that Kate had been right. Ed had feelings for her. He wanted something more than friendship from her and all other factors aside (like his wife and children), she didn't feel the same way about him. She had needed a friend so badly that she let herself ignore the obvious signs.

She sat up and grabbed her phone.

"It stinks we never see each other anymore," his text said.

It was almost ten o'clock. She wondered if he was in bed with his wife.

Linda dropped the phone back on the night table without responding and collapsed face down on her pillow.

The next afternoon Linda stopped by the SmilePosts office to pick up paperwork for an upcoming retake job.

She stepped out of her car and there was Ed, leaving the office for home after a morning retake of his own.

His face brightened. He waved. Linda stood still.

They approached each other in the middle of the parking lot.

"Hi!" said Ed. "This is nice running into you today."

"Yeah."

"How are you?"

"I'm okay."

"Got a retake tomorrow?"

"Yeah."

"I had one today," said Ed, "In Elkins Park. It was pretty easy."

"Ed."

"Yeah?"

"How exactly do you view our relationship?" said Linda.

Ed's face remained placid. At first he said nothing. He looked up at a nearby tree. A squirrel raced across a thin branch. The branch careened up and down from the squirrel's body weight, but the animal seemed unfazed by the precarious imbalance.

"What do you mean?" said Ed, inscrutable.

"It's just... You've been texting a lot," said Linda. "And it seems like you might feel something... And I wanted to say that I really like having you as a friend, but that's all I feel."

Ed avoided her eye contact. He looked back at the tree. The squirrel was gone.

"I don't know what you're talking about," he said.

Tears filled Linda's eyes, though she tried to hold them back. Her voice wavered.

"I really need a friend right now," she said. She felt so terribly fragile. *I haven't always been this way*, she thought. *I used to be stronger, didn't I?* "This friendship has meant a lot to me and I really don't want to lose it, but I needed to say that friendship is all I feel."

Ed still had not looked at her.

There was a long moment of silence.

"Look, I don't know what you think exactly," he finally said. "But I'm married."

His eyes turned back to her. His expression was filled with a confidence that was not present a moment before. His tone was subtly curt.

"I don't know what got into your head," he said, "but I have a wife and kids. Whatever it is you thought, you misread it."

Now it was Linda's turn to look away. As Ed became more poised, the scale of their conversation tipped, and she felt yet more insecure and vulnerable. He had denied her with such conviction that she couldn't help feeling silly and embarrassed, despite in her heart of hearts suspecting she had been right.

"I don't want to lose you as a friend," she said.

"Well I am a friend, so you won't. We just established that's all I am. You're the one who's imagining things."

She looked up at him. She wiped her eyes.

"I'm sorry," she said, apologizing out of compulsion and feeling ashamed by her apology. This was how it used to be with Jeff. He'd say something rotten and then she'd be the one who apologized. She always apologized. It was a crutch and she hated that she did it so automatically, but she couldn't help herself.

"It's fine," he said. "Anyway, I gotta get home. I'll see you around."

He got into his car and drove off.

Linda took a moment to gather herself, then walked into the office.

A few hours later, Ed ate dinner with his family, as he did every night. The same seats. The same time. One of the same few meals they made over and over again. The same people looking at him, wearing the same clothes.

The boys shoveled the food in their mouths, like they always did, looking at their phones while eating, like they always did.

"How was your day, Mason?" said Ed.

"Good," said the boy, through a mouthful of meat.

"How about you, Caleb?" said Ed.

"Mmh?" said Caleb.

"Your day. How was it?"

"Oh. Mmh," he said.

"Is that an answer?"

Caleb nodded.

Ed turned to Carrie. "How about you? How was your day?"

Carrie looked at him suspiciously. She could hear the odd edge in his tone and see the streak of tension in his forehead.

"Are you alright?" she said.

"Am I alright? Is a guy not allowed to ask his family how their day was?"

"Was your day okay?" she said.

"I was asking about you."

"Yeah, my day was fine," she said.

"Well so was mine!" he yelled, slamming his fist on the table.

The boys looked up from their phones. Carrie stared at him, worried.

"Ed?"

"What?! What the fuck is it?!"

They all stared at him, unsure of what to say or do. The swearing outburst was entirely out of character. The boys had never heard him use the

F-word.

Throughout their marriage, Carrie thought Ed's primary nature was docile, but lately she had sensed him poised for attack, like a long-caged lion who only now comprehended its imprisonment.

"Boys, why don't you get started on your homework?" said Carrie after a long, tense silence.

The boys paused, stuck between fleeing the table in terror at their dad's outburst and frozen in fascination, unable to turn away from the blazing fatherly crash occurring before their eyes.

"Boys," said Carrie, more insistent.

They saw her intense glare and retreated upstairs.

Ed had not moved, but his anger had quickly and pathetically deflated, replaced by a shoulder slump of defeat.

Carrie watched him for a long time until he finally met her eyes, looking shamed. He almost wished to reignite his spark of anger because of the false pride that came with it, but he was unable to find the fuse.

Carrie reached over and took his hand.

"It's okay," she said.

Ed was hesitant, cautious. He was unsure where Carrie planned to take the conversation.

She sighed.

"I know you've been having a rough time lately," she said. "It's okay. We'll get through it."

Ed looked at her.

The night they met flashed through his mind.

He was introduced to her at that dimly lit, overcrowded dorm party at Penn State. They began to talk and didn't stop, struggling to hear each other over the raucous crowd, retreating to the equally raucous, but less loud, sidewalks outside. They talked all night. Just talking. Nothing more than that on the first night. Each of them was a little reserved, a little more devoted to religious modesty than most of their peers. He asked her on a proper date, and he walked her to her door. He couldn't fall asleep, consumed by the thought of her. (He also couldn't fall asleep because of the asshole playing trumpet in the courtyard at four A.M. and the people screaming at the asshole to quit playing trumpet, threatening to beat his ass. The ensuing fight and the police sirens that resulted were of equally little help in falling asleep.)

Dating Carrie was so easy. So natural. It wasn't a burning wildfire but a nice simmering flame that cooked the meal perfectly. It was a healthy and consistent relationship and he loved her.

But the truth was, after eighteen years of marriage and twenty-two years of dating, their relationship had become boring. *There it is*, Ed thought to himself, feeling a strange sense of relief at being able to admit it. The strange thing was, at the present moment, sitting at the kitchen table with Carrie holding his hand, boring didn't seem all that bad.

Ed had felt angry after his conversation with Linda that morning. He had been slowly boiling all day. It was inevitable that the lid would pop off. He was angry at Linda, though not because she didn't want him. When she rejected him, he realized that he would never have acted on his feelings. (And yes, he *did have feelings*, he finally admitted.)

He was angry at her for violating the fantasy. He had liked pretending that he was that middle school version of Ed again, nursing a crush that would never go anywhere, still stuck in that place of unfulfilled hope because it was a good place to be stuck, if you had to pick one. A better place, in theory, than a mundane marriage with nothing new to offer. But the truth was, even if Linda had said she was in love with him, he wouldn't have done a damn thing about it. He knew that now. He loved his wife. He loved his family. It was precisely the fact that his fantasy would remain a fantasy that had been appealing. It was easy to thrill in the crush because there was no threat of it disrupting his life.

Carrie continued to hold his hand at the dinner table. He turned his palm upward and linked their fingers.

"I'm sorry," he said softly, meaning more than she knew.

Yes, their relationship was often boring. But that boredom was a side effect of knowing that the other person would be there day in and day out, consistently and powerfully always there when you needed them. And for that, he was grateful.

SEVEN
CHRISTMAS PARTY
(OR: A WELL-EARNED NAP)

THE SOUTHEASTERN PENNSYLVANIA SmilePosts territory's annual Christmas party was held that year at Marty's Tavern. Marty's was a red wooded mainstay of lower Montgomery County where smoking was still allowed indoors, despite state laws, and the bathrooms were outdoors, despite common decency. George had catered the party with several trays of traditional Christmas buffalo wings. No mild, only hot. George "liked his wings like he liked his women." He told me that alongside a group of male co-workers, in an uncomfortable interaction that I tried to forget about and didn't mention to any of the women present. I do believe George was merely trying to impress us in a misguided attempt at asserting his masculinity. I cringed at his buffalo sauce misogyny, but the other guys clapped him on the back like proud parents, all of them openly declaring agreement that hot girls were the best and they should feel super cool for being attracted to them.

The tavern was decorated with a lazy string of old Christmas lights, only two thirds of which were illuminated, and a shaggy Christmas tree that had been leaned upright against the corner walls, without a base. I witnessed the tree fall on three different people over the course of the evening.

When she arrived at the party, Linda looked around for Ed, but there was no sign of him. They had not spoken since her declarations in the parking lot. She had been tempted to text him, to try to salvage their friendship from the flaming pyre of that uncomfortable conversation, but it was too awkward. She thought that if he really wanted to be friends and nothing more, he would reach out to her. His silence indicated that she had probably been right in her suspicions. Unless, of course, she had ruined the friendship by falsely accusing him of having feelings. There was no way to know for sure.

Despite the uncertainty, Linda felt less regret about the situation than she expected. One way or another, she knew that she had said what was necessary. It was nice to feel confident about something for a change.

Linda moseyed into the party. She casually said hello to some of her co-workers. She ordered a beer and took a plate of buffalo wings. She leaned against an unclaimed high-top table in the vicinity of people she knew, but not directly next to anyone. She bit into a wing and her mouth turned to fire from the hot sauce and she drank her beer because it was the only liquid around. She felt the beer go to her head quickly and immediately regretted not pacing herself. Though she was hungry, she pushed the tray of wings away, not wanting to subject herself to any further pain.

She looked around at everyone conversing and she took out her phone. She scrolled through Instagram mindlessly, not really looking at any of the posts, wanting to do more than stand alone pathetically next to an un-eaten plate of wings.

"How's it going?"

Linda looked up from her phone. It was Josie. She had joined Linda at the high top, with a beer of her own.

"Oh hi. Good," said Linda.

"You made it through the season. Few do. Congrats," said Josie.

"Yeah thanks," said Linda.

"So what do you think of this shit show?"

"Huh?"

"You know. SmilePosts. What do you think?"

"Oh. I like it," said Linda.

"Really?"

"Yeah. You don't?"

"To me, it's like going to the dentist. Necessary, but I'd avoid it if I had better teeth."

Linda nodded, not entirely sure what Josie meant.

There was a pause in the conversation. They each took a sip from their beers to fill the silence. Linda glanced back towards her phone, trying to save Josie the trouble of talking to her by pretending like she had something important to check.

"So, you don't talk a lot, do you?" said Josie.

"What?" said Linda.

"My point exactly."

"Oh no. I talk."

"And you're proving it splendidly."

"Well, what do you want to talk about?"

"I don't know. Watching any good TV shows right now?"

"Umm. I've been watching *Orange is the New Black*."

"Oh, I love that show! Taystee is my favorite."

"Oh yeah, she's great. I like Red a lot."

"Yeah, that's a really great show. I just started watching *The Americans*. Have you seen it?"

"I haven't."

"Oh, you need to check it out. It's really great. It takes place in the eighties and it's about these Russian spies posing as a normal American couple."

Anyway, I don't need to recap all the details of Linda and Josie's conversation. You get the gist. It was a normal, pleasant, surface level talk between two people about pop culture. It was the kind of friendly, ordinary conversation two people have all the time, which doesn't make for riveting dialogue in a novel, but is the kind of uncomplicated socialization that keeps people going in real life. We need these conversations even if they don't translate into captivating entertainment in a book or on a television screen, completely out of place within the very TV shows Josie and Linda were discussing.

Leave it to Josie to get Linda talking. Josie was completely uninterested in conversing with so many people, but she spotted one of her ilk from a mile away. When she considered you a friend, there was no one warmer. You were a member of her own exclusive circle of worthwhile people and to be liked by someone who judged much of the world so harshly was an honor.

But I'm jumping ahead. It's not time to tell Josie's story yet.

Linda and Josie talked for a while and then Rita, the spunky tattooed vet who was friends with Josie, came and joined them at their table. Soon after, Cal and Stacy, two other vets, came over as well. They were all friendly and very complimentary to Linda about the job she had done that season. They told her stories of some of the co-workers from hell they had seen during their time at SmilePosts – rage-filled hot heads who cursed at the kids and unrelenting dolts who posed the children facing away from the camera. They told her that she was one of the good ones and they hoped to see her back again for the spring season. (They kindly paid me the same compliments after Josie waved me over to join their table.)

Linda started to wonder why exactly she and Ed had decided the veteran photographers were so unfriendly and stand-offish. Had she made that judgment on her own or had Ed suggested it first? Had Ed declared the veterans aloof because he wanted Linda all to himself? Why did she always misjudge the men in her life so thoroughly? Would she ever find love again?

Stop.

She cut off her thoughts before they continued any further. Now was not the time for an internal pity party. She was talking to people. She was having a good time. She wanted to enjoy the present moment like everyone was always telling her to do, because, for once, the present moment was rather nice.

Linda didn't know it then, but she had seen Ed for the last time. He never texted her over winter break and Linda, feeling too awkward, never texted him either. When she returned to SmilePosts for spring training in late January, Ed was nowhere to be seen. She asked Dee and was told that Ed had gotten another job. She felt sad about losing his friendship, but also accepting. Disappointments were an unavoidable facet of getting older and it was time she stopped dreading them.

Linda's financial and emotional struggles were far from over. Many questions about her future lingered. They might never have a satisfying answer.

That night at the Christmas party, wrapped in the warm blanket of small talk, Linda glanced over at the Jesus ornament on the unsecured Christmas tree and remembered her prayer to God from the beginning of the season. She had prayed that everything would be okay.

Maybe it was the glow of the Christmas lights and the cheerful holiday music or maybe it was her inclusion in the conversation, but, for a time, Linda's worries took a well-earned nap. In a way, her prayer had been answered.

IV.
DANA & ETHAN

ONE
THE LAST THING ON HER MIND

ETHAN DUNLAP NEVER PRAYED and if he had been forced to, he would have prayed for everyone to "chill the fuck out – I mean who really gives a shit, you know?"

It was a sentiment he put into practice and most people loved him for it.

Back in that first August at SmilePosts training, while Linda ruminated about her past and I ruminated about the future, Ethan took stock of the personalities surrounding him and realized he could run the show if he wanted. He'd always had a talent for being the center of attention. He was charming and funny in an uncomplicated way. He was the first one to make a joke, not because he was exceedingly clever, but because he had the guts to disrupt stale moments and spout the obvious bit of humor everyone else was too reserved to say. (As a child, there was not a fart that evaded his attention.) Ethan was charming because he was good-looking and felt no need to pretend that girls weren't interested. Everyone admired fearlessness as long as you weren't "fucking unhinged." (His words, not mine.) Ethan knew how to behave properly when it was necessary, but most of the time he didn't think it was necessary. At school or at work, he might not be the top student or the employee of the month but he'd have a good time and he'd get by and he'd get laid, and really, he thought, *who needed much more?*

I liked him, I have to admit. I'm sort of ashamed to say it, but it's the truth. Any objective description of Ethan's personality inevitably makes him sound hateable, but in person there was a winking geniality to him that was undeniable. When you spoke to Ethan, you felt that all he wanted in the world was for the people around him to be happy, even as he openly admitted that everything he said and did was for his own selfish pleasure. And though you believed his claim of selfishness – because there was no questioning the love he held for himself – his flippant nature entertained everybody and we forgave him his flaws, the way you might with a cute, bratty toddler.

Ethan took every opportunity to boldly lighten the proceedings. During a break on day two of training, he approached George. Several others, spotting the mischievous twinkle in Ethan's eye, gathered around to listen.

"So you want us to touch the children's lives, huh?" Ethan said, referencing George's notorious opening speech.

"Yes! Get out there and touch them!" said George.

"Guys, the boss says we gotta touch the children – right in the gaping open hole of their lives! Let's all remember that in court," said Ethan.

The others laughed loudly. They swooned in admiration of Ethan's audacity.

Dee watched from close by. She had been truly hoping that the trainees would move on from George's oblivious speech. She didn't want to have to tell her innocent manager about the illicit way his words had been heard by every single other person in the room. George was often like a child, endearingly unaware of the muck of cynicism and vulgarity where everyone else constantly plodded. His cherubic optimism was his strongest characteristic, but also his most frequent flaw. He lived in a candy-coated world and he was frequently blind to the reality surrounding him.

Dee decided to let George know how his speech had been interpreted, not only to prevent more embarrassment, but also to fend off any legal liability. She sidled up to him and clued him in quietly.

The others watched George as Dee spoke to him. Sadness spread across his face.

"That's not how I meant it," he said, glum. "You know that."

"I know," said Dee, trying to comfort.

By then, Ethan had moved on.

Ethan treated that first day of training like a politician at a swing-state diner, meandering from group to group, shaking hands, making friends, lightening the mood. He sold his charismatic persona while keeping his policies vague. If there had been a baby around, he surely would have kissed it for good measure. Though heaven forbid he actually got elected. He clearly would have disregarded any legitimate hard work that the office required.

Ethan's core constituents were any attractive girls, of which the Smile-Posts training offered quite a few.

Ethan, respectfully, didn't feel the need to comment on the wealth of beauty out loud, unlike a fellow trainee in my own group named Clint, an unrepentant bro, who within moments of meeting me actually said the words, "there's so much pussy here," in a workplace. Clint seemed to feel we were of the same ilk, probably because he noticed that I couldn't stop staring at redheaded Hailey, much as I tried, which I guess was not all that hard. More on that later.

Ethan eyed up the pretty females in the room like a wine connoisseur in a Napa Valley cellar, thrilled by the choices arranged in front of him. Various colors of hair and shades of skin. No preferences for Ethan. He enjoyed beauty in all its forms – or hoped to anyway.

Proving his sense of equality to no one in particular, he began his flirtation blitz with an extremely nice black girl named Shayla who declined him with a polite "no thank you, I have a boyfriend."

He smiled at her rejection without an ounce of bitterness. Never in the least discouraged, he moved on.

He got better reactions from the Korean girl and the Russian girl, both named Jen. He filed them away as possibilities for conquest.

I watched from across the room, in panic, as Ethan flirted with Hailey. I quickly began to despair, worrying that she would prefer a guy like him to a guy like me. But when he walked away from her, I restarted my engine of optimism and longing without a beat.

Ethan flirted with Gabby, the veteran girl running his and Linda's training group. He considered flirting with Linda, thinking that she was kind of a MILF, despite having no knowledge as to whether she was a mother. But he thought better of it when he saw how distracted and frazzled she was. She was too much to deal with, clearly, so Ethan moved on to heavily tanned Mackenzie, who dressed, acted, and made herself up like a hot girl, although Ethan thought she was only a six or seven, at best, on the widely accepted ten-point scale of hotness. On the plus side, Mackenzie was obviously into him, taking a selfie with him on her beloved iPhone within minutes of their meeting. She spent more time posting Instagram stories about her new job that day than training for it. Mackenzie would put out, Ethan had no doubt. He figured he'd save her for a rainy day.

As we were about to break for lunch, Ethan noticed a pretty young brunette with blonde streaks and a boatload of bracelets on her wrists. She was standing quietly on the far side of the final training group. Though she stood out in the open, he had the sense she was hiding. Ethan wanted to do a full inventory of all the possible women available to him. He made his way over to her.

"Didn't see you there," he said.

Bracelets looked up at him. Ethan smiled brightly.

"Okay," she said.

She did not smile back.

"Ethan," he said, holding out his hand in introduction.

"Dana," she said, keeping her own hand to herself.

"You're gonna leave me hanging?" he said.

"Appears that way," she said.

"How are you enjoying the new job so far?"

"Fine."

"Did you enjoy George's speech?"

"It was fine."

He looked at her for a moment, trying to get a read. She looked away, made uncomfortable by his stare.

Ethan laughed, entertained by how thoroughly Dana wanted the interaction to be over. He shrugged his shoulders. *Can't win 'em all.*

"Nice to meet you, Dana," he said, and walked away, mentally scratching her off of his list.

Meeting a man was the last thing on Dana Luciany's mind.

She drove home from her first day of SmilePosts feeling overwhelmed and exhausted. Dana was glad to have employment in some objective, detached way, but in reality, she dreaded it. She was twenty. She had never had a full-time job. She had worked part-time for the last couple years at an American Eagle store in the mall. Training for that job had been simple. Nothing like her overwhelming first day at SmilePosts.

They had thrown so much information at her. There was too much equipment and too many rules. She struggled to keep track of it all. It didn't help that her veteran trainer, a goateed, kind of pudgy guy named Cal, seemed to relish his role of power. He treated training like boot camp and took the opportunity to be a drill sergeant, whipping the unpromising new recruits into shape.

"Is that the button I said to push?" Cal said, with a stern wrinkle of his nose, when Dana hit the key light settings instead of the main light settings. She couldn't remember which of the lights was which. He had gone over them so quickly. Instead of nicely correcting her, he embarrassed her with his condescending question. *Want to try to teach me how to do it right, instead of being an asshole about it?*, she wanted to spit back in his face.

"Cal's actually really nice," another veteran named Stacy told Dana and the members of Cal's training group, during one of the breaks. "He just doesn't make the best first impression," she said.

The fact that Stacy felt the need to apologize for Cal, unprompted, didn't exactly raise their confidence that there was a hidden pearl hiding within his scaly shell. They looked at him. During the break, he stood at their training set as if guarding it, his arms crossed, frowning. He was a devoted watchman, determined to prevent any fun from storming into the city gates. Several of the girls in Dana's group laughed at his self-seriousness. Dana didn't. She was too stressed out.

Dana tried really hard to learn all the information Cal threw at them. She knew it was only her first day, but she already felt like a failure. She wanted to work hard but Cal's description of the job sounded overwhelming. He scared his group with tales of whole schools of poorly behaved kids running ragged through the equipment like wild beasts. "He exaggerates," said Stacy. "Most of the kids are pretty nice." Naughty or nice, the thought of corralling so many children was daunting. Dana could hardly take care of just one.

Dana pulled off of Cottman Avenue in the heart of Northeast Philly, driving her mom's car, and parked on the side street where she lived with her parents. Dana's mom, Molly, had let her use the Dodge Neon for work, since Dana couldn't afford her own vehicle. Molly only worked part-time and she insisted that she could take the bus to work. Dana accepted the generosity without argument because SmilePosts required driving and it was the best job she had been able to find without a college degree.

Dana felt grateful now that her parents had forced her to at least get a high school diploma. Her initial instinct had been to drop out when she became pregnant with Madison.

Dana approached the left side of the duplex where she lived with her family, opened the front door, and was immediately greeted by her two-year-old daughter flinging herself across the room.

"Mommy!" said Madison with glee. She wrapped herself around Dana's leg.

Dana bent down to kiss and hug her baby girl.

Madison was her "mini-me" as Dana liked to call her. Same shade of light brown hair. Same little dimples and green eyes.

She loved her daughter more than anything, even though her existence had completely upended Dana's life.

"How was the first day of work?" asked Molly, grimacing with stiffness as she stood up from the living room carpet where she had been playing with Madison. "Ugh. I'm too young to be this sore," she said. She was forty-six.

"It was fine," said Dana. She didn't want to say *I'm in over my head*, which was how she felt.

"And how was your day?" Dana said to Madison.

"I ate with granma," she said in her adorable, muffled toddler tone.

"Oh good. Did you have a good meal?"

"Yeah," she said.

"That's good."

"Mama, wanna watch Elsa?"

"You already watched Elsa earlier," said Molly. Elsa was Madison's way of referring to Frozen, her favorite movie, which she could watch for hours and days on end without ever tiring of the Disney musical.

"You mind watching her a little longer while I take a shower?" Dana said to her mother. "They had us set up and break down this set of equipment like three times. I'm like sweating all over."

Molly gave Dana a quick unfiltered look, which Dana interpreted as, *Of course I'll watch her – she's more my responsibility than she is yours*, a sentiment which pissed Dana off, even if her mom didn't vocalize it.

"Sure," said Molly.

"Thanks," said Dana, through gritted teeth, trying to hold back her annoyance.

On the way up the stairs, Dana walked past her dad Steve. They exchanged a quick glance of greeting and proceeded their separate ways.

Dana's rift with her dad had been going on too long for her to actively feel bad about it. When she first found out that she was pregnant and told her parents, Steve's silence and scorn had shattered her. She had always been so close with him. An only child, she was daddy's little girl. He had loved her and spoiled her with their limited resources. Molly was the one with whom Dana had always had tension. Molly was the disciplinarian. She was the one who clashed with Dana when she came home after curfew or failed a math test. Steve was always quick to forgive her, assuring Molly that Dana would do better next time. Molly thought he undermined her. Dana loved him for it.

Her relationships with her parents flipped when she got pregnant.

When she broke the news, her dad had looked away from her. He refused to make eye contact. There was an argument to be made that he had never truly looked at her again since.

They were a Christian family. There was no debate about whether she would have the baby. In Dana's mind, based on how she had been raised, abortion was the same as committing a murder.

There was some debate, at least by Molly, as to whether Dana should keep the baby once she gave birth. Molly argued that there were a lot of loving married couples who had trouble conceiving who might give the child a good home. Steve was silent on the issue. Neither keeping the baby nor giving it away were options he wanted to discuss, because doing so would verbally confirm that Dana was pregnant, a fact he refused to openly acknowledge.

At first, Dana did not offer her own opinion on what to do with the baby that was growing inside her. The whole situation was impossible to comprehend. She knew she was pregnant in some removed factual way, but she couldn't feel it. Emotionally, she was empty.

Dana didn't know if Steve was ashamed of her because she had gotten knocked up or if he was simply appalled that his daughter was having sex at all. She didn't know because he wouldn't talk to her about this or anything else.

Eventually, Dana decided to keep the baby. Her parents had forced her to stay in school, despite her pleas to the contrary, and once all of her classmates had seen her with an enormous child-bearing stomach, it became too shameful to tell them she was handing the little life off. Her pride wouldn't allow it. If those assholes wanted to shame her for the results of a broken condom, so be it (at least she had used one, unlike most of the other unfairly lucky girls she knew). She would be a great mother and love her kid to pieces and show all of those fuckers that the hellish nine months of embarrassment she spent among them weren't for nothing.

By default, Molly abruptly became the closer parent. Steve wouldn't speak to Dana. Molly did what she needed to do to make sure her granddaughter would be loved and cared for.

What made Dana the saddest was that Steve barely talked to Madison either. Steve, who had been so loving and playful when Dana herself was a baby, as proven by photos and VHS home movies, treated Madison like a roommate he didn't particularly get along with. It made Dana furious. It made her want to scream at him: *Hold your stupid grudge against me but don't take it out on Madison!* She never found the courage. She was too heartbroken by the way her father's affection had vanished. She sat by and watched as his supposed Christian values about sin destroyed their relationship.

Exhausted from training, Dana collapsed on the larger bed in the bedroom she shared with her daughter, enjoying a moment of quiet before she took a shower. She knew she was spoiled, having Molly as basically a second, more responsible, mother to Madison. She knew that a big part of parenting was watching your kid when you didn't feel like it, but Dana needed moments to herself sometimes. What was wrong with taking time when you could get it?

Dana turned facedown into her pillow.

The thing was – she didn't feel regretful anymore. She certainly didn't regret keeping Madison and she didn't even regret the broken condom.

She loved Madison so much that anything in life which led to her existence was retroactively a good thing. Madison was everything to her. Dana simply needed a break from her once in a while.

A small doubt voiced itself in Dana's head. *But wouldn't life be easier without her?* said the doubt. *Wouldn't it be nice to be a normal twenty-year-old?*

Shut the fuck up, Dana thought, in reply.

She didn't like those doubts. In fact, she hated those doubts and pretended they didn't exist. *Stupid fucking doubts.*

Dana hopped in the shower. She washed off the day and tried to reset her mind for the days to come. She wanted to make money. She wanted to do a good job and show her parents that she could someday support her own child. Even if the idea of taking care of Madison alone secretly terrified her.

You don't have to be alone.

That was what her friends said. They kept telling her – "You're hot. Go meet a guy! Find a husband."

"What guy wants somebody with a two-year-old?" she said.

"Some guy will," said the friends.

She didn't believe them, though fear of rejection was not the reason she hadn't been dating. She had too much else in her life going on. She had Madison to focus on and she needed to make money. Now most of her mental capacity would be taken up by trying to remember how to read a light meter and adjust something called an "f-stop" on the main light, key light, and background light, if she could ever remember which light was which.

"You'll find the right guy," her friends said.

Would you all shut the fuck up and let me be, she thought.

She didn't want a guy and she didn't need a guy. She didn't have time for their bullshit.

She was a mother now.

TWO
HOW LITTLE HE CARED

FIVE A.M. The phone tooted with its artificial guitar tune of idyllic country life, christened as "Strum" by the tastemakers at Apple. It was Ethan's least favorite ring tone. He thought it was cheesy and stupid. It got under his skin every time he heard it. That's why he chose it for his wakeup alarm. He needed his alarm to be a sound so irritating that he was forced to wake up at that ungodly hour to turn it off. Otherwise, he would never leave his bed.

It was a mid-September morning two weeks into the fall SmilePosts season. Ethan groaned. He twisted in his sheets. He listened to the horrible mockery of music coming from the phone on his dresser and tried to force himself up. His head ached. He was hungover. Drinking six beers on a Thursday night and getting only four hours of sleep will do that to you.

Ethan had deliberately put his phone on his dresser instead of his night table so that he would have to get out of bed to silence the atrocious ring tone. That Friday morning, not even Apple's nauseating mechanical approximation of sunny life on the river could get him going. His body was incapable of movement. His muscles were like jelly. His eyelids refused to be pried open.

He grabbed a box of tissues on his night table and threw it at his phone. This did nothing to silence the ear poison repeating itself on loop.

"Turn your fucking alarm off!" yelled Ethan's roommate Jake from the other bedroom. The walls were thin.

Ethan didn't say anything back, so that later he could convincingly lie, telling Jake he had slept through his alarm, as well as Jake's screams of protest.

Finally, Ethan forced himself out of bed, but he let the alarm sound go on for another minute. He didn't want the song to vanish too quickly after Jake's demands. He didn't want to give him the satisfaction. After all, it was partially Jake's fault that Ethan was so hungover. When Ethan had brought home two six packs the night before and asked Jake to drink with him, Jake had agreed. They both knew that Ethan had to get up early, so it was both their faults, if you really thought about it. That was Ethan's logic anyway.

Ethan stepped into the bathroom and pissed out what seemed like a gallon of pee. He splashed hot water onto his face at the sink. He had no time to take a shower but he took one anyway. He switched the temperature back rapidly from cold to hot, trying to shock his senses into an alert, sober state.

He got out and looked at the clock.

"Fuck," he said to himself. He should have been on the road five minutes ago.

He had no time to do anything but throw on the pair of khaki pants he had worn for twelve straight workdays without washing them, plus his SmilePosts-issued collared blue shirt, which was equally unclean, rush into his car, hit the gas petal, and speed down the highway all the way to Our Mother of Grace K-12 Catholic school in Lansdale.

He certainly didn't have time to pick up a cup of coffee.

But really, how was he supposed to drive safely to work without any caffeine in his system, when he was so hungover and didn't get enough sleep? Getting coffee was the right thing to do, both for his own well-being and for the safety of the others on the road with him.

He stopped at Wawa and bought a large cup of joe and a glazed donut.

By the time he hopped on 476, he was twenty-five minutes behind schedule. He got into the left lane and kicked the speedometer up to ninety.

When Ethan arrived at the school, he was only twelve minutes late.

He thought it was rather impressive, cutting his lateness in half by sheer force of aggressive speeding. Stacy, the rule-following veteran photographer who waited for him, felt otherwise. Instead of showing a proper appreciation for his feat of driving, Stacy lectured him on the necessity of punctuality. She was nearly shaking from the anxiety his lateness had caused her. She had debated going into the school without him to ensure that at least one of them was set up on time. She deliberated on this decision for nine minutes. At that point, she figured she might as well wait six more minutes, allowing him a gracious leeway of fifteen minutes total. Stacy always believed it was better to show a unified front at a school. If photographers walked in separately, the school would assume they were a team divided and therefore untrustworthy. She cared about the job. She wanted to execute each day to the best of her ability. It gave her pride to do good work and show competence in every area. Also, she was a little obsessive.

Ethan didn't catch much of what Stacy said to him. While she was droning on, he was internally debating whether he had time to grab another cup of coffee. He looked at the vein in Stacy's forehead, which bulged as she lectured him. He decided against the coffee run, as much as he was craving it. *Perhaps*, he thought, *I can steal some coffee from the teachers' lounge.*

Life was good for Ethan Dunlap, as far as he was concerned. He missed college and the rollicking party life that was dormitory living, but he didn't let his supposed adulthood prevent him from having fun. (For example, Thursday nights had always been party nights on campus and Ethan didn't let something as silly as having work the next day stop him from continuing to get wasted on Thursdays now.) So many of his friends had bowed to totalitarian parental and societal pressure to give up all their joys just because their school years were behind them. Not Ethan. He saw no reason why accepting a diploma needed to imply a chaste life of sobriety and responsibility.

If you were to ask him if he drank most nights, he would respond "fuck yeah!" If you were to ask him why he drank, he would reply, "because I like beer!"

If you were to ask him what his future plans were, as his dad did every time he saw him, he would say, "I don't know, I'll figure it out, I'm still young aren't I?"

I suppose Ethan's dad took this as a marginally acceptable argument because he kept giving Ethan money to pay for his apartment rent. Either that or his dad simply had too much to worry about at his high-pressure job to get involved in his son's life. A sternly voiced question about the future, asked on a semi-regular basis, was the best he could do.

Ethan was spoiled. He admitted it. His dad admitted it. His mom admitted it. Everyone seemed to agree on the issue, but no one seemed to do anything about it, least of all Ethan, who felt no shame in using his parents' money. "They have enough of it," he would say.

Ethan had grown up in the heart of the Main Line, a well-established belt of wealth in the suburbs west of Philadelphia. His parents were both lawyers. They often worked late and on weekends, which allowed Ethan plenty of nights to invite his friends over to smoke marijuana and drink beer. They never had any trouble acquiring their contraband. There was always a weird long-haired dude in a conch shell necklace or a thrift store Nirvana shirt in practically every class who had weed and booze to sell out of the back of his BMW at the close of the school day. Money for buying these drugs wasn't a problem. Ethan and his friends all had allowances so large they could barely spend them.

Ethan lost his virginity at fifteen. He immediately decided that sex was the meaning of life and anyone who spent any amount of time debating our purpose in this world couldn't possibly be getting laid.

He had proudly slept with twelve girls so far in his eight years of sexual activity and he intended to make it a baker's dozen as soon as possible. He saw no way that thirteen could be an unlucky number in this context.

In college, he had majored in business at his dad's behest. It didn't make much difference to Ethan. Work was work. It was boring and pointless, other than the money it provided. Most of his college buddies were money obsessed. It was all they could talk about. Ethan didn't care about money. Some said that was an easy sentiment to espouse for someone who always had money. In part, this was a valid accusation. But it was also oversimplifying the matter. Ethan's college cohorts had come from equally well-off families and they were also given large allowances. Their thirst for cash was unquenchable, while Ethan's was easily sated. Maybe it was because he was better looking than all of them. He was confident in his ability to continually sleep with attractive girls no matter how large or small his bank account was. The others were not. Of course, he truly had no conception of what it was like to live without a safety net.

When Ethan graduated, his parents expected him to find a good job in some Center City high rise building, where he would work sixty-hour weeks and start a 401K. In truth, he expected this as well. Then he graduated and he thought *fuck this shit* and he took the summer to do nothing but drink with his high school friends and buy weed from that same conch-shell-wearing weirdo who was still selling and still wearing that conch shell necklace, despite that fact that it was the 2010s. Ethan got an apartment in King of Prussia with his high school buddy Jake and he hooked up a bunch of times with a girl named Becky who was a waitress at a TGI Fridays. He broke it off with her when she had the gall to ask him if he ever planned to get a job. *Like what she was doing was so great.* That pissed him off. But it was fine. He was ready to move on.

Eventually he decided that he did want a job. For one thing, his parents' voiced concerns were getting marginally larger and he wanted to get them off his back. For another, he wanted to have some of his own income. He was not entirely immune to the pride of self-sufficiency, as loose as his parameters of the concept were. He had also become kind of bored during the daytime, waiting for friends to get out of work and the bars to populate with girls worth talking to.

Ethan looked at the job listings, expecting to finally give in to the glass-walled prisons in the business district downtown. But he felt so empty reading those job descriptions that he gave up on the idea almost immediately. Instead, he turned to Craigslist and after some brief meandering, he came across the ad for SmilePosts in the vaguely titled "Gigs" section.

Something about the SmilePosts ad appealed to him, though he wasn't sure what. My theory is that he was so unconsciously determined to hang onto his youth as long as possible that a job spent in schools was enticing. Though perhaps I'm giving Ethan credit for being deeper than he is. The appeal might have simply been that the position only involved heavy work through Thanksgiving. It wasn't a major long-term commitment. It was a job he could take without dreading the idea of doing it for the rest of his life. There was a comfort in that. Whatever his reasons, he applied, he got hired (like almost every single other person who applied) and once he showed up at training and saw all of the cute girls around, he pledged himself to the position. If it hadn't been for all of those girls he wanted to sleep with, he might have quit within the first week.

The exceedingly early hours and long, drawn-out days of the SmilePosts September schedule did little to alter Ethan's lifestyle. He smoked and drank when he got home. He went out to bars on weeknights. He persuaded Jake to smoke and drink with him, and Jake gave into the pressure at least half the time. He stayed up nightly until two A.M, not caring about when he had to get up.

Ethan didn't feel as though his lifestyle was affecting his job performance. He thought he was doing a perfectly good job taking pictures because he always assumed his own success at everything, though he rarely put in any effort.

The main conflict in his life was deciding which girl at SmilePosts he wanted to hook up with first. He had narrowed the choices of his initial conquest down to a few primary options: Mackenzie, who was an all-systems-go sure thing, Jen Zolitnikov and Jen Li ("the Jens"), who were slightly less certain conquests, and Hailey, who was the cutest of the selected bunch, but more resistant to obvious flirtation. It was about time for him to make a choice and pounce.

Throughout the day at Our Mother of Grace, a 1980s Catholic school building in the basement of a Church that smelled of mold and repression, Ethan noticed Stacy staring at him while he worked. Normally, he would have assumed this meant that she was into him, but this was not the typical stare of physical admiration. This was the tense look that a mother gives to an untrustworthy friend of her child, afraid to leave her kid alone in a room with their delinquent companion for even a minute. It irritated him. He considered deliberately fucking up his photos out of spite. That would show her.

Ethan tried to ignore Stacy and focus on the kids. The classes arrived in age order. They had begun with the kindergartners and slowly made their way up to the high school seniors.

When the twelfth-grade classes arrived, Ethan felt an uncomfortable swell of desire watching the graduating girls in their Catholic school uniforms. *No, not girls. Women!* He thought, trying to justify his lust. *They're probably eighteen*, he thought. *Or seventeen at the youngest. What's the real difference between eighteen and seventeen anyway?*

When a twelfth-grade boy arrived at the photo station, Ethan instructed him on the proper pose in a dull uncaring monotone and took one shot per person, obviously not caring what the boy looked like in his picture. When a twelfth-grade girl approached him, on the other hand, he became enthusiastic and flirtatious, complimenting her on how exceedingly well she followed his instructions. He took her picture two or three times, hardly making any adjustments, allowing her multiple opportunities to smile attractively and look right at him while he clicked the trigger. After he took one particular girl's photo four times, he looked to his right and saw Stacy staring at him with revulsion.

He thought he had been subtle in his interactions. He was mistaken.

"What?" he said out loud.

Stacy scoffed and turned back to her set.

She didn't say a word to him until an hour and a half later when they were safely outside the school, packing up their cars.

"It's not appropriate to flirt with the students, you know," she said to him.

"What?" he said.

"I saw you talking to those girls. It's disgusting."

He stopped loading up his car. He stood still and stared at her. She looked intimidated by his confident, angry expression, which pleased him.

"First of all, I wasn't doing anything," he said. "And second of all, those girls are only like three years younger than me."

"Right. So you weren't flirting with them, but if you were it's perfectly legal?"

"Exactly," he said.

"Whatever you say," she said.

They stood still and quiet. Ethan felt confused. He was sure he had won the argument, but something was amiss.

Stacy resumed loading her car, but Ethan still felt as though someone was staring at him. He looked around. A statue of the Virgin Mary looked down upon him from across a garden with a peaceful pitying expression that seemed to say, *I forgive you.*

What? Ethan said to her defiantly in his head.

He threw the rest of his equipment in his car and plugged the Smile-Posts office address into his GPS.

Fuck her, he thought, referring to Stacy, although the Virgin Mary wasn't far out of his crosshairs. It wasn't as if he needed to hit on high school girls anyway. He had plenty of options waiting for him back at the SmilePosts office. *Unlike you,* he thought, looking at Stacy, who packed her own car with a pitiable precision, brushing stray leaves off her seats with a brush. *Nobody wants to go out with you.* He was pleased by the internal insult.

He got in his car, slammed on the gas pedal, and sped out of the parking lot at sixty miles-per-hour.

Ethan felt a noticeable uptick in the energy of the office when he entered the room, carrying his day's haul of package orders and his unfinished paperwork. He arrived before Stacy who never drove even one mile-per-hour over the speed limit.

The other photographers who had recently returned from their schools brightened when they saw him. They knew he would bring some entertainment to the otherwise dull atmosphere. Ethan never tired of seeing that look in people's eyes. He cherished his ability to bust open the piñata of everyday decorum and pour candy over everybody's heads. Here were a bunch of people who had spent a long, arduous day coaxing cranky kids to hold still for thirty goddamn seconds, driving fifty plus miles to a school and then back to the office, sitting in the exhaust fumes of traffic, without the bravery or the skill to inject any levity into their weary work. Here they sat at these shoddy folding tables, adding up their package totals on their paperwork, crunching numbers and calculating cash hauls they would never get a piece of. A little dose of Ethan was exactly what they needed to send them home on a high note.

He dropped his stuff at an open seat and made the rounds.

He stopped over at a table occupied by the grouping of Otto, Pristine, and Bonnie. Otto and Pristine were fellow newbies. Otto was an overweight, gregarious guy who talked far too loud and Pristine was a shy, nerdy Indian girl who looked away with embarrassment at Ethan's mere eye contact. Bonnie was a raspy-voiced veteran in her mid-thirties who already had three kids at home and was newly pregnant with a fourth. Bonnie could be as tough as a bull and as sweet as a Cadbury Cream Egg. She took no shit but gave out cookies. She was always baking and always bringing her sugary confections to the office.

"How're you folks doing today?" Ethan said to their group.

"Hi Ethan," said Bonnie. "Would you like a ginger snap?"

She held up a Tupperware filled with her previous night's baking output.

"Don't mind if I do," said Ethan. He took a big bite of the snap. "Mmmm, delicious! Bonnie, your husband must really love you."

"Because I bake all the time?"

"Yeah, that and the fact that he can't seem to keep his hands off of you," Ethan said. He motioned to her pregnant belly.

Bonnie chuckled. Otto guffawed. Any reference to sex made Otto burst in bellowing laughter. He was an easy target. Pristine looked awkwardly down at her shoes. Any reference to sex made her try to pretend that she was invisible, and no one around knew that she existed.

"Ethan, I'm taking your DVD."

Ethan looked across the room. Dee was speaking to him from the table where he had dropped his paperwork.

"You got it," he said.

At the end of each workday, we burned a DVD of all of the high-resolution images we had taken that day. These DVDs were used by the company to produce and print all of the photos the children purchased. Before the discs were shipped off to corporate headquarters, Dee or George would take a look at them to review our pictures. For established veterans this was a speedy process, performed mostly to be sure that no glaring errors had slipped through the cracks for which the company could be sued. For example: A kid subtly giving the middle finger at the bottom of the screen. Or an unnoticed drawing of a penis on the inner arms of a t-shirt. Dee or George would flag the offensive picture before it was printed and sent to the school for distribution. These situations were a rarity. Even the worst SmilePosts employees were usually aware enough to notice if a kid wrote "fuck" on their forehead. (Though amazingly, one idiotic new hire proved it possible to miss this during my third year.) For the most part, the review process existed for the newbies to be judged on the quality of their pictures. They were told which aspects of their work needed improvement – whether it was kids' postures, grooming, photo framing, or basically every detail of their pictures. If, day after day, a photographer's work proved to be below the company's standard, they would be fired.

Some of the photographers would stand anxiously over Dee or George's shoulders while their photos were reviewed, waiting to hear the verdict. Ethan did not. He figured Dee would let him know if something was wrong. After all, she always did.

Ethan let Dee do her thing and made his way over to a table populated by Jen Zolotnikov, Ed, and Mackenzie.

"Sup Edward?" he said.

"Hi Ethan," said Ed.

Ethan sat down in the seat next to Ed, across from Mackenzie and Jen. They smiled as he joined their table. He handled the ladies in the way he thought would be best for his chances at sleeping with them. He ignored them and talked to Ed.

"You gonna watch the Birds game this weekend?" said Ethan, using the colloquial nickname for the Philadelphia Eagles.

"For sure," said Ed.

"What do you think?"

"The Giants don't have a defense. I think it's gonna be a big win."

"That's my boy."

Ethan slapped Ed hard on the shoulder. Ed grimaced.

Ethan looked at Jen and Mackenzie. He saw the eager anticipation in their eyes. They wanted him to talk to them. He let his eyesight linger long enough for them to believe they would get their wish, then he turned back to Ed. It was a somewhat cruel game, but one he knew would work in his favor. They were chomping at the bit.

"You put any money on the game?" said Ethan.

"No, I'm not a gambler," said Ed.

"But if you're so sure about the victory?"

"Gambling's all about the spread."

"Right, of course, the spread. I know what you mean," said Ethan. Ethan didn't know what a spread was.

Okay. Ethan was ready to turn his attention to the girls.

"And how are you today, ladies?"

"Good," said Jen.

"Pretty good," said Mackenzie.

Ethan opened his mouth to continue, but he was rudely interrupted by Dee across the room.

"Hey Ethan," said Dee.

"Yesssssss?" said Ethan, his extension of the word aptly conveying his complete lack of interest in whatever Dee had to say at the present moment.

"Can you come over for a minute?" she said.

"Surrrrrrrrre," he said. He stood up at a glacial pace, keeping his eyes on Jen and Mackenzie all the while. His overstated expression told the girls how little he wanted to leave them and join Dee. They laughed with approval. Ethan had learned over the years that disrespect for authority was a one-hundred-percent guaranteed method for impressing women. Whether they admitted it or not. The most rule-book-following adherent of law and order felt herself swoon with desire when he showed how little he cared to follow instructions.

He strolled casually over to Dee and plopped down in the chair next to her at the computer station.

"How was your day?" she said in the polite, measured way Dee had of speaking. Dee never got mad, nor did she ever get overexcited. While George was a constant thrum of color and energy, exhibiting poorly disguised highs and lows at every turn, Dee, the vice-administrator, was a source of reassuring, even temperament. She had to be. Yin naturally required yang and Dee did what was required.

"Great," said Ethan. "It was a great day."

"I'm glad," said Dee.

It would be false to say that Dee and Ethan didn't like each other. In a way, they were developing an almost sibling-like relationship, their frustration with one another tempered by a base affection. Dee was the responsible older sister who kept the machine churning along in an orderly manner. Ethan was the smirking, rebellious baby brother she needed to keep an eye on. Despite their fondness for each other's personalities, they had opposing roles at the office and they were bound to clash.

They spoke in pleasant tones, but, like rival siblings, there was an obvious subtext of one-upmanship beneath their words. Ethan pushed every interaction to see how much he could get away with and they both knew it. Dee looked back at him with unwavering confidence, imparting to him that there was a limit and she would happily impose her authority if she had to.

"Let's take a look at your pictures," she said.

"Sounds like a delightful use of our time," said Ethan.

"I'm sure it will be," said Dee.

She scrolled through the images slowly. There were two hundred and seventy-one pictures on the disc and she let each one breathe for a full second of observation. She said nothing. The silence caught Ethan off-guard. During all of the previous reviews he had experienced, Dee or George had clicked quickly through most of the pictures and paused on the weakest examples to point out exactly what he could improve. Dee's new silence was a jarring tactic. Ethan was unsure what to make of it.

He was never one to be easily shaken. He would play her little game. He sensed, without knowing why, that speaking up or questioning Dee would grant her a victory. So he remained quiet, following her lead, and waited as patiently as he could for this interminably long viewing session to reach the final photo.

After four and a half minutes, the disc reached Ethan's "END" slate and Dee turned towards him.

"What did you think?" she said.

"Of what?" he said.

"Of your pictures."

"Oh," he said. He tried to surmise what she wanted to hear and decide whether or not he wanted to tell her what she wanted to hear, if he could, in fact, figure out what it was. Which as it happens, he couldn't. "I don't know," he said, feeling stupid, "What did you think?"

"I thought they were rather poor," she said.

"You did?" he said.

"I did," she said.

There was a long awkward pause. He looked at her, waiting for her to say more. She waited for him to contribute. Ethan sensed that the power dynamic of the interaction had shifted entirely in her favor. He hated it.

"Well, what's wrong with them?" he finally said, annoyed, his jolly shield of sarcasm cracking.

"This isn't the first time we've sat down together these last two weeks."

"No," he said. "It's not."

"What did we discuss before?"

Ethan searched his memory.

"You said my framing isn't consistent enough. Sometimes the kids are too low in the frame, sometimes they're too high. You said that my expressions aren't good enough. It's okay if a few moody kids refuse to smile, but I need to do a better job of encouraging them to smile. You said that I need to use my combs more to fix messed-up hair. You said sometimes my kids aren't looking right into the camera and I need to make sure I tell them where to look."

"Yes, that's all correct."

"Okay."

"Have you made any effort to try to fix those issues? Because when I look at these images, I don't see much improvement."

"I mean, yeah, I'm trying." Ethan did not sound very convincing and he knew it. He conveyed a lack of care extremely well, but he did not naturally wear its opposite.

GREAT BIG SMILE

Dee's expression suddenly softened. She looked around. No one was listening in to their conversation, but she leaned in closer anyway.

"Ethan, everybody likes you," she said. "I like you. It's good to have people such as yourself on the team. People who bring some levity to help get through the day. Work can be hard."

"Thanks," he said, on unstable ground, not sure where this was going.

"But," she said, "we can't keep someone on the team who is consistently turning in pictures of this quality. I feel like you're entirely capable of doing better. I really do. I think if you stop needing to impress everyone so much with how little you care, you can do a good job. At least I hope so, because I'd like to see you stick around."

She waited for his response.

"I'd like to stick around," he said. He meant it too.

"Good. Then on Monday, when you're at your next school, think about the things we've talked about, and pay attention to them when you're taking your pictures."

"I will," he said.

"I'm glad to hear it."

Dee turned back to the computer and ejected his disc. She handed it back to him to put in his paperwork bag, thus dismissing him.

He got up. While he had been with Dee, Stacy had arrived back at the office. She was nearly finished with their paperwork. He looked at Stacy. He knew he should join her to finish what little work there was left to do. He looked over at Jen and Mackenzie who were checking the next day's schedule and getting ready to wrap up their own day at the office.

For a minute he entertained a fantasy of dramatically quitting. He'd shove the DVD back in Dee's face and bandage his wounded pride by leaving the conversation on top.

But he liked Dee and didn't want to shove a DVD in her face. She spoke to him like he was worth something and he appreciated that. She was just doing her job, even if she was being a hard-ass. Besides, what would he do if he quit? Get one of those stupid high-rise jobs? How many cute girls would be available to him there?

He looked over at Stacy, hard at work filling in data. *She's got the paperwork covered*, he thought. *I'll give her my DVD in a minute.* He walked over to Jen and Mackenzie. They smiled at his approach.

He flashed his movie star grin.

"So where are you ladies headed tomorrow?" he said.

THREE
THE FAMILIAR FIRE OF RESISTANCE

WHENEVER one of the veterans offered her advice, Dana tried her hardest to entertain it. It was contrary to her instincts to accept guidance without a combative rebuke, but she was working on it. Back in high school, a teacher's mild criticism would trigger a full mental lockdown, inner alarms blaring, unconscious security team gathering forces to thwart the attacking enemy. At her best, she would retreat to hardened silence as she stared bullets at the teacher, wordlessly warning them not to press the issue. At her worst, she unleashed a foul-mouthed word or two and got sent to the principal's office. There, she was lectured about behavior and decorum. She always felt guilty after she had mouthed off, although she didn't admit that to anyone. To the authority figures, she maintained her act of silent imperviousness and to her friends she feigned pride over her rebellion. Inside, she felt out of control of herself, unable to resist her exhausting stubbornness, unable to quell the insecure sense that if she needed improvement, it meant she wasn't worth enough to begin with.

Dana had more perspective now that she had Madison. It was still unnatural for her to accept instruction and her inner fire still ignited whenever anyone told her what to do, but she knew she had responsibilities. She wanted to keep her job, which required doing a good job, which meant stifling her natural obstinance.

Someone might offer a comment on the body positioning in her photographs, pointing out that the children were too flatly angled to the camera. Or they might drop a suggestion on how to make a frowning kindergartener break from his shell with an unexpected joke about "farts." (Kids reliably smile when they hear the word "fart.")

On one occasion, Dana noticed George staring at her as she talked to a student. He had stopped by the school to observe, as he sometimes did. When the student left her station, George recommended that Dana smile more herself when she snapped her photos. Her first instinct was to tell him to fuck off. She was far too accustomed to creepy men leering at her and telling her that she should smile more. She knew she suffered from what some referred to as "resting bitch face," a term that her female friends giddily embraced, but which Dana thought was insulting to the max. Dana felt as entitled to be moody as the asshole men surrounding her, competing in the constant dick-measuring contest they called "toughness." A guy who walked around frowning was a "man's man" or a "bad-ass," but a female who frowned was a "cold bitch" or an "ice queen." The double standard infuriated her and most of the time there wasn't anything to smile about anyway.

When George gave his advice about smiling, Dana took a deep breath and stopped herself from being swallowed up by her natural bitterness. George had been nothing but a nice guy in their interactions so far. He was likely coming from a place of helpful instructiveness, rather than dormant objectification. Through gritted teeth, she allowed him to continue talking.

"You're telling them to 'smile,' and they hear the word and it goes in one ear and out the other," he said. "It's funny, the kids mirror you, sometimes it's completely involuntary, but as soon as I start smiling, they can't help smiling too, it's incredible."

"Okay," she said. Not 'thank you,' but just 'okay.' That was the best she could do.

When she tried out his advice, he was right. She received much better expressions from the children when she smiled herself, even if her own smile was forced.

That afternoon during her photo review, Dee complimented Dana on her steady improvement. She told Dana that her expressions were looking good, but the posture and grooming of her students could still use some work.

Dana felt the familiar fire of resistance flare up. With effort, she suffocated the flame – the smoky haze of it lingering, but the heat removed.

She made a new conscious decision. Instead of deflecting advice, she would go against all her instincts and seek it out. It felt good to be complimented. Praise that balanced out the criticism had been few and far between in her school days. She wanted more of it. She wanted to be one of the best damn photographers in the company. She wanted to be considered an asset rather than an exhausting hindrance, for once in her life. She wanted to feel like a productive adult who could maybe one day be a full-fledged parent to her child, instead of a glorified older sister, which, she hated to admit, was her real role. She would show all the doubters that she was a competent adult: her co-workers, her parents, and those high school teachers who had thought she would amount to nothing, especially once she showed up at school pregnant.

At the end of her junior year of high school, Dana received a slip of paper with her class rank written on it.

"298 out of 457," it read.

Woo, top 300, she thought in a sarcastic tone.

Truthfully, the rank meant nothing to her. She was only concerned with the grade point average next to it, which was a "71.35." C-minus. A passing grade in other words. As long as she moved on to her senior year, all was right with the world.

Dana did, for a brief moment, feel a twinge of low self-esteem at the fact that two hundred and ninety-seven of the bozos around her had managed to achieve higher marks. Sure, there were thirty to fifty smart kids in the honors classes but what about the other... uh... two hundred?

(She quickly gave up on the math. If she had been able to calculate numbers in her head, she probably would have achieved a higher rank.) Did this mean that Chris Montague who sat next to her in Chemistry and who laughed each and every time Mr. Kaufman said "boron" (she guessed, because it sounded like moron?) was a better student than her? Or what about Iona Albescu who once lit up a cigarette during a U.S. History lecture and then got pissed off when meek Miss Lincow gathered up her courage and asked her to put it out? Did the statistics imply that these disgraces were smarter than Dana? Or were there still enough people behind her in the ranks that she could continue feeling superior to the jabronies who populated her classes? She wasn't sure. (Again, she was not very good at math.)

Her concern quickly passed.

In order to be a good student, one generally has to want to be a good student, and Dana did not. Academics were something she *had* to do rather than something she *wanted* to do and the gap between requirement and desire was never one she was able to bridge.

She felt unhappy a good deal of the time, but studying and putting more effort into homework was never something she thought would help the cause.

Junior year ended and Dana spent a lazy summer, hanging with her friends and her boyfriend Pat. They smoked and drank at whichever person's house was free of parental oversight. Most of the crowd were still seventeen years old, but a couple of the boys who had been held back were eighteen and bought cigarettes for everybody. Alcohol was not much harder to come by. Several older siblings could be convinced for a fee and if all else failed, Dana or one of the other girls would flirt with the older men at the liquor store or the beer distributor and convince them to buy a case of Keystone Light or a bottle of knockoff brand Jack Daniels for the deprived teenagers who only wanted to "have some fun and drink responsibly." Some of the men refused and a guy here or there would get all handsy and demanding after helping them out. But Pat and the other guys were always standing by, ready and eager to fight. So things almost never got too touchy.

She slept with Pat, just as she had slept with her two previous boyfriends. Her parents and the people at her church could preach chastity all they wanted, but in Dana's experience, a guy wouldn't keep going out with her unless she put out. Besides, she liked it. She didn't go around blabbing about her sex life like some girls, but she wasn't ashamed and the people who implied she should be pissed her off. If she wanted to sleep with a guy she was going out with or a guy she wasn't, that was her own decision and nobody else's. She liked getting drunk and she liked having sex. The partying helped her forget how sad she felt.

Of course, not all of the guys were nice about it. Some of them started pulling off her clothes when she didn't want them to and then called her a bitch when she slapped them away. She wasn't going to be a pushover about it. She was tougher than the other girls and she liked it that way.

The judgmental girls were more annoying to deal with than the pushy guys. There was a group of popular girls from the smart classes who lorded their good grades over Dana and her friends. These hypocrites felt no shame in attending the same parties as Dana's crew so they could flirt with the C-average boys who were better-looking than the nerds in their own classes. Among this gaggle of shamelessly flirty A-students was Melissa Laskaris, Dana's former best friend from second through fourth grade. Melissa led the charge of calling Dana a slut for sleeping with guys, while she hypocritically slept around herself. When Dana pushed Melissa against the wall at a late-August party, following one such insult and several shots of faux Jack Daniels, Melissa screamed such a high-pitched wail that Amanda Conley, who was hosting the party, checked her parents' glassware cabinet to make sure none of the glasses had shattered like in a cartoon when a fat opera singer bellows her highest note. Melissa yelled that she was "going to sue Dana for assault." She said she "would have to go to the doctor to make sure she didn't have any STDs now that Dana's filthy hands had touched her." As if Melissa hadn't gotten an A-plus in

Sex-Ed and didn't know exactly how sexually transmitted diseases were spread. She dumbed herself down to turn on the dolts from the football team like Seth or Marcus, who probably did have STDs.

In truth, Dana's contentious relationship with Melissa made her deeply sad. She remembered the elementary school afternoons at each other's houses, playing with Barbies or kicking around the soccer ball in the backyard. Roaming around the neighborhood, searching for flowers to pick, finding weeds and pretending they were flowers. Ringing doorbells on random houses and then running away. It made her sad that a friendship could transform into a monstrous rivalry. Of course, she didn't express this to Melissa.

Instead, she said, "fuck you," and told Melissa if she sued her that she would "fucking knock her teeth out."

No matter how Dana spent those high school nights, she always made sure to return home and be in bed by the time her parents woke up. When Dana said good morning (in what was technically the afternoon), she had a hangover and she inevitably felt a wave of crushing sadness that she didn't know how to acknowledge. She opened her window and smoked a cigarette hanging halfway outside. She thought nothing of the future and not much more of the present. She had no aspirations, but also no impetus to question the value of her actions. She followed her impulses and never fantasized about alternatives. In the back of her mind, she expected to someday get married and have kids and be a better Christian than she was in high school, but her future self was vague and uncomforting.

Senior year began. Dana's classes did little to alter her routine.

She smoked. She drank. She partied. She did enough homework to maintain her C-minus average. She got together with friends most nights. She and Pat had broken up at the end of the summer because they were tired of each other, but they kept sleeping together anyway. Most of the time he used a condom. Sometimes he didn't.

On the night Dana figured she had gotten pregnant, she knew Pat had worn a condom. She had insisted because she was close to her period. The condom broke, but she didn't panic or think much of it. It never really occurred to her that she might get pregnant, though she had seen other pregnant girls wandering the school.

Dana hated the way her teachers looked at her when her baby bump appeared. Or rather, the way they stopped looking at her. As soon as it became obvious that Dana was pregnant, her educators had given up on her for good. They avoided eye contact as one might with a panhandler walking by the driver side window with a cardboard sign. They pretended that she wasn't there and hoped she wouldn't initiate verbal contact. It was easier to not acknowledge her existence. It was a delicate game: the upstanding member of society somehow believing that their avoidance of charity was less immoral if they feigned the invisibility of the less fortunate.

Her teachers had decided that Dana was one of the unsalvageable. Even though she had never particularly cared about her teachers' approval, their judgment stung.

Eventually, it was easier to accept her assigned identity than to fight it. It was her teachers' fault, she thought, that she put in so little effort in her senior year and barely graduated. (Willfully ignoring the fact that her grades hadn't been much better in her freshman, sophomore, and junior years and that she had spitefully ignored all her senior year homework to protest her mom forcing her to stay in school.) The teachers were to blame. They had marked her for failure and who was she to argue with the authority figures. (Willfully ignoring the fact that all her life, she had done nothing but argue with authority figures.)

Once she got pregnant, Pat, not surprisingly, ignored Dana even more thoroughly than her teachers did. He avoided her gaze completely in the hallways and consistently vanished around the nearest corner the moment she appeared. Anybody paying attention knew that Pat was the father, but she didn't force him to acknowledge it, either publicly or privately. She let him be. Once he realized she was pregnant, he never talked to her again. She thought he was an asshole for it, but she never really expected him to behave any differently. She didn't confront him or ask him if he wanted to be a part of the kid's life. What would have been the point?

On the surface, Dana's friends treated her the same as they always had, but she felt a subtle, inescapable isolation when she was around them. She was a pariah, who had suffered the consequences of the actions they all undertook. They didn't want to stop their own behavior and every time they saw Dana, she was a visual lecture they didn't want to hear. She was an uncomfortable reminder of what could happen if things went wrong.

If you thought that the previous mentions of Melissa Laskaris were leading to some sort of heartwarming, narratively satisfying reunion with Dana during her time of trouble, then you have a poor understanding of teenagers. During Dana's pregnancy, Melissa was crueler than ever. Melissa basked in the ability to confirm Dana's slutiness every time she saw her. How could Dana deny she was a slut? She had the belly that proved it.

After she gave birth to Madison, Dana returned to the final weeks of school with an air of defiance. Instead of trying to pretend her pregnancy had never happened, brushing the whole incident under the rug like some of the other formerly pregnant girls in her class, Dana proudly flashed photos of Madison on her phone, determined to spit in the face of the shame people wanted her to feel.

It was an act – she did feel ashamed, exhausted, and lost – but the act worked. Her friends were now warmer to her. They gushed over Madison's cuteness and they all wanted to stop by the house to play with her.

Graduation day came. All dressed in her gown and ready to collect her diploma, Dana decided to skip out on the ceremony at the last minute. As the procession of seniors proceeded onto the school's football field, Dana looked back at Clarissa and Alyssa Luvell, fraternal twins who were her closest friends (proximity wise) in the alphabetically arranged line. She pulled a pack of cigarettes out of her pocket and motioned with the corner of her square cap to the shadowy recesses underneath the bleachers. While Tim Decklinger, the valedictorian, gave his insufferably predictable speech about chasing one's dreams, filled with half-understood quotations from Albert Einstein, Dr. Seuss, and things supposedly said by Abraham Lincoln that were never actually said by Abraham Lincoln (quotes acquired without any real research from the internet, that bustling beehive of made-up information), Dana and the Luvell sisters inhaled their cigs. In the bleachers above, Beth Filcher's mom choked on the upward moving smoke. This caused quite the scene when Mrs. Filcher, searching for a source of the smoke, spotted Javon Pellom's dad with an e-cigarette and threatened to sue him for negligence, screaming about secondhand smoke and lung cancer and also global warming, for some reason. Mr. Pellom responded by blowing his odorless e-smoke in her face, which he considered an effective rebuttal. Slaps were thrown, saliva was spewed, and Tim Decklinger briefly had to pause his unoriginal thoughts on how "life is a journey" while Mr. Downey, the gym teacher, ran into the stands and attempted to separate the brawling sides. No one thought this commotion was particularly unusual as they were in Northeast Philadelphia, after all.

When the Luvell twins asked Dana what her plans were for the future, she remained silent. She couldn't think of a lie. The future was a blank nothingness. She had no future and she knew it.

She lied much easier to her mom, when Molly said she had been unable to locate Dana during graduation. There were too many graduates for the principal to hand out individual diplomas during the ceremony, so Dana was effectively able to claim she must have been lost in the crowd "like one of them Waldo books." She sealed her lie by saying how much she enjoyed Tim Decklinger's thoughts on how "life is a journey," which Dana made up off the top of her head, but which, of course, was something Tim had said in his speech. Steve had chosen not to attend graduation, so he was unable to offer an opinion.

The summer after high school is a time in which many college-bound teenagers attack their social life with an almost desperate hunger, in fear that their childhood will officially end the moment they set foot in their freshman dorm. They bask in the imagined last light of their youth, getting together with friends every night, singing cliché songs together with little irony as they aimlessly drive in overpacked cars from one unsatisfying social outpost to another. They loiter in donut shops and all-night diners. One among ten might buy a single donut or a five-dollar appetizer to split. As the wait-staff stares on in bitterness, the teens laugh until they cry at inside jokes that no one else would find funny. The perceived monumental ending looms large and gives every dumb joke an exaggerated sense of meaning. They hug each other at each night's end as if the departure for college is deployment to an overseas war from which they are unlikely to return. (They are surprised, when they return home from first semester for their month-long winter break, that everything is pretty much the same, minus the emotional gravitas that colored the previous summer.)

This is the experience of many teens. Not Dana.

Shortly after graduation, Dana's cloud of persistent, hovering sadness descended on her. No layers of distraction were left to dissipate it. She lay in bed, day after day, watching her mother formula feed Madison. Dana refused to attempt breast-feeding, which angered Molly until she decided that resignation was her new permanent state for any matter concerning her daughter. Dana stayed in bed as much of the day as she was able. She told her mom and her friends that she felt "tired" and "sick." This was not entirely a lie. But it was a misunderstanding of her own condition. She was not ill in the sense that she claimed. She did not have a stuffed nose nor a sore throat. She did not have a fever. She was depressed. She felt hopeless and gripped by an imprisonment of lethargy. Her limbs moved slowly and her appetite receded. She ignored texts and calls. She left her window drapes closed all day, each day, as June and July blended together into a featureless slog of time. Molly told her she was depressed. Dana denied it. Molly told her to get outside, see friends. Molly said she would take care of Madison, as if it needed to be said, as if she wasn't taking care of Madison already. Dana said she was "fine" and politely asked her mom to "leave her alone – God!" Dana was too stubborn to admit she was gripped by an emotional affliction that weak, prissy girls whined about having. She thought that girls said they were depressed when they wanted an excuse for why Johnny didn't ask them to the prom or why they didn't get into their first choice of college. Dana didn't feel as though she needed an excuse for anything – she simply had nothing she desired to do and so she stayed in bed, day after day, because there was nowhere more appealing to go. Besides, she thought, people who were depressed cried all the time. Dana didn't cry at all. She felt completely dull inside, as if she couldn't possibly summon tears even if she wanted to.

Molly implored Steve to speak to their daughter. She asked him to either forgive Dana and lovingly encourage her that a happy adult life was still possible, or threaten to cut her off, taking a parental hard line that would force her into fending for herself. But he refused to talk to her altogether. "She's made it clear she's going to do what she wants," he said.

Right when it seemed to Dana that this suffocating condition would continue for the rest of her life, something remarkable happened.

Dana fell in love with her daughter and it changed everything.

Madison started smiling, then she started speaking little adorable words, and her face started to form into a miniature recreation of Dana's own. From the peeking eyes of her torpor, Dana watched Molly bounce Madison on her knee and saw the little girl coo with delight. Dana felt a faint light struggling to emerge in the darkness. As she began to dip her toe in the ocean of a relationship with her daughter, the light grew. She was still wandering in a dark cavern, but at least she could see.

The first time Madison called her "mama," it was as if Jesus himself had whispered in her ear: "This. This is why you go on."

With Molly's encouragement, Dana roused herself to the point where she applied for positions at several stores at Pennypack Mall and was eventually hired for a part-time gig at American Eagle. She hated working, but every time she came home from a shift and saw her Madison, sometimes awake, sometimes asleep, looking more and more like Dana with every passing day, she understood that being an adult meant sacrificing what she wanted for the sake of her daughter. Being an adult meant putting in hard, boring work, day after day, so that you could provide for a person you loved more than yourself.

Having a purpose improved Dana's well-being in all areas. She got back in touch with her friends, some of whom had gone off to college, some of whom had not. She managed to have a mild social life again. She avoided the parties that most of her crew still devotedly attended and instead invited them over to play with Madison or went shopping with them on a Saturday afternoon.

When the American Eagle at Pennypack Mall closed, the latest victim of the declining state of retail spurred on by world-conquering Amazon, Dana decided to pursue something more full-time. She applied for full-time positions at other stores, but the retail decline had made these positions surprisingly competitive and she was beaten out by those with more experience. She was offered several other part-time roles that she bitterly turned down, denied what she wanted.

She came across the SmilePosts job when scanning through Craigslist on a whim. It paid only a little more than the minimum wage she was being offered in retail, but provided more consistent work, at least during the fall. She was glad to find the job, though she was now daily overwhelmed and felt constantly on the brink of failure. The unemployment in between jobs had been frightening. She didn't want to fall into another depressed state. She never wanted to feel that way again. She couldn't – for Madison's sake.

The next time George and Dee gave Dana advice on her pictures, she made herself listen to it. She made herself take their advice completely to heart and apply it as much as she could. Every time she forced herself to swallow her pride and listen to what someone else told her to do, she became a little less resistant. There was a little more slack in the tightly wound band of her irrational pride. And her pictures got better.

Dana became a more valuable employee with each bit of conscious effort and that held an unexpected pride all its own. It was a pride unlike any she had ever known. A pride independent of defiance and rebellion. A pride that did not define itself in opposition to others, but rather, in conjunction with them and their needs.

It was the pride of growing up.

FOUR
WHO DOESN'T LIKE BACON?

BEFORE SHE LEFT the house for her painfully early drive to work, Dana took one last look at her daughter, sleeping soundly in their shared bedroom.

Madison loved her big-girl bed, which was only a cot. Dana wished they could give her something more comfortable to sleep on but there wasn't enough space to fit a real bed. Luckily, Madison didn't know the difference. Her only point of comparison was her crib, to which her cot was a huge improvement.

Occasionally Dana fantasized about getting her own place for the two of them, but the realities quickly dissolved the daydream before it could gain any footing. She couldn't afford the rent and the concept of sole parental responsibility was still terrifying. Molly's assistance was invaluable. Dana couldn't comprehend how a single parent could work and take care of their child at the same time. To her, the two tasks were complete opposites. She felt like Madison with her cute shapes puzzle toy, trying to jam the star piece into the triangle slot. The piece and the slot didn't fit together, and they never would no matter how strongly her stubborn daughter tried to force it. It was the same with work and parenting. Dana couldn't envision fitting the two together as a happy whole.

Dana watched Madison breathe her cute little breaths as her hair fell into her mouth, soaked in the drool of her deep sleep. She wanted her daughter's life to be better than her own. She hoped that whatever happened, Madison would never have to leave the house for work at five-thirty in the morning.

Dana hit the road. She had an hour-and-fifteen-minute drive ahead of her, even with no traffic expected at this pre-dawn time. She was headed to an enormous middle school in Northern Lehigh County, at the farthest edge of the SmilePosts territory.

Dana pulled into the parking lot of Elderbridge Middle School a few minutes before the scheduled arrival time. The only other cars in the parking lot at this hour belonged to fellow SmilePosts employees. There were a large group of them who had been sent to this two-thousand child behemoth of a school. Dana pulled into a spot in the set of designated visitor's spaces. On her left was Shayla, a fellow new photographer. She had not spoken to Shayla much, but she seemed nice enough.

In general, Dana liked her newbie co-workers. They were as green as she was and didn't try to tell her what to do, so they were easy to bond with. She had become friendly with Hailey, Mackenzie, both Jens, and a few other women her own age. During a recent day on the job with Jen Li, she had casually mentioned Madison. Jen hadn't judged her at all for having a kid so young. She had asked to see pictures of Madison and gushed over how cute she was. These days the most common reaction she received when she revealed that she had a daughter was not the judgment and condescension she feared, but a visible sense of relief in the face of the other person, thankful that their own life choices had not led to such a colossal mistake. They were happy for Dana that she had an adorable child to love, but they were also glad that they themselves did not.

One minute before the mass exodus of SmilePosts workers from their vehicles at the scheduled arrival time, one last car pulled into the visitor's spot to Dana's right.

Dana looked over to see who it was. She was greeted by a big toothy smile from Ethan. She turned back face forward without reacting.

Mackenzie, Hailey, and the Jens all thought Ethan was charming and hot and at least three out of the four of them had said they would seriously consider making out with him if he asked. Dana was not nearly as impressed. She thought he tried far too hard. He ploughed into every gathering of people like a defensive lineman, knocking over other conversations to say, "Look at me! I'm so great!" Dana had a hard time trusting people with such high self-esteem. There was something annoying about individuals who couldn't see that they were as flawed as everybody else.

Everyone at the office thought Ethan was an endless treasure trove of humor. Despite her general dislike, there were times Dana would secretly laugh to herself at something he said. The previous week at the office, he had made fun of a kid whose picture he had taken with the unfortunate first name of "Semen." Ethan proved his claim by showing off the poor boy's camera card to every person in the room. When Stacy pointed out that the name probably wasn't pronounced the vulgar way he was saying it and he was being prejudiced towards people from foreign cultures, Ethan had said "Oh CUMMMMMMMM on," raising his eyebrows and emphasizing his dirty wordplay in such an over-the-top manner that Dana couldn't help but laugh along with the rest of the room. She was caught up in the contagious embrace of how gloriously stupid the whole thing was. She hid her face, not wanting Ethan to see that his jokes had gotten through to her.

At six-forty-five A.M., Rita, the senior-most SmilePosts employee of the Elderbridge Middle School battalion, stepped out of her car and everyone else followed.

"Good morning sunshine," Ethan said to Dana as they stepped out of their cars.

This was the first time he had talked to her directly since she had shot him down at training. Now, he acted as if that rejection had never happened and they were close friends, simply because they were standing next to each other.

"How's your morning going so far?" he said.

"It's... early," she said. She wasn't sure how she wanted to respond to his chattiness or what impression she wished to give him, if any. It was far too early to process thoughts. She stuck a frown on her face and decided the safest thing was to keep it there.

"Tell me about it. These mornings are fucking rough. I can't function until I have my medicine," he said, holding up the coffee cup in his hand.

She looked at him suspiciously.

"Medicine?" she said.

"It's just coffee," he assured, catching her drift. "Though if I have to get up at four A.M. one more time, I may start a cocaine habit. It would probably be worth the investment."

"Yeah, maybe," she said, remaining vaguely unfriendly.

"What's up Ed?" said Ethan, spotting Ed and engaging in his usual tactic of pretending that he was more interested in Ed than the pretty girl at his side.

Dana followed the others into the school, Rita leading the way. The front door was open.

There was no one in the main office. They waited fruitlessly for several minutes for a secretary to arrive and give them official instructions. Finally, Rita decided for the group that no one was coming and they should seek out the gym on their own.

Mornings often followed this pattern. Schools would tell the SmilePosts account representatives what time they wanted us to be ready and our reps would tell them what time we needed to arrive. Despite this pre-agreed-upon plan, there was often no one to greet us or tell us where to go. So, we would wander the halls, searching for where to set up.

In truth, there was something I found personally peaceful about these early mornings at the schools, strolling through the empty echoing hallways. As a child, schools are always bustling places, staff and students either streaming through the halls in between bells or packed into classrooms with their teachers. The occasional trip to the bathroom with a hall pass provided a rare glimpse of unoccupied corridors, but there were always school aides checking the hall passes, trying to find delinquents cutting class. And any peace provided by the empty halls was tempered, at least for good students like me, by nerves about missing some crucial lesson in class, as well as the pain of the overfilled bladder that had necessitated the bathroom break in the first place. Those SmilePosts mornings, in contrast, were like passing through an abandoned city. All life was vanished from the building. You could hear the squeak of your sneakers on the floor and feel the tranquility left when humanity was drained from the typically overrun classrooms. Briefly, I might sense the calm that earth possessed before the human population exploded and the calm it will return to when we eventually extinguish from its midst.

I don't think many of my co-workers relished this experience the way I did. They were too busy trying to figure out where the hell they were going.

Finding an auditorium was easy. Auditoriums were always up front towards the office. That day, Dana, Ethan, and the others were scheduled to set up in the gym. Gyms were a little trickier to pinpoint, but their size made a substantial footprint in the school and you could use your nose as a guide. When you started smelling the waft of pubescent sweat, you knew you were close.

The usual tracking methods failed them that morning at Elderbridge Middle School. The massive structure was brand new. The school had not been around long enough for the stench of sweat to soak in and guide their noses.

The previously rural area of Northern Lehigh County had seen an real estate boom in the last twenty years as homebuilding companies had bought up cheap farmland and untapped patches of forest to build hundreds of townhouse developments in near identical style. The home exteriors were inevitably white or beige with green roofs and purely decorative window shutters. The smattering of farm families who previously made up the population were engulfed by a flood of young married couples looking for affordable three-bedroom, two-bathroom starter houses and decent schools where they could send the kids they planned on pumping out. This was the pattern for much of Southeastern

Pennsylvania. The first wave of suburban development, built in the golden age of post-WWII baby booming, had taken up much of the land in the immediate semi-circle surrounding Philadelphia. Now this millennial-induced second age, far less heralded than the first boom, perhaps because there was no generation-defining war that preceded it, had taken hold. Impoverished inner-city neighborhoods were gentrified by twenty-something hipsters, pricing out the people who had always lived there, until these same city neighborhoods became so popular that the hipsters were priced out themselves by overpaid thirty-something professionals. The people below the poverty line were callously tossed from neighborhood to neighborhood like a mast in a hurricane, not much societal concern given to where they would live when their rent became overpriced after the arrival of the local five-star gastropub. Poor families were pushed to the city's outer edges, causing the middle-class families who had occupied those territories for the past fifty years to flee like rats from a sinking ship, terrified of sinking property values and increased racial diversity. Digging their nails into their middle-class status, these folks bought up the affordable new townhouses deep in the surrounding counties. Faced with the population growth, school districts like Central Lehigh invested in big, new education buildings to contain the glut of privileged white kids legally entitled to attend them.

The school district had wanted to curb the message board complaints of parents who, like most internet users in the 2010s, sat down at their keyboards each day looking for a fight. The district put all their resources into a state-of-the-art mega structure of a middle school and an even more gargantuan high school, hoping that the level of tech and scale would appease the unappeasable parents. Parents still complained, of course. They complained about their kids' grades or the fact that their lunches weren't healthy enough or that their lunches were *too* healthy or any number of other issues, but for the most part they were pleased with the buildings.

Rita, Dana, Ethan, and the whole group saw plenty of the state-of-the-art building of Elderbridge Middle School as they roamed the halls, failing to locate the gym. The bright white hallways had twenty-foot-high ceilings capped with open skylight glass. The labyrinthian passageways weaved in and out of specialty corridors. There were computer labs around every turn. Roombas roamed the classroom floors, cleaning up globs of spilled snacks. Turn after turn, the group came across surprising and unexpected classrooms such as a pottery studio, a yoga room, and a full movie editing suite, but no sign of the gym.

They felt lost and trapped. Rita, usually awash with confidence, wiped her brow of the small beads of perspiration that gathered as everyone looked to her for guidance. Dana wondered if they would even be able to find their way back to the office.

"Who goes there?" a voice said somewhere behind them.

They turned their heads in various directions, searching for the source of the voice.

Dana spotted an older man in faded dirty jeans, an old flannel, and a custodial jacket at the end of a side hallway. The man looked wary.

"Over there," Dana said to Rita.

Rita looked over to spot the custodian.

"I said who goes there?" he repeated, sticking with the anachronistic phrasing of a knight guarding a medieval castle.

"We're from SmilePosts," said Rita.

In an instant his suspicious, unfriendly expression lifted and a big smile spread across his wrinkled face.

"Well why didn't you say so?" he said. "Name's Girard. Pleasure to meet you."

Girard went down the line and shook the hands of every photographer.

"You guys must have a lot of equipment. You always bring in so much equipment. I never understand it. They make all you little ladies carry so much. It ain't right. But you're strong. So much stronger than your little muscles there look."

"Uh... yeah," said Rita.

"Let me show you where the gym is," said Girard.

"Yes, please!" said Rita.

As it turned out, the gym was below ground in a basement none of them had realized existed. Towards the back of the school was an elevator painted to look so flush with the wall that they had mistaken it for the wall itself.

The custodian told them they should use door eighteen to enter the building. He gave them directions for which way to drive through the parking lot and pull their cars up. He said he would meet them at the door.

Of course, getting to their cars required retracing their steps back to the office and nobody bothered to ask him those directions. They turned down several new and unfamiliar paths and it took them over eight minutes to locate the front of the school. Then, when they finally got in their cars, they all followed Rita, who was the only one who listened to Girard's instructions. None of the others paid attention because they figured Rita would. Rita took a wrong turn somewhere or other and they all ended up in some strange dead end and had to turn around and drive back the way they came. They were in the car for another seven minutes before they finally found door eighteen.

At this point, this whole process of walking and searching and driving had already taken up over thirty-five minutes and they were getting significantly behind set-up schedule. As they got out of their cars, Rita rapidly pulled her cases from her small trunk.

"Let's go, let's go!" she said, increasingly frazzled as she looked at her watch.

Some of the others tried to hurry, but most of them didn't.

Ethan made no extra effort. He may have been psychologically incapable of feeling urgency. He talked to Dana as he casually pulled out one case at a time.

"Man, that guy Girard was creepy right? Are we sure that he's not a ghost?"

Dana tried to increase her pace, but quickly gave up. The cases were too damn heavy. It was impossible to move them any faster than she always did. Being set up on time wasn't worth breaking her back.

"I think he's alive," said Dana.

"I don't know," said Ethan. "I wouldn't be surprised if he disappears and then some secretary says to us, 'Girard? Why, he's been dead for FIFTEEN YEARS!' Like in one of those horror movies."

As he guarded the open side door, Girard the custodian, who was a living human, further disrupted their speed with his chattiness. He wanted to know everything about the job: What schools they went to, what kind of camera they used, how they took good photographs. He continually commented on the extreme number of heavy cases they carried, declaring over and over again how it was cruel to make small women carry the equipment without help, while never once offering any help himself. At one point, he went off on a tangent about a cousin of his who supposedly had been the real person to invent Whole Foods and who had unsuccessfully sued the company. No one was sure why exactly he had started talking about that and at least half of them assumed there wasn't any truth to the story.

When they finally got to the gym, Rita raced to set up her equipment, utilizing underused thigh muscles and every ounce of energy she had to build her photography station before eight o'clock, when they were supposed to be ready. When Rita calibrated her camera and snapped her start slate, she looked down at her watch with great satisfaction. She beat the deadline by two minutes. She gazed upon her monument of accomplishment – camera, lights, and background, all ready to shoot, flash, and be in the background of people, respectively. She felt good.

Rita caught her breath and turned to assess the progress of her coworkers. She had been so consumed with her own set up that she had paid no attention to the efforts of the others. She hoped that some of them were close to finished.

The air caught in her throat when she looked out upon the gym.

Her co-workers, to a person, had barely unfurled their mats. One or two had set up a single light stand. Ethan only then was carrying in his final case from outside.

It was incomprehensible to Rita. *How could they have possibly made such little progress? What had they been doing?!?*

She had no time to answer her question. The first three classes walked in at eight on the dot and Rita was the only one available to take them. She buckled down and prepared for the onslaught.

"Over here," she called in the grim tones of a front-line soldier, knowing her only job was to be slaughtered so the later lines could stop the enemy.

By the time the first big rush ceased, Rita's spiky hair was wilting, sweat was dripping down her tattooed arms, and she felt about ready to pass out. She had sailed through the children at a remarkable clip of fifteen seconds per student. She didn't imagine that the photos were anywhere near her best work, but she had taken three classes on her own and lived to tell the tale.

She looked around, assuming that by now the rest of her co-workers would be ready.

But there they were, affixing their last lights, snapping their cords into their power stations, still five to ten minutes away from their start slates. Ethan was only now setting up his light stands.

The next three classes arrived.

"I need to ask for a raise," Rita said to herself.

Once everyone was finally set up, the day at Elderbridge Middle School went rather smoothly. Rita photographed about a quarter of the school on her own, but the others contributed as they could and the large number of cameras allowed them to plow through the deluge of ever arriving classes.

At eleven thirty, already halfway through the day, they were granted a half-hour for lunch.

Ethan walked over to Dana as the last students left the gym.

"Do you think she's alright?" he said, laughing.

He indicated Rita who was staring at her twitching left hand.

"I hope so," said Dana, serious.

(Rita was okay. The twitching subsided after a few minutes and she regained her usual composure once she got some food in her stomach. Photographing at an intense clip was an unfortunate hazard of life as a veteran SmilePosts photographer. You had to pick up the slack for the slow newbies around you. This is something I've learned again and again as the years have passed.)

The crew pulled their seat boxes against a side wall in the gym and gathered together to eat the lunches they had packed. Ed ate a turkey, lettuce, and tomato sandwich on white bread. Shayla ate a homemade salad. Rita ate some leftover pasta out of a glass Tupperware. Dana ate a chicken salad sandwich. Ethan had two boxes of Pringles. (Though he had money to spare, Ethan hated going to the supermarket and was lazy about making a lunch, even when he had food at home.)

As they ate their lunches, Shayla scrolled through her phone and showed the others a picture of her adorable basset hound, whose name was LL Cool Dog.

The picture elicited a chorus of laughs and "awws." Several of the other photographers all lit up now that the conversation had turned to the delights of their pooches. Their thumbs scrolled on their own phones, whipping out pictures and videos of their own beloved pets.

"Okay, I have to admit something weird," said Shayla in a strange tone that was both shy and illicit.

The others were intrigued.

"Tell us please," said Ethan.

Shayla hesitated. She seemed reluctant to move forward with her revelation now that she had dangled it in front of them.

"Now I'm a little scared," said Ethan. "Is this something we're going to have to report to the police?"

"What? No!" said Shayla, laughing. She fortified herself. "Okay. So my dog does this weird thing, where he likes to eat my underwear." She immediately covered her face with her hands as soon as the word underwear escaped her lips.

"Eww," said Rita. "Why does he do that?" She was both grossed out and legitimately intrigued.

"I don't know!" said Shayla.

"Were these clean or dirty underwear?" asked Ethan, in the mocking tones of a serious detective, determined to get to the bottom of an unfolding mystery.

"Gross Ethan," said Rita.

Ed hid his own face in his hands, flushing red by the turn the conversation had taken.

"It's a legitimate question!" said Ethan.

The others all turned their heads towards Shayla, with looks of anticipation. Though they were too embarrassed to voice their support of Ethan's question, they wanted to know the answer all the same. Shayla realized she was socially required to respond.

"They were clean!" she said.

"Sure. *We all believe you*," said Ethan sarcastically.

"Really!"

"Okay, important follow-up question," said Ethan, after soaking in as much bashful laughter as he was likely to get for the previous joke.

Shayla waited, terrified by the possibilities of what he might ask. The others leaned in, equally eager to hear, though grateful they weren't his target. He glanced over at Dana. Though she had said nothing throughout this conversation he could see she was listening. He smiled at her, then turned his attention back to Shayla.

"Were these edible underwear?" he asked.

They all laughed, including Shayla, now that the tension had been released.

Ed was embarrassed to the point that he was beaming red and literally said "gosh," out loud.

"No, they were not," said Shayla through a chuckle.

"Listen, I don't know what you and your boyfriend are into, but edible underwear is a real thing," he said.

"I'm aware it is, but they weren't—," she said, before Ethan cut her off.

"And that would explain LL Cool Dog's desire to eat your underwear."

"I swear they weren't edible underwear!" said Shayla.

"What is edible underwear anyway?" said one of the others. "Like what kind of food is it? Does it come in different flavors?"

"It's usually cherry," said Rita.

They all looked at Rita. Wordlessly, they demanded to know why she possessed that knowledge. Ethan decided to take the reins.

"You answered that pretty fast Rita," he said. "Do you have some insider knowledge we should know about?"

"I just... know what it comes in," she said unconvincingly. She immensely regretted drawing this attention on herself.

"Yeah, you just know what it comes in... what it feels like to wear... that's all you know, right?" said Ethan.

"I've never worn edible underwear," said Rita.

"Never worn," said Ethan. "So, you're the one who did the eating. I see."

Rita covered her face in her hands.

"What is the consistency? Is it like a cake?" asked one of the others.

Their eyes bore down on Rita. She clearly knew the answer but was reluctant to share it. Their stares were oppressive, unrelenting.

"It's kind of like a fruit roll up," she said.

"Ahh," said the others, simultaneously.

"That makes sense and is also gross," said Shayla. "It really only comes in the one flavor? There's no chocolate? Everything comes in chocolate."

"Looks like Shayla's putting chocolate underwear on her wish list," said Ethan.

Shayla blushed, but did not deny it.

"Gosh," Ed said once again.

They all looked to Rita once more. Annoyed, she realized they were waiting for her to answer the question about whether there was chocolate underwear.

"I've only heard of cherry. *Heard of,*" she insisted to deaf ears. "Just heard of."

"It's okay if some boyfriend has eaten your underwear," said Ethan. "We don't judge."

"Some girlfriend," corrected Rita. This was a revelation to some of those around her, though they made an effort not to remark on it.

"If I had a girlfriend," said Ethan, "I'd want her to get a pair of bacon-flavored panties."

Embarrassed laughter and disgusted groans abounded.

"What?" said Ethan, with faux innocence, "Who doesn't like bacon?"

They all laughed. Ethan caught Dana's eye. Though she hadn't said a word throughout the conversation, she was laughing with the others.

Much to her annoyance, Dana felt her heartbeat increase when he looked at her. *What are you getting nervous for?,* she thought, angry with herself. *And why are you laughing? It's not funny, it's just gross.* She tried to stifle her laughter, not wanting to give him the satisfaction. But struggling to hold it in only made the whole thing seem funnier and she laughed again.

Ethan's gaze lingered. Dana felt annoyed with herself because there was an unexpected part of her that wanted him to keep looking.

"Umm excuse me?" said a small voice from across the gym.

They looked over. A small, pre-puberty, sixth grade boy had walked into the gym with a photo envelope.

"I was late to school," said the boy. "Could someone take my picture?"

The various members of the SmilePosts crew looked at each other, all fresh in the memory of their X-rated conversation, Ethan's gross use of the word "panties" still ringing in their ears. They all burst out in laughter, reminded that they were in a school, filled with children, and their discussion had been far outside of the bounds of what was appropriate.

"Of course," said Rita, well aware that no one else would volunteer. She wiped her own reluctant tears of laughter from her eyes and directed the boy to her camera station.

The photographers all finished their lunches and the huddle dissipated. As the others returned to their cameras, Ethan looked at Dana and wondered whether there was something there he had not previously considered.

A couple of hours later, during a planned break in the schedule, Dana looked up from her station and saw Ethan approaching.

A rush of anticipation swelled through her. Her skin prickled. Dana found this reaction extremely irritating and wished her body would knock it off.

She was annoyed that she had laughed at Ethan's jokes and she was annoyed that she was excited by his approach. *What the hell was going on anyway?* How could she hold two such opposing instincts at the same time? How could she feel a fresh spark of attraction while maintaining a dislike of Ethan's delinquent charm? How could she be burnt by the scorching sting of anticipation while consciously judging him as an off-putting narcissist capable of many levels of assholery?

"Hiya," he said.

"Hi," she said.

She remained guarded but did not turn away.

"This school's got a million fucking kids," he said.

"Yeah, they just keep on coming," she said.

"So where do you live, Dana?"

"Huh?" She tightened.

"I don't mean like your address. I'm not trying to rob you or something." He laughed. "I meant like what area do you live in?"

"Oh," she said, forcing a laugh, embarrassed that he had spotted her fear. "I live in Northeast Philly. How 'bout you?"

"I'm in King of Prussia," he said. "It's pretty chill. I'd like to be in the city though. Maybe Manayunk or something."

"Not in the Northeast."

"No, certainly not. I don't hate myself."

She laughed.

"I grew up there. I live with my parents," she admitted.

And then she paused. *I should mention Madison*, she thought. But for some reason, she didn't.

"Hey, no judgment here," he said. "It's hard out there. I have a roommate. My buddy Jake. I'd prefer to have my own place, but, you know, money," he said, pretending he didn't have plenty of it.

"Tell me about it," she said. "I can barely afford to eat."

"I could get Ed's bag of snacks for you if you're hungry."

They looked over at Ed, who was stuffing pretzels into his mouth at his camera station.

"I think I'm good," she said, holding back a laugh, trying once again to be unfriendly, but failing.

He looked at her, with the smile of a private detective who solves cases primarily to sleep with the distressed damsels who hire him.

"High standards I see," he said.

"The highest," she said.

"Well, I guess I'll have to raise my game then."

"I guess so."

Why am I encouraging him? she thought. *This is not a guy I want to go out with.*

"I could certainly steal some food from the cafeteria. A school this fancy, they're probably cooking lobster down there or some shit."

"Nah. They probably still have the same nasty rectangular pizza," she said.

He laughed. "I used to like that pizza," he said.

"Yeah, me too," she admitted. "I don't know why. It was fucking gross."

"Better than those cardboard hamburgers."

"Yeah, I'm pretty sure those weren't meat."

"Definitely not," he said. "So, what do you like to eat?"

"I don't know. Edible food."

He laughed. He looked at her with wanting eyes and she tried to summon the feeling of distaste she had felt for him previously, but the negative feelings ignored her call.

I should mention Madison, she thought again. *Why don't I want to mention Madison?* There was a lull in the conversation. It was a good opportunity.

A frightening possibility occurred to Dana: her reluctance to mention Madison wasn't caused by a desire to keep Ethan out of her life, but just the opposite. Madison's existence might scare him away. It was a discomfiting notion. *He doesn't need to know about her*, she justified. Ethan was a stranger. She didn't have to tell him about the existence of her daughter if she didn't want to.

The break ended. The new classes arrived.

Ethan hesitated for a moment before returning to his camera.

"I'll tell you what. You got some spunk Dana," he said.

Then he walked off, carried along by the inrushing tide of adolescents.

FIVE
SOME SORT OF LAZY, PURPOSELESS WASTE OF SPACE

THE UNNATURAL ODOR of disinfected vomit; the sound of drunk males celebrating their own drunkenness through idiotic, aggressive challenges to fellow drunk males; the feel of bodies pushing in from every angle as the proprietor flagrantly exceeds the legal capacity limit; a general attitude summed up in the phrase, "Here, every day is St. Patrick's Day."

It must have been Saturday night at one of Philadelphia's Irish pubs, at least three of which are uncreatively named "The Irish Pub," and it must have been Ethan out with his friends, looking to get plastered.

"How about this one? Look at that ass," said Ethan, indicating a woman, standing underneath one of the many Celtic artworks hanging on the Pub's walls.

"It's very nice," said Ethan's friend Larry, who was in a committed relationship and was highly uncomfortable objectifying women, but who still looked at the butt, despite his higher instincts.

"Or that one's got a nice ass," said Ethan, pointing out a different woman. He had been running the conversation along these rather repetitive lines for several minutes now.

"MmmmHummmm," said Joe, another friend, who was already well past his alcohol limit at 11:34 P.M. and had stopped speaking in words.

Ethan, Larry, and Joe were accompanied by A.J., Walt, and Ethan's roommate Jake, all of whom had paced themselves far more successfully than Joe.

"You meeting any girls at this new job?" Walt asked Ethan.

"Girls who aren't, like, eight years old, I believe Walt means," said A.J.

"Yeah, I got my eyes on one or two," said Ethan. Dana immediately flashed into his mind. He wasn't entirely sure why, but she had leaped to the top of his prospect list. She was far less friendly towards him than the Jens or Mackenzie. Half the time, when he said hello to her, she wouldn't say anything back at all, even after their conversational breakthrough at Elderbridge. Maybe that was exactly why he wanted her – the thrill of the chase.

"There's a few hotties," said Ethan.

"Again, want to be sure you're not talking about the children," said A.J.

"Nope. I'm talking about adult women," said Ethan. "How about this one's ass?" he said, motioning to a new woman in his immediate sightline.

"I like that one," said Jake. "That's a nice ass."

"Burrrrrrrrr," said Joe.

"Anybody going to talk to any of these girls or we just going to look at them?" said Walt.

"Looking's half the fun," said Jake.

"What about the other half?" said Walt.

"If I wanted to do math, I'd be in school right now," said Jake.

This was not an overly intellectual group of men.

"Nobody else finds it weird that Ethan is hanging out with children all day?" said A.J.

"Jake, you consider one half plus one half to be difficult math?" said Walt.

"How is that job going, Ethan?" said Larry.

"The picture day job? It's fine. It does the trick." said Ethan.

"What trick?" said A.J.

"I know what a half plus a half equals," said Jake.

"The trick of getting my parents off my back about having a job," said Ethan.

"What does it equal?" said Walt.

"Is that all you're looking for?" said Larry.

"One whole! It equals one fucking whole! Like two butt cheeks make one nice ass," said Jake.

"What do you mean, is it all I'm looking for? I'm looking to have a fun, good life. That's what I'm looking for," said Ethan.

"WhurrrrrrrrrMopppppppp," said Joe.

"Somebody give this guy a fucking gold star! He can do first grade math," said Walt.

"Fuck you," said Jake.

"But aren't you afraid that you have no real career prospects and no future plans to build a life around?" said Larry.

"Oh shit," said A.J.

The others all turned their attention to Larry and Ethan. A line had been drawn in the sand. Their attentions were magnetized to Larry's bold question and the surely volatile way Ethan would respond.

"What the fuck are you trying to say?" said Ethan.

"It's a question that comes from a place of friendship," said Larry. "We're all wondering it."

"Oh yeah?"

Ethan looked at the others. They all averted their eyes and looked at their shoes, or their beers, or the assorted butt cheeks of the women they had been staring at. None were willing to openly back Larry up, but they also wouldn't dispute his point.

"So," said Ethan, "you all think I'm some sort of lazy, purposeless waste of space?"

"Yeah, I guess that about sums it up," said A.J., only half joking.

"What are you guys doing that's so great?" said Ethan.

"Well, I have a job at Pfizer, A.J. is working for Liberty Mutual, Jake's got that gig at the Urban Outfitters HQ, Walt's getting his M.B.A. at Delaware, Joe is at TD Bank..." They all looked at Joe who was blowing bubbles with his saliva. Larry didn't let this distract from his point. "Look, we all had a great, fun summer, with lots of parties and fun, but I mean, we're out of college. We're in the real world now," said Larry.

"If Jake can get a good job, you certainly can," said Walt.

"Shut up," said Jake.

"Oh, so you don't think Ethan can get as good a job as you can?" said Walt.

"That's not what I meant," said Jake.

"It's what you said," said Walt.

"Shut up," said Jake.

"Jake, I think you should apologize to Ethan," said Walt.

"Guys..." for a quick moment Ethan felt angry, ready to lash out at this blindsided attack from his friends, but his ire vanished before he formed a sentence. "Don't you think you're all being a little dramatic? We just graduated. I've got plenty of time."

"You've got time, but what are you working towards?" said Larry. "You're a smart guy, we don't want you to waste your time."

"Thanks Dad," said Ethan.

"Ethan can do what he wants," said Walt.

"You don't agree that Ethan's wasting his potential?" said Larry.

"Of course I do, but he can still do what he wants," said Walt.

Ethan glanced back and forth amongst his friends, all of whom at one point or another had looked to him for social guidance. Back in high school, he was their charismatic leader, who slashed through the guards of awkwardness and hesitance so that they might all have an adventure they would have been too chicken-shit to have otherwise. He was the advanced one, never afraid to talk to girls, friendly with senior boys when they were only freshmen. He was fearless and they looked up to him. Now their pity-filled eyes avoided his own. He huffed, still certain that he had more courage than the rest of them combined. It wasn't so much their opinion about his career path that bothered him. They were simple guys who had bought, hook, line, and sinker into the idea of a post-college life endlessly propagated by their parents and teachers; this absurd, hard-lined concept that you were only a worthwhile adult if you let society pummel you into an unbearable job and heart-disease-inducing stress. If everyone was going to die someday, Ethan didn't see the point in his short life being regulated by miserable conditions. Their opinion about his work ethic (or lack of it) didn't bother him at all, since he thought the reasoning behind it was a "crock of turds." He disregarded Larry's concerns without a second thought. What upset him was that his buddies felt superior to him. It didn't matter the reason. What mattered was that a group of guys who had always admired him and aspired to be like him had now gotten it into their heads that he was second rate – an object of pity. They felt bad for him. It was infuriating.

Ethan gulped down the rest of his half-full beer glass and slammed it on the table. He stood up so quickly that the blood rushed to his head and he nearly collapsed.

He steadied himself before any further embarrassment.

"Are we gonna have a sausage fest all night or are any of us gonna talk to any of these girls?" said Ethan.

They looked at him, warily. They obviously suspected that he was running from the subject because he felt as ashamed as they thought he should be. That pissed him off further.

"Gaaaaaaa," said Joe.

The rest were silent.

"Fine. I guess I'm the only one who's getting laid tonight."

Ethan stormed off into the overstuffed human casserole that was The Irish Pub, squeezing his body through shoulders, thighs, and disconcertingly unidentifiable body parts, looking for a pretty face or a stray large boob to attract his attention.

He bumped chest-first into a wasted blonde, who immediately started talking to him about her bitchy boss before he had even said hello.

He said some things to her. Basic flirty lines about how "her boss must be jealous" and how "she really stood out in the crowd." You know, whatever came to mind. He wasn't thinking too hard about it. He offered to buy her a drink. She touched his forearm and said "thank you" in such a deep, profound way that you would have thought he had performed life-saving surgery on her. They drank. She laughed. She continued to attack her boss's character.

"She thinks responsibility is some like inherent good," she said. "And just because I forget to do some things, I'm like a worse person than her? It's really judgmental."

Ethan intended to back her up, but he couldn't find the energy to formulate words so instead he kissed her. Sometimes this kind of physically forward act backfired if it was unleashed too quickly, resulting in a slap in the face. But this girl was attracted enough or drunk enough to kiss him back and to be turned on by his aggression. When their lips separated, she slapped him on the butt.

"That's for being naughty," she said.

A fantasy of Dana flashed through Ethan's mind, overlaying the situation in front of him. He imagined Dana in the place of this blonde, whose name he still did not know or particularly care to know. He pictured Dana at this bar, standing where the blonde stood. He pictured kissing her in the same unprompted, unexpected way he had kissed the blonde. Dream Dana punched him. Hard. With righteous anger. She punched him repeatedly and accused him of assault.

Both Ethans smiled – dream and real – at Dana's self-defense and her charming antagonism. He had no idea why Dana's hard edges appealed to him. His crush on her was confusing but also undeniable. He figured he probably had the hots for Dana because he liked a challenge, but then again, that seemed too simple a diagnosis for this particular ailment. (The thought that he might be attracted to strong-will in a woman never occurred to him.) Either way, the idea of continuing to talk to the drunk blonde in front of him who was now insulting her boss's cat (an "ugly cat fuck" with a "stupid cat face") lost all of its appeal. Ethan excused himself. He said that he had to go to the bathroom, but instead he left the bar without saying goodbye to the blonde or to any of his friends.

He made his way through the Saturday night Center City streets, the bars overflowing onto Chestnut Street below the towering view of the Comcast Building. This was the nice part of urban Philadelphia he was used to, so much cleaner and more modern than the impoverished North Philly neighborhood he had photographed at on the Friday before. He was shocked that the city he spent all his life in contained such vast swaths of poverty. Until then, he had only ever passed by those neighborhoods on the highway, not giving them a second thought. It made him want to help those less fortunate in some way, but he had no idea what that might be.

Thoughts of economic inequality didn't last long. As he walked to his car, Ethan pulled out his phone and scrolled to Dana's number. He had programmed her digits in when they had worked together at Elderbridge Middle, snatching her number off the SmilePosts phone list.

He came very close to texting Dana, right then. But remarkably, he showed some restraint and decided that a drunk text, a few minutes past midnight on a Saturday, when they had never once communicated by phone, was the wrong tactic.

He arrived at his car. For a brief moment he considered whether he was too drunk to drive and should Uber home.

He thought about what his friends would say. They would tell him to be responsible with driving just as they thought he should be responsible with his career decisions. Those jackasses who had needed Ethan to guide them out of their boring lives, to take chances and grab life by the horns, or whatever the fuck the expression was, now thought they were so much fucking better than him.

"Fuck this, I'm not a pussy," he said, out loud, to himself. He hopped behind the wheel.

The following Monday, when Ethan pulled into the SmilePosts parking lot, he came across Dana, loading a new touchscreen computer case into her car. Her old computer had gone floozy during the day. Two kids into a line of seventy-five impatient first graders, the touchscreen had stopped responding to her touch, defeating its entire purpose.

The incensed parent-helper moms at Dana's school were furious about the malfunctioning equipment. They demanded that she fix the problem immediately, speaking at her through condescending gritted teeth, as if Dana herself was a misbehaving child.

(We were often accompanied at picture days by parent-helper volunteers. Typically, these were stay-at-home moms who would hand out combs, organize traffic flow of students, and not-so-subtly sneak behind our shoulders so that they could criticize our work. They would watch us pose and speak harsh judgments in voices that were soft enough to pretend they didn't intend us to hear, but loud enough to ensure that we would.)

Dana had frantically called George when the computer stopped working. He had assured her that someone would rush over with a backup computer, but she was way out deep in Chester County and the closest co-worker who wasn't using her equipment was Bonnie, who was at least forty-five minutes away. George told Dana that in the meantime she should pose the children for Josie, who was the only other photographer at the school. Josie had her own line of seventy-five first graders to contend with, which now became a joint line of one hundred and fifty kids. Dana joined Josie, forcing the six-year-olds into place, shifting their bodies and tilting their heads. As soon as she slid out of the way, Josie, who had been busy entering the package info into her own touchscreen, snapped the photos. They worked at a good clip this way, but not nearly fast enough to get back on schedule or make any dent in the ever-expanding logjam of students.

The parent-helper moms yelled at them that they were getting behind. But the moms didn't bother to tell any of the teachers to hold back on sending their classes, despite a schedule that was already overloaded prior to any technical malfunction. The moms also didn't bother to stop combing every single child's hair with an exhausting thoroughness, which created periodic gaps when Josie and Dana stood around, waiting impatiently for the moms to stop combing so they could photograph. And yet when the teachers arrived with their classes, incensed by the enormous line that made the procession at turn-of-the-century Ellis Island look like a quick jaunt to the front of the queue, the parent helpers held out their hands in mystified contempt and widened their eyes with helpless outrage, decrying the "horrible," "unprofessional," and "sickening," effort being put forth by the "incompetent" photographers.

When the office secretaries filled out the daily scorecard that SmilePosts employees always had to give to the school at the end of the day, the secretaries (who were good friends with the parent moms) gave Dana and Josie "poor" ratings with the note "Terrible job! The classes were backed up into the schoolyard! Computers didn't work! Sad!"

All of which is to say that Dana wasn't in a great mood when Ethan approached her.

"Howdy!" Ethan said, for some reason, immediately feeling like a dweeb. (Or in his words, "a fuckin' loser.") "Shit, sorry. Howdy? I don't know where the fuck that came from, I sound like a fuckin' loser," he said.

"Hi," said Dana, quietly.

"How was your day?"

Dana didn't want to say that her day was bad, which was the honest answer, because then he would ask why, and she would have to tell the whole story of what happened to her. The thought of recapping it all was unfathomable right now. She already felt unfocused and gauzy, like her old, depressed self, after the day's discouraging experience. She felt like a deflated parade float, stuffed awkwardly and impossibly into a confining shoebox, all the air sucked out of her and not enough space to breathe. She didn't want to talk to anybody at all. She wanted to crawl into her bed and close her eyes.

She didn't want to say her day was good either, because that was a clear lie, and though she had never had much of a moral issue with lying for her own benefit in the past, she felt reluctant to give that horrible day any credit for being worthwhile. Plus, she didn't think she could successfully back up the word "good" with her tone of voice. Her hatred and exhaustion would shine through.

"It was fine," she said, deciding on the middle ground. Still a lie, she supposed, but a less egregious one. Everyone knew that "fine" meant "bad" anyway.

"Nice, nice," he said, oblivious to her rotten mood.

He lingered. She closed her car trunk and avoided his eyes. An irate Canadian goose nearby honked at them as it passed through the parking lot with its gooselings. Ethan gave the goose the middle finger.

"Fuckin' geese," he said.

"Right," said Dana. "Well, I'm heading out."

She got into her car and closed the door.

Ethan felt an incredible swell of disappointment in the pit of his stomach. Or maybe it was the three Taco Bell Doritos Locos Tacos he had eaten on the way back the office. Either way, he didn't want to see Dana go so soon.

His mind rushed through romantic plans and schemes. He thought of ways to woo her and impress her – feats of strength he might display or practical jokes he might enact on others to make her laugh so much that she'd want to stick her tongue in his mouth. (It did not occur to Ethan to buy her flowers or pay her compliments. He only thought of how to impress her by showing off his own exceptional personality.) He quickly tried to calculate when he might run into her again by counting how often he had run into her at the office on average, but the math was confusing and the only result of this effort was frustration.

The goose honked at him again. He kicked at it.

He quickly regretted this. Not because he cared about being mean to a bird, but because he thought that getting into a physical fight with a wild animal might make a bad impression on Dana. Luckily, she had been looking away.

In fact, she was still looking away. So he kicked towards the goose again. *Fuckin' goose.* The goose scrambled off.

It felt good taking out his frustration on the goose. He couldn't remember ever feeling this thwarted when trying to coax a romantic conquest. It had been, what, a week since he decided he liked Dana and nothing had happened yet? Outrageous! That's what it was. Outrageous.

The conversation with Ethan's friends at The Irish Pub dropped into his mind again like a poorly balanced sack of bricks at a construction site, causing all sorts of death, dismemberment, and lawsuits. His buddies' unjustified superiority surged through his veins like an electric shock. It pissed him off. Where was the fuckin' goose? He wanted to kick at it again.

But the goose was nowhere to be found, so he did the next best thing. He marched up to Dana's window. As she started to drive away, he pounded on the glass.

She hit the brakes, terrified. She held her chest, her heart beating from the fright, and rolled down the window.

I'm not a pussy – I can ask out a fuckin girl, Ethan thought as he stared at her with what he imagined to be a look of determination, but to Dana looked like murderous rage.

"Jesus Christ," said Dana. "What the fuck? You scared the shit out of me."

"You want to go out sometime?" he said.

It took her a moment to reconcile his look of anger with his words. She replayed what he said in her mind to make sure he hadn't threatened her in the way his expression implied.

"What?" she said.

He saw the look of fear on her face and took a moment to process his own clenched fists and general agitation. He reached into his inner satchel of personalities and slapped on his trademark indifferent charm.

The change in his demeanor was abrupt and disconcerting.

"I mean, you know, we could go out if you want to. Up to you," he said.

Dana stared at him. All was quiet. At least until the goose returned and started screaming at Ethan. He held back on his nearly overpowering desire to tackle the bird to the ground. It wasn't the right moment.

Ethan figured that Dana's hesitation in saying yes was a result of letting his uncharacteristic anger get the best of him, which only made him angrier, but he locked his emotions inside. He put an awkward, forced smile on his face and held it there. He would not betray himself again.

His assumption about her hesitation was wrong. Dana knew she would say yes, though heaven knew why. Too late to question it, in any case. She was attracted to him and there was no stopping that train now. The reason it took her a moment to respond was that she was debating once again whether she should mention Madison. There was, of course, the very real chance that as soon as she mentioned her daughter, Ethan's interest would deflate like a punctured balloon. More than a chance. With this particular handsome douchebag, it was a likelihood. He seemed to thrive on his untethered nature.

Even if he was still interested in her once he learned she was a mother, he was clearly far from father material. Dana tried not to think too long term at the moment.

"Look, let's not worry about the workplace awkwardness," said Ethan, though that was a concern that neither of them had. "They can't tell us what to do."

Ethan always liked a good piece of rebellion, including when it was unwarranted.

I should really mention Madison, thought Dana.

"Sure, I'll go out with you," she said, not mentioning Madison.

At that, she rolled up her window and drove away.

Ethan smiled as he watched the car pull out of the lot. He unjustifiably took Dana's "yes" as a complete victory over his friends and their concerns, though the two matters were in no way related. He fell back in the comforting arms of certainty about his own greatness. The goose snuck up behind him and bit him in the shin.

"Fuck!" he shouted.

As Dana drove away, she suddenly and painfully realized that she had never been on a real date in her entire life.

In high school, she mostly hung with guys in group settings and at parties. The time they spent alone together was mostly in their bedrooms at their parents' houses, getting quietly naked and exploring each other's bodies. No guy ever took her out to dinner or paid for her to go see a movie while they held hands. Pat had ostensibly been her boyfriend and he never took her out. They sat on his couch and watched movies and made out and had sex. Or they smoked weed with friends behind the laser tag place. Those nights certainly didn't count as dates. Or at least, she didn't want them to.

She imagined that Ethan, for all his faults, would probably at least pick her up, take her to a bar, and buy her a drink.

That was a nice thought.

SIX
A NORMAL TWENTY-YEAR-OLD FOR THE NIGHT

"HOW DO I LOOK?"

There stood Dana, Molly's twenty-year-old daughter, ready to go out on her first official date as a single mom. She wore a light blue church dress she had not worn in three years, because it was the nicest piece of clothing she owned.

Dana asked Molly's opinion, then sneered at an expected insult before Molly responded. Molly presumed that Dana was daring her to say anything negative so that she could storm off in a satisfying fit of presumed disrespect and generational imbalance.

Dana, Molly's little girl, was a grown woman with a child of her own. But to Molly, Dana was still a teenager stuck in the limbo that pregnancy had created, knocking her out of sync from the maturation process and now teetering her back and forth from child to adult, nothing to slow down the confusing careen. Molly could not place Dana in any life stage and so when she looked at her, she saw all of them at once. How did her daughter look? She looked like she was too young to be a mother, like a ten-year-old girl play-acting adulthood by sneaking into the makeup drawer. And she looked too old, like a wizened forty-something trying to recapture youth in her teenage dress, tragically removed from the pure first date excitement she should be able to feel at her true, young age.

As all of this went through Molly's mind, Dana continued to wait for a response. At first, she appeared annoyed by the delay, but then Molly noticed something else – a more subtle craving that peeked out from beneath the closed blinds of Dana's testiness.

Did Dana genuinely care what Molly thought? Was her stance of defiance inspired by how little Molly's opinion mattered to her or was it a thin outer coating, hiding the vulnerable little girl inside? Was she waiting and waiting for a response, not out of obligation to the mother who paid most of her bills and raised her child, but because she desperately wanted validation? Inside, was she secretly still that crying infant who needed to be clutched and soothed and assured that everything would be okay, even though it might not?

"You look good," said Molly.

Dana nodded with a neutral acceptance.

They looked at each other, blank.

A car horn honked outside. Dana peeked out the window.

"That's him. Gotta run."

Dana ran over to Madison and gave her a big bear hug.

"Love you, be good for grandma," she said.

Dana didn't tell Madison where she was going. She grabbed her purse and left the house. Molly wanted to tell her to take a jacket, but she held her tongue.

Molly knew that one day they would have to explain Dana's dates to the little one, but that was an issue for a later time. Right now, Molly assured herself, Madison thought nothing of Dana leaving. The child was used to Molly as her primary caretaker. She was used to having a mom who was still a child herself.

Ethan took Dana to a four star (out of five) Italian restaurant called Spumoni's. He had some money to throw around, so he figured, why not make an impression? White tablecloths and wine glasses always lit up a girl's eyes. He deliberately picked a place that hadn't earned that extra star so that he would later have room to improve.

His restaurant choice was also dictated by the fact that Luciany,

Dana's last name, sounded like an Italian name and he figured Dana was Italian. He wasn't a hundred percent certain on the point. He knew if there was an "I" or an "O" on the end of a name, it was probably Italian, but what about "Y," that sometime vowel? Either way, Italian was supposed to be the food of romance, or some shit like that, so it was a good choice for the date.

Seated in a dim, candlelit corner of Spumoni's, up against the blood red walls, Ethan ordered a beer and Dana followed suit, both oblivious to the waiter's sneer at their disregard for the wine list. Luckily, the waiter did not ask to see Dana's ID since she wouldn't be twenty-one for another three months.

Dana felt more nervous than she was comfortable with. There were warring instincts inside of her. There was her responsible, adult side. This side didn't want to give an inch to Ethan's schmoozing character, knowing that he only had one thing on his mind and all his charm was merely a tactic to get her clothes off. But then there was her fluttery, surprisingly vulnerable, immature side. This part of her felt more excited for this evening than she could rationally justify; this side, now that she was here, with Ethan, on an actual date, felt nothing more complicated than the anxious hopes of a teenage girl, hoping the cute boy across the table would like her. The two sides pushed and pulled, grappling for control.

"So, what do you think of the job so far?" asked Ethan.

"It's alright," she said. "The little kids are cute."

"Yeah. Some of the older kids can be real assholes though."

"That's true," she said. "And awkward."

"For sure."

Dana thought of a particular incident. She laughed to herself involuntarily.

"What?" said Ethan.

"It's nothing," she said.

"I think it was something."

"It was an awkward kid thing I was thinking about."

"Oh well, now you gotta tell me."

"I... it's... nothing," she said.

"It's clearly something," he said, his handsome grin spreading from one dimple to the other. "C'mon you gotta tell me now. The suspense is killing me."

"Well..." she said. "The other day this kid came up my to camera and he had, like, a full-on boner."

Ethan laughed so hard that he startled the sixty-something couple at the next table. They glared at him, incensed, as if insulted by the idea that anyone would take that much pleasure in anything.

"You're shitting me?" said Ethan.

"I am not," said Dana. "He had on those like, awkward mesh shorts, so there was no hiding it. He didn't seem embarrassed or anything. I guess he didn't think I noticed."

"I bet you're giving all the thirteen-year-olds wood."

"Uh... thank you?"

"You're welcome."

While Ethan was issuing his classy compliment, the waiter arrived with the beer. He seemed petrified by the conversation he had entered. He presented them with their beers and took their food orders with a ghostly pallor, hoping he could escape as quickly as possible.

When he left, Ethan laughed.

"I love how that waiter acts so mortified at walking in on a conversation about boners. I bet he's hard himself right now," said Ethan.

Dana shook her head, holding in embarrassed laughter.

"Probably jerking off in the kitchen," said Ethan. "Probably not safe to touch any of the food he brings us."

Dana continued to stifle laughter underneath her breath.

"Don't think I don't see you there, Dana," said Ethan.

"What do you mean?" she said.

"I know you try to be all serious and everything, but I see the fun girl underneath. I think you're wilder than you let on."

Dana thought about how to respond to his brazen assessment. One instinct was to slap him and storm out, another was to lean across the table, grab his collar, and kiss him.

Her perpendicular desires confounded her.

Was his comment an insult or a compliment? Or was it both? And how could it possibly be both? Her one side so desperately wanted to be a mature, respectable adult. The type of person who could be a responsible mother. This type of person did not laugh at boner jokes. There was simply no central cross-section on a Venn diagram between people who laughed at erections and responsible mothers. Just two separate circles with an enormous gap in between them.

On the other hand, every time she forced herself to stifle a laugh at some bout of immaturity, every time she turned down some bit of fun with her friends, every time she forced herself to focus as her mom explained some bit of adulting like paying a bill or filling out a check, she felt like she was living a lie. The effort to be mature was driving her back into that terrible fugue state of sadness. That was no recipe for proper motherhood either.

She missed her care-free teenage life of parties, sex, and booze. Feeling nostalgic, she sifted out any memory clumps of emptiness in high school and now primarily recollected the highs.

And she missed weed. God, did she miss weed.

"You got any weed?" she said.

It was as good a response to Ethan's observation as any.

A slow smile crept across Ethan's face like an expanding accordion.

"As a matter of fact, I have some in the car," he said.

"Fuck this place," she said. "Let's go get high."

"Who am I to argue with that?" said Ethan. He threw down a twenty for the beers, and they rushed to the parking lot.

Ethan considered pulling the car onto a side street before they lit up, but it was more of a turn on for both of them to smoke right there in the parking lot.

GREAT BIG SMILE

He rolled a joint. They passed it back and forth. The sixty-something couple passed by them on their way out of the restaurant, scandalized by the blatant criminal action in a public place. *Go to the five-star place if you want to be so high and mighty*, thought Ethan. He laughed to himself. The pot was already taking effect.

"What?" said Dana.

"Oh, just these old folks. Look at 'em. You'd think we were sitting on a pile of dead bodies, the way they're looking at us."

Dana burst out in laughter and she wasn't particularly high yet. The smell of marijuana alone was enough to make her let loose.

Ethan rolled down the window and blew smoke towards the couple. The terrified wife pulled the husband along by the arm and said "Ken, please, let's get in the car!" in the same tone of terror Ethan imagined her using with a mugger or an innocent black man. *Racist fucks*, thought Ethan.

"Oh god, that's nice," said Dana after taking a long hit.

"See, this is the Dana I like," said Ethan.

"You don't like the other Dana?"

"No, I like that Dana too. After all, the primary thing I look for in a girl is fear she might punch me in the nuts at any time."

Dana burst out in uncontained laughter.

"There it is," said Ethan.

"You like getting punched in the nuts, huh?"

"Only by a soft, supple female hand."

"I don't know how soft and supple my hands are."

"Let me see."

Ethan leaned down and planted a long, seductive kiss on Dana's hand.

Dana laughed harder at this cheesy gesture than at his joke about getting punched in the nuts.

"Okayyyy," she said, the syllables soaked in sarcasm

"What, you don't believe that I'm a romantic gentleman?" said Ethan.

"I believe that you wanna get in my pants," said Dana.

"I mean, no reason both things can't be true at the same time."

"That's all this is, right? You're just tryin' to seduce the tough girl to prove you can?"

"Are you uninterested in my seduction?"

"No."

"There you go."

"Why me?"

"What?"

"Why not those other girls at work?"

"Who says I'm not seducing them too?"

Dana stared at him with the exact "I'm gonna punch you in the nuts look" Ethan had referenced.

"I'm joking!" he said. Then in mock reassurance: "I'm not gonna seduce them until after I get in your pants."

This time she did punch him in the nuts.

"Fuck!" he said.

She laughed as if it was the funniest thing she had ever done, which perhaps it was.

"I was kidding!" he said.

"I know," she said. She took a long hit on the joint.

"That's what I like about us together," he said. "The constant threat of violence."

A rolling wave of giggles from Dana. She couldn't stop her laughter now that she had gotten a little high.

"Happy to sacrifice any future children I might have for your enjoyment," he said, massaging his wounded crotch.

Dana's giggles abruptly cut off like a door had been slammed in her face.

Ethan's joke had reminded her of her own child, who she had still neglected to mention. At this point, her silence about Madison went well beyond any conversational lapse and was becoming a deliberate lie of omission.

All the immature fun was drained from the moment and Dana's responsible side grabbed the reins.

"You okay?" said Ethan, noticing the shift in her mood. "My balls are gonna be fine you know."

"Yeah, I know," she said, wrapped in her thoughts. Then she registered his joke and said, "I'm not worried about your balls."

"Good," he said. "I think."

Dana took a long look at him. She took one last hit of the almost finished joint.

"What?" he said.

Dana felt a geyser of pressure rise up within her. Her cheek bones swelled with the information that begged for escape. She hated this moment. She hated wanting to keep the daughter she loved so much a secret. She also hated the fact that she had a daughter and had to be put in a situation like this at age twenty. It wasn't fair. And she hated herself for thinking such a horrible thing. She wouldn't give up Madison for anything.

For a few moments, smoking some pot in a car, she had forgotten that she had catapulted herself directly out of her teenage years into responsibilities she could not ignore.

There wasn't anything to do about it now. The reminder was there and it wasn't going away.

"I have a kid," she said. "Madison. She's two."

Ethan was still trying to downplay the overpowering pain in his testicles (which he figured was his own fault for introducing the ball punching joke in the first place) and he was a bit high from the weed, so it took him a moment to process Dana's words and realize what she was saying.

"Wait, what?" he said.

That's that, thought Dana. She saw his interest dissolve away as he processed this new reality in his marijuana-slowed brain. She knew the fun was over.

So much for living like a normal twenty-year-old for the night.

Dana had approached the cliff's edge that I know all too well. That sudden abrupt fall from the heights of imagined possibility down to reality's lower depths. One moment you're skipping along on mountainous peaks of hope, then like Wile E. Coyote, you look down and find that you left the solid surface behind many steps ago. You're hovering over nothing. And you plunge, landing in a cloud of dust, all your fantastical expectations racing away with the speed of the dimwitted Roadrunner.

I always felt bad for Wile E. Coyote. Look – I know, I know. He's the villain. He's got those evil eyebrows. And he wants to eat the Roadrunner. But he's a carnivore, what do you expect him to eat? It's the circle of life and all that. He's in the middle of the desert. It's barren. There are probably snakes and scorpions trying to sting and bite him all the time. He's thirsty and he's starving. Have you seen how thin he is? The Roadrunner is his natural prey! And yet, time after time, Mr. Coyote (Yes, I'm giving him the proper respect he deserves) is foiled from getting the only thing in the world he's ever really wanted. Time and time again, he fails to achieve his dream. But he never stops hoping. He never stops trying. Even though every single person watching knows that it's a children's cartoon and we're never going to see him murder the Roadrunner and consume the bird's flesh. There's something so sad in Mr. Coyote's endless optimism and inevitable defeat. Am I the same as him? Is all my hope and effort for naught? If an audience of children were watching me, would they laugh at my repeated attempts at achieving my dreams, every time foolishly expecting that the newest ACME product will be the one to capture my elusive desires? Will I never be nourished by the fantasies that fuel me to keep moving forward? And if I never catch up to my own personal Roadrunner, what does that mean for my future? How do you live a life when you've given up on finding the things you've been searching for as long as you can remember?

For Dana, in that smoke-filled car, things weren't as immediately dire. Or rather, I should say, Ethan didn't flee as quickly as she expected. Whether or not this was a good thing, I'll leave up to your individual judgment.

"A kid? You have a kid?" said Ethan.

"Yeah," she said.

"Like a baby?"

"She's two."

"So... like a baby?"

"She talks and walks and stuff."

"Man. And you like... gave birth to her?"

Somewhere in his mind Ethan realized how stupid he sounded. But the pot had gummed up his processing center. His thoughts were stuck in molasses now and by the time they dripped down to his vocal cords, any intelligent expression was left gooey on the walls of his brain.

"Yes. I gave birth to her," said Dana.

Dana had a higher tolerance for marijuana than Ethan.

"Shit," he said.

Ethan shut his mouth. He shook his head around and hoped to loosen some of the muck. He needed to think about this. As he shook his head, it occurred to him that the back and forth sideways motion of his neck might make Dana think that he was saying "no," to the situation, which he was not ready to do, so he transitioned to a steady upward and downward nod, but this seemed too clear of a "yes," which he definitely didn't want to commit to, so he started rotating his head in a strange diagonal pattern, the sideways figure eight of an infinity symbol, but this made him feel ill, so he stopped moving his head all together and tried to think.

Think. Think.

As Ethan's silence went on, Dana felt increasingly guilty. She had been lying to him and now he was in the awkward position of determining how to escape from her in an acceptable way. They worked together at Smile-Posts, so he couldn't just open the door and run off, though she wouldn't blame him if he did. She should never have put him in that position.

"I'm sorry," she said. "I should've told you. That was shitty. You can do whatever. It's fine if you don't want to date again."

Ethan looked at her. He saw the fragility in her tired eyes.

He definitely didn't want to date someone who had a kid. Even high, he knew that. It was such an obvious fact that it didn't require thinking about. It was a factory setting template of his desires. An automatic feature – no set-up required.

And yes, he was horny. And yes, when he was horny, any possible drawbacks to touching a pretty girl sitting in a car with him might be cast aside like expired milk, but his aversion to dating someone with a kid came built in with an emergency escape switch that overruled the claim of any erection.

If his system were working properly, he would have run from the car and traveled a minimum of two states away from the threat flashing red in front of him.

But he didn't.

What counteracted his immediate, and if we're being honest, sensible instincts was the thought of his fucking friends and their fucking judgmental attitudes from the previous weekend. (Again, his use of the f-bomb, not mine.) He imagined his friends hovering over his shoulders like those pesky, condescending mini-angels in one of those cartoons he used to watch on Nickelodeon – *man, those were great*, he thought, *remember the one where there was that talking Australian dog or something named Rocko, and his weird cow friend, man that show was weird... wait, what was I thinking about?* (Ethan was extremely high), *oh right* – and his annoying friends in their little white angel costumes were saying, "Ethan, you can't watch over a kid. You can barely take of yourself. Wait, scratch that. You can't take care of yourself AT ALL. If you were to watch after a kid, it might be an actual CRIME. They might ARREST you, you fucking loser." *Shut up*, Ethan thought, *shut the fuck up, I can do whatever I goddamn please. Fucking assholes.*

"So what?" he said, out loud, though he didn't realize he had spoken until Dana looked at him with wide attentive eyes. At that point, he figured he should say something else, though the time in between this statement and his next was far longer than his perception of it.

"I don't care," he said, at last (or quickly after, depending on whether we're using Ethan's reality or objective clock time). "You have a kid. So what? Doesn't bother me."

Dana was astounded.

She didn't know if she should fully believe him. She didn't know if he was only high and horny and would change his tune when the daylight hit.

She was not as high as Ethan, but she was still high, and in her current state she didn't give her doubts the time and consideration they probably deserved.

She primarily felt a powerful rush of relief. The cat was out of the bag and it could meow freely and chase mice and do whatever else it is that cats do. (She was more of a dog person.) The secret of Madison had been this heavy weight and now she felt so much lighter. Telling him about her daughter had been like playing Russian roulette with five bullets in the revolver. She was sure a bullet would be lodged in her head, but much to her surprise, the trigger had clicked innocuously and she sat here alive, next to a cute guy, who liked her, out for the night for a goddamn change, and for the moment, her hesitations slipped away.

She grabbed Ethan's shirt and pulled him close. They made out in the parking lot for a half hour. In the process, he tried to take off her shirt a couple times, but she slapped his hand away. She was loose and elated, but not enough to let him sleep with her on the first date and she knew any nakedness was a slippery slope. Eventually the same waiter they had walked out on in the restaurant knocked on their window and demanded they leave, because the "paying customers" were complaining.

Neither of them registered the insult. They were too happy.

SEVEN
A SECOND KIND OF HAPPINESS

"**REALLY GOOD** photos today, Dana," said George, as he handed Dana back her DVD. "Smiles are good, expressions are good, framing is good, lighting is good, focus is good, head position is good, eye direction is good, all really good photos, good work."

"Thanks," said Dana. She turned away, bashful. She didn't want it to be too obvious how much the praise meant to her. For once in her life, she was decent at something. It was a new sensation to feel like a contributor to a cause rather than a roadblock someone else had to pass through on their way to something better.

"Also, you look hot," Ethan whispered into her ear as he passed by on the way to the overflow candy jar. George had been keeping candy on his desk since Halloween.

Dana's eyes snapped at him with reprimand. Ethan looked back with a sly smile as he popped a root beer lollipop into his mouth.

Dana and Ethan had decided to keep their new relationship private. They didn't need the scrutiny of their co-workers, who tended to eat up every stray morsel of gossip with a voracious appetite. Also, Dana was relishing her new identity as a quality worker and didn't want her image sullied through association with Ethan. She didn't tell him about the second part.

Ethan had agreed it was best to keep their dating life to themselves, but his behavior showed that he primarily liked secrecy as a flirtation game. Zipped lips were a way to build illicit desire.

He licked his lollipop in a suggestive manner as he passed Dana again on the way back to his table. She assumed that these lusty licks were the only reason he had taken the lollipop in the first place. Ethan was hardly a candy addict like George, who routinely went through three packs of M&Ms and six Jolly Ranchers in the course of a half hour.

As Dana's eyes followed Ethan to his table, she caught Bonnie staring at her with uneasy consideration. It was a mother's stare, ripe with concern for a young, innocent girl digging herself into a hole with a bad boy's shovel.

Dana snapped her head in the other direction with more guilt than she intended. She worried that Ethan's unsubtle overtures made their coupling obvious to the others.

"Are you hooking up with Ethan?" said Mackenzie, when Dana sat back down at her own table.

"What?" said Dana, caught off guard by the direct question. "No."

Mackenzie looked back at Ethan and then again at Dana.

"You're hooking up with him," said Mackenzie with confidence. "Lucky. How is it?"

"How's what?"

"Yeah okay."

Hmmm. So keeping a relationship hidden at SmilePosts wasn't particularly easy, Dana admitted to herself. She still had no intention of discussing it with the others.

"I don't know what you're talking about," said Dana.

For the next couple of weeks, this is how things went:

Dana worked hard. Ethan did not. At least, no harder than he needed to. Whenever they crossed paths at a school or at the office, Ethan would pull Dana around a quiet hallway corner or into a broom closet and they would make out for a couple minutes before Dana got ahold of herself and pushed him away.

Word of their coupling spread like wildfire amongst the SmilePosts employees, though both Dana and Ethan denied it whenever they were asked. Dana, not unexpectedly, had a better poker face than Ethan. When he was pressed on the question, he would smile the "I know something you don't know" smile of a mischievous child. This was the same smile he used to indicate to his friends that he "was gettin' some" when they "weren't gettin' any," though in this case, he actually wasn't "gettin' some," because "some" clearly meant sex, and Dana wasn't willing to cross that particular bridge yet.

Dana was more affected by the office's transparent knowledge of their relationship than Ethan. All he seemed to feel was pride at having bagged Dana and further pride in taunting everyone else by refusing to admit it. Dana felt judgment. She spotted the changed way that Dee, Bonnie, Josie, and the other veteran women looked at her. They all liked Ethan and thought he was entertaining, but they pitied a girl who could fall for his act. Dee might be grading her pictures, saying something nice about the kids' expressions, but underneath she looked at Dana like she was sifting through a pile of spoiled fruit, hoping to find one ripe piece among the wreckage. Josie, who had been very friendly to Dana previously when they worked together, now flipped past her like an episode of garbage TV that wasn't worth her time. Worse, was the behavior of the newbie friends Dana had made like Mackenzie, Hailey, and the Jens. Unlike the older gals, they didn't judge her negatively for dating Ethan. They were mad at her for refusing to admit it. Her silence on the topic gave off the impression that she thought she was better than them – too high and mighty to share the spoils of her love life with the lesser beings around her. It was hard being ostracized by her new friends and Dana seriously considered being open, but every time she approached them, she stopped. Because as soon as she publicly declared that she was dating Ethan, she would enter a new stage of commitment with him that she was not ready to take.

Dana was having a ton of fun on her dates. But she had a hard time ever imagining Ethan as a father figure to her daughter, and so the whole enterprise seemed destined to crumble within a matter of weeks. Solidified within Dana's mind was the rule that she would not sleep with a suitor who was incapable of remaining in her life. She now knew the consequences of irresponsible sex and she was not willing to take that risk without the proper vetting. Whenever they started fooling around, her immature side argued that she should say "fuck it" and go all the way, but she held strong.

No. She would not sleep with someone who could not be a father to Madison.

She didn't tell her SmilePosts friends about Ethan because she knew it would get back to him. Then he and everyone else would think they were boyfriend and girlfriend and he would expect her to spread her legs for him. And she wasn't ready to do that, goddammit.

One Saturday night in late November, Ethan and Dana were lying on Ethan's bed in his apartment, watching YouTube videos of clumsy skateboarders crashing into light poles and falling down staircases, laughing their asses off. (Ethan and Dana were laughing, that is, not the skateboarders, who were screaming in pain.) They had been dating for three weeks.

Ethan looked at her and thought, *I really like this girl,* and then, speaking his next thought out loud before considering it internally, he said, "I want to meet your daughter."

Dana's laughter abruptly stopped. The only sound in the room was the cry of agony from a skateboarder who had fallen from a metallic rail, coming from Ethan's laptop speakers.

"What?" she finally said, although she had heard him perfectly well. She was buying time to process how she wanted to respond.

Ethan sat up on his crumpled bed sheets, which had not been washed in three weeks. His linens were high quality because his mother had bought them, but she didn't come to his apartment and force him to do laundry. He had too few possessions in his room for it to be considered a proper mess, though he never dusted and the grime buildup was palpable. Dana wasn't any cleaner herself, in her own room, and she wasn't bothered. Mostly, she was impressed with the quality of his things: The big screen TV in the living room, the speaker system in his bedroom, the LED clock, which scrolled news stories and sports scores. Going to his apartment, she realized, as she had not before, that Ethan was kind of wealthy. The scattered objects shone a spotlight on his family's money and made his aloof manner less defiant or purposeless, than pre-ordained by destiny. He didn't work hard, not only because he didn't want to, but also because he didn't have to. A crucial difference.

"I said I'd like to meet your daughter," he answered her, as if it was the most casual thing in the world. As if he was commenting on the weather. He smiled the charming smile that made her feel completely out of control of her impulses.

As Ethan smiled at her, maintaining his look of nonchalance while fully aware of his character being assessed at the most fundamental level, his thoughts caught up to his bold declaration. He formulated his reasons for wanting to meet Madison.

For one, he really liked Dana. That was a nice, unfiltered truth that was not always the case when it came to girls he tried to sleep with. Speaking of which, he did really want to sleep with her. She was obviously holding back until she fully trusted him and it was getting increasingly torturous. She had started coming over to his place and they had started getting half-naked and doing everything with each other's bodies except that final, culminating act. He knew she would trust him more if she saw he was good with her daughter, and why shouldn't he be? He worked with kids. He liked working with kids and kids liked him. He always joked around with the six and seven-year-olds, giving them high fives and asking them about how much school sucked. The fact that Dee and George kept criticizing his pictures didn't mean he wasn't good with the kids, it just meant that he didn't have the impossible standards for photographs that his managers did. Madison would love him. Everybody loved him. *But are you really ready to be a father?* he asked himself. *Well, no*, he admitted. But he wasn't exactly asking Dana to marry him.

He thought about what his friends would say. They kept popping into his mind lately, telling him he wasn't good enough, telling him that he was digging himself into a hole he wouldn't be able to get out of. This time, he imagined his buddies warning him with a big red stop sign that he was not responsible or mature enough to be a father or even a father figure. They told him he was in over his head and should run away as fast as he could. Ethan was so bored of his friends and their recriminations. (Though these recriminations came from a fictional version of his friends, rather than the actual human beings.) The guys were so boring, so monotonously tied to their concrete life plans, refusing to let life carry them down any interesting, unexpected paths. Maybe he would bond with the kid. Maybe he would marry Dana and become a father. Who's to say what he might do? There wasn't anyone who could tell him how to live his life but himself.

Damn he was horny.

"Okay," Dana finally said, hesitantly capitulating to his request. "Okayyyy," she repeated, holding on the "y" with a noncommittal, question mark in her voice.

"Great!" said Ethan. "Maybe next weekend we can hang at your place?"

"Yeah, okay," she said, looking like someone who had taken an unidentified pill at a party and was terrified to see what the effects might be.

"Awesome," he said.

Ethan shut his laptop screen and stuck his hand down Dana's pants.

Ethan took his hand out of his jacket pocket and offered it to Dana's father for an introductory handshake.

"Pleasure to meet you, sir," said Ethan.

Steve glared at Dana silently. He refused to look at Ethan.

As Ethan continued to awkwardly hold his hand out, he realized that Steve would not reciprocate. He considered making a joke of it. "What are you, some sort of germaphobe?" he might say. Instead, he read the room and smartly held his tongue.

"Okay," said Ethan as everyone watched him awkwardly lower his arm.

"Here she is," said Molly from the staircase. Dana's mother carried Madison into the room. The girl clutched her stuffed animal of Elsa from Frozen. (Question: Is it still a stuffed animal when it's a human character? Is it a stuffed human? Just wondering.)

"Hey baby," said Dana. She took Madison's hand. "I want you to meet a friend of mine." Dana directed her towards Ethan, but the girl's feet remained planted. Shy, Madison turned her head into Dana's leg. "C'mon," said Dana. Madison would not budge. "C'mon," Dana repeated, with growing insistence.

"She's a little shy," said Molly. She looked at Ethan apologetically as she spoke, but her words were directed at Dana in reprimand. The clear subtext was, "leave her be."

"It's okay," Ethan said, speaking directly to Madison in the child-friendly voice he used at schools. "I'm shy too."

Dana snorted at this brazen lie, but no one else noticed.

"Whatcha got there?" he said. He approached Madison confidently. "That looks like Elsa to me."

This got Madison's attention. She peeled her forehead away from Dana's leg and looked at him.

"It is Elsa," Madison confirmed.

"I knew it!" said Ethan. "She's pretty cool. She's got those magical powers. I wish I could freeze *my* enemies in blocks of ice."

"I like Elsa," said Madison.

"As you should," said Ethan. "She's a good female role model. Much like your mom here. I like strong women."

Dana smirked as he literally winked at her. The cheese was overwhelming, but also wonderful.

"Can I see her?" said Ethan.

"No," said Madison, matter-of-factly.

Ethan laughed. "Well, like I said, I like strong women and you don't have to share Elsa. No means no."

Dana blushed. Her parents were in the room, after all, and Ethan was making playful sexual assault jokes with her daughter. Still, he was being rather sweet with her.

"I'm going to the living room," said Steve, to no one in particular, then he walked out. Dana's heart ached, like it did each and every time her dad presented his new icy, uncaring persona to her. Some wounds would never heal.

"Can you show me your other toys?" Ethan asked the girl.

"Yeah okay," said Madison. Then she sprinted up the stairs.

Ethan gave Dana a smile that said, "I guess this is happening," then followed the girl in her race to the second floor.

Molly looked at Dana. They were the only two left in the room.

"He seems nice," said Molly, though her voice betrayed a hesitancy that her words did not.

"He is nice," said Dana, though it felt like a lie. There were a lot of things she liked about Ethan, but kindness was not the first quality that came to mind.

She turned and followed him up the stairs.

When Dana entered her room, Ethan and Madison were sitting on the floor. She was showing him her set of colored magnet tiles and multiple Elmo figurines.

"This is Elmo. This is Elmo."

"Two Elmos with one stone, huh?" said Ethan.

"Yeah," said Madison.

"I'm more of a Grover guy myself," said Ethan.

"This is *Elmo*," insisted Madison.

Ethan laughed. "Yes, I know. It's Elmo."

"Not Grover."

"No, it's not Grover."

Madison seemed satisfied that she had won the debate and handed

Ethan one of the Elmos.

"Oh thank you! How generous," he said.

Dana lingered in the doorway and watched as the conversation continued. Ethan looked back at her and smiled his heart-melting smile.

She watched Ethan and her daughter play like that for several minutes. She observed from a distance before she eventually joined them on the floor and jumped into the game. As she watched Ethan charm Madison in the same way he so effortlessly won over the people at SmilePosts, with his attitude-expressed belief in fun above all other things, she considered a possibility she had not previously allowed herself to think. There was a small chance that Ethan was legitimate boyfriend material. Maybe he wasn't just the hard candy you guiltily snuck for a sugar-rush. Maybe he could also be the fresh fruit, which tasted sweet while containing benefits to your health.

Maybe he could be the guy she was looking for, though she had previously decided that she wasn't looking for a guy at all.

"I'm pretty jealous of your toys, Madison," said Ethan.

"Yeah," said Madison.

The next time they got together at Ethan's, Dana slept with him.

"Ethan & Dana" changed quickly from a coupling that everyone at SmilePosts secretly knew was happening to one that everyone openly knew was happening.

Dana made up with her newbie friends, apologizing for her secrecy. "Honestly, I didn't think it would last," she told them.

"Yeah, neither did we," said Mackenzie, sounding disappointed that it had.

Ethan relished the new status, taking every opportunity to steal PDA from Dana at the office, relishing in the mild annoyance she expressed each time he hugged or kissed her. He thought her angry bashfulness was entertaining. He was a conquering king who wanted to be sure everyone

GREAT BIG SMILE

in the kingdom knew of his exploits. He was a master hunter who had captured the savannah's most elusive prey. He was the alpha dog, and he was pissing on everything to leave his claim.

Beyond the intense ego satisfaction of everyone knowing he was getting laid by the hot girl at the office who had initially wanted nothing to do with him, Ethan was happy with the relationship itself.

He really liked Dana. He liked her bitter snark and hard edges. He liked the fragility peeking underneath and the way she melted when she was with her kid. He also really liked Madison, much more than he would've thought possible. The tyke had a spunk of her own, clearly inherited from her mom. She was a blast to play with. She had a zest for fun and an inquisitive nature and a stubbornness that was hilarious in such a little person. The nights at Dana's place, when they played with Madison and watched Disney movies, were almost as enjoyable as the nights at his place when he and Dana had sex. Almost. Okay, the nights when he had sex were definitely preferable, but the point was, he enjoyed the nights with Madison.

"What grade would you give yourself for the season?"

"Uh... I don't know. B?" said Ethan.

Dee looked skeptical.

"B-minus?" offered Ethan.

It was the Friday of the SmilePosts Christmas party. Ethan's mind was already on alcoholic eggnog and unwrapping his own present of Dana's naked body.

"Please list ten things you did well this season and ten things you could improve on, in order from most good to least good and from most improvement needed to least improvement needed," said George.

"What?" said Ethan.

"How about one of each," said Dee. "Something good you did and something you can improve on."

Ethan was meeting privately with George and Dee. At the end of each season, the manager and his unofficial co-manager met individually with each photographer to conduct a review. It was exactly the kind of corporate minutiae that Ethan despised. He was doing his best to pay as little attention to his bosses as possible and get done with it.

"Alright," he said. "I was good at talking to the kids and I could improve on... um... I don't know... you know... I don't know. I think I'm doing good."

"But you gave yourself a B-minus," said Dee.

"That's true. So yeah, I guess I could do better. Sure, why not," said Ethan. "Hey, is there going to be food at this party later?"

George and Dee looked at each other. It was the look of parents about to tell their child that they were getting a divorce. They turned back towards him, silent, concerned, measuring their words.

"No food?" he said, although he doubted that was what inspired their grave expressions.

"Ethan," said Dee, "George and I have some concerns about bringing you back for the spring."

George turned away. Actual tears welled up in the corner of his eyes.

"I always hate this," said George, dabbing at his eyes with a nearby napkin.

Ethan felt his defenses fortify. *Fuck you*, he thought preemptively, at any insult that was about to come from George and Dee's mouth.

But then, oddly, he thought of Madison. His hostility turned to fear for reasons he could not quite grasp. He dreaded whatever Dee was going to say next.

"We've given you a lot of notes on your photos," continued Dee, "and yet the work continues to be below our standards. You've also been late to work on a number of occasions."

"I hate this," said George, "excuse me, sorry," George shuffled off, unable to control his tears.

Even in the current tense atmosphere, Ethan thought George's melodramatic breakdown was a thing of great comedy to remember to tell Dana about.

"It's hard to justify continuing your employment here," said Dee. Then she waited.

There was a window. Despite her words, Dee seemed to be giving Ethan a chance to offer a rebuttal. She was taking a moment to allow him to defend himself and see if he was willing to take a stand.

Ethan's friends and family and everyone in his life seemed to judge him for his refusal to embrace adulthood, or society's concept of it, as if he should be jumping for joy at the coming avalanche of responsibility.

Everyone embraced hard work as if it were something other than a burden, which was a viewpoint that he had never been able to comprehend. (This was in great part because he had never had a glimpse of financial struggle, but he was too blind to his own blind spot to realize he had one.) Up until now, Ethan had always thought that maturity was inextricably linked to a crushing sense of boredom.

But at this crucial life moment, offered the chance to either submit to values that everyone else held or keep on fighting the good fight, the good fight suddenly seemed unimportant. He thought of Dana and Madison. He liked the way Dana looked at him when he played with her daughter. It was a way of being seen that was so unfamiliar to him that he didn't recognize it at first. She looked at him like someone who could make something of himself. People always liked Ethan, but no one ever expected him to accomplish anything because he wasn't mature. But what if he could be? Maturity waited before him, ready to be seized if only he could quiet his ego long enough to grab it.

"I can do better," he said, quietly, averting his eyes. "Give me a chance. I don't want to lose this job."

Dee brightened. She seemed pleasantly shocked that Ethan had taken her bait.

"Why should we believe that you'll do better?" she asked, with a tone of encouragement, rather than malice. She hoped he would give a good answer. She was rooting for him.

Perhaps happiness comes in different forms, thought Ethan, as he pictured himself giving Madison an airplane ride in his arms, while Dana gazed upon him with admiration. Perhaps freedom from responsibility leads to one sort of happiness and responsibility leads to another. A second kind of happiness, which he has never known.

"I have to do better," said Ethan. "I will do better because I have to. It's the only way people will see that I can make something of myself."

Dee silently observed him for a moment, as if they were engaged in a game of chess and she was thinking long and hard about her next move.

"I'll have to talk to George," she finally said. "But that's good enough for me."

Ethan breathed a deep sigh of relief. He didn't realize how nervous he was until Dee issued her verdict.

"But," she said, "you're on your final chance. Any more lateness or mess-ups in the spring and that's gonna be it."

"I understand," said Ethan, flashing his Cheshire Cat smile.

Ethan drove to Dana's house as soon as the meeting was over. He texted her that he wanted to give her a ride to the Christmas party that night, though he had already been at work and was close to the bar where the event was held. (Dana had her far more positive review meeting with Dee and George the day before.) Ethan texted that he wouldn't take no for an answer because he was too excited to see her. Dana replied with a smiley face emoji.

On the way over, he was buzzing with exhilaration. He felt the electric charge of change. A new dawn was upon him and he was ready to embrace it.

His friends were wrong. He could be an adult after all. It wasn't that hard. He'd probably be better at it than all of them, those fucking losers.

He pulled into a parking space across from Dana's house at about forty-five miles per hour, slamming on his breaks and terrifying the freezing old woman who was out letting her dog poop on the slushy remains of an early winter snowfall.

He rushed out of the car and texted that he had arrived – which is what people under the age of thirty do instead of ringing doorbells. He waited impatiently, thinking that Dana should have been anxiously waiting for his text and primed to open the door as soon as she received it.

His excitement grew. The expression "turning over a new leaf" passed through his head and then he wondered what the fuck that was supposed to mean. *A new leaf?*

He didn't go too deep down that linguistic rabbit hole because Dana answered the door, Madison in her arms.

"Maddy, look who it is!" said Dana. "It's Ethan, here to see us."

Madison beamed, then tucked her face into Dana's shoulder, blushing, as if embarrassed by how glad she was to see him.

Somewhere inside Ethan a panic ignited, encouraging him to run away from all of this, get the hell away from a single mother with a kid, get to a bar, get drunk, get laid, quit his job, abandon any pretense at wanting to do better and promising he'll do better, hating the idea that he was on thin ice and had to behave and stay within pre-set boundaries.

Fuck you, he told the panic.

He stepped inside the house.

EIGHT
THE EXPOSED, GENUINE ARTIFACT

AT THE TAIL END of a long, cold January, on the day of Smile-Posts spring training, Ethan managed to isolate Dana for a moment as she stepped into the hall to use the bathroom.

"Can we just talk for a minute?" he said quietly, not wishing anyone else to hear. He was repentant, but also annoyed with her. "You won't respond to any of my texts."

Behind Dana in the photographer room, the vastly truncated group of returning employees were learning the new spring portrait program.

The spring pictures varied from year to year, offering parents a fun twist. Instead of the standard pastel-colored background of fall, in the spring, the child might stand in front of a woodsy cabin, or an out-of-focus field of flowers, or a white picket fence. Instead of the standard torso-to-forehead framing, we might offer poses varying from a body-length shot with hands in pockets (for boys) to hands on hips (for girls) to an elaborately complicated horizontal shot of the child sprawled on the ground, ankles crossed, cheek leaning against an open palm. The latter is supposed to be adorable, but usually comes off as either physically strenuous or discomfortingly seductive depending on the child's age, arm length, and/or advanced cleavage.

This year, the portraits involved a façade windowsill with fake flowers, in which the children cherubically placed their chins in their hands and gazed out at the off-screen spring day.

In the hall, Dana looked towards the bathroom door. She really did have to pee.

"I have to pee," she said.

"I said I was sorry," said Ethan. "I don't know what I did that was so bad."

Dana looked at Ethan. He was smiling at her with a politician's look of contrition. And it was working. The fact was, she did miss him. She also didn't want to crumble, weak-kneed before him, absolving him of his behavior with a simple wave of her hands.

"I have to pee," she repeated, sternly.

Then she went into the bathroom.

Dana had seen Ethan nearly every day of the month-long unemployment known as SmilePosts Christmas break.

Neither of them had realized quite how extended the time off would be before returning for spring training in late January. Unemployment compensation turned out to be the unexpected gift that kept giving. Dana marveled at it.

"We get money for doing nothing," she said to Ethan repeatedly, in disbelief at this miracle.

Ethan, who had been getting money for doing nothing from his parents for years, was less impressed.

"Yeah, it's cool," he said, without any of Dana's reverence.

In many ways, it was the best period of time in Dana's entire life.

She had employment, but she didn't have to work. She got to stay at home and bond with her daughter, guilt free, knowing that she was doing her part to provide for Madison, even as she slept in until ten A.M. most mornings and spent half her nights at Ethan's apartment.

Though she would have never said it out loud, Dana thought she might have been falling in love with Ethan.

"I hate you," was what she said instead, repeatedly, sarcastically, whenever he unleashed a bit of his sneering humor. She retorted to his jokes with "I hate you," so frequently that it was obvious she meant exactly the opposite.

Never had she been with someone and felt so wanted and cared for. Her high school boyfriends like Pat had been awkward and aloof. She saw that now. Ethan was so smooth, so present. He was far from perfect, she knew. There were aspects of the schmoozy, self-serving, frat boy within him that simply could not be denied. But he also cared for her. He expressed his affection for her openly, with words, which would have been unheard of with Pat, who had never vocally expressed an emotion in his entire life.

Madison was also falling in love with Ethan, which was a more dangerous occurrence than Dana's own love. The girl giddily ran to him whenever he arrived, her hair bobbing in the self-created breeze of her sprint. She wrapped around his legs with her little arms and he reached down and lifted her upside down into the air until she spun right side up once more on his shoulder, laughing the whole time as if it was the funniest thing that had ever happened to anyone.

She talked about him near constantly when he wasn't around. Etan this and Etan that. (She wasn't yet capable of pronouncing a "th" sound.) Is Etan sleepin? Is Etan up? Where Etan? Etan play with me, she would say, playing with her own toys when Ethan wasn't even there.

Molly clearly thought the situation was a bit worrisome. Dana could see it in her eyes whenever Madison went off on one of her Ethan love fests.

"She's getting awful close to him," Molly would say to Dana, with terror in her voice.

"That's a good thing," Dana would say, defiantly, never wanting to agree with Molly, while inside she felt the same irascible fear. *What if he doesn't stick around? What will that do to my kid?*

Dana didn't allow herself to venture too far down that path of thinking. Life was good. She didn't want to taint the joy of it with thoughts of how it might spoil.

Everything went off track at 2:47 A.M. on a Thursday in the third week of January.

There was a loud knock on the door. A burst of drunken laughter behind it.

What the fuck? thought Dana. She peered out her window to catch a glimpse of the person pounding on their front door.

It was Ethan. Ethan and some friend. They were laughing and almost certainly drunk.

Annoyed, Dana slipped out of her sheets. Graciously, Madison was still asleep despite the racket. Dana quietly slipped into the hallway, where her parents were already waiting, Molly pressed against the wall in fright, Steve stewing with anger.

"I'm going to call the police," said Steve.

"Wait, don't," said Dana. "It's Ethan."

"I know," said Steve.

Still woozy at having been jarred out of sleep, Dana searched her father's eyes for some sympathy and found none.

"Dana!" yelled Ethan as he pounded on the door once more. "Hey Dana!" followed by fits of laughter on their front stoop.

"He's going to wake up the whole neighborhood," said Steve.

Dana's bedroom door inched open. Madison appeared in the hallway.

"Mommy. Grammy." She was on the verge of tears, scared by the knocking and yelling in the middle of the night.

"Oh sweetie, it's okay," said Molly. She picked Madison up and held her tight.

"Let me go talk to him," Dana said to her parents. "I don't believe this shit," she said to herself, as she raced down the stairs.

Dana threw the door open.

"What the fuck are you doing?" she said quietly.

"Dana!" said Ethan, full volume. He pulled her in and kissed her. She pushed him off.

"Jesus, you reek," she said. His breath stunk of alcohol.

"This is her?" said the other guy with Ethan.

"Who the fuck are you?" said Dana.

"This is A.J.!" said Ethan. "The guys wouldn't believe me that I'm like basically a dad now, so I told 'em I'd prove it."

"Ethan, you're drunk. Go home," said Dana.

"A.J. wants to meet Madison."

"I don't care."

"C'mon. Why you being so mean?"

"Leave right now or I'm going to call the police," said Steve, busting into the conversation. He apparently felt that Dana's time limit to smooth out the situation had expired.

"Dad, please, give me a minute," said Dana.

"I gave you a minute. The minute's up. I'm calling the police."

"Shit, why is everybody so serious?" said A.J., bursting out in more laughter.

"Did you drive like this?" said Dana, quietly, to Ethan.

"I'm fine," he said. "I just wanted to see you and Maddy and introduce you to A.J. He's my bro."

"It's nice to meet you," said A.J.

Dana glared at Ethan.

"Why are you doing this?" she said.

"Doing what? I wanted to see you," said Ethan.

"I'm calling the police," said Steve.

"Dad, would you please give me a fucking minute! Jesus Christ."

"Etan?" said Madison.

Molly had walked halfway down the stairs and Madison spotted Ethan.

"There she is," said Ethan, pushing past Dana to get to Madison.

"Ethan, don't," said Dana.

"Nice to meet you," A.J. said to Steve, holding out his hand for an introductory shake.

Steve looked back at him like he would murder him on the spot if it was legal.

"Ethan, I think maybe we should go," said A.J.

Ethan ignored him.

"Hey there Maddy," said Ethan. "Can I see her?" he said to Molly.

"I don't think that's the best idea," said Molly.

"C'mon, just for a minute. Maddy, can I see you?"

He leaned in close, breathing on her.

"You smell," said Maddy, who looked frightened.

Ethan laughed, uncontrollably.

"Well that's not very nice to say!" he said.

Dana grabbed him by the arm.

"Enough. You're leaving."

"I just got here. You're not happy to see me?"

"Let's go, I'm driving you home," she said.

"You're not going anywhere," said Steve.

"I'm not letting them drive like this!" she said. "And why do you suddenly care what I do?"

Steve opened up his mouth to respond. Then closed it. He paused a moment, then he walked up the stairs without saying another word.

"I don't understand what the big deal is," said Ethan. "I wanted to see you and Maddy. I wanted A.J. to see me with the kid. The guys didn't believe me."

"We believed you," said A.J. "We were fucking with you."

"You didn't fucking believe me, and you know it. This kid loves me," he said, motioning to Madison who had started to cry.

"Please drive safely," Molly said sternly to Dana. She turned around with Madison and walked up the stairs.

"Bye Maddy!" said Ethan.

"I'll drive Ethan's car and stay at his place. I'll come back tomorrow. I'll take the train or something," Dana said to Molly, but her mom had stopped listening. "Give me your fucking keys," she said to Ethan.

"Are you mad at me?" said Ethan.

"What the fuck do you think?" she said.

Back at spring training, Dana walked out of the bathroom. Ethan was standing right outside the door.

"What, did you listen to me pee?" she said.

"No," he said. "Well, maybe a little. I mean, I wasn't trying to. They need a fan in there or something."

"Jesus."

"Can we talk now?"

"We need to get back to training."

"I'm so sorry. I got drunk and I got excited to see you. Is that such a crime?"

Dana had been thrown for an intense loop by Ethan's drunken appearance at her house. It wasn't that anything about his obnoxious drop-by was particularly surprising or out of character. It was the opposite. It was all so in line with what she knew about him that it terrified her. Here, it seemed, was the real Ethan, the exposed, genuine artifact, so undiluted that he truly couldn't grasp what was wrong with his actions.

"You can't do that shit. You can't upset Madison," she said.

"I would never upset Madison," he said.

"Well you did."

"Look, are we hanging onto this endlessly? Or are we gonna go back to having a good time?"

There was a tear in the relationship fabric that Ethan wanted to pretend wasn't there. Ideally, Dana wanted to patch it up, but first she wanted Ethan to feel the cold air coming through the rip.

"Now is not the time," she said.

Back in the office, Stacy, who was at the training helm for the moment, was introducing the subject of sibling photographs. Often, in the spring, schools would allow siblings to take portraits together. It was a learned skill, knowing how to stuff these family sets into a photography

GREAT BIG SMILE

station designed for one subject. Most of the time, a sibling photo would consist of two or, at worst, three members of a family who attended the same school. But occasionally, some exceptionally frisky parents would have pumped out a family of four, five, or even six kids within a school's age range, never having heard of birth control or the cost of college tuition. Cramming all of these children from the same gene pool into your station was a practical impossibility and these photos were comically overstuffed. When the parents found enough time to stop reproducing, they furiously called up our customer service department, shouting an earful of expletives about the terrible family photo they had received.

It was basically impossible to prepare for photographing clans the size of the Von Trapp Family Singers, but the vets did their best to teach us how to shoot duos and trios.

Stacy asked for volunteers to demonstrate a sibling pose.

"I'll do it!" said Cal, the grumpy veteran, showing off an uncharacteristic bit of enthusiasm, which confused everyone in the room.

Cal ran over to the station. "Always happy to help you Stacy," said Cal.

"Thanks Cal, I appreciate that," said Stacy.

"You're quite welcome Stacy," said Cal.

They looked at each other and blushed. There was an awkward silence as the rest of the room stared at this odd bit of flirtation.

"Okay..." said Ethan, diffusing the awkward romantic tension. "I'll be your brother, Cal."

Ethan scurried over to where Cal was standing on the mat. He stood behind Cal, wrapped his arms around Cal's waist, and spooned the veteran, resting his head on Cal's shoulder.

The room exploded in laughter. Cal turned a bright shade of red.

"Get offa me!" he said. He tried to peel Ethan from his body, but Ethan held on tight.

"C'mon big bro, let's take our photo!" said Ethan.

"Ethan, please," said Stacy, looking at Cal with ashamed apology. Cal avoided her eyes, mortified.

"Is this not how we should pose the kids?" said Ethan, with maximum feigned innocence.

Holding on to Cal for dear life, Ethan scanned the room and found Dana. She was laughing with all the rest of them.

"I'm sorry," said Ethan.

The rest of the room assumed he was talking to Cal, who he continued to clutch with a steel grip.

Dana knew he was talking to her.

She turned away from his look. She started talking to Hailey, standing next to her.

Out of the corner of her eye, she saw Ethan clutch Cal a little tighter. Perhaps, this time, not to make everyone laugh, though they did, but to comfort himself, to hug someone, distracted by the sad thought that his stupid drunken action may have cost him the best relationship he'd ever had.

Dana was ready to forgive him, she decided, as she talked to Hailey about sibling photos, barely cognizant of her own words. She figured she had tortured him long enough. The message had been conveyed that she wouldn't take any more shit. Still, she thought she'd let him sweat it out for the rest of the day.

Several hours later, as training wrapped and they were headed to their cars, she pulled Ethan aside.

"You and Cal make a cute couple," said Dana.

Ethan, who had been uncharacteristically subdued all afternoon, was surprised by Dana's conversational olive branch. His confidence had taken a major hit with Dana's seeming-refusal to forgive him. He wasn't used to teetering on the precipice of heartbreak.

He quickly regained his footing.

"Well our complexions really complement one another," he said.

"Can I come over tonight?" she said.

Relief flooded through him. "That would be great."

"Okay good."

Dana turned to walk away, then stopped herself. A thought occurred to her now that the tension had been alleviated.

"Hey," she said, "when you came over drunk that night, you said something about feeling like a dad to Madison. Did you mean that?"

Ethan hesitated for the briefest moment before answering.

"Of course, she's a great kid. You know how much I like her," he said.

She smiled. She walked over and kissed him lightly.

"I'll see you tonight," she said.

NINE
HONESTY

"YOU SAID SOMETHING about feeling like a dad to Madison. Did you mean that?"

Dana's words screeched in Ethan's head like a dying hawk plummeting to the earth.

Ethan watched Dana get in her car at the end of that spring training day, following the conversation that repaired their relationship. He smiled at her, all the while combusting inside, wanting to run home, pack his suitcases, flee the state, and never talk to anyone he had ever known again. Such was his panic at realizing that he had drunkenly called himself a dad to Madison.

And now he had doubled down on this assertion, affirming while sober that he had meant it. You could always take back something you said while drunk. Sober statements were a different story.

Why the fuck did I say that? He thought on repeat, about a thousand times, during the drive home.

For over a week, all he had wanted was for Dana to talk to him again. He had missed her worse than he had thought possible. He thought his suffering would cease the moment that she forgave him, but he had now dug himself a much deeper grave.

When Ethan entered his apartment, Jake was on the couch, playing one of those disturbingly realistic World War II games, where you fire machine guns at Nazis and charge ever-forward like a sociopath, emotionally unaffected by your best friends dying beside you.

"What's going on?" said Jake, as he knifed a German soldier to death.

"Shut the fuck up Jake!" said Ethan, all wound up like a Happy Meal toy.

"Bad day?" said Jake.

"Are you alright?" said Dana, later that night, as they lay in Ethan's bed. Ethan stared at the ceiling, petrified like a victim of Medusa, not looking at Dana, barely speaking.

"I'm fine," said Ethan, through gritted teeth.

"You don't seem fine. Are you mad that I didn't talk to you for a week? Because that was your own fault."

"I'm not mad. I'm super happy," Ethan said, with all the enthusiasm of a person having his toenails peeled off.

"Okay," said Dana, entirely unconvinced.

They continued to lay there silently.

"So do you want to have sex or...?" said Dana.

"Yes, of course I do," said Ethan, with maximum affront.

They pulled each other's clothes off and all the while Ethan kept thinking, *why the fuck did I say that?* Over. And over. And over.

That weekend, Ethan went over Dana's house. In the intervening days he had managed to calm himself down. His statement about being a dad was a small misstep, an insignificant blunder. He convinced himself that Dana didn't think anything of it.

He rang the doorbell.

Dana answered, holding Madison in her arms.

"Maddy, look who it is!" said Dana.

I'm not her fucking father! thought Ethan.

"Etan!" said Madison.

"Yep, it's me," said Ethan, his skin crawling.

He stood on the doorstep, not moving an inch.

"Are you gonna come in?" said Dana.

"What? Oh yeah."

He stayed still.

"Are you okay?" asked Dana.

"I'm great!" said Ethan. He forced himself over the threshold.

"Etan, play wit me?" said Madison, forcing herself out of Dana's arms, to the floor.

Madison ran to the playroom. Ethan stared off into the distance.

"You're being super weird," said Dana.

Ethan attempted to slap a smile on his face, but it was like churning milk into butter. Dana saw the struggle of his widening mouth, his cheeks trembling as he tried to raise them. His dimples were over-stretched rubber bands, at the point of snapping.

"Let's go somewhere," he said. "Let's go to a bar or something."

"Okay, she said. "We should spend some time with Maddy first. She's excited to see you."

"Can't your mom watch her?"

Dana looked at him like she had bit into something sour.

"Yeah... I mean, she's upstairs right now, I told her we'd spend some time with Maddy," she said. "My mom doesn't watch her all the time, you know. I watch her too."

"Sure, but can your mom watch her now so we can get outta here?"

"Etan!" said Maddy, who ran back into the room, clutching a tiger toy by the tail.

"I don't want to play right now, okay Maddy," he said, harshly.

"What is wrong with you?" said Dana.

"I want to go to a bar. Can't we go to a bar? Jesus."

"You know, I'm not twenty-one yet," said Dana.

"What does that have to do with anything?" said Ethan.

Madison stood still, holding her tiger toy. She began to cry.

"Oh honey," said Dana. She ran over to her daughter and held her tight. She looked up at Ethan, who was not expressing an ounce of sympathy. "Maybe you should go," she said to him.

"You drink with me all the time," he said.

"What?" said Dana, as Maddy continued to cry in her arms.

"This bullshit about not being twenty-one. I don't know what that's supposed to mean," he said.

"It's okay sweetie," Dana said to Maddy. "Ethan's being a jerk. Sometimes boys are jerks."

"Oh okay. Now I'm a jerk because I feel like having a night out." He was getting increasingly agitated. "This is such bullshit."

"Would you stop saying that word? She's a two-year-old."

"She doesn't know what it means."

Dana shook her head at Ethan, in a seamless blend of perplexity and distaste.

"It's the poop that comes out of a male cow," he said. "And it's when someone says something that's totally made up and makes no sense. That's bullshit. There, now she knows."

Maddy continued to cry. "Etan?"

"I don't want to play Maddy. I'm not in the mood to play, okay!"

"Would you get the hell out of here?" said Dana.

"Oh, so hell's okay, but bullshit isn't?" said Ethan.

"Is there a problem here?" It was Steve. He had entered from the living room.

"No problem," said Dana. "Ethan was just leaving."

"Jesus Christ," said Ethan, exasperated.

He slammed the door on the way out with all the force he could muster.

📷

Dana went right back to ignoring Ethan after that. She wouldn't answer his calls or texts, and whenever she saw him at the office, she would look the other way, taking refuge in the crowd of female co-workers, who protectively shrouded her. They all stared daggers at Ethan as if he were a bloodthirsty wolf intent on sinking his teeth into their innocent flock of lady sheep.

He knew, somewhere inside, that he had been a dick that night at Dana's house. Yet all he could consciously feel, despite rational thoughts to the contrary, was that he was the one who had been wronged, that Dana was acting like a total bitch, and that she was torturing him for no other reason than her own sadism.

He knew that if he wanted Dana back – which he did, desperately, she was all he could think about – the best course of action was to apologize, but the thought of apologizing, as absolutely earned as the apology would be, was a knife repeatedly stabbed in his gut.

"Ethan, my man, what's shaking?"

Ethan looked up from his camera station. It was 7:13 A.M. on a Monday. He was jammed into an unused kindergarten classroom in West Philly, depressingly ratty old toys covered in dust flanking him in every direction and an out-of-place poster for the Nicholas Cage film *Con-Air* unpeeling itself from the wall over his head.

It was Otto talking to him. Otto, the overweight, self-described "sneaker-head" co-worker who bragged about his own Instagram, which supposedly had "like a shit-ton of followers." Otto tried his best to get as many laughs as Ethan in the office by telling three times as many jokes, with a very low batting average of successful comedy.

"Not much Otto. Not much," Ethan replied, deliberately refraining from the typical response, *how about you?* He was not in the mood to encourage a conversation.

"This Saturday," said Otto. "BIG party at my house. Folks are out of town. I'm making mojitos!"

"Okay," said Ethan.

"I mean, Dana probably told you about it. You gotta be there. Everybody's coming. Hailey. Mackenzie. The Jens. Josie. Blake. Pristine. Clint. Cal. Stacy. Dana. Even fucking Linda—"

"Dana's gonna be there?" said Ethan.

"Yeah, she said she would when I asked the girls. They said they'd all come. Have you not talked to her? Is there trouble in paradise?"

"Is this where I come for the haircut?" said a small voice at the door. It was a second-grade boy.

"No..." said Ethan and Otto simultaneously, confused by the question.

"Okay," said the boy. He walked away without another word.

"No, there's not trouble in paradise," said Ethan, incensed. "Dana and me are fine. I just didn't talk to her about it yet."

"Oh," said Otto. "It's all good. So, you'll be there?"

Ethan thought about it. This would be a good opportunity to win Dana back. And, if nothing else, there would be free mojitos.

"Yeah, I'll be there," said Ethan.

"Do you know where I go for the haircut?" said the second-grader who had reappeared at the door.

"No..." said Otto and Ethan.

"Okay," said the boy.

He stayed in the doorway, staring at them.

Otto lived in Richboro, a wealthy pocket of Bucks County with a fittingly direct name.

He had called the party for eight P.M. Ethan showed up at ten-fifteen, figuring he would be one of the first ones there, since no self-respecting person showed up at a house party before ten, but the place was full when he arrived. Otto's friends and his SmilePosts co-workers were obviously all quite lame.

When Ethan walked in, Otto was nodding his head to the Iggy Azalea song blasting on the speaker, while holding court to Jen Zolotov and Clint, our co-worker who was a bro straight out of a bro catalogue. Otto was discussing the instruction booklet that comes with a pack of condoms.

"Spermicide is such a weird word," said Otto. "It sounds like homicide or suicide. Like it's death by sperm."

Jen looked completely revolted by every single thing Otto had to say, but she was fawning over Clint, who had gelled his hair for the party to the point that it looked cryogenically frozen.

"I don't know man, I'm a lover not a fighter," said Clint, somewhat incongruously.

Jen laughed delightedly at Clint's words. She was a sucker for a good set of pecs.

Otto spotted Ethan. He reacted like a prisoner-of-the-state told that his nation had been liberated from centuries of oppressive rule.

"ETHAN! MY MAN!"

He ran over and man-hugged Ethan, hitting Ethan square on the back with his big open fist as if he were trying to dislodge a piece of food from Ethan's throat.

Ethan was extremely glad when the hug was over.

"Can I get you something to drink?" said Otto.

"Yeah – whatever you have," said Ethan.

"One homemade mojito coming up!"

"Let's start with beer," said Ethan.

"You got it hombre."

Otto skipped off like an excited schoolgirl. Jen and Clint, finally left alone, commenced making out.

Ethan scanned the house for Dana.

She was in the corner of the living room with Mackenzie, Jen Li, and some guys who Ethan didn't know. In theory, the strangers were friends of Otto's, but the girls might have brought their own boys to make sure the party wasn't insufferable.

Dana looked up, spotted him, then immediately looked away.

Ethan walked over towards her.

He passed right by me. I was awkwardly chatting with Hailey by the record player, engaged in a poorly disguised and poorly executed attempt at flirting.

Ethan went past a group of the vets – Gabby, Josie, Cal, Stacy, and Rita – talking in a circle he had absolutely no interest in joining.

He walked past poor shy Pristine, visibly trembling like a lost mouse as she held her beer and tried to work up the courage to join a conversation. Any conversation.

He walked with purpose towards Dana, but she spotted him first and stepped further inside her circle, so blatantly avoiding him that it made his heart ache and killed any forward momentum.

He sat down on the couch, feeling a wild craving for Dana that tunneled inward and barreled outward in stomach-churning unison. It had never been like this before with any of the girls he had been with. Even the actual girlfriends, the ones who had stuck in his life for a bit, had never inspired this sense of painful severance, as if Dana was a crucial biological organ and her rejection sent his system into panic, unsure how to compensate for the missing part.

"Here you are. One mojito!" said Otto, returning to Ethan's side with a green drink that definitely should have been clear.

"Fuck it," said Ethan.

He had asked for a beer, but he took the mojito, or whatever the disgusting drink really was, and drank it in one big gulp.

"Drink, drink, drink!" Otto started chanting too late, after Ethan had already consumed the whole mojito.

Ethan looked back over at Dana – she was talking with some blonde guy with long surfer hair.

"Get me another," Ethan said to Otto.

"Aye aye captain!" said Otto – running off in grateful servitude.

Ethan remained on the couch and stewed.

Then, feeling restless, he stood up and walked in the opposite direction of Dana, not sure where he was going, only knowing that he couldn't sit there and watch her talk to another guy. He wanted to throw up or cry or kick someone in the face, unsure which would provide the greatest relief from this terrible unmoored feeling.

He bumped into someone with a great deal of force. Their beer spilled on his shirt.

"Shit," he said.

"Oh god, sorry," he heard a female voice say, apparently apologizing for the beer spill, though the collision was entirely his fault.

He looked up. It was Linda, the older newbie at the office he had barely spoken to since training. She was clutching what remained of her beer. Lucky her that she had managed to find one and avoided the disgusting fauxhito.

They looked at each other. His anguish over Dana must have been poorly disguised because the next thing she said was, "Are you alright?" and she clearly wasn't concerned about him feeling damp.

"I'm pretty shitty," he said.

"Oh." She was surprised by the honest answer.

"Dana won't talk to me."

"Oh." After an uncomfortably long pause in which Ethan didn't provide anything more but didn't walk away from her either, she added, "You had a fight?"

He sighed. "I guess," he said, honestly not sure what to call the abrupt collapse of their relationship.

"I'm sorry," she said. "Relationships are tough."

"I don't want to lose her," he said.

He was prepared to open up and he wasn't sure why. He was in such a state of vulnerability that the words came out on their own.

"Oh," Linda said once more. Being a confidant or advisor was unnatural to her, but Ethan looked so sad, such a pitiable version of his normal, assured self, that she felt like she had to say something to help him. "You should talk to her."

"And say what?" he said.

"I don't know. Be honest?" she offered, completely unsure that honesty ever solved anything.

"Honest."

"Yeah. Tell her how you feel. Tell her the truth. Women like that," she said, immediately thinking of a number of times in which a guy had been honest with her and it had led to nothing but pain.

"Honest," he repeated. "You're right."

"Yeah..." she said, uncertainly.

"Thanks Linda," he said. "You're a real pal." He looked closely at Linda for the first time. She had gussied herself up for the party. Nice makeup, nice form-fitting dress. "You look good tonight," he told her.

Linda blushed. "Oh. Thanks."

He gathered himself to tell Dana the truth about how he felt. He turned around, walked over to her, brushed right past the surfer-dude, ignoring his "what the shit?" response, ignoring Jen Li's scoff and Mackenzie's smile and the vacant stares of the other bros in the circle. He stood right in the middle of all of them and looked at Dana, nobody else.

"I need to talk to you," he said.

"I don't want to talk to you," she said.

"I want to be honest with you," he said.

She was silent.

"I miss you so bad. Please can I talk to you for a minute?"

"Anything you can say to her, you can say to us," said Jen.

Dana seemed to think this declaration was a bit over the line and Ethan was grateful for the absurdity of Jen's gang warfare.

"Fine," said Dana, assenting to him. "Come on."

They found a door that led to the garage and walked inside for some privacy.

"Okay, what do you want?" she said.

"Do you not have feelings for me anymore?"

She sighed and looked at her feet.

"Okay," he continued. "I'll take that as you do still have feelings for me. Well I really like you too. This is killing me not talking to you. And I know you're mad at me because I was a dick to Madison. And I'm sorry. That was fucked up."

She looked up.

"It was fucked up," she said.

"I don't want us to break up. I don't want this to end."

"Neither do I."

"Maddy's such a sweet girl. I shouldn't have been a dick. But I was all fucked up that night because of what you told me I said. About feeling like a dad to her. The truth is I don't remember saying that. I was drunk. And I don't want to be a dad to her. I'm not ready to talk about being a dad. I just want to hang with you and not think about that shit. Because spending time with you is great. So, can we be together and not think about that other stuff? Like being a parent? We're too young to worry about that stuff."

Ethan felt an immense sense of relief getting it all off his chest. He was grateful to Linda for her advice. He had been honest and he instantly felt a thousand times better.

He held out his arms, ready to hold Dana against his body. It was then he realized that she looked like she wanted to murder him.

"What?" he said, genuinely perplexed.

"We're too young to worry about being parents... I am a parent, Ethan! I can't just not be a parent! It's not that easy."

He struggled to respond. "I mean your mom does a lot of it, right? You having a kid shouldn't affect what we have."

She was a pot about to boil over. Her breaths were rapid, her eyes narrowed.

"Fuck you!" she yelled at the top of her lungs.

"Don't you want to be with me?" he said.

"Yes! But I can't be with you if you don't want to be with my daughter."

"I'm cool with hanging with her sometimes, I don't want to be a dad, that's all. I'm twenty-three years old."

"I can't talk to you right now," she said.

She stormed out of the garage.

"Goddammit!" He kicked a bicycle that was standing in the corner – it crashed to the ground. He kicked it again, leaving a dent in the spoke.

He made his way to the kitchen, found the beer, and drank a whole bottle of Miller High Life in about twenty seconds. Then he took another. He looked over toward the doorway and spotted Linda, putting on her coat.

"You're not leaving, are you?" he called to her.

"Oh, uh," she was obviously leaving, but was reluctant to confirm it.

"You're not leaving," he told her. "Take off that coat and come have a drink with me."

Linda paused, hesitant. "Okay," she said.

Three beers, two fauxhitos, and two shots of tequila later for Ethan, two beers, one fauxhito, and one shot of tequila later for Linda, Ethan said:

"You're pretty."

"You're nice," she said.

"I mean it. You're really pretty. And you're smart, not like these stupid young girls. You like honesty. You're not scared of it."

"I'm scared of a lot of things."

"Like what?"

"I don't know. Failure. Loneliness."

"Why be lonely? You're here talking to me."

"That's true," she said.

"You're pretty," he repeated.

She blushed. She knew this exchange was heavily influenced by alcohol, but she still enjoyed being complimented.

"Let's find a bedroom. This place has like five of 'em," he said.

"I don't know if that's a good idea," she said.

He leaned in close and kissed her.

"Come on," he said.

He took Linda's hand and led her to the staircase. Her drunkenness getting the better of her, she followed him, thinking all the while that she should turn back around, walk away. But she never did.

As they walked upstairs, Ethan spotted Dana. He caught her eye. She looked appalled and wounded.

He smiled his movie star grin and disappeared with Linda up the landing.

TEN
THE CEASELESS FLOW OF CHILDREN'S BLADDERS

A WEEK AND A HALF after Otto's party, Dana had the unfortunate luck of being scheduled with Ethan at Reed Elementary in Chalfont. Gabby and Stacy were also there and with their assistance she was able to successfully ignore him all morning.

Shortly after the clock struck noon, Dana's fortitude waned. During a break between classes, she stormed over to him across the auditorium stage.

"Did you sleep with Linda?" she said.

"What do you care? You broke up with me," he said.

"I didn't break up with you."

"You said you couldn't be with me if I wouldn't be a dad to Madison."

"That was not what I said."

"I'm pretty sure it was."

"I didn't need you to say you wanted to be her dad right now. I just needed you to be a part of her life, if you want to be a part of mine."

"Well, that's not what you said."

"So, did you sleep with her?"

He paused. He didn't answer.

She slapped him across the face.

"Jesus!" he said at the top of his lungs.

Gabby and Stacy looked over from their own camera stations.

"Everything all right?" said Stacy.

Dana started to cry. She ran off the stage.

Stacy gave Ethan a dirty look and got up to go after Dana, but right then four classes arrived and she couldn't abandon her camera.

Stacy was set up closest to Ethan. In a brief pause in between children, she spoke to him.

"You're not a good person, you know that?" she said. "Dana's a sweet girl and you don't deserve her."

"Go fuck yourself Mother Teresa," he said.

Stacy's jaw dropped. In a huff, she returned to the next child in line.

"Come in. Stand on the red feet," Ethan said to the first-grader waiting at his own station.

The kid didn't move. He stood still, swaying from side to side.

"C'mon let's go. Time for your picture," Ethan said with no patience.

The kid trembled.

"Let's go. Red feet. Stand on them. Now." Ethan repeated.

The kid waddled in, nervous, shaking. Ethan knew he should pose the boy into the proper position, but he was in no mood. He didn't care how his pictures looked right now.

"Look over here," said Ethan.

The kid looked down, still quivering.

"C'mon kid," said Ethan. "All I need you to do is look at the camera."

He wouldn't look.

Ethan groaned. He walked over, grabbed the boy's head, and moved his face into place, holding it still.

"Hold there. Look at me," said Ethan, without a trace of sympathy.

"I have to go to the bathroom," said the little boy.

"What?" said Ethan.

Like a switch had been flicked, the dam broke and the boy peed all over Ethan's mat, Ethan's shoes, and the bottom of Ethan's pants. It was an absurd amount of urine. It must have been half the kid's body weight.

"Shit," said Ethan. "Stacy!"

"What?" she said, in no mood to talk to him. She looked over.

"This kid pissed all over me!" he said.

Stacy looked at him for a long moment. Then she exploded in laughter.

Dana badly needed a cigarette. Aware that if she was spotted smoking on a school's grounds she could be fired on the spot, she ran outside, still crying, and found a shadowy hideout behind a tree across the street from the building. She inhaled the first breath of smoke from her Parliament like it was a life-saving breath of CPR.

Also aware that she could get in trouble for disappearing from a school for an extended period of time, especially with Stacy present and probably timing the length of her absence, she smoked rapidly and tried to gather herself.

Her relationship with Ethan was over. Even while angrily ignoring him and knowing that she would never stay with someone who could be cruel to Madison, she had not fully abandoned her feelings for him. She was still confusingly awash in the blissful high that she had felt in December. It was only a little over a month earlier that she had been infused with a life-giving affection for him. But cheating on her by sleeping with Linda, that was absolutely not something she would stand for. He did it openly, at a party with all of their co-workers. Everybody knew about it. The shame of walking into the office now and seeing everyone pity her for her personal troubles was unbearable.

She felt herself tumbling. She remembered all that time after high school, after giving birth to Madison, when her energy had vanished. When she had been lethargic and joyless. When she had been depressed – okay, she admitted it, she had been depressed, sad, miserable, unable to latch on to any sense of purpose, any reason to get up in the morning and keep going. She could feel the beginnings of that incapacitating feeling encroaching upon her again like a spreading oil spill and it made her furious. She didn't want to feel that way again. When she had been depressed, she had been useless. She couldn't let herself go missing from life again because of some stupid boy.

Dana took a deep inhale of her cigarette and looked out at the calm mid-day suburban street. The only sounds were a few birds chirping and the background cacophony of recess on the other side of the school building. There were a few scattered snow drifts on the lawns from a mostly melted recent storm. People were at work, driveways empty. The sky was clear blue. It was thirty-two degrees outside and Dana should have been freezing because she didn't grab her coat, but she didn't notice the cold, too wrapped up in her thoughts.

She inhaled once more and she felt the depression recede into the caverns from which it came. She breathed the smoke in. She blew it out. Breathed in. Breathed out.

And suddenly she was calm. Not because of the nicotine, but because of an abrupt realization at the immaturity of her thoughts. They were the thoughts of a teenage girl, spiraling into madness because of some idiot boy. She wasn't a girl anymore. She was a woman now. She had a child. She had a job. She had responsibilities. All this worry and stress about a stupid relationship was incredibly silly. Guys came and went. She was entitled to enjoy herself and then cast a guy aside for the person who really mattered – Madison.

She dropped her cigarette to the ground and snuffed it out.

She had to get back to work. She had a child to provide for.

When Ethan got back to the office, his pants stinking of urine and covered with the scattered scraps of soapy paper towels he had vigorously scrubbed himself with in the boys' room at Reed Elementary, Dee asked him to join her. Stacy, Gabby, and Dana were already at a table doing the paperwork. The three of them had ignored him the entire day after he had been peed on and he saw no point in joining them. He threw his paperwork and money envelope bag in their direction and made his way over to Dee's desk.

Dee saw his pants and smelled the odor.

"You get peed on?" she said, as if it was the most normal thing in the world.

"Yeah," he assented, quietly, not wanting anyone else in the office to hear.

"It happens," she said.

For a moment neither of them said anything. They remained silent and thought about the ceaseless flow of children's bladders.

"Can we go talk somewhere for a moment?" she said.

Ethan nodded, then followed her into the equipment room, which was unoccupied.

"Ethan," she said, "I'm afraid this isn't working out."

"What?"

"Your position here."

Covered in pee, his cheek still stinging from Dana's slap, his heart still shattered from the confusing, abrupt end of his relationship with Dana, Ethan couldn't believe the low blow of this apparent firing. Fury arose within.

"Is this because I cursed out Stacy, that fucking baby tattletale? She deserved it. I bet she came crying to mommy as soon as she got back here."

Dee took a step back from him. Her face hardened.

"I haven't talked to Stacy," she said.

"Oh," he said.

All compassion vanished from Dee's voice after Ethan's outburst.

"No, Ethan, the reason we're letting you go is because, despite multiple opportunities, your pictures have continued to be sub-par and you've continued to show up late to work."

Ethan still felt angry but he was also cowed. There was no way out of this except for shameful submission.

"I'm sorry," he said, forcing the words out with much strain. "I can do better."

"Honestly," said Dee, with a sigh, "I'm not sure that you can."

For once, Ethan had no response.

"You'll have to turn in your equipment by the end of the day," said Dee. "Fill out your timesheet and your last check will be mailed to your residence."

Their conversation was interrupted as the door to the equipment room was opened. It was Otto.

Dee left the room without paying Ethan another glance. Otto held the door for her.

"Ethan my man," said Otto. He inched close to Ethan and whispered. "Hey, listen, I have to ask... Did you bang Linda in my sister's room? I mean, I'm not mad. But you could have given me a heads up. I would've washed her sheets after..."

Ethan said nothing. He stood still, staring into the distance.

"Dude," said Otto. "You smell like piss."

ELEVEN
EXACTLY THE OPPOSITE

TWO MONTHS LATER.
It was early April and the first warm currents were putting cracks in the icy armor of lingering winter.

Ethan was not enjoying the nice weather. He was locked in his room, smoking himself into a stupor. This had been his routine for the last two months of unemployment. Shades down, windows closed, a near-permanent cloud of marijuana smoke hovering near the ceiling, he contemplated whether he wanted to watch porn for the third time that day because there was not much else to do, but he felt too empty to be aroused.

It was nearing five P.M., not that Ethan was aware of the time. Clocks held no interest for him at the moment, since any time was pretty much the same as any other.

His cell phone rang.

Rang. Actually rang. Not blooped to indicate a text, as was its primary mode of communication, but rang, as if someone were calling him, like it was 1995 or something.

"What the fuck?" he said.

He grabbed the phone, didn't recognize the number, figured it was some robocall, but answered anyway.

"Who is it?" he said, wanting to sound angry, but only sounding high.

"Ethan?" said a female voice he couldn't place.

"Yeah," he assented frostily.

"It's Linda. From SmilePosts."

That piqued his interest. It also made him fearful for reasons he couldn't place. He sat up.

"Linda... what's up?"

"How are you?" she said.

"Fine," he said.

"Things are good?" she asked.

"Yep," he said.

"Um... are you at work?" she said.

"No," he said.

"Oh, okay. Did you get a new job? I wasn't sure why you left Smile-Posts."

"They fired me."

"Oh, okay."

"What do you want Linda?"

A long pause on the other end of the phone. Ethan waited, tense. His armpits were soaked in sweat. He wasn't sure if the phone call was responsible or if his armpits had already been that way and he hadn't previously noticed.

"So listen, you remember that night at Otto's party?" she said.

"Yeah," he said.

"Well, the thing is... this is crazy..."

"Yeah?"

"See... I was never able to get pregnant. They told me I couldn't get pregnant. I tried and tried for years..."

Ethan stood up, panic shooting up his spine. His foot tripped on a dirty pair of boxers and he fell. His head banged on the floor.

"Shit," he said.

"Are you okay?" asked Linda.

He grunted in response, sat up, rubbing the back of his head, desperately wanting the conversation to be over.

Linda waited. He didn't say anything else so she continued.

"Um... so like I was saying, they told me I could never get pregnant. Or that it was like near impossible, or very unlikely, you know. I mean I tried IVF and everything and it didn't take. It was really hard. To go through."

Silence.

"Okay," he said.

"Right. So I wasn't worried about you using protection because... I mean I was drunk, we should have never done that in the first place, but... I was feeling lonely and... I mean I know it would have been smart to use a condom anyway, because I don't know who you've been with... I mean I'm really sorry it happened, I never should have let it happen..."

"Spit it out Linda. Please." His head ached, he was having trouble focusing. It felt like each one of his individual bones was trembling.

"Right, sorry," she said. "The thing is. I'm pregnant."

He was quiet.

"I'm pregnant," she repeated and there was an undeniable lilt of joy in her speech. She was trying to disguise her happiness, because she knew this news would probably be a black pit of dire terror to Ethan, but she couldn't hold it back. She was ecstatic.

"Okay," he said.

"It's yours," she said, needlessly.

"Okay," he said.

"I'm going to keep it. It's what I've always wanted," she said, instantly giving up the charade of concealing her bliss, which pissed Ethan off.

"Okay," he said.

"I wanted you to know, I'm not expecting anything from you. I mean, of course, if you want to be involved, you can, but—"

"I don't want to be involved," he said.

"Okay," she said, not sounding the least bit disappointed.

Ethan clutched the back of his head.

"Was there anything else?" he said.

"No. Just that," she said, laughing awkwardly.

"Okay. Bye Linda." He hung up. He tossed the phone up onto his bed and leaned against his dresser.

Then, completely taking himself by surprise, he began to cry.

Even though he was still high, the pot-induced stupor he had kept himself in the last couple months was pierced by his crying and a stark, shattering glimpse of clarity pounded him, forcing him to face the thoughts he had been running from since Dee had laid him off.

For the past two months, he had locked himself in his room and barely spoken to anyone. At first, his concerned friends had texted him frequently. But he stopped responding back, trying so hard to ignore the fact that all of their criticisms were probably right.

He had no purpose. He had no ambitions. He had no sense of any excitement for the future and nothing to look forward to.

He had no idea what he was doing with his life.

The thought of a kid popped into his mind, but it wasn't the unborn child Linda was carrying. He wanted nothing to do with that kid. Let Linda raise it. Let him never hear anything about it again if at all possible.

No, the kid on his mind was Madison.

I miss that kid, he thought.

And that took him back to that terrible last day at SmilePosts when Dana slapped him and a kid pissed on him and Dee fired him and Stacy told him he was a bad person.

Am I a bad person? he wondered.

He examined the evidence and was honestly unsure. Was he cruel? Was he uncaring? He knew he was immature, he admitted that. But did that make him morally unfit?

He never intentionally wanted to do anyone else any harm. He wanted exactly the opposite. He wanted to cheer everybody up, to make everybody around him feel happy.

He remembered the stricken look on Madison's face when he had yelled at her, telling her he wasn't in the mood to play. It broke his heart to think about it.

He remembered Dee saying that she wasn't sure if he was capable of being better.

Ethan realized that he wasn't sure either. And he had no idea where that left him.

TWELVE
SOMETHING NEW

WHEN LINDA pulled Dana aside in mid-April after the weekly SmilePosts meeting, Dana wasn't sure what to expect.

Though they were civil to one another, they had mostly avoided contact since Otto's party. This was not too difficult as they had barely spoken before Linda slept with Ethan. Linda had become friends with the vets. Dana had her own crew of Mackenzie, Hailey, and the Jens, who all had her back and snubbed Linda in solidarity. Dana would never have asked them to do that, but she appreciated it anyway.

Dana was fairly sure that every single person in the office knew what had happened, even Dee and George. It was likely no coincidence that she and Linda had not been scheduled to work at the same school since the party.

Linda asked Dana to step outside the office, into the parking lot. They both looked around to see if there were any eavesdroppers. The coast appeared clear.

"First, I wanted to say I'm sorry," said Linda. "I should have said that long ago."

"Okay," said Dana.

The truth was, Dana had never really held a grudge towards Linda. The lion's share of her rage was directed at Ethan and that anger also dissipated quickly along with the revelation that she didn't want to be dragged down by a stupid boy. Still, it wasn't in her nature to offer lovey dovey forgiveness.

"But that's not why I wanted to talk to you," said Linda. "What I wanted to tell you is that I'm pregnant."

That was a turn that Dana had not expected the conversation to take.

"I didn't want you to be taken by surprise when it becomes obvious."

Dana was thrown off balance. She wasn't sure what Linda was asking of her or what she wanted.

"Okay," she said.

"Because it's Ethan's," said Linda, spelling it out. "But he's not going to be involved."

Dana searched herself. She wondered if she felt any of the lasting damage or heartbreak that Linda obviously expected her to feel. She examined herself to see if she cared about this news at all.

"Your life is your life," she said to Linda. "I have to get my paperwork for tomorrow."

Dana walked back into the office. She had no time for this drama. There was work that needed to be done.

At the end of the season, Dana received a glowing review from Dee and George.

"Your pictures have improved tremendously from the beginning of the year," said Dee.

"Yeah, you're doing really great, really great, the people like you, the kids like you, you're consistent, you're reliable, you take good pictures, we'd love to have you back in the fall," said George.

"I'd love to be back," said Dana, feeling an emotion she wasn't all that familiar with: pride.

She returned the next season and the season after that and she's still working at SmilePosts with me today. Unlike me, Dana has no mixed feelings about her extended time period at the job. She's grateful to have employment and to be doing something she's good at. She's grateful to be able to provide for her daughter.

That summer after her first year on the job, Dana basked in the continued miracle of unemployment compensation and spent as much time as possible with Madison.

Slowly, she tried to prove to Molly that she was capable of watching Maddy for a full day at a time. She started cooking Maddy's meals and taking her to the doctor and being a real mother to her. She still relied on Molly for a lot of things, but she did her best to acknowledge Molly's contribution and be openly thankful. It wasn't Dana's instinct to express gratitude, but she forced herself to do it because she knew it was important.

One night, in early July, Molly was out having dinner with her own group of friends, who she had not caught up with in some time.

Dana was happily at home with Madison, watching episodes of the Backyardigans in the living room, when Steve stepped in the room, looking for the morning's newspaper.

Dana looked up at him and felt a crushing wave of sadness. She missed him.

"Hey Dad," she said.

"Hmmm," he looked up at her.

"Why don't you come watch with us?"

Steve looked at the poorly animated animals on the TV screen.

"No thanks," he said.

He found the paper and retreated to the kitchen.

An hour later, after Dana had put Madison to bed, she went to the kitchen and sat across from Steve at the kitchen table. He held the sports section of the Philadelphia Inquirer in front of her, blocking her view of his face with images of the 76ers.

"Dad," she said.

"Hmmm," he said, behind the paper.

"Let's do this."

"What's that?"

"Let's have it out. This has gone on for way too long," she said.

Slowly he lowered the paper. The only sound in the room was the crinkling of those long, gray sheets.

"Hmmm?" he said, tentative.

"Don't play like that," she said, dead serious. "We used to be close. And we're not anymore. And you barely talk to Madison. And it's not fair," she said.

He said nothing. She wasn't sure if he was being intentionally silent or if he couldn't find the words to respond.

"What do you want me to say?" she said. "That I regret getting pregnant at seventeen? I mean, I do. Of course I do. But I also don't. If I hadn't gotten pregnant, I wouldn't have Madison."

He still said nothing, but he was looking at her, really looking at her, with unbroken eye contact and that was a start. It had been a long time since he looked at her with such unfiltered attention.

"I miss you," she said. "So much. I want you to be a part of my life. A real part. Not this person hanging in the background. I want you to be a part of Maddy's life. She didn't do anything wrong. She deserves to know you. She deserves to have you as a grandpop. I don't know what to do anymore. It's been over two years. It's too hard not talking to you."

She waited. The overhead light glinted off his watery eyes. He didn't look away.

Quietly, nearly whispering, clutching the newspaper in his hands tightly and getting smeared with newsprint, he said "I didn't know how to stop."

"What do you mean?" she said, encouraging.

He was struggling, but he continued.

"I was so mad at you. So mad at my little girl for doing that. For ruining her life."

"I didn't ruin my life."

"I know, I know, but it felt like you did. And I was so mad. But even when I stopped being mad, I didn't know how to make it better. I didn't know how to go back to normal."

"Dad," she said. She reached over and touched his newsprint-covered hand. "It's okay. Can't we go back to how things were before?"

He considered her.

"No, I don't think we can," he said.

Dana took back her hand and collapsed into the chair, discouraged.

"But maybe we can move forward to something new," said Steve, cautiously.

Dana perked up.

"Yeah," she said. "Maybe we can."

V.
ME & JOSIE

ONE
AT A CROSSROADS

SOMETIMES I WONDER, is there a difference between resignation and acceptance?

I'm embarrassed to admit that I've recently been reading "self-help" books.

They come in all types. There are the bright yellow texts written by silver haired psychologists with perfect teeth – books with names like *You Can Be Happy Too* and its sequel *You Can Be Happy Too 2*. There are science books about the brain's neurology and how to best use our evolutionary patterns to our benefit. There are new-age tracts about mindfulness and reconnecting with the pure energies of consciousness floating all around us. There are even celebrity autobiographies that pose as memoir but are, in fact, lectures on how your favorite aging movie star broke free of their depression and with enough pluck you can follow their lead! (Spoiler alert: The transition involved more sobriety and fewer nude scenes.)

I suppose I started reading these books out of desperation. I continued because for every bit of brazen fantasy I couldn't buy into, I found an insight that helped, at least for a moment. I've never taken any drugs, so my main method of combating the honking thrum of restlessness and dissatisfaction has always been mental. I seek that cool drip of relief when the machinery slows, not through pharmaceuticals but through ideas that coat my anxieties like a melted lozenge.

I know when I've read some theory that connects with me on a physical level. It feels like the truth, not because of some balance-checking intellectual exercise, but because the written thought immediately provides relief. It's similar to when a loud background noise you've gotten used to suddenly shuts off and the balm of silence becomes an active quality in and of itself.

Not to be one of those people who goes around saying, "there are two kinds of _____ in this world..." because those people are annoying and most of the time such statements are extremely reductive, but I have decided that self-help guides fall into one of two categories.

There are the books that think the best way to improve your life is to get off your ass and TAKE ACTION! This action might be external – putting in the work to find a better job, putting in the effort to create a better relationship, and so forth – or it might be internal – working to actively change your thoughts and intentionally think positive ideas. Either way, the conclusion of these books is that effort is essential for gaining happiness.

Then there are the books that are mostly about acceptance. These volumes encourage observing life in all its messy truth and not fighting too much with reality, because it's a brawl you'll never win. Sit back, stop struggling, and enjoy the ride for what it is, which is a mixed bag.

As much as I would like to buy into the gospel sold by the action books, since I have been a card-carrying member of their philosophy most of my life, it's the latter books that are connecting with me at the present.

Having lived twenty-eight years now, it feels like they're telling the truth.

I have tried effort. I have tried and tried to put in the work to improve myself and improve my life and the best it ever gets me is a feeling of optimism for the future, but never fulfilment in the present.

The acceptance books talk about "mindfulness," the act of paying attention to your thoughts and feelings without trying to influence them, relinquishing some of your mind's power by not fighting or embracing your inner vicissitudes. Closing your eyes and paying attention to your thoughts is an eye-opening experience. (Metaphorically speaking, since your eyes are closed.) You realize how inconsistent your mind is. You constantly desire contradictory things simultaneously. You're internally assaulted at all times by a barrage of wants and needs and inadequacies that you unquestioningly take as gospel.

But acceptance goes beyond these acts of meditation. It includes looking at the story of your life and admitting the primacy of present circumstances, rather than lingering in some hard-to-grasp dream of future fulfillment.

For if I operate under the belief that having a wife or becoming a Hollywood screenwriter will make me happy, then how can I be happy now, if I don't have those things? If I say, "I will be happy when..." then my current contentment is cut off at the source, depleted without the required fuel.

Which brings me back to my initial question – what's the difference between acceptance and resignation?

If acceptance involves taking life as it comes and not trying to achieve your dreams, because pursuing something that you don't have will inevitably leave you unsatisfied, stripped from contentment in the very act of wanting – isn't this a form of giving up, throwing in the towel, calling it a day and letting life pull you along like a broken down car hooked up to a spiritual tow truck? Is defeated resignation really the most peaceful way to live?

I'm not so certain I want to give up on my dreams, even if they cause me distress.

I'm at a crossroads – unsure how to live my life.

It's not that I'm incapable of being happy these days, it's more that happiness used to be effortless and now it requires work. When I was younger, it was all so effortless.

I miss being a kid.

TWO
A REAL PHOTOGRAPHER

I SPOTTED HAILEY as soon as she walked in the room on my first day of training at SmilePosts, back when I was twenty-three. I couldn't take my eyes off her.

Love at first sight is a ridiculous concept, perpetuated with reckless frequency in the movies I love. Two beautiful people spot each other across a crowded room and lock eyes. The camera slowly pushes in towards each of them. The background and the surrounding extras recede out of focus. They smile at one another with full bright smiles, showing off all their glorious, perfect teeth, and the audience knows that an immaculate romantic bond has been formed that will melt away the many convoluted conflicts which arise to keep them apart.

Have you ever tried smiling at a stranger with teeth showing? It feels incredibly unnatural. Seriously, try it right now. Put the book down, pretend that you spotted the love of your life at the other end of the bar and smile at him/her/them with your biggest Tom Cruise or Julia Roberts inspired smile of pearly glinting whites and impossible charm. It feels weird, right? Like you're posing for a picture, but there's no camera anywhere. You feel like a goddamn crazy person.

Just another manufactured dream of cinema.

(Deep sigh.)

Love at first sight is a fiction. But infatuation at first sight, that's something that happens to billions of people daily. If you're a hopeless romantic like me, you often mistake infatuation at a distance for love, despite all your inner reason. You spot a girl across a room and you are pulled by a force as strong as gravity towards a crush that will consume at least sixty percent of your waking thoughts, as well as a good deal of your dreaming ones.

I was seated at one of the stained folding tables in the photographer basement on that first day of work. I was one of the first trainees to arrive. I'm chronically terrified of being late, always showing up uncomfortably early wherever I'm supposed to be. I'm the guy who arrives at the movie theater before the pre-preview commercials and shows up to parties when the host is still tidying up and putting out the snacks.

When I entered the SmilePosts office, the only people there were Shirley, the older woman who would quit after only a week of work, and Dee, who sat at her desk, drinking coffee. As we inched closer to a reasonable arrival time, I watched the others slowly trickle in and didn't think much about any of them. I was busy mulling over a screenplay idea I was developing. A script that I assumed would launch me like a rocket into the galaxy of film industry stardom.

Then Hailey arrived. Cute, pale skin, freckled face, buried in her phone, texting away with Lord-knows-who at seven fifty-three A.M., her strands of wavy red hair falling in her eyes and not bothering her in the least. Five feet tall and smiling to herself. An angel.

I am not what you would call a "tall" man. In fact, you might accurately say that I'm a short one. If the previously mentioned diminutive superstar Tom Cruise and I were in a class together and the line was arranged in height order, I would still be in front.

I'm five-foot-four. I guess there's no reason to beat around the bush. Cruise is five-six. Supposedly.

For the record, I think Tom Cruise is a pretty great actor. I judge him on his excellent performances rather than his alleged personal quirks.

But I'm getting distracted. The point is that I was attracted to Hailey's small stature because of my own height, or lack of it.

Hailey sat down at a table parallel to mine, in my clear sight path. I thought of all those movie scenes filled with romantic cross-room eye contact and I looked at her and smiled. (Though not with teeth, because I'm not a creep.)

She did not look at me once.

"Sure is a lot of pussy here." I turned my head and saw Clint, fellow trainee and the type of guy who wore a sleeveless muscle shirt to his first day at a new job. Because the universe is a cruel, indifferent place, he had sat down next to me.

"You got your eyes on that redhead, huh?" he said.

"No," I said.

"You're staring at her."

"I'm not staring."

"Hey, she's fucking hot, I don't blame you. I kind of like that Asian chick over there."

He indicated Jen Li.

"Woowee," Clint said. "We're gonna have our pick, my man."

I had no idea what to say to that.

"Name's Clint," he said.

I introduced myself reluctantly. "Blake."

Clint spoke with a slight Southern lilt, despite having lived all his life in Delaware County, Pennsylvania. He loved going to the gym, which I knew because he spent the next twenty minutes talking to me about the exercises that he did for each individual muscle, still talking after George had begun his introductory speech. I'd never heard the word "deltoids" so many times in my life.

After George finished his uncomfortable lecture about how we needed to "touch children's lives," which has been mentioned several times in the previous chapters, we were broken up into training groups, and, what do you know, this division was based on the tables where we were sitting.

"We're training buds," said Clint. He held up his hand for a high five. I raised my hand for him to slap, feeling shamefully embarrassed, too cowardly to deny him his high five, as I looked around the room and hoped no one was watching. Clint must have used those delts he kept talking about for the high five because he hit my hand with the force of a Mack Truck. The clap of our hands echoed throughout the room and Hailey looked over at me for the first time to see what had caused the outrageous noise. I clutched my hand in pain as we made eye contact. She quickly turned away.

Off to a great start.

So while Linda and Ethan followed Gabby to begin their training and Dana went with Cal, Hailey joined Bonnie, who was her designated group leader, and my tablemates and I were introduced to Josie.

"Welcome to SmilePosts," Josie said to us with an impressive lack of enthusiasm. "Let's clear away these tables and get started."

It was Josie's third season at SmilePosts. She was the sole surviving representative of her own training class from two years prior. When she arrived that morning, George congratulated her on the accomplishment.

"You're the only one still here from your year! Well done! You made it!" he said, with the awed praise you might shower upon a marathon runner entering the final stretch of the race.

George's words curdled in her stomach. To Josie, outlasting all of the people who started with her was not an accomplishment, but a failure.

She seriously questioned what was wrong with her that all of the other idiots hired two years before had managed to escape the SmilePosts shackles, while she lingered, with no escape plan, terrified of becoming at home in her prison cell.

The other veterans, like Bonnie and Cal and Stacy, treated Josie with esteem for her membership in their elite club of established vets. Only Rita, who had been hired the year before Josie, seemed to understand that this survival feat was not a source of pride.

"Congratulations," Rita had said to her, with biting cheer, as the two huddled in the corner during George's opening speech. "You went all

Hunger Games on those people who started with you and you're the only one left standing."

"Are we talking like Hunger Games part one where Jennifer Lawrence is a hero, or like Hunger Games three where everyone is depressed and everything is terrible?" said Josie.

"I don't know, I haven't actually seen or read any of them."

"Oh, you should, they're pretty good."

"That's what I hear."

"Anyway, I don't know what I'm still doing here," said Josie. "I'll probably quit after today. I collected my summer's worth of unemployment. Time to hit the road."

"I'll miss you," said Rita.

"And I, you."

They were distracted from their conversation by George's speech.

"Did George just tell the newbies to 'touch the children?'" said Rita. They listened in.

"Touch their lives. Their *lives*, Rita," said Josie.

"Poor, sweet George."

"He means well."

"He does," said Rita. "You're not really going to quit, are you?"

"Where would I go? What could I possibly do that would be more fulfilling than SmilePosts?" she said, dripping with sarcasm.

"There's always prostitution. Oldest profession in the world."

"That's why I like you Rita. You're always looking out for me."

"What are friends for?"

"Looks like we're breaking into groups. Oh goodie. I got Betty White," said Josie, indicating elderly Shirley from my table. "Can't wait for her to last all of a week."

She and Rita bid each other good luck and Josie joined our group.

Unlike Bonnie, who was boisterously getting to know Hailey, the Jens, and the rest of her training squad before any instructions were given, asking each of them to share their name and something interesting about themselves like they were at an overnight camp orientation, Josie wasted no time with idle chat and began her lesson immediately, avoiding any personal connection to the best of her ability.

Throughout Josie's opening explanation of the various pieces of equipment, Clint continued to chat with me. He whispered away about his daily workout regimen, talking about exercises I'd never heard of, with names like kippers, Supermans, and Turkish presses. Josie gave us a dirty look, but didn't bother telling us to be quiet, not really caring whether any of us listened to her. If there was anything the first two years of SmilePosts had taught her, it was that most of the new hires would be gone by the end of September anyway.

I didn't comprehend her mindset at the time and I felt judged by Josie's dirty look, still a conscientious student at heart who didn't want to disrespect the teacher. I gave her a pleading stare, trying to assure her that the conversation taking place was not consensual. My attempts to convey this psychic message were unsuccessful. Josie avoided my eye contact. That seemed to be going around. I looked over at Hailey once again and Clint noticed. "Yeah, boy," he said in the tone of a white guy who thinks he's cool because he listens to rap. "You're gonna get it," he said. I inched slowly away from him and he followed each step without hesitation.

"Can you repeat that last part?" asked Shirley, to Josie, in a feeble, confused voice, interrupting the monotone description of the equipment.

"Which part?" said Josie.

"All of it," said Shirley.

Though Josie had already been working at SmilePosts for two years and I had recently graduated college, we were both twenty-three. Josie had attended a two-year photography program at a local arts school called Arcola. In high school she had been a solid B student and could have gotten into a four-year university program if she had wanted to, but neither of her parents offered much support (either emotionally or financially). Josie decided not to bury herself under a larger hill of student loans than necessary. Her mother Nicki and her father Lou were of the "fend for yourself" philosophy when it came to their children. Josie sometimes tried to convince herself that her parents' hands-off style was an intentional decision, meant to inspire independence and resilience in Josie and her younger brother Landon, but most of the time she thought her folks were too caught up in their own drama to pay their kids any mind. Ignoring Josie was not an active decision, but a passive one. They forgot about her, though she still lived with them. There were moments when Josie wished that she were more fucked-up, so that Lou and Nicki could see what a terrible job they had done and feel guilty about it. Landon's repeated failing grades in school and burgeoning drug habit might do the trick, but perhaps she was giving her parents too much credit. More likely, they would stay uninvolved in their children's lives even if Josie and Landon went on a public murder spree or became porn stars or both. The children's failures had nothing to do with them. Josie and Landon were separate entities, living unrelated lives.

"You got a roof over your head, don't you?" said Nicki, when Josie had complained about the lack of support she received.

She did have a roof over her head. And Josie desperately needed to get out from under it. But how the hell was she supposed to afford her own place? Her SmilePosts wages certainly weren't enough and her true career goals provided no easy path to pursue.

Photography had been Josie's passion for as long as she could remember. She was good at it. Everyone told her so – her friends, her teachers, random commenters on Instagram, although part of her hated Instagram. She thought digital filters were poisonous to the art form.

She had picked up her first camera at the age of seven. Her father's. He was furious when he saw how much film she had "wasted," though in her opinion the images she had captured as a third grader were superior

GREAT BIG SMILE

to anything that Lou had ever shot. As soon as she was legally allowed to get a job, at thirteen, as a CIT (or "counselor in training") at a nearby summer camp, she saved up her seventy-five dollars a week and used it all to buy a Nikon F80 film camera, with twenty rolls of film. She started out taking portraits of her friends and photos of trees in the woods that surrounded her middle school, but as she got older and bolder, she took the train into Center City Philly and snuck shots of interesting-looking strangers on the streets. She liked photos of people who had character in their faces. A curmudgeonly old man selling soft pretzels. A sharp-nosed businesswoman screaming publicly into her outdated, enormous cell phone.

Josie loved to search for old pictures from Life Magazine on the internet. She stood in the photography aisle of Barnes and Noble for hours, perusing collections of the world's greatest photographs, reading instructional guides on lighting and framing techniques, and making her way through memoirs from the great photojournalists. She read stories of brave photographers charging forward into war-torn countries, remarkably keeping their cameras in focus as bullets flew inches past their heads and explosions nearly collapsed their ear drums. She went to the library and paged through thirty years' worth of National Geographics, marveling at the images obtained of tribal cultures, endangered animals, and exotic foreign cities.

This became her dream – to travel the world as a photojournalist. Few other professions existed at this cross-section of important insight and artistic expression. She could share hidden images with the rest of the world. She could put the impoverished on display, broadcasting their humanity. When you heard about people suffering half the world away, empathy remained remote, but if you showed someone a picture of a starving child or a weeping widow, they became emotionally invested. They might actually contribute to the cause in some meaningful way as a result of the image. Photography held that power. She wanted to convey these pictures of horror and be a courageous message-bearer, but she also wished to see the beautiful locales and varied cultures spread throughout the Earth. There was so much more to the world than the suburb of Plymouth Meeting, Pennsylvania and the downtown hub of Center City Philadelphia. Josie had hardly been anywhere and she wanted to be everywhere. She wanted to explore and photograph. She wanted to be a real photographer.

But how to achieve these dreams? It remained an unanswered question.

Either way, she couldn't stay much longer at SmilePosts. SmilePosts was not real photography.

"SmilePosts isn't real photography," Josie said to the group when shy Pristine, shaking with nerves at her first turn at the camera, admitted that she knew nothing about photography. Pristine held her head in shame, like a Catholic at confession, wishing to be pardoned for her sins. She summoned all her courage to look up at Josie, unsure if she was being submitted to some cruel test and sure she would fail even if she wasn't.

"Really," said Josie, "you don't need any skills at all to do this, except basic human competence and sometimes not even that."

I laughed. I didn't mean to. It was not the sort of laugh you force out kindly to acknowledge a joke has been made – whether a throat scratching chuckle or pushing a bit of air through your nostrils. It was a genuine, unintentional laugh, which I think we can all agree is the best kind. Josie didn't intend for the group to find her statement funny, mocking us from her own island of cynicism.

She looked over at me. I smiled, again not because I meant to, but because the aftereffects of the laugh still lingered.

She smiled back. She was surprised but grateful that someone appreciated her sarcasm. She turned back to Pristine.

"Seriously though. All this job requires is memorizing a very specific set of steps and then repeating that set of steps hundreds or thousands of times. And, I guess, knowing how to talk to children without being a creep."

"Talk to children?" said Pristine, her left eye starting to twitch. She was panicking.

"Yes...," said Josie. "Taking pictures of children requires... speaking to them."

I laughed again. Josie looked at me and shook her head in mild disbelief at what she had to deal with. She seemed glad to have a comrade who was on the same page.

Philip, another member of our little group, who was wearing a wool winter hat, indoors, on an 88-degree August day, jealously picked up on the headway I had made at becoming our trainer's favorite pupil and forced out an outrageous false laugh. Philip was an ambitious social climber. His enormous ego made him want to be at the center of every human grouping, though he lacked the likeability to accomplish this goal. Josie and I heard the outrageous squeal he intended as a laugh. We rubbed our damaged eardrums, then looked at each other and laughed ourselves, not hiding our mockery as much as we should have.

Trying to compensate for his obvious embarrassment, Philip doubled down by unleashing on poor Pristine.

"Yes, how do you expect to talk to children without talking to children?" he said to Pristine, in the sniveling tone he might use with a waiter who had screwed up an expensive meal. "The act of talking to children requires talking to children, you know. How else to talk to a child except to talk to them?"

Pristine was shaking. She looked about ready to explode into a cloud of dust.

"Are you finished?" Josie said to Philip. *Are you finished, asshole*, was implied, but unsaid.

Philip had overplayed his hand. He was trying to convince everyone that a pair of threes was a full house and Josie was like, *what cards? I'm not even playing.*

"You'll be fine," Josie reassured Pristine. "It's really not that hard."

Pristine was fine, by the way. She always took good photos, although she was constantly petrified that she had disappointed someone or other.

Philip, on the other hand, was gone from the job after a week. Ostensibly he was fired because he showed up to a school an hour and forty-five minutes late and didn't bother to call anyone, but I like to think he was let go because his irritating schmoozing crossed a line that the managers could not abide. After his brief tenure at SmilePosts, he spent the next several years passing from one job to another, always acting like the cock of the walk, always trapped in his own world of ballooned confidence, never noticing the hatred he inspired all around him. Eventually, he was recruited for some scam credit card debt relief business by a cousin of his who had recently been released from prison. Miraculously, their crimes went unnoticed by the authorities, but they failed at their scheme, losing more than they made, and the enterprise collapsed. Philip rebounded by marrying a fifty-four-year-old wealthy window he met on Tinder, when he was only thirty-one. They were divorced two years later after she fell in love with an even poorer man her own age. Philip, who had not the patience nor the intelligence to have read over his pre-nuptial agreement, assumed he would "make bank" from the divorce. He ended up with nothing.

As training continued, we ran through the set up procedure and then moved on to taking test portraits of one another.

Clint continued to talk my ear off about his body-building routine, sharing a long list of muscle powders and protein shakes that he digested on a bi-hourly basis because he wanted to get "big," not just "cut," because "you can't see abs through a t-shirt, though you can try."

Luckily, at this point, Josie was able to sense the one-sided nature of our interaction. When it was Clint's turn to pose, he snapped automatically into a sideways flex that I later learned was his usual shirtless mirror pose for social media postings. Pristine was acting as his photographer, trying and failing to convince him to relax his posture and shift into the proper position. Clint was determined to not have any picture taken of him in which his pecs were not bulging out of his too-small muscle shirt. Josie intervened and asked him to "turn his obliques" to his left, which gave us both a good, stifled laugh. Clint obeyed without hesitation – she was speaking his language.

At lunch I grabbed my paper bagged salami sandwich and hoped to snag a seat at a table with Hailey, but she left the office with Mackenzie and the Jens to grab takeout at a nearby Chick-fil-A. I was nowhere near bold enough to suggest accompanying this gaggle of girls. I had a brief moment of respite from Clint, who was in the parking lot doing three-hundred crunches. I spotted Josie and Rita eating their salads at a table in the corner.

"Hey, mind if I join you guys?"

"Have a seat," said Josie.

"I'm Rita," Rita introduced herself.

"Blake," I said.

"Yes, I can see that on your name tag," said Rita.

"How come you guys don't have to wear these?"

"We do. We just aren't," said Josie.

"Ah," I said.

"How come you're not out there doing sit-ups with your buddy?" said Josie.

"I already got in my thousand crunches before I came to work, so..." I said.

"Right, of course," said Josie.

"Is that guy your friend?" asked Rita, cautiously, not completely sure if she was in on the joke.

"No, it appears he locked onto Blake like a barnacle on a whale and Blake is too nice to scrape him off," said Josie.

"We were at the same table," I said, as an excuse.

"I'm sorry to hear that," said Rita.

"Thanks," I said.

"So is this job really as bad as you make it out to be?" I asked Josie.

"Did Josie imply she didn't like working here? No way. What a shock," said Rita, without any shock whatsoever.

"I don't know why George asks me to train," said Josie. "He has to know I'm going to have a bad attitude. Nate likes to call me a menace to society. It's one of his pet names for me."

"Who's Nate?" I said.

"My boyfriend," said Josie. "He doesn't work here. He doesn't hate himself."

"George asks you to train because you're good at your job, whether you want to be or not," said Rita. "Plus, there are only so many veterans. He needs everybody he can get."

"Yeah, I think it's more the numbers game. He lets me corrupt the youth because he has to."

"The youth?" I said. "How old are you?"

"Didn't anyone ever tell you not to ask a woman her age?" said Rita.

"Twenty-three," said Josie. "If I don't answer, he's going to think I'm some old wretch with good plastic surgery."

"Oh okay. I'm twenty-three too," I said. "Or also, I mean. Not twenty-three-two. Twenty-three, as well."

"God, I feel so old," said Rita. "And no, I'm not going to tell you how old specifically, so shut your mouth."

It was hard to tell if Rita was still joking. I didn't press the issue.

"So is the job that bad?" I said to Josie, repeating the earlier question to bring the conversation out of the dangerous territory it had entered.

"Josie likes to talk shit and put on airs," said Rita. "She's really good at her job and she loves it here."

"I don't *love* it," Josie insisted. "It's fine. Some of the people are nice. And some of the kids are not annoying. It's a source of money."

"She loves it." Rita reaffirmed.

I laughed.

"You guys make it sound so exciting. I can't wait to jump in!" I said with mock excitement.

They laughed.

"I like this one," said Rita.

"Yeah, he might not fail," said Josie.

They were joking about my failure, but I wanted them to know I didn't plan to stick around SmilePosts long. I wanted to tell them about my screenwriting aspirations. I wanted them to know I wasn't another unambitious cog in the machine, only trying to get by. I was different. I was going to make something of myself. One day, they would see my name up on the big screen and knowing me would be an anecdote they could tell friends and family about – the time they met the famous Hollywood screenwriter.

I wanted to tell them all this, but I didn't want to start tooting my own horn without any context, like a douchebag. I wanted it to come up naturally. It didn't. I brought it up anyway.

"I went to film school. I'm just here long enough to save up money to move to L.A.," I said, which wasn't truthfully my plan at the time, but saying I was going to move to L.A. made me sound important. It made my life bigger than the small lives of those around us, so I said it.

"That's cool," said Rita. "I hear L.A. has a great food scene."

Josie said nothing.

She was thinking about her own unfulfilled ambitions and wondering whether the future she wanted would ever arrive.

THREE
THE SUPPOSEDLY UNBREAKABLE MATHEMATICAL LAWS OF THE UNIVERSE

LOST IN A HAZY, borderless swirl of thoughts about Hailey, I didn't notice my dad talking to me at the dinner table.

"How much are they paying you?" he asked.

"What?" I said.

"The kiddie pics," he said.

"Don't call them kiddie pics," I said, feeling icky as I repeated the phrase. "What was the question?"

"How much are they paying you?"

"Twelve dollars an hour."

"Hmmm," he said, cutting his chicken with condescension directed both at me and the overcooked dead bird. My mom had a constantly vocalized, deep-seated fear of eating underdone meat and my dad, who cooked most of the meals, had spitefully roasted every last drop of moisture out of the chicken as if to punish all of us for Mom's pestering.

"It's not my career," I said. "It's a temporary thing until I sell a screenplay."

"It's good that he's working," said Mom.

"I'm not saying that it's not," said Dad.

Then we all waited. 5, 4, 3, 2...

"But...," said Dad. There was always a *but*. "But... writing is a hard way to make a living and it might not hurt to get a job that can lead to growth while you are trying to become an *artist*." He said the word "artist" with the same skepticism that one might speak of UFOs or werewolves. As if the existence of artists was only a myth, proliferated by conspiracy theorists.

"I know. You've said that," I replied. We had literally had this same conversation forty-seven times. I had counted. "First of all, I don't want to be an artist, I want to be an entertainer." This was a sentiment I had expressed in rebuttal twenty-three times. (Although it was bullshit. I did want to be an artist. I just didn't want to give him the satisfaction of being right.) "Entertainers make money," I said.

"It's a tough road," said my dad, for what must have been the thousandth time. It had been said so many times I had lost count.

There was a collective groan from the rest of us at the table – myself, my mom, and my younger sister Rebecca. Becca supported my exasperation with Dad completely, though at only sixteen she had her career path entirely planned out. She wanted to be a lawyer, much to Dad's relief.

"Dad, you've said this a million times," said Becca.

"I have? I'm sorry." His usual response. He seemed to genuinely feel each time we had this conversation that he was expressing a new concern. It was mind-boggling.

"It's okay," I said, hoping foolishly that this was the end of it.

There were a few moments of silence as we all chewed the overcooked chicken and tried to wash down the dry fragments with our glasses of water.

"Hard to make a living on twelve dollars an hour," Dad said, quietly into his chest, but obviously loud enough for us all to hear, as if he expected us to be less annoyed with his harping if he pretended that he was talking to himself.

"Honey!" / "Oh my god!" / "Dad!" my mom, sister, and I remarked, simultaneously.

"I won't say another word!" said Dad.

We stayed on the topic for another twenty minutes.

As irritating to me as my dad's anxiousness about my career was, it did encourage me to get busy writing. I wanted to prove to him and everyone else what I could make of myself.

I started slaving away in every spare moment on a be-all, say-all, intentionally elaborate screenplay of intersecting lives and casual magic, intended to be a thesis statement about life itself.

I pictured accepting the Oscar about two years later, a remarkable feat for a first-time screenwriter. I knew my movie would be that good. I practiced my acceptance speech nightly in the shower.

When I wasn't dreaming about my meteoric rise in the film industry, I was dreaming about Hailey. The discussion with my dad at the dinner table was hardly the only time that thoughts of her interrupted whatever it was I was supposed to be doing.

I might be driving to work at six A.M. in the middle lane of the Pennsylvania Turnpike, picturing myself holding Hailey close in some narratively climactic slow dance, when I would miss my GPS telling me to take exit 330B. (Where I thought we would be slow dancing, I have no idea – outside of proms, I'm not sure that slow dancing exists anymore.) *Did someone say something?* I would think somewhere in my half-awake mind, then I would glance down at the map screen, which rested in my cup holder. The next exit on the state toll-road wouldn't be for another nine miles and my estimated arrival time would jump from comfortably thirteen minutes early to one minute late. "Shit," I would say out loud, increasing my speed to fifteen miles over the speed limit, praying that I wouldn't be pulled over by a state trooper while I tried to make up that crucial minute.

Or... I might be setting up my equipment after loading all of my cases onto a school's auditorium stage. I'd be lulled by the minimal yellow stage lights, which were the only lights I could find without tracking down a custodian, too nervous to start flipping the unlabeled levers in the metal box on the side wall. My eyes would half close as the flickering dirty light bounced off the dark wooden stage, while slipping into musings of holding Hailey's hand and watching the sunset together in some undefined beautiful locale. Then suddenly Cal would approach with his usual look of theatrical anger, yelling at me that I had screwed my background light in the opposite direction from where it should be facing. Such an obvious mistake to look at it, but easily made while distracted by the imagined sensation of Hailey's fingers linked in mine.

In my daydreams I often inserted Hailey and myself into a replica of the climactic scene in *Jerry Maguire*. I would picture storming into the SmilePosts office, as all our co-workers watched, saying hello to everyone, and then telling Hailey that I had sold my first screenplay, the only achievement I had ever wanted... but the moment wasn't complete, because I didn't have her to share it with. "You complete me," I would say, like Tom Cruise had. Like Renée Zellweger, she would tell me, "Shut up. You had me at hello. You had me at hello," and we would fall into each other's arms as those around us cheered.

The main barrier to this scenario becoming reality was that Hailey and I had not technically met. If I "had her at hello," it was primarily because "hello," was the only thing I had ever said to her.

I needed to talk to her. I needed to get to know her as a real person, untangling her from the Hailey of my imagination. Figuring out how to do this in a natural manner was the challenge.

Though we had yet to be scheduled together at a school, every two or three days I would see Hailey at the office. I would cherish these lucky moments when we returned at the same time to drop off our day's paperwork.

Here and there, I started creating excuses to exchange a few words with her, all without ever having officially introduced myself.

She might be in the supply closet. I would casually walk in at the same time.

"Hmmm, they're almost out of rubber bands," I would say, seeing her reach into the nearly empty bag of bands.

"Yeah," she would say, then walk out of the closet.

Or she would be at the paperwork bin, collecting her packet for the next day's job.

"Where are you headed?" I would say.

She would look at me, somewhat confused as to why I was talking with her. I would maintain an innocent expression, implying (falsely) that I was only being polite and there was nothing I wanted from her.

"Derricksville Elementary," she would say.

"Oh nice. Where's that?" I'd say.

"Derricksville," she would reply.

"Makes sense," I'd say.

Then she would walk away and I would storm off to the bathroom so no one could hear the pounding drum of my heartbeat.

I imagined us slowly getting to know each other in this incremental fashion. Each interaction would add a slight, but crucial, bit of unfulfilled romantic longing to the charge produced by our polar personalities. Our longing for one another would grow like the world's most gradual snowball, taking its good old time to roll down the hill, but gathering force and circumference, until it could not be ignored by the terrified village of Scandinavians below.

What I've always wanted even more than someone to love, is the growing possibility of love, unfolding over the episodes of my life like a classic will-they-or-won't-they television coupling. I've wanted my own pre-destined beau, like Sam and Diane on *Cheers* or Jim and Pam on *The Office*. There's something so romantic to the unexpressed certainty of affection. Something wonderful in the knowledge that unspoken feelings exist between two people, as the charge builds in one flirtatious interaction after another. Until finally you reach that culminating season finale moment and all the unsaid romance comes to a transcendent revelation.

I'm okay with waiting. In fact, I prefer it. It adds to the drama. It makes the love story more meaningful than if I were to simply ask someone out

GREAT BIG SMILE

on a date. I want not only happiness, but poignancy, and if poignancy requires a certain amount of ache, by definition, that's okay, because it makes the culmination all the sweeter.

Waiting for the storyline of my eventual romance with Hailey to begin in earnest, every day I'd get in line over at Dee's desk, where she posted the daily schedule. As I waited impatiently for those in front of me to take their excessively long looks at the 8.5x11 piece of paper, I hoped with an embarrassing intensity that I would see my name next to Hailey's. More than once, I wrote in my journal that Hailey made me feel like a starving man craving food, which I know is such a stupid, privileged white person thing to say about having a crush – I mean there are actual starving people out there – but my mind had become so gripped around the thought of getting to know Hailey that liberal considerations weren't taken into account when forming my metaphors.

Day after day, I swelled with anticipation as I prepared to look at that scheduling chart, ever-optimistic that this would be the time Hailey and I would be scheduled together. It seemed a matter of simple math. At some point, the numbers dictated, we would have to cross paths. If you rolled the dice enough times, eventually you would land on a six. Right? *Right?!* I mean, I was never that strong of a math student. I was more of a humanities guy, obviously, but I still counted on the supposedly unbreakable mathematical laws of the universe to ensure that at some point or another I would get to spend a whole day at a school with Hailey.

Each day, I looked slowly across that daily schedule, scanning the column of school assignments with the sharpened focus of a spy scanning stolen documents for hidden code. Each day, I reached the blank margin on the bottom of the sheet without having found the elusive Waldo of my name linked with Hailey's. Each day, disappointment ignited in my stomach and launched into my heart like a space shuttle. Each day, I turned my head and sauntered towards the window, looking out at the gray smear of the parking lot, not sure where to go or what to do, hope expunged once again. And each and every time, just my luck, Clint would be around at this moment of darkness, the universe outrageously flaunting the statistical likelihoods I kept foolishly expecting to behave in my favor. He would walk over to me with his veiny shoulders popping out of his SmilePosts t-shirt, always with that hungry glare, like he was about to pound a cheesesteak down his gullet and then bench two-hundred pounds to turn the food into muscle. He'd say, sympathetically, "not scheduled with Hailey again, huh?," this human meat-slab infuriatingly gifted with incredible insight into other peoples' secret desires.

"What, no? I don't know what you're talking about," I would say to Clint unconvincingly, now hungry for a cheesesteak myself.

"You should talk to her. Ask her to hang out. She's right over there," he would say, pointing her out.

"Look, I'm really hungry Clint," I'd say, apropos of nothing.

"Dude, I know," he'd say, effortlessly staying with me like a Pro Bowl cornerback after a cutting receiver. "Wanna order a pizza?"

"What, like now, to the office?"

"Yeah man. Why the fuck not?"

In truth, the idea of a pizza sounded appealing and I'd be about to say yes when I remembered that Clint was a simple-minded bro who I was annoyed with because of his pinpoint observational skills.

"No, Clint, we're not ordering a pizza to the office," I'd say like an adult who relished in refuting the existence of Santa Claus to children.

"Whatever," he'd say, then pull a Slim Jim out of his pocket and snap into it with all the vigor that Macho Man Randy Savage had always encouraged.

I would look over at Hailey. Her paperwork gathered for the next day, she would be chatting with Dana or Mackenzie or one of the Jens as they left the office. Each time, I watched her cross the lot and longed for the day when I might get to know her.

There are different kinds of attraction. There are subjective levels that exist within you, burning and bubbling, separate from the objective rankings of beauty and hotness. I know in some definitive place of judgment that Victoria's Secret model Adriana Lima is better-looking than Amy Deckland from the Ancient Greek Myths class I took during my sophomore year of college. But the image of Adriana Lima has never burrowed its way into my soul and clanged repeatedly like an alarm clock I can't turn off in the way that Amy's fair skin and strawberry blonde hair did, often making me miss what Theseus or Apollo was getting up to, because I was too focused on trying to not repeatedly look at Amy.

It was the same way with Hailey. Objectively, she was not the best-looking girl at the SmilePosts office. That probably would've been Jen Zolotov or maybe Dana. But something about Hailey's particular construction fit exactly with my desired "type," an image of profound desire that came from who knows where. Her image shook my mind and every time I saw her, I wanted to look at her. Honestly, I felt powerless.

I certainly didn't want to be the creep who kept staring at the girl he liked. It's awkward. And the last thing I want to do is make someone uncomfortable. The world is rough for women with all the leering men out there. I didn't want to join the thrum, aware of my behavior but unable to stop. I just couldn't help myself. I was so attracted to her it was almost painful.

Slap, slap.

That's me slapping myself across the face as I write this, trying to get a grip on myself. Sometimes I think life would be so much easier if you could remove sexual desire from your system like a burst appendix.

"Did you know that we're in the No Bully Zone right now?" said Josie.

"I can't say that I did," I replied.

"Take a look," said Josie, motioning behind us.

Hanging on the wall was a poster with the words "No Bully Zone" written in bold imposing print on a white background. The word "Bully" was contained within one of those red circles with a slash through it that always made me think of *Ghostbusters*.

Josie and I were photographing at Buchanan Middle School in Norristown, one of those pockets of poverty swaddled within stretches of suburban wealth that the gerrymandering political map makers went out of their way to draw around, creating a jagged, haphazard non-shape that avoided anyone with a low income voting for their representatives.

(Seriously, take a look at the shape of Pennsylvania's 7th congressional district. It's insane.

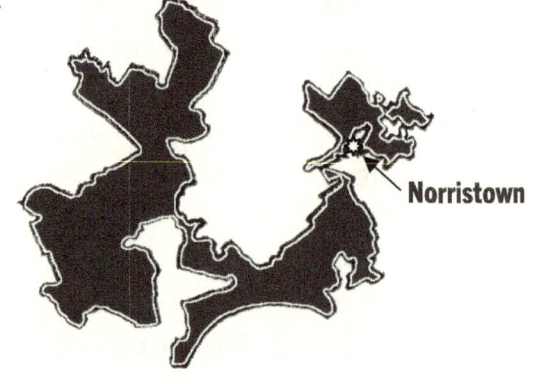

There's Norristown in a concave crevice in the upper right corner, expertly avoided by the map makers. It's such a blatantly unnatural way to draw the voting lines that, looking at it, I'm less infuriated and more awestruck with the gall of politicians who claim this map makes any sense whatsoever.)

Buchanan Middle was a large orange brick building from the 1960s, designed in that era's vision of the twenty first century. It was a strange mold of science fiction, circular windows, and solid colors, with mod designs and the furniture equivalent of beehive haircuts.

We were set up in a weird, octagon-shaped corridor of the hallway, designed like an amphitheater with no seats.

"Hmmm," I said, considering the "No Bully Zone" poster. "So if we're in the no bully zone here, does that mean that there are parts of the school where bullying is permissible? And as long as you practice your bullying in the legally designated places, you're all good?"

"That's just what I was wondering," said Josie, excited that we were on the same page. "Anyway, you're lucky that we're in the no bully zone, because if bullying were permitted here, I'd tear you a new asshole."

I laughed. The vulgarity took me by surprise.

"Yes, that is lucky," I said.

"Where do you think the borders of the zone end?" she said.

"Hard to say. They should be more clearly marked so the bullies know whether they're operating within the bounds of the law."

"Yeah, this set-up is pretty unfair to bullies."

"Absolutely. Society never gives a fair shake to bullies anymore."

"So, how's the job treating you?" she asked. It was late September, a month into the season. We had worked together at a couple of massive schools with enrollments of two thousand kids in the first week of the season, but we had not been scheduled together again until photographing at Buchanan.

"Pretty good," I said. In truth, I had been too focused on thoughts of Hailey and the continual frustration of waiting to be scheduled with her to get bogged down by the frustrations of the job. When I wasn't thinking about Hailey, I was focused on my screenplay, tinkering endlessly with the outline, starting in on scenes I felt confident about in Final Draft, dreaming of the glory of winning a major contest. At the time, my opinions about working at SmilePosts were minimal because I assumed my time there would be temporary. I had bigger fish to fry, as they say. I didn't yet feel that the hopeful light at the end of the tunnel was receding, the way Josie did in her third year. I was not yet acquainted with the gnawing sense that maybe your dreams were nothing other than dreams after all, with no basis in the waking world, and the escape hatch you had planned to drop out of was in fact a solid floor. Nowhere to go, nothing to become but who you already were.

"Let me know how you feel in October when we start going to Philly schools," she said.

"I will," I said.

And I did. When I went to my first exceedingly rough school in North Philly in the first week of October and a second grader attacked my photo background with a pair of scissors, slicing a strip right in the center of it, then running freely around the mold-scented auditorium since no one wanted to corral him while he was wielding a sharp object, the first person I thought of telling was Josie.

I texted her, "So a second grader sliced open my background with a pair of scissors."

She replied, "Sounds like he was bullying you. Are you in a no bully zone?"

"I'm not," I said.

"There's your problem," she said.

From then on, Josie and I established a regular text friendship, utilizing each other to comment on some of the more absurd observations and occurrences that happened at schools.

I texted her when I took a picture of a gym teacher who insisted on dressing up like a clown for his yearbook photo.

She texted me about a boy who gave her a note from his mom that said, "please don't show his double chin." The poor boy was eleven years old and certainly capable of reading the insulting note.

I texted her about a music teacher who had stormed into the music room I had been told to photograph in. He screamed about losing his classroom and pounded the drum set in a fit of vein bursting fury. It was the kind of anger that was hilarious to everyone except the person suffering from it.

Photographing in a school library, she texted me the image of a children's science book called *How Big is a Stick?*, a supposedly innocent exploration of two cartoon boys comparing stick sizes and stick shapes, which the authors must have realized was a thinly veiled discussion of penises.

All this texting happened later, though.

Back at Buchanan Middle School that day, our conversation was interrupted by the arrival of two classes that came straight from gym, all of their carefully coifed hairdos and freshly pressed clothes drenched with sweat.

Josie groaned. "I hate when they send kids to gym class right before we're about to take their pictures. They pay us to come and take photos and then they get mad when the kids look like they've just run a mile. As if it's our fault."

"Our equipment should come with some sort of portable shower for a situation like this," I said, trying to respond with something clever.

"Okay Blake. You want to give the children showers? Real appropriate," she said with comical judgment.

"That's not what I meant," I said, sheepish.

"Didn't know I was working with a creep," she said, but she laughed.

The whiff of children's body odor came so near that we knew we had to return to our stations and photograph the classes. Our conversation took a break. Holding our breath as best we could, we called the children to our cameras.

On a Friday in mid-October, after a long day at a stuffy school deep in Chester County where the suburbs dissipate into farmland, after a stifling hour and a half drive in the early rush hour traffic of the week's last work day, my joints sore, so tired that I nearly fell asleep when I closed my eyes for a moment after pulling into the SmilePosts parking lot, I walked into the office and my patience was finally rewarded.

There, on the schedule for Monday of the next week, was my name written next to Hailey's. We were going to the same school. Gallagher Middle School in Quakertown.

All the frustrations and exhaustion of the day were immediately forgotten. I was thrilled and terrified. It was finally happening – my chance to talk to Hailey – and I couldn't waste it. What would I say? What would I do? So much was riding on this single day. Unfortunately, we would not be alone. We were going to a large middle school with two other photographers: Bonnie, who was super nice, although also super talkative, which in this case was not to my benefit, and Clint, who was being thrust upon me repeatedly as a punishment for some crime I had committed in a previous life.

(I'm being facetious. I don't believe in past lives. Or future ones for that matter. Besides all the other reasons, let's consider the basic math of the proposition. According to a United Nations data report, in the year 10,000 B.C., around when it is speculated that the agricultural revolution first took place, changing us forever from the hunter-gather species we were to the eventual creators of cities and civilizations, there were around four million people living in the world. Around the birth of Christ in year zero, there were approximately two hundred million people. We didn't hit a global population of one billion until around 1800 A.D. The current world population is seven and a half billion. This all leads to an important question. I know what you're thinking – how can we possibly maintain enough natural resources to support this exponential growth of humans? It's a great question but not the one I'm asking here. My question is this: If past lives exist, how exactly does everyone claim to have lived all these previous existences when there weren't enough past people to have inhabited all the current lives? I once posed this quandary to a reincarnation believer and they suggested that a lot of souls are simply new souls, fresh out of the oven. But no one ever goes to a past lives psychic and is told "I'm seeing nothing, you must be brand new!" It's basic math, people, that's all I'm saying...)

I was the first person from our Gallagher Middle School group to be at the office, so I took the paperwork and texted everyone else the arrival information.

My fingers trembled as I typed in Hailey's number, looking at the phone list, trying not to memorize her number because who memorizes phone numbers anymore, but I couldn't help myself. With each remembered numeral I felt the illicit thrill of peeking into her life.

GREAT BIG SMILE

Normally I'd send the information to all three people in one large group text, but in this case, I texted them all separately. I wanted my own private correspondence with Hailey.

"Hey Hailey, it's Blake! From SmilePosts!" I texted her. "We're working together Monday! Here's the school info!" I typed the address and arrival time, then wrote, "looking forward to working together!"

As soon as I clicked send, I became nearly catatonic, my anticipation anxiety kicked into overdrive. I stared at the phone for several minutes, waiting for a response.

The phone buzzed. My heart beat like a crazed animal.

But the text was from Clint, responding to the less enthusiastic version of the arrival info I had sent him.

"Thx bro cya Mon," he wrote.

"Are you feeling okay Blake, want a Jolly Rancher?" said George, across the office.

Much to my embarrassment, he had spotted my emotional heart attack of anticipation. "I just love Jolly Ranchers," he said. "When I was a kid, my mom always got me Jolly Ranchers, I like the green ones, I like Starburst too, pink, and red, and sometimes orange, not yellow though, don't know why."

"No thanks," I said.

Realizing that I had no further reason to be at the office, I gathered the Monday paperwork bag, got in my car, and headed home.

Ten minutes into the drive, my phone buzzed again. While I know it's dangerous to look at your phone while driving, I did anyway, rational notions of safety no match for my desire to see words Hailey had written on my screen. *It's probably Bonnie*, I thought, pre-discouraged, but there was Hailey's name (which I had programmed into my phone). It was remarkable that I didn't swerve into oncoming traffic.

Her message was only one short word that looked like gibberish. At the next slowdown of traffic, I unlocked the screen and read the message closely.

"ty," she wrote.

Ty? TY? Who or what the fuck is TY?, I thought frantically, before I remembered that it was an abbreviation some people used for "thank you."

She had only written two letters, practically the bare minimum possible response, yet still my mind churned the rest of the drive home, plotting what I could text back as soon as I got off the highway and came to a full stop.

After driving down the off-ramp and coming to a red light, I snatched the phone and quickly typed back "You're welcome! See you Monday! Should be fun!"

I waited the rest of the night to see if she would reply to my second message.

She never did.

It was a long weekend of anticipation, but that Monday, there was Hailey, already parked in the lot of Gallagher Middle School when I pulled up next to her. I caught her eye and waved enthusiastically.

She did not see me. She was looking at her phone.

"Morning!" I said when we got out of our cars.

"Hi," she said.

Hi, I replayed in my head over and over.

The secretary at the school showed us the gym where we would set up for the day. We pulled our cars around to unload our equipment and I engaged in the awkward dance of ensuring that my camera station was set up next to Hailey's.

I lifted my camera bag and waited, since Hailey was still digging in her trunk. She slowly packed her cases onto her cart and I tried to match her pace. Bonnie was already wheeling her set into the school. Clint was lifting two cases at a time on his shoulder and carrying them into the gym, refusing to use the cart, because he saw this as a good opportunity to "work on biceps and triceps." Distracted by the mystifying sight of Clint carrying the wheeled cart itself over his head into the school, despite the certainty that he would never utilize it and the fact that, you know, it had wheels, I missed Hailey wheeling her own cart into the school. I sped up with my own cart to catch up to her, accelerating like a NASCAR driver. I had my ten cases precariously stacked. It was a feat of engineering to get all the cases on the cart in one trip, and the G-forces created by my burst of speed along the curve of the sidewalk made the background case tumble off the top of the stack and into a nearby bush. I quickly tried to calculate the time differential of grabbing the background tube from the bush and placing it back on my cart, but I saw Hailey passing through the doorway and I knew it was a time to act and not think. I left the abandoned case behind.

In the gym, Bonnie had already claimed the far left spot along the wall where we were told to set up. Clint had plopped his pile of cases by the door, splitting his entry workout into two sessions. As Hailey wheeled in, I raced up behind her. Clint was clutching the first two cases of his second session in his arms, and the three of us all proceeded towards Bonnie at the far wall. We were in our lanes like track-stars, jockeying for position, Hailey out in front, no one aware that it was a race except for me.

Hailey got to Bonnie first, her early lead too much to overcome. Clint and I were neck and neck. I made a last push and overtook him, the screeching rubber of my tires leaving a mark on the gym floor as I swung into place beside Hailey.

I looked over at her and smiled wide, flushed with victory. She was looking at her phone and did not see me.

📷

"Dude, some of these girls, I don't know how I'm supposed to not get their cleavage in the picture!" Clint said, far too loudly, after a class of eighth graders had departed the gym. I shot an embarrassed look towards Hailey. She had gone straight to her phone during every break. I had been desperately searching for a way to engage her in conversation but had come up short.

What to say? An inquiry about what TV shows she was currently watching? A deep dive into the latest celebrity gossip? A thoughtful analysis of world politics? A question about what the hell she was looking at on her damn phone screen all day?

A discussion of student cleavage was definitely not the conversational breakthrough I was seeking. Luckily, with her head buried in her screen as always, Hailey seemed not to have heard Clint's comment. Bonnie, who was always listening to everybody, was gratefully in the bathroom and missed the cleavage talk altogether.

"I bring my camera all the way down so I'm not shooting right into their boobs," continued Clint, "but some of these girls wear really tight shirts with really big boobs and the cleavage shows and I can't get rid of it. My camera is practically on the ground and you're still seeing the curve of their boobs. I don't know what to do."

Clint was genuinely distraught over his failure to avoid photographing cleavage. His face was furrowed in puzzlement.

"Well for one," I said quietly, "you should probably stop saying the word 'boobs' in a middle school."

Miracle of miracles, I heard a small, feminine laugh out of my left ear. I turned and there was Hailey, looking up at me, apparently listening to the whole exchange after all, even though she had been staring at her phone screen. She gave me a quick look of appreciation for my retort, shaking her head and rolling her eyes with a smirk at the gross masculine buffoonery of our co-worker.

Clint didn't realize I was making fun of him.

"Right. Don't say boobs. Got it," said Clint, earnestly. "But how do I not show the boo—I mean... the breasts?"

Hailey burst out laughing and I joined her. We looked at each other, completely in sync, sharing the moment. A hot current passed through my entire body.

Clint did have his uses. This was the second time that mocking his nonsense had helped me shatter a barrier between me and a woman.

"Just tell them to pull up their shirt," said Bonnie, who had returned from the bathroom and heard Clint's last question. "It's not that hard. If they're flashing you, tell them to pull up their shirt. Don't make it awkward."

"That makes sense," said Clint.

During the next break between classes, Clint loudly announced that he "had to take a shit," and I took advantage of the opportunity to try talking to Hailey. I took several deep breaths, trying to control the full body convulsions that were forming. I looked over at Bonnie, who was distracted momentarily by counting the name cards each student handed us when we took their picture. I hoped Bonnie wouldn't interrupt.

"I'm scheduled to work with Clint almost every day," I said quietly to Hailey.

"I'm sorry to hear that," she said.

"Thanks."

"Jen Li likes him," she said. "She thinks he's hot."

"Oh." I hated hearing Hailey mention that a guy was "hot," even if she was only speaking secondhand through another girl. I wanted to ask her if she also thought Clint was hot, but I couldn't bare the possibility of an affirmative response.

"So... see anything good on the internet today?" I asked, sounding like an undercover cop who was trying to pretend he was a high schooler.

"Yeah, look at this," she said, astoundingly unfazed by my awkwardness, lifting up her phone and showing me a video of a dog riding a merry-go-round. She laughed. I laughed. We looked at each other.

"That's great," I said. *I'm in love*, I thought.

It was one of the happiest moments of my life.

FOUR
PURE MOMENTS TO BE FOUND AMIDST THE SUPERFICIALITY (OR: THOSE PHOTOS ARE WEEEEIRD)

JOSIE'S WORN WHITE CONVERSES crunched in the untouched snow, the thin sneakers providing little protection for her frigid feet. She had snow boots somewhere at home, but for her spontaneous trip into the woods after work, her normal footwear would have to do.

She stepped quietly though the pretty leafless gray birches, the thin trees blending in with the blanket of white. She tried to ignore the messages that drunk teens had carved in the innocent trees – all the hearts scratched on the bark, filled with initials, signifying young relationships that were likely long expired. Such a selfish thing to do, Josie thought, to deface these trees, vandalizing nature. It was a juvenile and futile attempt at leaving a permanent mark on the landscape. Her high school boyfriend Billy had once suggested they carve their initials into a similar tree and she had adamantly refused him. That incident and the fact that he still called himself Billy at age sixteen were strong indications the relationship was doomed.

Josie was somewhere near Valley Forge National Historical Park, in one of the hallowed stretches of untouched forestry still surviving amidst the suburbs. The five o'clock winter sunset had been in its earliest stages as she left the SmilePosts office for the day and she was inspired to capture some pictures of the orange sky over the white ground. She had bypassed her normal highway exit and taken a detour of local roads towards a patch of solid green on Google Maps, signifying unoccupied land. She hoped to find a private, natural space to photograph. She pulled over onto an open bit of shoulder, took her film camera out of her glove compartment, and walked into the woods, freezing, but unbothered for the moment by the February chill that typically angered her.

She looked around and she listened. There was a small reverb of car traffic from the not-too-far-off highway and the occasional airplane over head. Impossible to escape society entirely, but all things considered it was nearly silent. A few birds fluttered overhead. A squirrel scampered. The wind beat against the creaking, bare branches.

Sometimes, when she felt overwhelmed by life and the mounting pressure of all that society required of her, Josie liked to imagine what the earth was like before people. She would step out into a patch of woods and look around at the trees and attempt to mentally erase herself from the scene, picturing the vast landscape of plants and animals unaffected by human development. There was a great peace that came with these images. All thoughts of phone bills and insurance payments melted away because those were human inventions that had no place in this pure untouched world, free of the suffocating, inescapable human designs of her daily life.

She looked at the woods and pretended that it was fifty thousand years ago. She felt briefly relieved from the pressing burden of her future.

She looked west towards the vanishing crest of the crimson sun, the purples and oranges filling the gaps between the trees, creating beautiful alternating stripes in the landscape. She slowly and carefully raised her camera towards her eye, as if too-brusque a movement would awaken the woods to its place in modern times.

She adjusted the aperture for the quickly vanishing light.

She clicked the shutter, ensnaring the lost serenity in a photograph.

When she arrived home, Josie's parents were having a row. ("They're having a row," was how Josie liked to describe her parents' fights to her boyfriend Nate, sometimes throwing on a British accent for full effect when she said it.) She could hear their screams before she opened the door, though not the content of the argument, which Josie usually did her best to ignore. She reluctantly entered the house.

"I told you that before!" said her mom Nicki.

"No you didn't!" said her dad Lou.

"Yes! I did!"

"If you had told me, I would know!"

"I did tell you, you just weren't fucking listening!"

"I was listening, you just didn't fucking tell me!"

The conflicts never ran particularly deep. Josie assumed that half the time her parents didn't know what it was they were fighting about – all they wanted was to scream at their spouse, reasoning be damned.

Josie's mom and dad hated each other, with an almost impressive degree of openness. It was hard for her to envision them as the hippie college students they once were, getting stoned, embracing free love, participating in orgies with their friends. (The latter fact being a putrid revelation Josie desperately wished she could unhear.) Together, their bodies wrapped in tie-dye rags, embracing in the rain as they protested both the Vietnam war and the practice of wearing deodorant; passionately in love back then, as they both separately told it; neither yet clued in to the other's nefariousness; each now furious at the egregious act of wool being pulled over their eyes that they had maliciously suffered at the other's hands. When Josie boiled it down, she thought that her mom had held true through the years to those early hippie values, doubling down on them to an irritating extreme, and her dad had abandoned the values for a corporate, conservative (or as he called it, "mature adult") life. Nicki said that Lou "had sold out." Lou said that Nicki "should take a shower once in a while because she smells like shit."

They fought about money. Nicki decried it as the root of all evil while using Lou's income to fund her supply of healing crystals and herbal creams. Lou said that Nicki was still living like a naïve teenager and money could be a great thing when saved and invested with intelligence. Meanwhile he spent hundreds of dollars a week on horse racing bets and booze.

They fought about morality. They had both cheated on one another, Josie was certain. Lou, while staying out overnight for extended "work trips." Nicki, while having her yoga instructor Marvin over the house for long afternoons, during which Josie blasted music in her bedroom to drown out what she might overhear. Both of her parents still believed in God, a practice which Josie had long ago abandoned, but their religious beliefs clashed like everything else. Lou had become a regular churchgoer. He disguised his alcohol breath with a mint long enough to spend Sunday mornings at the chapel. He judged the rest of the family for their heretic abandonment of the Church when he returned home and cracked open the latest bottle of scotch. Nicki espoused the beliefs of a New Age philosophy, haphazardly combining aspects of Judeo-Christianity, Buddhism, Hinduism and Who-knows-ism. She always talked about reincarnation and networks of souls, veganism, and tarot cards. For some reason, she also had a vendetta against halogen lamps, a crusade for which Josie could never deduce the original source.

Despite their espoused beliefs in spiritual forces larger than themselves, both of her parents seemed to get most of their inner fulfillment from yelling at each other. Wrath and disdain were more tangible satisfactions than meditation or prayer, apparently.

You might think that in a household of such marital division, the mom and dad might take more interest in their kids – at least in the selfish service of trying to recruit support to their side – but you would be wrong. As previously mentioned, Josie's parents paid her and her brother Landon little mind. They only had (angry) eyes for one another.

On that February night, Josie slipped in the house and entered the kitchen, easily unnoticed as the fighting match continued. She stuck a Marie Callender's frozen linguine dish in the microwave for the four minutes and thirty seconds that the packaging requested, set her phone alarm, and paced the hall.

She walked past Landon's room. Landon was almost never home anymore and when he was, he was always so high from one pill or another that Josie didn't bother trying to talk to him.

She was alone in this house, even when other people were around.

She used the hallway bathroom, waited for the food to be done, grabbed the meal from the microwave, and took a fork from the silverware drawer as Lou and Nicki's screams continued unhindered. She retreated to her bedroom, put the steaming plastic meal down on her desk, and shut the door to her room for the night. She turned on her speakers, pressed play on the latest Tame Impala album, and turned the volume all the way up to drown out her parents.

When she finished eating, she turned down the music by two-fifths on the dial to a steadily perfected level where she could muffle her parents' arguments but also call Nate. They talked each night when he got home from class.

"What are you listening to?" asked Nate, hearing her music in the background after answering her call.

"Tonight, my folks' fighting is sponsored by Lonerism," said Josie.

"Who's that?"

"It's a Tame Impala album."

"Isn't that a car?"

"You're thinking of the Chevy Impala."

"Oh."

"The Chevy Impala, while having a nice leather interior, doesn't put on a particularly engaging live show."

Josie was passionate about music. Nate less so. She loved going down to Union Transfer or the Electric Factory in Philly to see all the popular indie and alternative bands, keeping up with the newest hyped artists, regularly listening to full albums. Nate's musical knowledge didn't go much deeper than the most overplayed Beatles tracks and, more recently, the radio hits of Taylor Swift, whose talent he emphatically praised on a regular basis. ("I'm just saying, she's a really good songwriter," he said adorably.) Despite his musical limits, he always accompanied Josie to concerts of bands he had never heard of, each show concluding with his same earnest, mildly surprised declaration of "that was good!" as he put the sports talk channel on the radio for the drive home.

"Tame Impala, huh?" said Nate. "It's a cool name. So, how are you doing tonight?"

"Oh, slowly wasting my life away," said Josie.

"A normal night then."

"Yeah, about average."

Josie and Nate had been together for a little over three years. They had met, like at least one out of every four modern couples, through an online dating service. Specifically, they connected on OkCupid, the most popular dating site for a brief period of time with a certain segment of culturally inclined, unreligious millennial singles, until it was overshadowed by Tinder's swipe-right, swipe-left revolution. Josie was exceedingly grateful that she had been spared ever having to use Tinder. Sure, she had gotten her fair share of disgusting messages from horny robotic douchebags on OkCupid, but at least she had some descriptive content to base her dates on. She could get a sense of a guy's personality and taste in movies and music before they went out. That was preferable to the barren husks that were profiles on that bottomless black hole of Tinder, featuring a few pictures and not much else.

On the same night that Nate had sent her an introductory greeting on OkCupid, she had received a message from a guy named Sunil. After looking at both their profiles, Josie decided she was fully on team Sunil. Nate was handsome, but his cultural taste was a little bare-bones. His favorites list was made up of unoriginal choices like *The Shawshank*

Redemption and *The Office*. Josie wanted her potential mate's interests to dig deeper. She wanted to learn about new things from the guy she dated. Sunil's favorites list included a bunch of foreign film titles like *L'Avventura* and authors like Don DeLillo. Nate didn't list any books at all.

Also, if she was being honest with herself, she liked the idea of going out with a non-white person. Her liberal pride was stoked by the notion of an interracial relationship. It was more than a preference; it was almost a requirement. She wanted to do her part to support diversity and tolerance in society. What stronger gesture could she make than choosing to spend her life with someone of a different race, standing alongside him, hand in hand, at any public place they would ever go?

She went on three dates with Sunil. He was a good-looking guy who was perfectly nice and definitely intelligent. But for whatever reason, they didn't click. This sort of thing happened a lot with online dating. On paper (or perhaps I should say "on screen") someone appeared to be an ideal match, but in person something in the chemistry failed. No rational reason for it, but the oven of attraction failed to ignite. It was exceedingly hard to gauge potential romantic harmony without meeting someone in real life first.

The day after her third date with Sunil, when they had both mutually acknowledged that their coupling wasn't leading anywhere, Josie felt discouraged. She was tired of the crush of consistent disappointment that was online dating. On a whim, she looked in her OkCupid inbox and was reminded of Nate's message, which she had never responded to.

"What's your favorite snack?" he had written.

She looked at Nate's profile once again. It didn't say much. He was studying to be a nurse. (That was one feminist check in his favor – some guys would never be willing to be a nurse, simply because of the gender role connotations.) He really liked pizza. He wrote that as someone in the medical field, he knew he should say he liked broccoli or salad or something, but really, he liked pizza. (An amusing if obvious observation.) He listed no religion. (Not as strong as saying he was an atheist or agnostic but it would do.)

She looked at his pictures again. He was quite handsome. And when it came right down to it, Josie loved *The Shawshank Redemption* and *The Office*, even if it was boring that everyone else did too.

"I like popcorn with melted M&Ms and Hershey syrup drizzled all over," she had replied to his message. "I'm exceptionally healthy. How about you? Let me guess... pizza?"

They had their first date a few days later. They went to a pizza place, albeit an artisanal one that Josie selected down in the hipster Philly neighborhood of Northern Liberties.

"I'm so excited we're eating pizza!" he said when they met, with the unreserved earnestness that was his signature. Josie laughed. She liked him right away.

As it turned out, Nate was much smarter than she had anticipated. He loved science and politics and could speak on these subjects with an informed understanding that was always humble and always acknowledged the limitations of his grasp. He was equally as liberal as she was, though in a less confrontational way. He believed in kindness and charity towards fellow humans and he practiced it. He was busy with his exhausting school schedule and he still found time to volunteer. That's right, he actually volunteered! Josie didn't volunteer. She only talked about wanting to volunteer and felt guilty that she didn't volunteer. Nate was the kind of guy who acted, rather than talked about doing things. He downplayed his own smarts, accomplishments, and giving nature, but his actions laid bare his natural inclination towards all three. He was not exceedingly funny, but he was clever when he wanted to be, and Josie preferred to be the funny one in the relationship anyway. And he adored her. He doted on her and looked upon her with admiration and desire. She loved being looked at like that. He was always there for her, always supportive. She felt naturally comfortable with him from almost the very beginning and that was a difficult quality to find in a relationship. The fact that he didn't know much about foreign films or indie music was a private disappointment, but it could be forgiven because of that incredible sense of comfort.

Now, three years later, Josie laid back on her bed and cuddled up with her phone against her pillow as she talked to him, still comforted by her boyfriend after all this time.

"How was class?" she asked.

"Good. Exhausting, but I learned a lot of important things."

Josie smiled. Nate was an eternal optimist, always putting a positive spin on every situation. It worked as a nice complement to her natural cynicism.

He was in year one of a three-year nursing grad program at a Delaware County college. The first year was mainly academic. Years two and three he would be training in a hospital.

The program hadn't been his first choice (that was a school in New Orleans), but he had decided to stay local because he didn't want to be separated from Josie by long distance. It was a sacrifice he downplayed, but Josie knew how important it had been for their relationship and appreciated him for it. At the same time, she wanted nothing more herself than to travel and escape from the confines of the place she had spent all her life. It was so frustrating that she couldn't have told him to attend the Louisiana program and offered to move there with him. She would have loved to live in New Orleans, eating gumbo and attending live jazz. But she couldn't afford to move from home until she had some sort of sustainable career. Her lack of money had failed them both. She never brought this frustration up with Nate, though he always encouraged her to be honest and open with her feelings. She didn't want to make him feel any worse about his selfless decision. She preferred to make him laugh.

"What sorts of important things did you learn?" she said to him on the phone. "Did they finally teach you what a vagina is?"

He laughed. "Not yet."

"Well I sure hope they get to that soon."

"Maybe you can show me," he said, displaying some atypical spice.

"Nate! Why I never," she said, putting on a southern belle impression.

"Sorry," he said. She could feel him blushing through the phone and she loved it.

"No, it's okay. I'll show you," she said. "School's failing you and I'm happy to do my part to teach the future nurse."

"Very kind of you."

"I'm a good person. People are always telling me that."

"I bet they are."

There was a pause in the conversation. It went on long enough for her parents' yells to seep in over the softened sounds of Lonerism.

"They're at it again, huh?" said Nate.

"Every night!" said Josie with a sarcastic chipperness.

"I'm sorry Josie, that's really tough. I know that's hard for you."

"I need to get the hell out of here. I wish we could move in together."

"You know that I'm not opposed to that. If it's what we want, we can figure out a way to make it work."

"I don't want to go any more in debt than I already am. And I don't want you any more in debt either."

"We've talked about this. I've told you what I think the financial options are."

"The financial options are – I need to find another job so I can afford for us to move in together."

"Yes, that's one option."

"It's a necessity."

"Have you been looking at the job listings at all?"

"Sometimes. There's not much that's appealing. I need to figure out how I can make money with photography."

"Have you looked into local newspapers? They always have photos. Maybe someplace needs a photographer."

"At small papers, those photos are usually taken by the writer, I think. And those photos are terrible. I would never want to take shitty photos like that."

"Maybe you could raise the quality of them."

"Again, I think it's the writer that takes them anyway. Like I just said."

"It was only a thought."

"It's not a real path to anything."

"Sometimes you have to start your own path if you can't find one."

"Did you read that on an inspirational magnet somewhere?"

"Maybe there's a contest you could enter."

"You've said that before."

"I'm just trying to be helpful."

"I know, but you don't need to repeat yourself. I listen when you talk."

"Sorry."

The conversation went quiet. Josie and Nate almost never fought. Josie hated arguing. Whenever she could feel the frequency of their conversation tuning itself towards conflict, she pivoted in some humorous direction to avoid the tension.

"It's okay," she said. "What can I expect from a guy who doesn't know what a vagina is."

He laughed. "That's a fair point." Then he added, "I'm only trying to help."

"I know," she said.

Nate often tried to engage Josie in hard truth discussions and the search for practical solutions. Josie often evaded those discussions, shutting any windows with a view of her own vulnerability, preferring to remain a hardened cynic. It was part of their dynamic.

"I love you," she added, happy to say it, fully meaning it.

"I love you too," he said.

A couple months later, on a Saturday night when Nate was swamped with homework, Josie decided to attend Otto's previously detailed party.

While Ethan was hitting on Linda and I was attempting to converse with my new acquaintance Hailey, holding my armpits close to my body to hide the waterfall of nervous sweat induced by small talk with my crush, Josie was chatting with her fellow vets Gabby, Cal, Stacy, and her pal Rita.

"Do you like butter or margarine on your toast?" Stacy said to Cal.

"I don't really like toast," said Cal.

"Really?" said Stacy, with too much fascination.

"I like French toast. Does that count?"

Gabby, Rita, and Josie watched Stacy and Cal's innocent and awkward flirtation. The bystanders inwardly smiled at the inevitable coupling that would occur when one of them found the courage to reveal their feelings. Might take a while, but they'd get there.

"Let me get your opinion on something," Rita said to Gabby and Josie, pulling out her Tinder profile. "So I've been talking to this girl who seems great, and she's hot, and the messages are funny and entertaining and I ask her to get together and she says she's only available on Wednesday afternoons."

"Was she making a joke?" said Gabby.

"That's what I thought," said Rita. "I said 'LOL. Sorry I usually work on Wednesday afternoons. How is your Thursday at three A.M.'?"

"Funny retort," said Josie.

"Thank you. I thought so," said Rita. "But then she was like, no I'm serious. That's the only time of the week I'm available."

"So, what is she like married or something?" said Gabby.

"That's what I was wondering," said Rita. "But I can't ask that, can I?"

"Let me see your phone," said Josie. Rita handed her the phone and Josie scrolled through the messages.

"I think she's still joking," said Josie.

"Really?" said Rita.

"Maybe," said Josie. "Hard to tell. Anyway, SmilePosts jobs are drying up at this time of year anyway. I'm sure you'll have a free Wednesday afternoon soon enough."

"But I don't want to go out with her if she's married," said Rita.

"I went out with a married guy," said Gabby.

"Gabby!" said Stacy, appalled by this illicit revelation and interrupting her conversation with Cal to express it.

"What? His wife sucked," said Gabby.

Josie laughed, humored by Gabby's reasoning.

"That's adultery," said Stacy. "That's a sin."

Josie laughed more.

"What is so funny?" said Stacy.

"Sorry," said Josie. She usually downplayed her atheism around her co-workers. Stacy, who was quite nice and who she generally rather liked, would surely turn into an intolerable soul-saving missionary if she knew that Josie was a nonbeliever, callously discarding her future spot in heaven.

"How did you meet him?" asked Rita.

"At his wedding. I was the photographer," said Gabby, now blushing.

"Damn girl," said Rita.

"I know..." said Gabby. "But his wife really did suck."

"So what happened? How come you're not still with him?" said Rita.

"He kind of sucked too," said Gabby, laughing.

"I can't believe what I'm hearing," said Stacy.

"Me neither. Disgusting," said Cal, with his trademark revolted vigor. "I'm with Stacy," he added, in case his dashing show of support for his romantic interest hadn't been made clear.

"Oh, but speaking of weddings," said Stacy, eager to change the subject and not be tainted by the muck of other people's transgressions. "I'm photographing a big one Saturday after next and I need a second person. Anyone interested?"

"I have my Grandpop's birthday that day," said Cal, discouraged. "Dammit!"

They all stood silently and looked at Cal, his outburst lingering in the air.

"Uh... I'm going to get a beer," said Cal. He walked off.

GREAT BIG SMILE

"I have a wedding that day myself," said Gabby. "Sorry."

"Not like she would want you there anyway, always stealing away the grooms," said Josie.

"Shut up," said Gabby. "That only happened a couple times."

Josie burst out laughing.

"Josie, you should do the wedding with Stacy," said Rita.

Josie looked at Rita, confused and on the precipice of annoyance.

"Weddings aren't my thing," said Josie. "You know that."

"You've never done one. How do you know they're not your thing?"

"I don't like that kind of photography."

"What do you mean?" said Stacy, unable to comprehend why anyone would dislike wedding pictures. (They were photos of a *wedding* – the most special, perfect day in a person's entire life! Unless of course, the wedding photographer saw fit to seduce the groom... Stacy really needed to have a talk with Gabby about the potential eternal punishments of her sins...)

"You're literally always complaining about how you need more money," said Rita. "You don't like SmilePosts photography either, but you do it for money. You need to be open to new things sometimes if you ever want to get what you want."

Since they were mainly work friends, Josie had only hung out with Rita while drinking a couple of times. She forgot how blunt Rita could be after some alcohol entered her system.

She wanted to fire back with some nasty assassination of Rita's character, but she forced herself to take a breath before responding. During her forced restraint, an irritating thought entered her head. *Maybe Rita's right. You do need the money.*

Before she knew what was happening, she heard herself say, "Okay, Stacy, I'll do the wedding with you."

"Really? That's so great!" said Stacy.

Rita looked at Josie, surprised that her provocation had worked.

"Send me a picture of the groom if he's cute," Gabby said to Josie.

"Gabby!" said Stacy.

"I'm kidding!" said Gabby.

The wedding was held at a country club on the Main Line, the wealthiest stretch of the Philadelphia suburbs, west of the city. Three hundred and fifty people were in attendance. Josie wasn't sure she could list three hundred and fifty people she had ever met, let alone would invite to her wedding. From what she overhead, the bride was the daughter of some business magnate and a third of the guests were clients who had never met the bride nor the groom.

If Josie's father insisted on inviting people she had never met to her own wedding, she would be furious. But this teeth-whitened couple from straight out of the photo frame were basking in the adulation and praise of the strangers. They were happy to be the central stars of this solar system of humanity, unconcerned about who any of the other planets were as long they rotated around them and handed them a card with a check in it.

The hall was decorated with thousands of white flowers and the guest list was as white as the bouquets. Josie strained her eyes searching for a single person of color and could not find one. The divisions of class and race were on full display.

The whole affair was an overpriced exhibition of excess and insularity, an under-glass slice of the privileged celebrating their own false importance with no self-awareness for how they came off. It was exactly the sort of wedding that made Josie hate most weddings.

"Isn't it lovely!" said Stacy, who had to wipe tears of joy away from her face after nearly every picture. "It's a dream come to life! I wish my wedding could be like this."

"Mmmhmm," said Josie, admirably succeeding at keeping her mouth shut.

Despite her aversion to the event, Josie did the best she could at the job she had been hired for. Stacy was spearheading the organized portraits, so Josie was left free to roam the party, focusing on candids. For this, she was grateful. She wasn't sure she would have been able to stomach the forced poses and smiles of the official wedding party session, but candid photos were her specialty. She liked capturing people unaware, in true postures and unperformed emotions. The wedding was populated by the upper-class, reeking of money and the entitlement that accompanies it, but individually they were still human beings and when they were caught unaware by the camera, some essence of truth could be captured in their behavior. That was what thrilled Josie – taking a photo of a person as they truly are, devoid of intentional presentation. Perhaps they were letting loose on the dance floor or sharing a drink and reminiscing with an old friend. There were pure moments to be found amidst the superficiality if she looked closely enough.

"Ooooh, can I see?" said a sweaty, drunk bridesmaid, running barefoot from the dance floor. She nearly tackled Josie to the ground.

Josie tucked her camera close to her like she was protecting an infant. She had just taken a photo of the sweaty bridesmaid grinding up against a seventy-year-old man, certain the image would never make the wedding album but unable to resist capturing it. Apparently, she had not been secretive enough because the bridesmaid had spotted her and abandoned her dance, to the old man's great disappointment.

"See what?" said Josie.

"The pictures!" said the bridesmaid.

"Uh, I don't want to share them yet. We'll pick the best ones and edit them and everything."

"Come onnnnnnnnnnnnnn."

The bridesmaid was breathing into the back of Josie's neck, her chest pushing up against Josie's back as she weaved her way into photo viewing position without Josie's approval.

"Fine," Josie said, desperate to do whatever was necessary to regain her personal space. "Just a few though."

"Kelsey! Marin! Come here! We're looking at pictures!"

Two of the other bridesmaids emerged from God-knows-where and surrounded Josie on all sides. They smelled like perfume, blush, and dirty socks.

"Oh yay!" said either Kelsey or Marin. Josie didn't much care to determine who was who.

"Just a few. Real quick," said Josie.

Josie held up the camera's view screen and began swiftly scanning through a selection of the hundreds of photos she had taken, proud of the images she had been able to squeeze out of such an annoying event.

She didn't notice the eerie silence of the loud ladies, which should have been a sign that something was amiss.

"Those photos are weeeeird," said the sweaty bridesmaid, when Josie had finished.

"Yeah, where are all the photos of us together?" said Kelsey or Marin.

"Stacy took those."

"Who. Is. Stacy?" said Kelsey or Marin.

"The other photographer," said Josie, losing her patience.

"I don't understand," said the sweaty bridesmaid. "What are these pictures supposed to be? Here, take a good picture – take one of the three of us!"

The bridesmaid pulled Kelsey and Marin close to her and all three simultaneously put their left hands on their left hips, popped out their right legs, and pursed their lips. Their uniformity did not appear to be a joke – they seemed to be under some absurd unconscious agreement that this alien pose looked sexy.

"I think I'm good," said Josie.

"Come on bitch just take the picture," said Kelsey or Marin.

"Kelsey!" said apparently Marin, laughing.

"What? She needs to do her job," said Kelsey, unremitting.

Josie, boiling inside, lifted the camera and snapped a quick shot.

"There, I took it."

"Let us see it!" said the sweaty bridesmaid.

They stuffed around Josie once again. Josie showed them the picture and they were delighted.

"Yesssss. It's sooooo good," said the sweaty bridesmaid. Kelsey and Marin seconded her.

"So good," said Kelsey. "You should take more pictures like *that*."

"Okay," said Josie.

Then a Britney Spears song started playing and they all screeched in Josie's ears and ran to the dance floor.

Driving home at midnight, after the wedding finally concluded, Josie's anger at the bridesmaids and the entire insufferable evening inflated to near-unbearable proportions. She had said a terse and, she knew, rather rude goodbye to Stacy, who had thanked her profusely for her help and given her a generous check for her contributions. Josie had packed up her camera bag as quickly as possible, rushed out of the country club parking lot to beat the traffic of drunk guests, and sped onto the highway, weaving in and out of lanes and constantly changing the radio station in furious restlessness on the way home.

She felt a disproportionate amount of hatred and self-righteousness directed at all those who had attended the wedding, as if she had worked at the party of some flagrantly evil dictator's child and was now covered in moral grime as a result, hating the dictator, hating his family, and hating herself for selling out to the murderous regime.

She knew, in some rational part of her mind, that her anger was unwarranted and unreasonable, but there was satisfaction in the hot wind of the emotion. Being angry towards others allowed her to deflect the spotlight off herself, and really, wasn't she the most mad at herself? Wasn't she disappointed and irate at herself for going nowhere and accomplishing nothing? For being no better than the other untalented photographers at

SmilePosts and accomplishing nothing higher than wedding photography? Was she destined to spend every weekend for the rest of her life at these pretentious ceremonies because her only skill was photography and these were the only gigs she would be able to get? She felt trapped and the only escape was hating every other person around her. All of them, all satisfied with the fake parameters of what society said a life should be. Marriage, kids, a house in the suburbs, a dead-end job, judging other people online while doing nothing to improve your own life or the world around you.

The whole thing made her want to scream.

So she did. She let loose at the top of her lungs, screaming as she drove twenty miles over the speed limit on the uncrowded highway, hoping that some car could hear the echo of her yells as she sped by.

It helped. At least for a moment.

When she got home at 12:37 A.M., the lights were still on downstairs in the house.

She entered and her parents were waiting quietly in the living room.

This calm, united late-night vigil was far more terrifying than their typical verbal brawls.

"Hey Josie, where have you been?" said Lou. It should have sounded like an accusation, but it didn't. He was tired and defeated.

"I was photographing a wedding" she said. "Just for some extra cash," she added, feeling the need to justify her selling out, though she knew her parents didn't care.

"That's nice," said Nicki.

The eerie quiet continued.

"What are you guys doing up?" said Josie.

"We were waiting for you," said Lou.

"We need to talk to you," said Nicki.

"Landon too, but who knows if he'll be home at any point," said Lou.

"What is it?" asked Josie. Goosebumps spread across her body. She felt woozy.

"Your dad and I have been talking a lot and we've decided the best thing would be for us to uncouple," said Nicki.

"Uncouple?" said Josie.

"Get divorced," said Lou, sighing with exasperation over his soon to be ex-wife's vocabulary.

It should have been the most inevitable news in the world, but it hit Josie like a nasty shock. She didn't understand her own reaction.

It's obvious they should get divorced, she thought. So why did she feel like crying?

"Your mom is going to stay in the house with you and Landon. I'm going to get a condo in the city."

Josie was having trouble breathing. She needed air.

"It's going to be better for everybody this way," said Nicki.

"Of course you think it's better if you're around the kids and I'm not," said Lou, irritated.

"We both agreed this is the best option," said Nicki.

"Doesn't mean you have to be so passive-aggressively pleased about getting me out of here," said Lou.

"I believe in expressing the truth. You know that," said Nicki.

Their burgeoning fight was interrupted by the click of a camera shutter. They looked up. Josie's face was obscured by the camera she held in front of her eyes. She had taken it out of her bag while they were distracted by bickering.

They both stared at her, utterly confused.

She took a second picture. And a third.

"Josie?" said her dad.

She lowered the camera down, revealing the tears that flooded her eyes.

Before they could say anything more, she stuffed the camera back in her bag and ran out the front door.

Nate was woozy and clearly jolted out of sleep by her call.

"Hey – I need to come over," said Josie.

"Hey," he said softly, half asleep, but still instantly sympathetic to the fragile sound of her voice. "What's the matter?"

"Can I just come over?"

"Yeah, of course. Text me when you get here. My parents are asleep."

When he opened the door, she fell into his arms.

"Hey," he said, concerned. "What happened?"

"My parents are getting a divorce," she said.

"Oh Josie. I'm really sorry. That's rough."

"Is it though?" she said.

She peeled away from him.

"They should get divorced," she said. "They hate each other."

"It's still not an easy thing to hear," he said.

"It should be though. It's the right thing. I don't even know why I'm upset. I'm upset with myself for *being* upset. That's what I'm most upset about."

"Jose..."

"I need to get out of there. I need to get out of that goddamn house."

"I know."

"I wanted to scream at them. But instead I started crying like a baby."

"It's okay to cry at a time like this."

She put her camera bag down. She sat on the floor, leaning up against the front door.

He sat down next to her, resting his arm up against hers in the intimacy of solidarity.

"You're dressed pretty fancy," he said.

"I was at that wedding."

"How was it?"

She didn't respond to his question. Instead, she said, "When we get married, let's not have a wedding."

She avoided his eyes for a moment, hesitant to see his reaction to her boundary crossing proposition.

They had never discussed getting married before. But when she gathered the courage to look, he was smiling.

"Okay," he said.

She kissed him on the cheek and leaned her head on his shoulder, breathing in his comforting scent of baseball glove leather and hand soap.

"Okay," she said.

FIVE
EVENTUALLY, THINGS TURN OUT ALL RIGHT

"**PLEASE LINE UP** from tallest to smallest," Josie told the class of second graders while I stood next to her, observing.

It was a week into my second fall as a SmilePosts photographer. I had been granted a responsibility that was only assigned to employees who made it past their first year. I was being taught classroom group photography, that fine art of arranging thirty children without hiding a single face, then miraculously convincing them all to look at the camera and smile simultaneously, avoiding a single blink or silly expression among the rabble.

"Tallest in the front of the line and the smallest in back," Josie said. She was met with the confused stares of twenty-seven second graders.

"We line up alphabetically," said the goody-two-shoes girl at the front of the line.

Josie looked at the teacher, hoping for some assistance. None was forthcoming. Mrs. Spanbrooke stared back at her defiantly. *I'm not doing it*, the teacher said with her eyes. *I deal with these kids all day – it's your turn.*

Josie turned back to the children.

"I'm sure that you normally line up alphabetically," Josie said to the prissy line leader and the rest of the group. "But right now, I need you to line up so the tallest person is in the front and the shortest person is in the back. Please line up in size order. Now."

The seven and eight-year-olds looked at each other, some delighted, some terrified by the requirements of this request. They dispersed into a chaotic cloud of movement until a few leaders emerged in the group to herd their fellow students. Over the course of a minute, they rearranged themselves. A boy, closer to my height than I would have liked, proudly took his place at the front of the line, a miniature doll of a girl took her place at the back, and a few debates carried on in the middle of the pack. Kids of near identical height compared themselves back to back, each vying for height supremacy.

"That's close enough," said Josie, to the children debating over millimeters of height difference. "Follow me."

Josie led the size-arranged class to the auditorium steps.

It was our third class of the day and I felt like I pretty much had the procedure down. Josie arranged the classes so that the tallest kids were standing on the top row and the shortest kids were sitting in chairs on the floor. She then told some of the children to take small steps to their left or their right, staggering every other row of faces like seats in a movie theater, or bricks on a building, so that no one was blocked by the person standing in front of them. She called this process, "windowing."

It all seemed simple enough but I was happy to let Josie take the reins until she specifically asked me to take over. Standing by and observing allowed me more time to wallow in thoughts about my life stalling out like the twenty-four-year-old vehicle it was, stranding me in the middle of my narrative highway as other cars zoomed past me in the left lane of success.

During that summer of unemployment after my first year at Smile-Posts, I had received a series of emails kindly letting me know that my screenplay had failed to place in any competition I had entered. It was a crushing series of blows and I was reeling, unsure of my next step.

Remarkable how twenty-four years' worth of dreaming gets shred of all its fantastical fat so soon after your school years end. Reality is an unimaginative butcher, cutting the flanks of circumstance to a practical, tasteless cut. You go through your sixteen years of schooling. All the while, you are taught to believe that good grades guarantee success waiting for you on the other side of the commencement gates. You believe that adulthood is idling on the other side of those gates, ready to give you a lift in an open-air convertible, happy to drive you to any career destination you choose. Instead, you're left waiting at the bus stop in the rain with no timetable for pickup or any guarantee that the buses are running at all.

My plan for success was thrown out the window and I had no idea how to develop a new strategy. This sudden sense of drifting without a map was compounded by the shakeup in my social life.

Half the friends I thought of calling were now a plane flight away (or at least an extended drive), having moved for jobs or having stayed in the cities where they went to college. Others were caught up in their relationships or their high-paying twelve-hour a day jobs or their attempts at becoming self-sustaining farmers (admittedly, this latter example was only one individual). As a result, the weekend nights with friends that used to come together so easily now required a depressing amount of effort. More and more Saturday nights I found myself alone, in my bedroom, watching Netflix.

Suddenly it was the end of that depressing summer. I felt lonely and confused and I didn't know what else to do but go back to SmilePosts.

And there I was, a leak in the cask of the unearned superiority I had felt when I was a newbie, sure at the time that my first season would be my only season because I was destined for greater things.

I tried to maintain a belief that I could patch the leak. I tried to brainstorm a new screenplay idea that could gain me traction in the contests. I wondered whether I should relocate to L.A. but was terrified by the realities of a cross-country move. I still hoped my life would naturally fall into place but I was increasingly uncertain as to what would cause the topple.

"You ready for a turn? I think it's time to see what you can do," said Josie, with a scheming smirk as a class of fifth graders approached. "I would hope these kids are old enough to figure out how tall they are."

She was right. They were.

The class of kindergartners after them, however, were not.

"Sorry buddy – I have to throw you to the sharks at some point and see how you do," said Josie, when I looked over at her with pleading eyes, hoping for help with the little ones. "It's the only way to learn," she added, shrugging her shoulders.

"It's not the only way to learn," I insisted. "There are all sorts of ways to learn."

"Nothing I can do," she said, then sat down at a nearby chair and kicked back as I flailed.

"Thanks," I said sarcastically and laughed. I turned to the kindergartners. "Okay, I need you guys to line up from tallest to smallest."

They stared at me blankly. One kid picked his nose.

"They're all pretty much the same size," said their exhausted teacher, Miss Ulmero. It had apparently taken a superhuman effort to get her class to the auditorium and she was in no mood to herd the beasts any further.

"Well..." I was hesitating. Hesitating was death in the game of classroom photography. "I guess I'll figure out their height order myself."

One by one, I selected kids from the class and told them where to stand on the steps. This went slowly. At some point, I glanced over at Josie. She tapped her wrist with her index finger in the universal gesture of "time's-a-wasting." She was having way too much fun at my expense.

When I finally had all the kids lined up – then readjusted several of them with itchy feet who had begun to shift from their spots – I ran back to the camera.

Right then a second class of kindergartners entered the room, arriving at the scheduled time for their own picture.

"I'll be with you in a couple minutes," I said.

Their teacher, Mrs. Wallack, groaned.

"You know, I have things to be doing," she said.

"Right, of course," I said.

"I can't be here all day," she said.

"Sure," I said, eagerly trying to end this exchange so that I could photograph the restlessly waiting class, every passing second increasing the risk that they would shift out of place.

"We were scheduled for right now."

"I get it," I said. "Let me just take this class and then I'll be right with you."

"I don't know what you're waiting for," said Mrs. Wallack.

I held my tongue. I focused on Miss Ulmero's class in front of me.

"Okay everybody smile!" I said.

One or two kids smiled. The rest looked around the room, ignoring me completely.

"What's that?" said a boy with glasses in the middle row, pointing towards Lord-knows-what.

"Everybody look at me please!" I said.

Now other kids were looking in the direction where the boy with glasses had pointed, trying to see what mysterious object had seized his attention.

"Oooh, look at that," said a girl with pigtails.

"Where?" said a boy in a John Cena shirt.

"Everybody please look at me!" I pleaded.

"This is going to take forever," said Mrs. Wallack.

"I don't see it," said a girl in a polka dot dress.

Now I turned to see what they were all looking at. I couldn't figure it out and I felt idiotic. I walked over close to Miss Ulmero's class to implore them to focus.

"Hey everybody, I really need you guys to look at me. Okay. Everybody look at me. Please." I pointed to my eyes. "Look. At. Me. Okay."

I ran back to the camera.

"Ready, give me a great big smile!" I took a picture. About two thirds of the students were looking at me in the photo. Four or five of them were smiling. Better. But still not good.

"Guys I need everybody to look at me and smile. On the count of three everybody say 'money,' okay? One. Two. Three!"

The entire class of children screamed "money" with the vigor of someone stranded on a desert island, yelling "help" at a passing plane. I checked the photo. Almost everyone was looking. They weren't exactly *smiling* as much as *yelling at the top of their lungs*, but it would have to do.

"Okay, thanks, you guys are all done."

I looked over at Josie. She mimed applause in appreciation. I took a small, sarcastic bow.

"Do you think I have all day?" screamed impatient Mrs. Wallack.

"I'll take over," said Josie.

My whole body sagged with relief. "Thank you," I said.

The truth was that returning to SmilePosts was disturbingly comforting.

The stress of that first fall – the pressure of learning the equipment, the adjustment to the early mornings and long drives – had receded, replaced by an ease of familiarity. I knew what to expect. I looked upon the fresh batch of first year photographers, dropping off one by one like characters in an Agatha Christie novel, some fired, some quitting, all wrapped up in the annual Hunger Games of their first SmilePosts season, and I felt superior. I had already proven myself. I had immunity to their plague.

Three quarters of the people I had started with from the previous fall were gone.

Clint was back, because I was apparently cursed to spend every day of the rest of my life with him. He greeted me in September with a bone-crunching hug that may have permanently dislodged several disks in my back. He instantly launched into a twenty-minute monologue about all of his drunken summer exploits. He told me about the "four and a half chicks" he had "banged." I did not ask for clarification on what constituted a half bang.

Linda was back that second fall, although she was visibly pregnant, and she only made it to October before the job became too physically stressful. I eventually heard from Stacy (who stayed in touch with her) that Linda had her baby (a boy) and that mom and child were both doing well. Linda never returned to SmilePosts after that. I have no idea what she's up to now.

Dana was also back, though both of the Jens were gone, along with Mackenzie. Shayla and Pristine had returned. Otto was back and seemed determined to take up Ethan's mantle as "funny, dirty joke guy" at the office, without any of Ethan's natural comedic charm. Otto would throw out the words "penis" or "dick" or "cock" at least once a week, sometimes completely devoid of any conversational context. Dee finally pulled him aside and told him that if he continued to be inappropriate at the workplace he would be fired. He walked around with his tail between his legs for about a week and then pivoted to fart humor, which I guess he thought was more appropriate. George seemingly agreed, because he broke down laughing every time Otto made a fart joke, nearly choking on his Jolly Ranchers.

Lastly, answering all of my summer prayers, Hailey had returned. (I'm using the term "prayers" loosely. I'm not religious and the last time I remember praying was at my Bar Mitzvah.)

Mutual members of the select group who had survived our first year, Hailey and I now interacted. We were friendly. We talked sometimes. She smiled at me when she said hello.

God, she had the best smile. (Again, not religious. Using "god" here as a term of exclamation, rather than a reference to an almighty being.)

During my first year, the month of September had seemed to last forever. That second year, it sped by and before I knew it, it was late October and retake season was upon me.

I realized that I didn't mind the job. Sometimes I even liked it.

This was disconcerting. I didn't want to become complacent. I wanted to stay hungry for something better. Comfort can be a hard ailment to overcome.

I couldn't allow myself to forget that SmilePosts was supposed to be a stopgap. I needed to work to achieve the life I wanted. I needed to develop a new screenplay idea or two and put all my effort into producing the scripts that would get my feet in the door.

That's what my mind should have been focused on.

But mostly, I thought about Hailey.

I had spent a large portion of the summer friending and following her on various forms of social media. I experienced a little high every time she posted something new on Facebook, Instagram, or Twitter. I scrolled through Hailey's past photos on Facebook and Instagram, my insides contracting in a breathless cringe whenever I saw some image of her with a guy, not wanting to think of her romantic history, but not averse enough to stop looking at every image of her I could find. Her Facebook page listed her as "single," which I took as an irrefutable fact. I would accept no other possibility, for the sake of my sanity.

I did feel a bit shamed by all this social media "stalking," as they call it. I know it's commonplace in these modern times, but there was still a sense of a voyeuristic violation. I sometimes felt like a creep. It was too easy. All these images were sitting there, online, attracting the unconstrained magnetism of my crush.

The internet is a pretty terrible place, in general. It brings out our worst instincts. It's basically a several-acre landfill that you know contains a few inches of precious gems. So you sift through heaps of reeking garbage, getting smeared with unidentifiable detritus, for the occasional chance at scavenging something glittery. And meanwhile, as you search, there are hundreds of anonymous voices hiding behind some pile of rotting food to berate you and shout about how worthless you are as a person. Some commenters say that your methods of finding the precious minerals are pitiful and others say that the gems you're holding are fake and everybody knows rubies suck and emeralds rule and you're a loser.

"But," some might say, "What about likes? Aren't they a source of communal support and positivity on the internet?" You would think so, wouldn't you? But you'd be wrong. YOU ARE WRONG. (See, this is what spending too much time on the internet does to a person. You start speaking in all caps and blowing your top at the slightest disagreement. My apologies. You're entitled to your opinion and every person has a different perspective and that's okay.) Receiving a like should be a nice little boost, a miniature compliment, a good tiding, a basket of fresh warm optimism, but instead, each like is a mini-drug, creating a cycle of craving for more likes, ever more likes, no amount of likes ever enough. When the likes stop coming on a post, you plummet and need more likes, have to have more likes, need to make a new post as soon as possible so that the likes can continue, each post ultimately fueling this unsatisfying cycle that ends in a pit of emptiness, from which only more likes can pull you from the depths.

This emptiness is compounded when it's only one particular person whose likes you really care about anyway.

That summer, I had made posts and watched the fifteen to thirty likes come in over a day or two and waited and waited to see Hailey's name on the list. And when her name occasionally appeared, it was more of a relief than a pleasure. I wondered why the anticipation of seeing her name on that "like" list was so necessary when it provided so little in the way of satisfaction. I had seen her at work. She scrolled through her phone and looked at each post for about a third of a second. It was mindless. There was no real value in receiving a like from her, but it was all I wanted in the world.

When the season resumed, Hailey greeted me with her soul melting smile. She asked me, unprompted, how my summer was and if I did anything fun.

I was ecstatically happy and an insane notion grew wings – *what if Hailey liked me back?*

Here and there I made a small overture. She posted an Instagram photo of her dog eating a steak and I wrote, "How does he order his steak?

Medium well?" She liked the comment. At work one day she mentioned an affection for the character Chandler from the TV show *Friends*. That night, I posted a YouTube montage of Chandler clips on her Facebook wall with the caption, "Could this montage BE any more up your alley?" She liked the post. In early October, on one of the rare, sacred days when we were scheduled together, we had a conversation where she mentioned loving animals. That night, I messaged her my favorite Wikipedia article in the world, a hilarious list of the official names for groupings of different animal species. This list goes far beyond the commonly known "swarm of bees" or "flock of geese" and extends to the regal "pride of lions," the haunting "murder of crows," and the jolly "parade of elephants." This glorious list ventures into the outright absurd, such as a "pandemonium of parrots," a "conspiracy of lemurs," and my all-time favorite, a "business of ferrets." I hear "business of ferrets" and I picture a bunch of ferrets in suits, holding briefcases, walking into the bank to apply for a small business loan. If there's a funnier imagined scene, I don't know what it is. I messaged Hailey the Wikipedia link, pointing out some of my favorite animal group terms, making the joke about the ferrets applying for a small business loan. I waited anxiously for her reply, excited for the witty banter I expected us to exchange. She replied, "lol." That's all she said.

    My flares fired over the internet ocean were a gauge of whether Hailey could like me as more than a friend. They were prophylactic-covered flirtation, trying to tell her I liked her while still maintaining plausible deniability about my feelings, should things get awkward. "I was only being friendly," I could say, if necessary. I didn't want to let the cat out of the bag unless I knew the mouse I was trying to catch wanted to be caught. The thought of open rejection was mortifying. Maybe some people at work could intuit that I liked Hailey, but as long as no one talked about it openly, I didn't have to run away in the humiliation of open rebuff.

    I balanced myself on the teetering tight rope belief of dreams becoming reality. I would never be with Hailey unless I made my feelings clear.

But I didn't want to tell her my feelings unless I was sure that she liked me. I didn't want to be a coward, always having been told that girls like it when guys are forward, but I was also cognizant of not making her uncomfortable, always having been told that men make women's lives a daily torture. It was a crippling balance.

I hovered in the hazy middle ground of indirect revelation, where I could bask in the illusion of possibility. I imagined us together in a satisfying daydream, ignoring the smart deduction, reached by the gathering tangible evidence, that she didn't reciprocate my feelings.

Each time I ran my internet offense, Hailey would be less friendly towards me the next time I saw her. I would catch her eye to say hello or make a *Friends* reference and she would walk right past me or give me a tepid smile while avoiding eye contact.

I would then retreat, making no overtures for a while, avoiding her at the office, though it was painful to be so close to her without interacting. When I had withdrawn for long enough, Hailey would be friendly again.

In all probability, she had (correctly) suspected that I liked her and, not feeling the same way, had wanted to discourage me. After my withdrawals, her suspicions receded and she would be friendly again, asking how my day was in the most inconsequential of small talk, which, to me, took on the heaviest meaning.

This was all a vicious loop. For as soon as she was friendly with me again, I would newly convince myself that she wanted to be my girlfriend. And I would once again find an excuse to post on her Facebook wall or comment on her Instagram post, and then she would once again act removed and distant until I gave up hope and stopped.

And so on.

Occasionally I would wonder if I knew Hailey at all. Did my crush have any real basis or was I completely shallow?

I attempted to describe her to myself. She was a pretty redhead with a great smile. Okay, sure but what about her personality? Ummm... well, she was a nice person, to the people that she liked, and she really enjoyed her smart phone. These personality assessments didn't go too deep and I couldn't decide if Hailey was a character of simplicity, who I was failing to accurately evaluate because of my overwhelming attraction, or whether it was my own superficiality I failed to see – obsessed with a woman only for her surface-level charms, never bothering to engage with the hidden depth beneath.

Either way, months passed by in the fog of my crush. I looked at the calendar and it was late November and I hadn't done any writing at all. I had no new screenplay ideas and nothing to show for the rapidly expiring days. I needed some clear, focused time to brainstorm ideas. But how was I supposed to do that when all I could do was think about Hailey all the time and try to scrounge up evidence for the ever-harder-to-support case that she might like me back?

At a family Hanukkah party in early December, I was caught staring longingly out the window by my dad's first cousin Jay, who I always felt I should call "uncle," but didn't. (He was technically my first cousin once removed.)

I was busy thinking about Hailey, as usual, getting frustrated with myself and trying to stop thinking about Hailey, which only made me think about her all the more, wondering what the two of us would even talk about if she wanted to go out with me, both bored and enthralled simultaneously by my repetitive thoughts about her, which were nebulous, circling around overused memories of her, breaking no new ground, providing no new context, discovering nothing revelatory in the slightest, but there she was, hovering at the back of my every thought, ill-defined and ever present.

"You alright there, sport?" said Jay, the cousin in question, who was the type of guy that called members of the younger generation "sport."

"Yeah, fine," I said, turning inward, noticing the smell of latkes emanating from the kitchen.

"It's been a while," he said.

"Yeah," I said.

It was the first time my dad's entire extended family had gotten together for Hanukkah in many years. When I was younger, these extended family parties were a yearly tradition, but after some of the older generation had passed away the parties had fallen by the wayside.

That year my Uncle Abe had decided to resume the tradition, bringing everyone back together for latkes, gelt, and awkward attempts to cover a decade's worth of life in a brief bit of small talk.

"You've gotten so big," said Jay. "I remember when you used to run around these parties with your wang hanging out."

"Sure," I said. Then I thought about it. "Wait, why would my wang have been hanging out?"

"What are you doing these days? Did you graduate college?" he asked, bypassing my question.

"I did," I said. "A year and a half ago."

"What are you doing for work?"

"I take pictures of children," I said.

"How's that?" Jay looked wary.

I misinterpreted his reaction. I thought he was disappointed in my career path.

"I know, I know, but it's only temporary," I said. "I went to school for film. I'm going to be a screenwriter."

(I was still saying "I'm going to be," instead of, "I want to be," at that time. The mental projection of my dreams was still strong. Not so much anymore...)

"So you're taking pictures of children until you become a screenwriter?" he said.

"Exactly."

"Do their parents know?" he said. "Should the police?"

"What?"

It suddenly dawned on me why he looked concerned. The sentence "take pictures of children," out of context, might be worrisome.

"No! I didn't mean it like that," I insisted. "I'm working as a photographer. A school picture day photographer."

"Ohhh," he said, relieved. "You might want to think about your phrasing."

"Yes, I can see that now."

"But you're going to be a big Hollywood screenwriter, huh?"

"Yes! Exactly."

"How's that going? It's a tough industry to make it, I hear."

"Yeah. It's going okay. I need to... well, I'm working on... It's kind of confusing, actually? Because in school they teach you how to write. And I know how to do that. And I need to be working on my writing more, I know that. But I also feel like I graduated and no one ever really told me how you sell a screenplay? I entered a bunch of contests, but, I don't know exactly what the proper procedure is?"

I'm not sure why I was suddenly so honest with Jay, this first cousin (once removed) who I hadn't spoken to in a dozen years. It was a completely different tone than I took at the nightly dinner table with my father, where I always projected false confidence so that I wouldn't have to hear his doubts and advice.

"Your twenties are a confusing time," said Jay.

"Yeah," I said.

"You're looking for a career and a spouse and everything is uncertain. And you still have these big aspirations for yourself that suddenly seem so much harder to attain than they did when you were a kid."

"Yes, that's totally it," I said, thinking that maybe I had underestimated cousin Jay. Who knew a guy who called you "sport," could offer such insight?

"But I got good news, sport," said Jay. "Eventually, things turn out all right."

"They do?"

"Absolutely. You struggle for a decade or so, but when you get to your thirties you settle and you give up on your dreams and you end up having a pretty good life. Don't worry. You'll get there."

"Oh," I said. "Thanks?"

"You got it kid. Can I get you something to drink? I know I need alcohol to get through this."

"The party?"

"No. Life. That's the other trick. Just drink a lot."

I wanted to laugh, hoping he was joking, but something told me that he wasn't.

"I can tell you don't believe me yet," he said. "You still think you'll be the exception, not the rule. That's fine. That's what your twenties are all about. Hang in there. And keep taking those kiddie pics. I'm getting a drink."

He smiled and walked off.

I didn't want to think about the shoddy infrastructure of my future dreams.

So I turned back to the window and thought about Hailey.

SIX
AN ALL-ENCOMPASSING QUESTION

IT WAS LATE in the season and Josie had the day off. Early December, with all of the newbies already laid off until the spring, the only jobs left on the schedule for the calendar year were a few scattered retake days divided among the veterans.

Josie sat at home while Nate was busy at the hospital, learning to be a nurse firsthand in the trenches of the ill. Josie cycled over and over through the same dozen apps and websites on her phone and then on her computer. There was nothing new to look at, and yet she kept scrolling through the same sites anyway, watching vapid Instagram stories and clicking on inane Facebook links as if they provided any enjoyment whatsoever.

Periodically, she would put her devices aside and try to read. She wanted to take advantage of the time off to get through at least one of the twenty-five unread books on her shelf, but her concentration was minimal. She kept abandoning the books and returning to the internet.

She missed the early part of the fall season when she had been busier. She hated herself for this thought. Any nostalgia for time working at SmilePosts was unacceptable and yet there it was, the day's boredom stubbornly slapping her in the face with a desire to be at work rather than at home. At home, she had to face the stalled-out journey of her adulthood.

She slammed her laptop closed. She threw her phone across the room. She collapsed, face down onto her bed and stuffed her head into her pillow. She curled up into the fetal position and tried to squeeze out the emptiness through force of physical comfort. It was ineffective. The tremors of aimlessness found her. They would not let her rest.

She was shaken out of her bed cocoon by a knock on her brother's bedroom door. One of Landon's teenage classmates-slash-customers. Her brother was now openly dealing drugs out of his bedroom, making little effort to disguise his illegal entrepreneurship with dad out of the house.

Josie wasn't certain how deep Landon's stockpile of drugs went and she didn't want to know. She hoped he only dealt weed and some lower-level pills, but she didn't inquire. She wanted to maintain plausible deniability should the police ever raid the house. Besides, it would have been hard to have a conversation with her brother about his illegal enterprise when they never talked at all.

Mom was totally oblivious. She could openly witness Landon hand a bag of pills to a classmate in exchange for money and think Landon was only "having some fun with his friends." Some protective (or damaged) part of Nicki's brain prevented a rational interpretation of events. Besides, she was too occupied with her incredibly annoying new boyfriend Jacque. Jacque had sideburns thick as an Azalea bush, smelled like burnt leather someone had sprayed with air freshener, and was fond of ranting about how evil it was to drink cow's milk. He regularly asked Nicki for money, which she happily shelled out in fifty-dollar increments. Josie did not know or care what Jacque spent his allowance on. She spent as little time around him as possible.

"Sup bro," Josie heard a guy say in the hallway when Landon opened his door. "You got that shit?"

Farther in the background, she heard her mother's screams of pleasure from her daytime lovemaking with Jacque. Josie tumbled back onto the bed and forced her pillow over her ears.

God, she needed to get out of the house.

Keeping her pillow held tight to her ears, Josie shuffled across the room, picked up her phone from the floor, and sprinted back into bed. She looked at the same dozen apps and websites again, very little having changed, and the changes that had occurred providing no entertainment or value. She felt herself tremble like a teapot coming to boil.

She couldn't take any more of this. She needed to leave and she needed to do something *worthwhile*. All of this meaningless internet content, all of this stifling family energy, and the ash heap of her unachieved dreams were all swirling together and draining her until she was a dried-out husk. Before she had any time to think of where she was going, she put on clothes that were more respectable than the pajamas she had been wearing all morning, grabbed her coat, keys, and a camera, and walked out the door.

She did not currently have the key to her mom's car. She would have had to ask Nicki for that key and she was not about to interrupt Jacque's guttural cries for any purpose.

The train station was a fifteen-minute walk away. The train, whenever it came, would carry her away from her house. As an initial goal, that was good enough.

Josie rode the regional rail towards Philly, unsure of where she would exit, watching the mélange of humanity stepping on and off the train. Here and there, subtly aiming her camera lens from within her coat flap, she captured a surreptitious picture of a stranger's face.

She listened to the conductor on the fuzzy overhead speaker announce each next stop. Any departure station was as good as any other, but Josie waited for her instincts to take over, carrying her into an unknown neighborhood.

The train entered the crowded urban landscape of North Philadelphia, that impoverished expanse where so many of the city's residents lived. Josie decided that she wanted to disembark before she hit the skyscrapers of Center City or the outer crust of hipsterdom in Northern Liberties and Fishtown. She had spent enough time in these familiar pockets of the city. They were safe and known. There was nothing to be learned or achieved by a visit there.

At the North Broad station, she shot up and hustled off the train.

Josie ran down the station steps and into the waiting neighborhood, wishing to plunge deep, to become enmeshed in the side streets of private lives. Off the beaten path, one might say, except in this case the more beaten the path the better. She wanted to immerse herself in the rough edges of the city, wanted to see the gritty unfiltered reality underneath the shining surface she normally observed.

She took out her camera and began snapping images of the area. An abandoned lot covered in graffiti, occupied by only one ravaged individual collapsed in a beach chair. A crowded street corner bodega, populated by a laughing crowd of teenagers. An elderly woman walking slowly through a litter-filled park. She was enthralled by her simulation of photojournalism, pretending she was a New York Times reporter in a foreign country. She captured images of the local population in their local lives to put a human face on the emotionally detached distant land.

Except... she was not in some foreign country. She was in her own city.

Josie paused after photographing a pack of young elementary school girls, racing home, unaccompanied, their plasticine backpacks hopping up and down behind them like trailing tails.

She lowered her camera.

Her moral instincts flashed with shame at the illicit thrill that she, a privileged suburban white girl, felt from walking around a black neighborhood and putting it under the glass of her camera's frames.

She thought about the first time SmilePosts had sent her to a school in North Philly, during her first season on the job. The segregation of the city, which she had always in some sense been aware of, had struck her with a primal, uncomfortable urgency.

Plymouth Meeting, where Josie had gone to school, had a small percentage of non-white students, but there was no question that where she grew up she had mostly been surrounded by people of her own race. Even as someone who had always believed that the democratic values of equality were an inherent good and racism was an undeniable evil, she had never given a second thought to the racial divisions of her own area.

The racial divide was visceral, traveling from school to school for SmilePosts. Almost every suburban area was mostly white, and the poorest pockets of the city were inevitably all black or Hispanic.

It was a shocking revelation of direct observation, a demographic breakdown that Josie had always known but had never thought about. Philadelphia was a Democrat voting city, far removed from the unambiguously racist laws of the historical South, yet here was an inarguable segregation of the races, dictated not by overt laws, but by time, lack of opportunity, and the vestiges of America's racist history, leaving marks of separation that could not be denied.

Josie was upset by this revelation that shouldn't have been a revelation at all. She remembered talking to a first-year co-worker about the topic, after they had left an all-black West Philly school and returned to the office.

"I never really thought about it before," Josie had said. "But it's pretty clear the after-effects of slavery are still affecting society today. All of the poorest neighborhoods in the city are black, and that has to be because of the racial subjugation throughout American history. The Civil War, after all, wasn't that long ago, in the larger scale of things."

"Yeah, I don't know," said the co-worker. "Anybody who works hard enough can get ahead. This is America."

Josie had then realized that she had blindly expected others to be empathetic to the plight of the disadvantaged. She expected others to care about their fellow man and be as horrified by inequality as she was.

This was an assumption that did not prove accurate.

But now here she was, walking around North Philly, hypocritically treating the black community as *other.* Acting like she was an anthropologist researching a strange tribe that she could photograph and then escape, returning to the warm, if stifling, comfort of her house in the suburbs. She was culturally appropriating, using images of black culture to make herself feel artistic and escape her own emptiness. But these were just people. All of them were trying to live their lives the best they could, support their families, enjoy times with friends, squeeze the most happiness and meaning they could out of the struggle of day-to-day existence, while being dealt a crappy hand of playing cards Josie could hardly conceive of.

A cop car drove by and Josie, without thinking, raised her camera. She took an image of several wary teens staring with a defiant glare at the white police officers passing through the neighborhood.

She thought about the growing Black Lives Matter movement and the disturbing insight into the divergent treatment of white and black citizens by the police. And she realized that her understanding of how the racial divides of the past had left indelible marks on the present didn't go far enough – to this day, there was a divide in how the races were treated. And she thought about the fear she sometimes felt venturing into the poorer neighborhoods, the reluctance to park her car on certain side streets when visiting city schools that didn't have parking lots, the reluctance to venture into North or West Philly at night because of a fear of crime and violence. It was a fear of impoverished areas that had existed within her as long as she could remember. A fear, though she didn't want to admit it, which perhaps included a corresponding fear of race.

She felt angry – at fear she didn't want to feel and at photographic aspirations she couldn't deny. She could imagine her photograph of the teens staring at the cop car in a gallery somewhere. It was exactly the sort of image that the privileged would appreciate, nodding their heads at their own perceived compassion and their understanding of systemic racism, while doing little to eradicate any of the problems. And was Josie any better?

Despite all her guilt, she couldn't help but feel a flash of fantasy: she daydreamed of showing her photographs from that day in a downtown gallery, wealthy old people in fancy coats looking upon her images, discussing them in ostentatious tones, and paying two hundred dollars for a print of her work so they too could live vicariously through the lower classes with whom they would never interact. Josie felt a high thinking of her work receiving analysis and praise, even as the pretentiousness and hypocrisy of the projected audience made her flush with further shame and self-criticism. She wanted to be revered. Where exactly were the lines of her principles drawn?

"Whatcha taking pictures of?"

It was a boy of maybe thirteen sitting on his front stoop. Josie felt a wave of apprehension at stepping out from behind the camera's protective glass lens and talking to a local. It was like stepping into the movie screen during a film, unexpectedly pulled into the story when you thought you were an audience member. She was once again ashamed of her fear. She needed to be better than the racist masses who would tell her not to go to "a bad neighborhood," making asinine judgments based on race and poverty. She approached the boy.

"All sorts of things," she said.

"Like, what? You take a picture of me?" he said.

"I didn't."

"You should. I'm the best-lookin' guy around here. I'll pose for you."

The boy stood up, flexed his biceps, and slapped on a cheesy grin.

Yep. It was not all that different here than at a stuffy wedding on the Main Line. Everywhere she went, she tried to take candid, genuine pictures of life as it occurred, unobserved, and her process was interrupted by someone wanting to strike a stupid pose. Cultural differences didn't cut that deep after all.

She took a picture of the boy.

"Let me see!" he said. He ran over to her side.

Also ubiquitous and inescapable were people who wanted to see their pictures immediately after they were taken. Reminded of the cruel comments those bridesmaids had made about her photography when she submitted to them, Josie tucked the camera close to her, protectively. Though on this occasion, she couldn't have shown the boy his picture even if she wanted to. She had brought her film camera instead of a digital one.

"What?" said the boy, snickering. "You scared I'm gonna steal your camera?"

"What, no," said Josie. "No, of course not."

"Let me see your camera then."

"It's film," she said.

"I know. It's a camera. I'm not stupid," he said.

"I don't think you're stupid," she said, insistent.

"Let me see my picture then."

"It's a film camera. I have to develop the film."

The boy was clearly unfamiliar with this concept.

"Can I see the camera anyway?"

Normally Josie would never let a stranger hold her precious Leica M6, but she was oversensitive at the moment about showing any racial prejudice. Overcompensating, she held the camera tentatively towards him, her fingers afraid to let it go because it was her baby.

The boy laughed. "Shit, look at you holding that camera out. You scared I'm gonna steal it."

"I'm not."

"Your arms are shaking. You barely letting go of it."

"Here. I don't think you're going to steal it. Take it," said Josie, getting annoyed.

"Thank you," said the boy, gently taking the camera from her hands.

Then he sprinted halfway down the street.

Josie stood still, mouth agape, her heart thrumming against her chest as she watched the boy run off. She felt paralyzed, unable to move and unsure of what to do.

At the end of the block the boy stopped, looked back at her, waved, and doubled over with laughter.

He walked slowly back towards her, clutching the camera with his right hand, his progress slowed by his breathy heaves of amusement.

"Shit," he said through his continuing laughter when he was within earshot. "You really thought I ran off with it. You should see the look on your face."

"Oh yeah. I guess I did."

"I should of taken a picture of YOU," he said, tears of hilarity dripping from his eyes.

"Yeah maybe," she said, eyeing the camera, focused only on getting it back in her hands.

The boy took a moment to look over the camera.

"Weird camera," he said. "You should get one where you can see the pictures. Then you know what they look like."

He handed the Leica back to her. She wanted to cradle it close like a rescued infant.

"Yeah maybe," she said.

He looked at her. She was still petrified from the stress of him running off with her camera. He laughed again, full and loud.

"You're funny," he said, walking back to his house. "Have fun taking pictures."

She was annoyed with herself for crumpling so easily. Nothing bad had happened. A boy had played a brief joke to pass the time. She did not want to feel unsafe, because that was giving in to the stereotypical fear of the masses. She hated the racial and class segregation that existed within so much of Philadelphia and the surrounding areas. She wanted to do her small part to fight racial inequality. But right now, all she wanted was to go home.

Josie abruptly felt adrift and lost in a sea of unfamiliarity. She looked around her, unsure on immediate glance which direction she had come from and which way she should walk to get back to the train station.

She took out her phone, mapped the route back to the North Broad station, tucked her camera close to her, and walked briskly towards the train.

There was a further indignity besides the privileged implications of her retreat. What did this panicked surrender say about her future as a photojournalist?

If she couldn't take the heat of a teenager's innocent practical joke in her own city, how was she supposed to handle the stress of wandering through foreign lands, not speaking the language, harangued by the threat of militant violence and hunger all around her? How was she supposed to dig herself into the dangerous trenches of world conflicts and photograph lives being taken, shrapnel careening past her on all sides, authoritarian forces threatening her freedom to photograph and to continue living, when a laughing kid sent her running home to hide under her bedsheets?

Was she really that much weaker than she wanted to be?

Back at the station, she purchased a ticket, hustled up the steps, and stared at the empty rails, waiting for that far-off sound of the train's approach.

Maybe, she thought, *I should stick to taking pictures of nature.*

Perhaps her photojournalist dreams were too ambitious. Or rather, they were not in tune with her personal frequency.

It was the National Geographic images of beautiful natural landscapes that were her true passion. She found the most peace taking pictures of places that were devoid of humanity, not overrun with it. This could be an important lesson in focusing her artistry. She didn't need to go to conflict-ravaged cities, she needed to go to lush rainforests and spare deserts. She needed to travel to towering, snowcapped mountains and sprawling swamps.

She felt optimistic for a moment, but the flame of positivity was quickly blown out by the winds of practicality.

How was it that she expected to go to any of these places? Cities or nature? She had never been anywhere and there was no reason to think that this precedent would end. She didn't have any money to spend. How was she going to traverse the globe with an empty bank account?

She took out her phone and searched a few sites, gauging the potential cost of airline flights to the rainforests of Costa Rica or the dunes of the

Sahara Desert. The prices were exorbitant. It cost thousands for the flights alone, never mind the lodging fees and all the daily costs of traveling.

She was furious at the injustice of her limitations. And then she was furious at her skewed, privileged sense of injustice.

She felt selfish and she felt trapped. She kicked a nearby trashcan. A man standing nearby snickered at her. To him, her anger was funny. She wanted to give him the finger, but held back. Instead she turned away and settled on a nearby bench.

What am I going to do? she thought, her face collapsing in her hands. An all-encompassing question.

She heard the rumble of the train. A few seconds later followed the whistle of approach. As the train pulled into the station, she gathered herself, held her camera tight, and boarded.

The next day, Josie had little enthusiasm for her retake.

She was at Delaware County Preparatory Academy, a K-12 private school. The principal allowed parents to come in on retake day and watch their children be photographed, since it was their final chance to get a picture they liked.

It was a SmilePosts photographer's worst nightmare.

Though Delco Prep was a small school – only 198 kids enrolled, only one class per grade – half the kids came back for pictures on retake day. How could the parents resist? The only reason the remaining students didn't do retakes was that they had two working parents who couldn't swing the day off.

Parents and children came down to the library where Josie was set up and returned their photo envelopes. Ninety percent of the time, the original pictures had no noticeable problems. Either the parents were so controlling that they refused to accept any pictures they hadn't personally approved or they thought that their kid's natural appearance was hideously ugly and wanted to instill in their children a lifetime of crippling self-hatred. Sometimes, it was both.

What was theoretically scheduled as a one-hour morning retake went on for nearly four hours. This was longer than it had taken the original photographer to take the whole school on the first picture day.

This was not the day that Josie needed. Her stressful quarter-life crisis from the day before lingered and burned.

Each new child was an excruciating experience. Their moms (as well as a few dads and one feisty grandmom) stood beside her at the camera, nitpicking each tiny wrinkle of clothing, every follicle of hair's specific position, and the millimeters of difference apparently separating a "real" smile from a "fake" one.

The latter, in particular, was an endlessly repeated battle cry.

"Give a real smile!" the parents repeated.

"I am!" their children insisted through the closed teeth of their attempted smiles, like second-rate ventriloquists trying to direct your attention back to their dummies.

Some of their smiles were good, some of their smiles were bad, but aside from a few rebellious kids determined to thwart their parents' wishes at all costs, Josie had no doubt that the students were trying their best. It was so frustrating to watch parent after parent cut their kid down and make them feel inferior for how they looked when the kids were trying their hardest to please. She was witness to a heap of future therapy fodder that day. She struggled not to intervene. It was especially difficult to hold her tongue when the parents turned their micromanaging towards her, critiquing her framing and grooming and general manner. She would have liked to punch many of them right in the face. But she held back. She was a professional. And she needed to keep her job, as much as she hated it sometimes.

She came especially close to losing it during an interaction with a special needs girl and her mother.

A sad normality of working at SmilePosts was photographing special needs classes of non-verbal, immobile children stuck to life in wheelchairs, sometimes in complete paralysis. These non-verbal children had their own small classrooms of four or five kids, separated from the higher functioning special needs children who walked around and talked to you and were usually friendlier than your average kid.

The higher functioning kids made you smile. They seemed fantastically unaware of the limitations society saw in them. Many came to the photography station with irrepressible verve. It was hard to convince them to focus, but when you caught them looking at the lens and smiling it was the proudest moment you experienced on the job. You were giving their parents something special, a rare still image of the child's inner spirit frozen in time.

The experience of photographing the children with more severe disabilities was a bit different.

I know I wasn't supposed to feel this way, but when I came across a kid like the girl Josie photographed that day – a nine-year-old who was completely motionless, her eyes staring consistently leftward, her nostrils connected to a breathing tube, her tongue continually hanging outside her mouth – it broke my heart. And I couldn't help but wonder what kind of a life that was. A child like that did not fall into the category of challenging, but ultimately rewarding, portrait subjects like the kids with more moderate disabilities. A child like that made you feel helpless. There was little you could do to take a good portrait other than to have the teacher turn their wheelchair towards you and put your camera up high to get a good angle of their reclined face. When you said, "give me a big smile," in your friendliest tone and received no acknowledged reaction from the child, you took the teacher's word for it that it was "the best you're gonna get." It must be tough to be the parent of a kid like that. To love them so much, but still, maybe sometimes secretly want more from them than they're capable of giving.

I say this to encourage empathy for the mother I'm about to mention. But also to request empathy for Josie and her rather harsh internal reaction to the mother.

In general, I find it's best to have empathy for everyone, whenever possible. Life, after all, is not easy.

The girl in question was Laurel, a nine-year old in a wheelchair, whose tongue, rather unfortunately, tended to hang outside her lips. Laurel's mother pushed her into Josie's camera station and handed Josie the envelope from the original picture day.

"These photos are terrible," Laurel's mother said, getting off on the wrong foot with Josie right away. Josie hated when someone came to where she worked and started insulting her. No "hello," no tinge of friendliness, no acknowledgement of shared humanity. Instant attack, pistols drawn.

Josie looked at the original photos. Then she looked at Laurel.

The picture of Laurel and the live version were identical.

Josie tried to give the angry mother the benefit of the doubt. Maybe whatever newbie was at Delco Prep the first day didn't make a real effort. Maybe Laurel was capable of tucking in her tongue and flashing a smile. It was worth trying. This mother deserved to have a nice picture of her daughter, even if she was being an asshole about it.

"Sorry. We'll try to do better," said Josie.

"Who is we?" said the mother.

"Me..." said Josie.

"You should take responsibility for your own actions," said the mother.

"I didn't take the original picture," said Josie, defensive.

"Blaming others gets you nowhere," said the mother.

Josie was about ready to explode. She took a deep breath.

"Okay," she said.

She walked behind her camera as the mother wheeled Laurel into place.

"Hey sweetie, it's time for your picture," the mother said lovingly, diametrically opposed to the harsh way she had spoken with Josie. She turned back to Josie and her gentleness disappeared. "Just be ready for

GREAT BIG SMILE 329

when she smiles," she said without an ounce of kindness.

"Okay," Josie repeated.

Josie was experienced in the split-second reactions needed to catch a good expression on a special needs student. She held her finger ready on the trigger, ready to snap the photo the moment a smile appeared.

The mother removed Laurel's breathing tube from her nose. Then something very odd happened.

Laurel's mother kneeled down on the ground, grabbed her daughter's wheelchair by the spokes and began to shake her child with the vigorousness of an athlete preparing a protein shake.

She shook and shook and shook her child for no discernible reason. Josie had no idea what this torture was supposed to accomplish.

She waited. With each passing moment, her desire grew to slap the poor mother and scream "leave your daughter alone!" But she waited.

Finally, wanting something to change in this interminable moment, Josie clicked her shutter and snapped a picture of Laurel.

The picture looked exactly like the original photo, which was sitting in the returned envelope on Josie's workstation.

Laurel's mother hustled over to see the picture.

"Horrible," she said. "She's not smiling at all. I told you to wait until she smiles."

"Okay," said Josie.

The mother ran back to Laurel and resumed treating her daughter like a bottle of Yoo-hoo.

"She usually smiles when I do this," said the mother.

How did you discover that? thought Josie, judgmentally.

The mother shook Laurel for another minute at least.

Meanwhile, the retake line of parents and kids had grown substantially behind them. Josie was receiving a number of impatient dirty looks from those waiting, all huddled together in the nonfiction section of the library.

"There, she's smiling, I think she's smiling," said Laurel's mother.

Josie snapped a picture.

She looked at it. Laurel looked exactly the same.

The mother hustled to see the photo.

Laurel's breathing apparatus started beeping. It had been disconnected from her nose for too long. This seemed an immediate concern to Josie but the mother ignored it. She considered the photo for a long time.

"I think we can do better," she finally said, a tinge of pitiful hope slipping through the cracks of her hardened exterior.

She ran back to Laurel and resumed the shaking, ignoring the insistent beeping of the breathing machine.

By the time Josie arrived back at the office, she was thoroughly exhausted and irritable.

It had been a grueling twenty-four hours that she was anxious to cast aside and forget.

When she walked in, I was standing over at the discarded photo table. At each retake day, the students were required to return their original envelopes so that they didn't dupe the company into getting two packages for the price of one. When we returned these envelopes to the office, we left them on a folding table for a time, before they made their way to the secure shredder bin. The purpose of this stopgap was ostensibly for the newbies to look over the mistakes they had made in the service of their continual improvement. But mostly when the photos were looked at, it tended to be as a source of entertainment for veterans such as myself. We laughed at the wretched framing and the horrid expressions of the students, questioning how some newbie (who had probably already been fired) had taken so terrible an image and then thought, *yep, this is a good representation of this human being.*

Josie threw her paperwork bag down on an empty chair and walked her large pile of discarded envelopes from Delco Prep to the reject table.

She audibly sighed as she released the weight of the envelopes from her hands.

I laughed. Both at the unusual bulk of envelopes and at her undisguised weariness.

"Tough day?" I asked.

"I mean it wasn't as bad as like storming the beaches of Normandy or vacationing in Chernobyl," said Josie.

"There you go. Glass half full," I said.

"Ugh" she said. "This school lets parents come to retake day, so basically more people bought pictures than on the first day. Remind me to tell you later about this mother who insisted on shaking her wheelchair-bound daughter like a rag doll. I'll tell you when I won't get so angry that I end up punching you in the face just to get out my frustration."

"I look forward to hearing that story and not getting punched in the face," I said.

"I look forward to telling the story and not punching you in the face," she said.

Josie looked over the refuse of abandoned images on the table.

"Anything good in here?" she said.

"Some major over-tipping," I said, pulling out a few photos of kids whose necks were tilted at complete ninety-degree angles. Their ears were practically parallel with the ground.

"Oh c'mon," said Josie, in total disbelief that some idiot newbie thought a parent would be okay with these images. "I wish I knew who took those."

Sadly, there was no way of knowing for sure which culprit was responsible for these photographic crimes. The envelopes were tragically unlabeled with our SmilePosts ID numbers.

"Here's a picture where a kid wore the exact same color as our blue screen background and now he's only a head," I said.

Josie laughed. "I love that," she said, mildly cheered up.

She joined me in the cathartic activity of searching through the photo pile.

"Here's a great smile," she said sarcastically, showing me an 8x10 of a girl with an expression that could only be described as "angry constipation."

"Rough," I said.

"The doctors aren't sure if she's going to make it," said Josie.

I laughed. "I'm sorry to hear that."

"Oooh, here's a great example of when retouching goes wrong!" said Josie.

SmilePosts offered a retouching add-on for photo packages. Mainly, this was useful for middle school kids with an outlier pimple or two. The blemishes could be removed by a computer program at corporate headquarters where our photos were finished and printed. But sometimes, when a kid had a face too full of acne for an easy computer makeover, the results ended up a little strange. This was the case for the photo that Josie held, in which an unsuspecting boy had his eyebrows graphically removed and his face blurred down until it looked like he was vanishing from history.

"I don't understand what's weird," I said, dryly. "He looks perfectly normal to me. If he walked in right now looking like that, I definitely wouldn't scream in terror and run as fast as I can from the building."

Josie continued sifting through the photos and sharing unearthed gems from the pile. She was not fully cheered up, but she was at least pleasantly distracted. I was experiencing a similar momentary reprieve. My family Hanukkah party had been that previous weekend and for the last several days Jay's speech about "settling" had been stabbing me with the sharp blade of looming disappointment. Making fun of children's pictures with Josie made me forget about my fear for the moment. I was having fun.

At some point in the process, we pivoted from mocking kids' looks to mocking their names – a favorite activity among SmilePosts employees.

"Here's a boy named Eagle," said Josie.

"Here's a girl named Special," I said.

"Here's a girl named Lollintine," said Josie. "Combination of lollipop and valentine perhaps?"

"Here's a boy name Schwing," I said. "I think that might be a reference to the erection sound in Wayne's World?"

"Ooooh," said Josie, "I've got a couple of dooosies here. You ready?"

"I am," I said, smiling with anticipation.

She held an envelope in each hand and flipped them towards me simultaneously, revealing the names. "I have one boy named Manmeet and another named... get this... Semen! Continuing your erection theme."

(I'm not sure whether or not this was the same "Semen" whose name Ethan had mocked at the office a year earlier. Either way, it was just as funny as it had been the first time.)

I laughed hard. But I did feel a little bad. "Those are just foreign names, I think. I kind of feel like we're being a little xenophobic laughing at them."

"You're right," she said, always culturally conscious herself. "But I mean, *Semen*, c'mon..."

"Yep, that kid is going to have a horrible childhood."

"Awful. He must hate every day of his life."

We both laughed, distracted from our own problems by poor Semen and the day-to-day horror that must be his existence in an American school. Surrounded by classmates who were as immature as we were and probably more openly cruel.

In a weird way, the joke reminded Josie of how much better she had it than so many others out there. It made her feel guilty about the self-pity she had been bathing in. Things could be so much worse. She could be poor and struggling to afford meals. She could be chronically ill. Or yes... she could be named Semen. Poor little bastard.

"Speaking of the kid named Eagle," I said, "have you ever looked up the names for different groups of animals? They're my favorite thing. A group of eagles is called a convocation."

"What?" she said with excitement. "I like the sound of this."

"Yeah, check it out," I pulled up the Wikipedia list on my phone and showed her.

"A parliament of owls?" she said, delighted. "I love imagining them in little barrister wigs debating English domestic policy."

"My favorite is business of ferrets," I said.

"Well everyone knows that ferrets are big fans of the invisible hand of the market."

"True," I said. "I still think it was a mistake for the government to bail out Big Ferret during the financial crisis."

"Hey, those ferrets' profits trickle down to us!" she said. "It's basic ferretnomics."

I laughed.

"I always like to picture a group of ferrets in little elongated ferret suits, walking into a bank and applying for a small business loan."

Josie burst out in laughter. "I love this list so much," she said.

We both knew that at some point we should get back to work.

But that could wait a little longer.

SEVEN
THE PUBLIC AND PRIVATE LIVES OF THOSE AROUND US

EARLY IN MY THIRD FALL SEASON, I was sent to Tomlinson Elementary, the bright red school building in Northeast Philadelphia I had attended from ages five to ten.

It was the first time I had returned to my old stomping grounds, as they say, since I was ten years old. It was the location of my formative years, as they also say, where I made friendships I still have and was taught multiplication problems that I could solve better at age nine than I can today. (Don't ask me what seven times nine is because I do not know!)

Most of the teachers from my school days were now retired and the ones who were still there didn't recognize me, to my relief. I would have been ashamed by them thinking that a career at SmilePosts was all I had accomplished in life.

It was strange being back. Partly for the expected reasons. All the rooms and hallways looked so much smaller than I remembered them. A random patch of school yard or a nook in a staircase triggered memories I'd long forgotten.

There were unexpected side-effects as well, not listed on the nostalgia warning label.

As I set up my equipment in the cheese yellow gym, on the floor covered in faded paint and decades worth of scratches, I was struck by the way that time felt shorter than it used to. It's a cliché that the years go faster as you get older, but never had my mind's eye been forced to look at such a direct comparison of one era and another. The five years I spent in elementary school felt like an epic stretch, time enough for a new species to have come and gone from the Earth. As for the previous five years – two at SmilePosts and three at college – they had passed in a blink. Time was becoming less solid, less full. Although I remembered more events from my recent years, they felt thinner and fast-forwarded. The calendar claimed that ages twenty to twenty-five were equal in length to ages five to ten, but the comparison refused to match up. The earlier period was clearly more substantial. It was like that optical illusion where two lines of equal length appeared to be different sizes. A ruler always proved the lines identical, but personal perception insisted otherwise.

As picture day began, a class of first graders made their way to the gym. They reflected the impressive diversity of Northeast Philly, one of the few areas we photographed where a racial mixture was the rule, rather than the exception. I was always grateful I had grown up in such a neighborhood.

As I began telling the six-year-olds how to pose, physically putting them into place when verbal attempts inevitably failed, I was struck by this thought: To these kids, their small community is the whole world. In their eyes, the neighborhood where they live is enormous and all-encompassing because it's all they know. My perception of the world was exactly the same when I was their age.

When I was ten, I used to walk the three-block distance to my friend Eric's house and it felt like I was on a cross-country expedition. I had to be driven to my friend Iggy's house, because he lived on the other side of busy Bustleton Avenue. It felt like I crossed oceans to get there. One end of my neighborhood to the other felt like the reaches of a great nation.

You get older and your mental map expands. You see different parts of the country (and maybe the world, though I haven't personally been outside the U.S.) and you realize how small your pocket of living is, how little impact your local fabric has on the larger quilt of civilization.

As a SmilePosts photographer, I've gone to school after school and the pattern inevitably repeats for children in each area. All these little people in all of these little places think that their own intimate, minimally impactful slice of the world is of paramount importance.

At Tomlinson Elementary, I photographed first graders sitting in the same gym where I once had my own picture taken, all of them as oblivious to the complications of growing up as I once was. I thought about what their futures held.

Here was Bobby Nardi, buzzed blonde hair, wearing a green Adidas shirt and yellow mesh shorts. His parents selected a twenty-six-dollar "A package" (one 8x10, three 5x7s, ten wallets) and a blue background. Bobby smiled with his mouth closed. He would grow up to be a stockbroker. He would be twice divorced and have three children, two thirds of whom would consider him an inadequate father.

Here was Santé Abreu, dark looping curls, wearing a long sleeve shirt with vertical red and yellow stripes and a pair of adorable six-year-old denim jeans. His parents selected an eleven-dollar "D package" (one 5x7, three wallets) and a red background, despite the red stripes on his shirt. He refused to look straight into the camera no matter how many times I asked, distracted by the bustle in the room. He smiled with his mouth wide open like a howling wolf. He would grow up to be a fine college baseball player and have a brief career in the professional minors, before fizzling out and falling into a decade-long depression. He would work for years as a busboy at a café owned by his aunt Ana, before taking over the place himself when Ana died of a sudden stroke. The tragedy of his aunt's death would turn his life around. Managing the café would become his driving purpose. He would meet his wife there when she stopped in for a weekly latte and they would have four children.

Here was Nyah Williams, hair braided in an elaborate bun, wearing a pink shirt and an attached skirt with Peppa Pig and the Pig family embroidered on the front. Her parents selected an eighteen-dollar "B package" (one 8x10, one 5x7, six wallets) and a green background. A strong student, Nyah would be ranked seventh in her high school class and would attend Boston University as a political science major. She would stay in

Massachusetts and eventually run for the state senate, losing her first election by a heartbreaking few hundred votes. Six years later, after much emotional and some financial struggle, she would achieve her dream. Two years into her term, however, her career would be nearly derailed when a political opponent unearthed a video from her college days of Nyah punching another girl in the face. But the internetsphere would join together to proclaim that the punched girl "had it coming" after a longer cut of the video revealed the offensive taunts that had set Nyah off. Her reputation was redeemed.

Sitting in the gym where I once sat for my own school pictures, so recently yet so long ago, I imagined the futures of these children and wished I could pause their lives for them. I wished I had a magical camera trigger which froze not only their image on my monitor, but also their aging process, creating a clan of Peter Pans, spared the cruel fate of adulthood. Spared having to reach age twenty-five and wonder if the best times had already passed by without them realizing it. Spared having to wonder whether the "future" was always a false promise.

During my lunch break that day, I wandered the halls of Tomlinson Elementary.

I peeked into my fifth-grade classroom, room 212, once home to Mrs. Ollireich with her fondness for patterned curtains and smelly teas, now occupied by a young second-grade teacher named Miss Plemmons. Science fair projects hung on the walls. I remembered the day in room 212 when my class performed a mock trial of the Big Bad Wolf versus the Three Little Pigs. I was a member of the prosecution team. Inexplicably, my jury of moron classmates let the wolf off with no time served. It was bullshit. He was clearly guilty.

I peeked into the cafeteria, with its long twenty-person tables and its rowdy children. Kids were running around the room with food in their mouths, always under threat of choking on a potato chip. I remembered a rainy day during my elementary years when we were locked in the lunchroom during recess and I played an elaborate murder mystery game with a dozen classmates. The game involved clues hidden beneath plastic cups and faux-profound accusations spouted out in an array of absurd British accents. Looking back, I'm fairly sure the game didn't make any sense at all, but we weren't concerned about logic, only fun, and there was plenty of fun on that soggy afternoon.

I glanced out into the busy schoolyard where children were running around and rough-housing like a pack of jubilant wild beasts. I remembered a day during my fifth-grade year when I had spoken to Nicole Jaracosicsz in the shady corner of the yard, right outside the art room window. Nicole was my first real crush. I have no memory of what we spoke about, but I remember the excitement of that conversation as if it were yesterday.

Terrified as I've been by the uncertainty of the future, unsure which direction to steer myself in the foggy realm of moments yet to come, it was soothing on that lunch break to retreat into the past. It was a comfort to lounge in the peaceful childhood days when the future hovered in the distance, out of frame, waiting to be fulfilled, and life existed on an intimate, manageable scale.

There's a security in how cemented the past feels. Unlike that anxiety geyser of the future, set to explode at any time with incurable unpredictability, the past is set in stone. The concrete has hardened, no longer vulnerable to the stressing handprints of choice.

The way in which these glimmers of the past sparkle through my head is both one of my great joys and great pains. There is a drug-like bliss to these bubbles of recollection, but they make living in the present more difficult. It's often hard to believe that the multi-sensational experiences that swing endlessly through my head are gone forever, shoddy deteriorating imprints of something vanished. They're so vivid. Not just visually, but emotionally. They're drenched with power and meaning. They come when called and when not. The oft-repeated and the long-forgotten. They swirl. Sometimes they're only a feeling, unclaimed by identifiable context, unconfirmed as any verifiable event, but more real and true than the fabric touching my skin or the light bouncing off my eyes. Fathoming the unreachability of these memories, their vaporous quality, breaks my heart. My life meaning is built on a bed of air that's nowhere to be found.

The past is made up of pebbles of remembrance. Small parcels of recollection that were strong enough to withstand decomposition. Sometimes it's obvious why a memory sticks around. Other times, the persistence of a spare moment is less clear. Something that seems important one moment becomes trivial later on. And a moment which seems indistinguishable from a million others stays with us our entire lives. What remains is powerful – it's a small sampling that stands in for everything we are.

The end of my lunch break came with the screeching sound of the school bell and I was shocked out of my reverie by the unpleasant sound. The swarm of small people in the halls scattered back towards their selective classrooms. The kids were sweaty from an active recess. I missed that pure burst of unrestrained energy that only children of a young age are socially unconscious enough to engage in, letting loose without fear of judgment. I wanted to take advantage of the now-empty yard and run as fast as I could across the blacktop, becoming a blur of memory and nothing else. I would let the fall breeze pound against my face as I sprinted, sniffing the air of long-lost days, forgetting that my childhood was past, never to return again.

I know that nostalgia isn't based on how things really were but rather a filtered version of them. But I remember the imagined daydream better than the outer shell of true context. I'm haunted by the glorious false memories of a fictional sun-drenched fulfillment that never truly existed. My body feels the warmth and recalls the fantasy of spring romance and friendship and perfection. Even when it's not spring. In my memory, it's always spring.

I know there are many who don't have the same nostalgia for childhood that I have. A lot of people hate their childhoods. Many wouldn't want to receive my magical gift of being frozen in temporal place. They would not want to spend their days in an ageless Neverland. They look forward to growing up and as adults they look back on their childhood and shudder, glad those days are long gone.

The belief that every individual sees life from the same viewpoint is a classic mistake. It's often difficult, if not impossible, to separate from your own perspective.

The screeching bell echoed in my eardrums. I returned to my camera station. I was working with Shayla that day. I had told her that I'd been a student at Tomlinson. When I came back, she asked how it felt to return to my old school.

I kept it basic.

"It's good," I said. "The place seems a lot smaller."

Yes, time does move faster these days.

My second, third, and fourth seasons at SmilePosts disappeared in a blink.

Events progressed in a loop, years passing with little demarcation.

In film school, you're taught to plot your screenplays around beats of progression and development. I kept waiting for the forward motion of my own life but there was only stasis and repetition.

I wrote a new screenplay. I entered contests. I failed to win or place in any of them.

I took pictures at SmilePosts. I crushed on Hailey.

I went home.

I wrote another new screenplay. I entered more contests. I failed to win or place in any of them.

I took pictures at SmilePosts. I crushed on Hailey.

I went home.

I learned that some of my college friends were moving to Los Angeles to pursue their careers in the heart of the industry. They encouraged me to follow them.

I told my friends that I was thinking of joining them out west, but it was a lie. I wanted success on my terms. I wanted to become an accomplished screenwriter first and only then move to L.A., if necessary. It was an unprecedented model of entertainment industry success, but it was what I wanted. At least, that's what I told myself.

Mostly, I was scared. I was scared of moving to L.A. and losing all my savings and still not making it as a writer, then crawling back home, destitute and desperate. I was terrified by the idea of failing in a place where I had no family or foundation. Better to fail at home, if one had to fail, I theorized.

Life was much the same for Josie as it was for me. Little progression or development. Only surrender and impatience for an ambiguous release that would not come.

She took more wedding gigs. Reluctantly at first, then without any hesitation, then almost eagerly. She even volunteered for a job when Gabby mentioned being offered a wedding on a Saturday she already had booked. Josie was as unenthusiastic about photographing weddings as always, but she needed the money.

She and Nate talked about moving in together. They talked about getting married. But first he wanted to finish his nursing program. And then he wanted to make sure he had a steady job. And then he wanted to make sure they had enough savings in the bank.

Josie never doubted the authenticity of Nate's desire to be with her, but the delay in moving forward was frustrating. She was so tired of living at home. She was so tired of feeling like a stunted teenager, caught in the purgatory of unending adolescence that would never evolve to maturity.

The years passed and she waited. She waited to leave her mom's house. She waited to marry Nate. And she waited for something else. Something undefinable. Something she knew she wanted but could not name or visualize.

The years passed and the SmilePosts seasons passed and many co-workers came and went with each successive fall.

Josie and I watched the revolving door spin and got in the habit of gossiping about our ever-changing supporting cast. She became my automatic confidant for all SmilePosts incidents and plots that needed conveying.

There was much to discuss.

Trapped in our own sluggish loops, we looked around, eyes open, observing and surmising the public and private lives of those around us. We snuck time to pow-wow at the office or file reports via text about the characters that emerged in our midst.

There was the daily soap opera of newbies Spencer and Megan during my third season. Fiery Megan and sizzling Spencer locked eyes on their first day of training, like hunters catching a prey in their sights. Except they were both the hunter, neither prey, prepared to devour one another in some sexual cannibalistic display that made the rest of us extremely uncomfortable. They hooked up that first day of training and by day two they couldn't keep their hands off one another, refusing to pose for test portraits unless they could stand on the red feet together, arms interlinked, cheeks touching. On the final day of training, they broke up for the first time, hurling a spew of invectives at each other in the parking lot at the tops of their lungs, scaring away birds from the nearby trees. But by the following Tuesday, they were back together, making out in the equipment room, pawing at each other with such aggressiveness that they fell into the background tubes, sending the stacked assortment of backgrounds rolling all over the ground, along with their bodies. Two Wednesdays later, they broke up again, apparently over some slight Megan had made towards the quality of Spencer's ham sandwich. "You do not insult a man's food!" Josie heard Spencer yelling into his phone at six thirty A.M. as they walked into a middle school. No surprise, Spencer and Megan were back together a few days later, passing a Jolly Rancher from George's candy jar back-and-forth between each other's mouths using only their tongues. "Guys, c'mon, that is not appropriate behavior at the office," said Dee, who was as exasperated with this hurtling comet of passion as the rest of us. Somehow this comment caused Spencer and Megan to break up again. I don't remember why. But they were back together soon enough, and the pile of background tubes was never safe. Spencer was not invited back in the spring due to his subpar portraits and word was that Megan refused to come back without him, falling on the sword in honor of her on-again-off-again lover. Josie friended and followed them on Facebook and Instagram, because she couldn't take her eyes away from the drama. Last she told me, they had been married and then divorced. And they had adopted a cat.

There was Vicky, the over-sharer, who joined us in the fall of my fourth season. Vicky had a habit of telling every person she worked with her entire, unfiltered life story. Someone would say, "hi good morning," and Vicky would respond with, "my boyfriend left me for another woman because he said she was more attractive than me," or "my mom never loved me, I don't think. At least that's what she told me. I always asked for Frosted Flakes cereal and she would buy me Special K, which she would claim was the same thing without the 'frost' and was better for my health. She said I was fat. But then she would eat Frosted Flakes right in front of me, after saying the store was out of them, and I would say, 'isn't that a box of Frosted Flakes?' and she would say that I had made a mistake." If you worked with Vicky, she would drone on in a ceaseless, upsetting monologue all day, even if you never said a single word to her in response. I mean this literally. Josie tried it. She photographed with Vicky at an elementary school and did not speak one word to her the entire day, and still she had to hear about Vicky's "excessively bloody first period," and "medically unusual foot fungus condition." And if you think that hearing one of Vicky's depressing stories once gave you immunity from hearing it again, you are naïve. Because she was also repetitive. One day I heard the Frosted Flakes story three different times. Josie, Rita, and I took to hiding around corners whenever we heard Vicky approach. We would duck under a table or run into the bathroom to avoid the barrage of ceaseless sharing. I did feel badly for her. It sounded like her life had been filled with a lot of trauma. But empathy only extended so far.

There was Sheila, who was hired my second season. Despite being in her fifties, Sheila resisted the curse of older employees and was undaunted by the physical constraints of the job. She was very physically fit, a self-proclaimed gym rat who, like Clint, preferred to carry her equipment into the buildings by hand. She and Clint got along well. They talked a lot about Muscle Milk. Sheila's photos were excellent – ideal examples of framing and expression that reflected exactly what SmilePosts wanted a portrait to be. The problem with Sheila was that she was terrifying. Her students posed properly only because they were afraid she was going to straight-out murder them if they didn't do what she wanted. Photographing next to her, it became clear she was a cross between a drill sergeant and an escaped mental patient, screaming at the children as they stepped into her camera station. Her unblinking eyes, red with veins, pierced into the children like she was going to swallow their souls just by looking at them. "SMILE RIGHT THIS INSTANT!" she would say. Followed by "DON'T LOOK SO SCARED!" Her pictures were always perfect, though they were birthed in authoritarian terror. But the schools complained about her and we received extremely low ratings wherever she was sent. George tried to convince her to be less aggressive in one of the most awkward exchanges that has ever occurred between two people. George actually used the expression, "go to your happy place," when encouraging her to be nicer. Sheila responded saying that the only way to teach a child was to "whip them until they break." It was unclear if she meant this to be metaphorical. In late October, after Sheila threatened "TO EAT" a particularly stubborn fifth grade boy if he didn't cooperate, George was forced to fire her. Children throughout the five-county area breathed a sigh of relief. So did Josie and I. We were both kind of scared of her too.

There was Sofia, the hippie chick from my third season who proposed eating Miracle-Gro. "There are benefits to your bones," she suggested.

"We're all plants when you come right down to it." Her actual words. Josie and I were pretty sure she was always high and we were shocked that no one suggested she take a drug test. Sofia offered everyone in the office free palm readings. Rita took one. Sofia told her that her "thighs were destined for great things." As for the rest of her, who knows? But my favorite Sofia moment came when someone said they had eaten tilapia for dinner and Sofia responded that she thought tilapia "sounded like a verb. I tilapia. You tilapia." Josie and I say that one a lot. "I really tilapiaed today" is a common refrain in our personal dialogue that, much like the versatile Hebrew "shalom," can convey several different meanings. Sofia is also the only person to ever work at SmilePosts who was happy when her equipment got peed on. She claimed that her mat had been "purified by the natural liquids of innocence." Gross Sofia. She quit SmilePosts that spring to go on a "Turkmenistani Safari," which I'm fairly certain is not a thing.

There was Sven who literally did not speak any English. The only word I ever heard him say that I recognized was "hello," which, again, much like the Hebrew "shalom," he used to mean both hello and goodbye. The rumor that went around the office was that Sven had shown up for a job interview, had met George, and had not been hired because he didn't speak any English. However, he didn't understand that he hadn't gotten the job and he had shown up for work on the first day of training anyway. He was told again he had not been hired, but he still didn't understand, and he kept showing up, despite not receiving any pay. (How, in this scenario, he understood what day we started, or where and when to show up to schools, I do not know.) Remarkably, Sven proved himself competent at taking pictures, using only gestures and the excited exclamations of a Scandinavian language. (Josie and I weren't sure which Scandinavian language he spoke.) After he had been sent to schools and made other newbies look bad by taking great photos without even speaking English, the company decided to start paying him. So went the rumor. "But that can't possibly be true?" said Josie, while we huddled by the supply closet, laughing at this absurd scenario that had supposedly made Sven a full-time employee. It probably wasn't true, but we liked to think that it was.

Sometimes Josie and I would spend our days at separate schools texting back and forth, debating about who was the worst co-worker we ever had.

"There was that guy who I'm pretty sure was a neo-nazi," she said once.

"He was just bald!" I retorted.

"And mean," she rebutted.

"And mean," I assented. "What about that girl who insisted on calling the kids 'my precious babies'," I said. "It gives me shivers thinking about it."

"Oh!" she said. "What about the guy who insisted on talking in a terrible French accent to everyone, including teachers and principals?"

"That guy was the worst," I said. "I can't remember his name."

"Me neither," she said.

"Was it Crestin?" I said. "I want to say it was Crestin."

"That can't be right," she said.

"I'm telling you, I think his name might have been Crestin."

She replied with a GIF of music and film star Ice Cube shaking his head in disgust.

Of course, our gossip was not limited to the one season wonders of quickly departed newbies. We also talked about the other veterans.

There was the constant wait for Cal and Stacy to ignite their slow-burn flirtation. We watched these two shy, petrified individuals circle around their obvious affection for one another, neither courageous enough to come in for a landing. Each time Stacy lectured Cal about being too mean to the new people or Cal yelled back at Stacy that she was too nice, before profusely apologizing, the fire was stoked and it became more obvious they needed to kiss each other and be done with it. Josie, Rita, and I had a betting pool going on when we would learn that Cal and Stacy had officially gotten together, diffusing the swollen tension. Rita won. She had bet on the summer between my second and third season.

We saw the evidence in the parking lot that fall when Cal and Stacy arrived to work together, holding hands. It was unbearably sweet.

Speaking of Rita, she had some love life troubles of her own. That same third season training day when we learned that Cal and Stacy had fulfilled their promise, Rita met a newbie named Lacey, who was that rarest of creatures – a conservative Christian who preferred dating other women. Rita had come out when she was thirteen and was infuriated by the notion that someone gay would support a political party and a movement that rejected equal rights for people of her sexual orientation. It was a form of self-hatred, she told me and Josie, fuming about this girl she had not yet spoken to, riled up in a way we had never seen her. Something more than political antagonism was bubbling beneath the surface of Rita's rant. It turned out that something was "the hots" for Lacey, which Rita had a large dose of, to her great dismay. "I can't have a crush on a conservative," Rita told Josie, never once removing her eyes from Lacey as she said it. To make matters worse, Lacey was excessively nice and was open to Rita's guilt-ridden flirtation. "This is so stupid," said Rita. "We shouldn't go out just because we're the only two openly gay people in the office." "Openly?" asked Josie. "Is there someone secretly gay?" Rita gave Josie a knowing look but refused to reveal her intel. This led Josie and me on a guessing game that neither of us were proud of, but which couldn't be helped. Answers remained inconclusive. Meanwhile, Rita, awash in shame, asked Lacey on a date. "How did it go?" Josie asked. "I hate myself," Rita responded, which turned out to mean that it went better than she wanted it to go. Rita and Lacey went out several more times, but they walked a tightrope and a slip was inevitable. One afternoon in early October, they were heard (by pretty much everyone) arguing in the office's bathroom hallway. The gist was that Lacey broke with the ideologies of her political party and religion in support of gay marriage, but she agreed with them on everything else. Rita insisted that this crack in Lacey's belief system should open a wider chasm of support for the disenfranchised and transform her judgments of what was morally right or wrong. But Lacey continued to spout offensive opinions about poor people and make disturbing remarks like, "affirmative action is a great crime." She was immovable in her views. That was the end of their brief coupling. Rita couldn't justify continuing to date her. For a while, Rita was a wreck. "I don't know why I'm so sad," she said to Josie. "She is so completely wrong for me." "I know," said Josie, "but our feelings don't always make sense. And that doesn't make them any less real." Ain't that the truth.

There was Clint, that meat slab of a human being, who I could not seem to shake. Clint, who was hiding around every corner, no matter where I turned, so omnipresent in my work life that Gabby once referred to him, without irony, as my best friend. (Josie laughed at my undisguised revulsion when Gabby said that, but Gabby didn't understand what was funny.) I've always believed in being kind and non-judgmental, but Clint's particular brand of meat-headed bro-losophy irritated me to no end, compounded by his obliviousness at my irritation. He too thought we were workplace besties. "Sup broseph!" he cried out at the start of our third season, after two months apart during the unemployed summer. Then he grabbed me and lifted me into the air, saying "I missed you bro," as I was held helplessly above the ground, unable to escape his iron clutch. But... even Clint proved to contain hidden depths I did not expect. Soon after, Josie showed me a surprising Instagram post. It was Clint, at a Sixers game, accompanied by a black boy of about eight years old. The photo was captioned "#bigbrother." I questioned Clint about it the next time we worked together. It turned out that he had been participating in the Philadelphia Big Brothers program for the past three years. He was admirably reluctant to brag about it or to accept the compliment that he was "a good person" for doing it. "I enjoy it," he insisted. "The kids are great. We have fun. We play basketball or ride bikes or go to a game. It's a blast," he said. A glass of guilt knocked over inside me, spilling everywhere. I made fun of Clint with Josie near-constantly and the truth was that he was never anything but nice to me. Sure, he was a bit dumb and undeniably oblivious, and yes, his unquestioned beliefs skewed towards casual misogyny, but he meant well. Who was I to judge someone's worth because I didn't think they were as smart as I am? I felt like an asshole and I was determined to treat Clint better. I decided that from then on, when he said something distasteful, I would point out the error of his words and refrain from mockery. A few weeks later, when he made a comment about not being sure whether Marcy, one of the newbies, "was fat or had big boobs," because "her shirt stuck out a bunch, but it might just be the boobs," I replied that it was offensive when he objectified women in this manner. "Oh, sorry bro," he responded, surprised. His brow was furrowed in deep thought for the next several minutes. I like to think he was overhauling his entire way of thinking about women. But it's more likely he was still trying to figure out Marcy's boob size.

There were the other worlds of the office. The upstairs employees, leading simultaneous but eternally separated lives from us photographers in the basement. The ladies in customer service who Josie and I liked to equate with the seven dwarves. There was Happy Mindy, always a smile on her face, always a compliment to dish out; Grumpy Ruth, who answered every customer phone call like it was an affront to basic morality; Bashful Tyra, who hid her face whenever anyone spoke to her and who spoke into the phone so quietly that it was impossible for the customers to hear her, causing Josie and I to suspect that these were fake phone calls and she was merely keeping the line occupied so no actual person could get through; Sleepy Val, poor Sleepy Val who had six children under the age of twelve and who always looked like she had pulled an all-nighter in the Amazonian wilderness; Also, Sneezy Jane. I don't know, I guess Josie heard her sneeze once and we needed a Sneezy, so Jane became Sneezy. Out of a sense of decorum, I won't say who our Dopey was. We're still searching for a Doc. Even more than the customer service ladies, Josie and I loved observing the salespeople. Our trio of well-dressed schmoozers with hard-edged, single syllable names: Vic, Al, and Kay. They would come to the schools in their business suits, saying things like, "We've got a great rapport, you wouldn't believe this rapport" and looking ready to sell their own mothers' ashes to maintain an account. Josie and I enjoyed the contrast between the Wall Street vibe emanating off the salespeople (along with their pungent colognes) and the innocent, alphabet-decorated halls of the elementary schools they visited. They were Gordon Gekkos guest starring on Sesame Street, driving the hard bargain while somewhere in the background a classroom of kindergartners sang "The Wheels on the Bus."

Of course, there were also stories unfolding outside of our view.

Take Shayla. Consistent, uncomplaining Shayla. Along with Clint, Dana, and Hailey, we were now the only survivors from my starting year. I wouldn't classify Shayla as quiet exactly. She was always friendly and happy to engage in a group conversation. She was funny at times, surprising you with a bit of dry humor when you least expected it. But she was private. She was never the subject of gossip, partially because she was kind and well-liked, but also because no one knew much about her personal life. Without ever mentioning it to a single SmilePosts co-worker, she had been working a second job at night, at an Acme Supermarket in Upper Darby where she lived, and a third job during the summers, as a counselor at her church's youth camp. Unbeknownst to any of us, she was helping to support both of her parents, both of whom had suffered from career-ending illnesses, neither of whom had prescription plans from the low-tier marketplace medical insurance they had signed up for after losing the benefits that came with their jobs. It was a struggle to afford the rising costs of the medications her parents needed and still put food on the table nightly, not only for the three of them, but also for her younger sister Nevaeh who was in tenth grade. Shayla wanted a life for herself. She wanted to get married to her boyfriend and she wanted her parents to be well enough that she could move into her own house and start her own family. She fought daily with the struggles of constriction, weighed down by obligations that would seemingly never cease, frustrated that she had to live her life for others instead of herself. But she never let her discouragement show, not to her family who needed her and certainly not in the workplace.

Then there was George. Our loquacious leader seemed like the last person who would be battling any inner demons. He charged into the office each day like a kid experiencing a sugar rush on the first day of summer vacation. Even at our earliest six A.M. arrivals, George might show up to oversee, glowing with energy like a new father, ready to inject his manic passion for school portraits into all our veins. There never seemed to be a cloudy day in George-land, no roadblock to slow the happy thoughts racing full speed out of his mind and into our ears. But the truth was, not everything was sunny in George's personal life. During my second season, George's marriage was falling apart and during my third season, he was going through a divorce. It was devastating. He couldn't comprehend what had gone wrong. He wanted to start a family and have children, but instead his five-year-old marriage had sputtered to the side of the road like a car trying to drive across the country on a single tank of gas. "It's not working," his wife told him, sympathetically. She still cared for him. But she was married to the most talkative man in the world and they couldn't find a single thing to discuss. They sat there in silence over dinner, George trying his hardest to jump start the conversation, but nothing worked, nothing kicked their stalled marriage into gear and nothing would, because the necessary fuel of love was not there. Divorce wasn't the only trauma George faced. Right as his marriage was ending, his mom had a stroke. She lost her ability to speak and to walk. She required immense therapy to get back to anything resembling a human life. George was an only child and his dad had died years before. He was the only person his mom had left. He used every spare minute not spent at SmilePosts or working through his divorce to help his mom get back in shape. She screamed at him without words, in immense discomfort, hitting him, wanting to give up on therapy, give up on life, be done with the struggle. But George would not allow it. George was a fighter. George would not let the world get him down. He would be there for his mother and he would persevere. And when he came to work, he would not let his

GREAT BIG SMILE

employees see anything from him other than a shining, irrepressible verve. Because it was their job to get smiles from children – the purest task in the world. If he wanted his employees to be sources of joy and harbingers of smiles for the young and the innocent, he needed to lead by example. He needed to show them nothing but optimism. So when George greeted us at six A.M. on an average weekday with bursting positivity, we should have appreciated him more. As we all slapped ourselves in our waiting cars and gulped coffee to stay awake, pushing into the day as through a vat of molasses, and George said, "Good morning, everybody! It's a great day, a great day, ready to get some smiles, ready to make children happy, ready to see the smiling faces and bring a little joy to the world, that's what the world needs, are we all excited, are we ready for the day?" we should have seen him as the great leader that he was. But mostly we groaned, annoyed, and thought, *it's too early for this shit.*

George showed us the value of his upbeat persistence last fall, a few weeks into my fourth year.

It was a Thursday afternoon. We received an all-photographer group text from Dee informing us of an afternoon meeting. This was odd because our weekly meetings were usually on Wednesdays. We'd had a long one only the day before. Dee's text was replied to with several GIFs of celebrities shaking their heads and rolling their eyes in exasperation. She did not respond back.

I arrived at the office around three-thirty, curious to see what the surprise meeting was all about. Josie was already there waiting. I looked at her to see if the mystery had been solved. She shook her head – no answers yet. I sat down with my day's group and we did our paperwork as other co-workers trickled in. There was an annoyed anticipation in the air, everyone wanting to know what egregious error had been made and who should be blamed for this second weekly meeting.

Once everyone had arrived, Dee took the floor. George stood beside her. It was immediately clear that something was wrong. They were far too serious. Even the worst of SmilePosts mistakes – letting a kid wear a shirt that said "Fuck" in their photo, talking back to a school principal and losing the company an account – didn't elicit this sort of solemn overture.

"Guys, can you stop talking please?" Dee said, silencing a few pockets of chatter in the room. "I have some sad news."

Dee was unable to finish what she was saying. She started to cry and excused herself.

That got our attention.

George stepped forward as Dee left the room.

"We've received some bad news about Greg," said George.

Greg was a new photographer who I had barely met. He had curly blonde hair and didn't say much. That was the extent of what I knew about him.

"Greg passed away last night," said George.

Someone in the room gasped. I'm not certain who.

"What happened?" someone asked, boldly.

George claimed they didn't know the specifics but by the following week the truth had spread, without any official announcement or any indication of how the facts had been gleaned. It was a suicide. Greg, that quiet, curly-haired guy I didn't know had, for one reason or another, taken his own life.

Josie and I learned what we could about Greg from those who had worked with him. Most of the conclusions were consistent with our own observations. He was quiet, he stayed away from the conversations. He seemed sullen and removed.

But were these after-the-fact judgments? Did we paint this sad composite of Greg in retrospect because we needed a person who died by suicide to fit a certain mold, in order to justify an incomprehensible event?

I could make up a backstory for Greg in these pages. I could invent facts about a troubled home life or a childhood of being bullied. I could dig into Greg's fictional doppelgänger, searching for a narrative that would make sense of his early exit from this Earth. But maybe there was no graspable reason. And making one up seems in bad taste.

What I will tell you is that George, whose irrepressible positivity had always seemed like a silly affectation, became the beating heart of an office in search of answers. While George was secretly dealing with a divorce and his mom's slow recovery, he took it upon himself to be the territory wide beacon of optimism. He knew which photographers were having a particularly hard time after Greg's death and he showed up at their schools without fail, ready to assist in the daily tasks of the job, going beyond what was expected of a manager. He posed children, he kept the lines moving, he helped set up equipment. He would often seem to be at two schools at once. We would discuss George sightings at the end of the day and his multiple reported appearances defied the logic of travel time. He was a churning motor. He was the Energizer Bunny. He was caffeine personified. With every spotted sad expression of an employee, he compensated with more energy and support.

A couple of weeks after the news about Greg, I was at a high-enrollment middle school when a newbie named Will started making fun of George. He performed an unflattering impression that sounded like Barney the Dinosaur after snorting a hefty bump of cocaine up his big purple nostrils. On a normal occasion, we all would have laughed. This time, something interesting happened. People got mad.

"Fuck you," said Dana, who was also at the school. "George is a good person. He's doing his best." My other co-workers seconded Dana's response. We had all been bolstered by George's unflagging spirit. He was exactly what we needed during that time, struggling as we were with our barely known co-worker's death.

George showed up at the school later that day to help us break down our equipment. He was greeted with a chorus of appreciation and gladness that surprised him, though he quickly embraced his new popularity without questioning it. He was happy everyone wanted to talk with him.

He loved to talk.

The surge in respect for George wasn't the only unexpected side-effect of Greg's death.

With a swell of guilt, I tell you that it also, inadvertently, led to one of my happiest moments.

It was the Monday after the somber Thursday meeting when we learned the news. I was scheduled to work with Hailey.

I wanted to feel less excited to spend the day with Hailey because of the grim news. I also wanted to feel less excited because I had given up on anything romantic ever happening between us. But the truth was that neither of those factors mattered. I was as excited as ever.

We were photographing at Graham Hill Elementary in Berks County, a school sixty miles Northwest of Philadelphia, out in the increasingly hilly regions that gradually transition into Appalachian Mountain towns. These are places of long abandoned steel mills and main streets built on a steep incline. Graham Hill Elementary's surrounding neighborhood was a small preview of the rural shift, but it felt like a different universe from Philly and the surrounding suburbs. I swear I saw someone in overalls and a straw hat walking a goat as I passed a local gas station. I saw them in my peripheral vision so I might have been mistaken. Perhaps the goat was a dog.

At the school were me, Hailey, and a newbie named Louisa, who mostly kept to herself.

From the start I could tell Hailey was off. I tried to talk to her and her sadness was striking. Her responses were short and distracted. Not even her phone provided a diversion. In between classes she stared off into the distance, a forlorn glare plastered on her pretty face.

During an extended late-morning break, I decided to broach the subject.

"Are you alright?" I asked.

"Kind of," she said. "It's so sad about Greg."

"Yeah totally."

She looked at me, considering. She averted her eyes but kept talking.

"I worked with him on his last day," she admitted.

"Oh god," I said. "That's hard."

"Yeah... I didn't talk to him," she said. "I never really talk to the new people. Unless they talk to me, I guess." She looked directly into the ground. Her eyes filled with tears. "What if I could have said something? It must have happened that night."

"Hailey..." I was overcome with a feeling of wanting to protect her. I wanted to hold her in my arms, but I knew I couldn't. "He must have been a really depressed guy," I said. "He would have to be, to do something like that. Don't put any blame on yourself. It's definitely a really tragic thing that happened. But don't do that to yourself. You're a really good person."

"You think so?" she said.

"I know so," I said. "You're really nice. Don't ever question whether you are."

"I think I could be nicer sometimes," she said.

"Look, none of us are perfect. I could give you a list of my flaws that would occupy us for the rest of the day."

"Like your refusal to get a new phone?" she said, smiling.

It was an established fact at the office that my phone was five years old, an eternity by modern definition to everyone else but me. From anyone else this barb would have annoyed me, but from Hailey it made my heart melt.

"I wasn't asking for volunteer submissions to the list," I said with a light, warm sarcasm.

"Sorry," she said with a little laugh. "I think you're really nice too."

There it was. A peak of unexpected happiness I would surely remember forever.

"Thanks, Hailey," I said, trying to disguise my own watery eyes.

I was so happy.

And then I remembered why. A co-worker had killed himself and it had given me a chance to comfort the girl I liked, at a moment when she was depressed.

I was mad at myself for finding any joy in this twisted scenario. I wondered if there was something fundamentally wrong with me.

But that didn't stop me from feeling happy.

EIGHT
UNCHARTED TERRITORY

IT WAS A FAIT ACCOMPLI that my crush on Hailey thrived, because I hadn't found anyone to replace her with. My mind always required an object of desire. The only way to boot one person from worship was to install another. The throne would not abide a power vacuum.

It's not as if I didn't try to depose Hailey.

Over the last four years, I've gone on nineteen online first dates.

Three of those nineteen progressed to a second date.

One of those three managed a third date.

I have yet to go on a fourth date.

Even if I got to a fourth date with someone, I'm not sure how we would advance any further. I still live at my parents' house. Nobody wants to date someone who lives with their parents. For logistical reasons more than anything. When my date comes over for a romantic night, she'll have to first pass through the living room and face my dad's questions about what kind of car she drives. Nothing kills the mood faster than a dad wondering how many miles you have on your vehicle. I don't know why I've bothered trying to date while living at home. I should have waited to have enough money for an apartment. Whenever that might be.

Besides, I find the whole online dating thing to be extremely awkward. In general, I'm more of a slowly-dip-my-toes-in-the-water guy and less of a dive-right-in-head-first guy. This is true both with swimming pools and romantic pursuits. I like to slowly build a rapport (to borrow the salespeople's favorite word), sensing the chemistry as layers of personality are gradually peeled back. I like to take my time, co-writing a romantic story.

Online dating shoots you out of a cannon.

There you are with some woman you've just met, at a restaurant or a café or a bar, immediately expecting the sparks to ignite so dramatically that they burn down the surrounding establishment, trapping you amidst the smoke and plummeting planks of roof, the two of you huddling together as you wrap your arms around her and protect her from inhalation. But instead, you spend the first half of the date readjusting your expectations of her personality, since she inevitably seems different from the person who you exchanged messages with for a week online. The second half of the date you continue to wait for that spark to ignite, not sure that you are *not* interested in her, but feeling no certainty that you are either. All the while your guilt grows about the jury of your brain deliberating on the worth of a human being you've *only just met*, who doesn't deserve to be judged so harshly on an hour's worth of her time.

(To acknowledge a seeming contradiction – I know I said earlier that I was infatuated with Hailey at first sight. This would appear to dispute my claim that it's hard to know whether I like a woman too quickly. But there is a crucial difference. I met Hailey under no obligation of potential romance. She saw me as only a co-worker and I was able to gestate in the fantasy of romance without the pressure of necessary action. Online dates do not provide this safe distance of fantasy. You're thrust into reality from the moment you decide to meet in-person. Each of you engages in an interior dialectic determining whether your date is worth your time. This is typically a "yes or no" proposition. Even if there's an attraction, it's difficult for infatuation to thrive under these harsh conditions.)

At the end of an online date, you always say some variation of "this was fun, let's talk soon," whether you intend to talk soon or not. You lecture yourself not to say "let's talk soon" if you don't really want to talk soon, but you always end up saying it regardless, because the date is ending and you have to say something dammit. Occasionally, when you say "let's talk soon" you mean it, thinking that there was something there this time, a tiny spark, not a big enough spark to burn down the restaurant but who knows, give it some time and maybe arson is possible in the future. Unfortunately, *she* didn't mean "let's talk soon" when she said "let's talk soon." And when you reach out to talk a couple days later, which is soon, by definition, she never responds. In online dating, silence after a single date is considered proper etiquette for conveying lack of interest. It's far kinder (or at least less terrifying) than telling a person you're not interested in them after spending only an hour together.

All of which is to say, I had no luck finding anyone to replace Hailey in my crush throne.

Year after year, I came back to SmilePosts and so did Hailey.

Each fall, a part of me wished that she wouldn't be there. Maybe, I thought, she'll have moved on to some new job, sparing me from my chronic desire. When I arrived and she greeted me with her welcome, returning smile, the spuriousness of these wishes was exposed and I swooned with relief, wondering how I would have coped if she were not there.

After our first couple of seasons, I gave up my attempts at trying to let Hailey know that I liked her. I reeled in my girlfriend fishing line and she eased around me, no longer on guard for the threat of a potential ask-out. The years went by and we were an established part of each other's work lives. I kept my feelings private and we became friends.

At some point during my fourth year, it became apparent that she had a boyfriend. I would overhear her talking about him to Dana at the office. I can't tell you much about the guy. I deliberately left the room whenever Hailey brought him up.

Over time, the rational part of me steadily acknowledged that Hailey was wrong for me. I could not envision a real scenario in which we were a couple. We were not a match. We were pieces from entirely separate puzzles. What would we talk about? What would we do together? These were open questions to which I had no satisfactory answer.

She was a placeholder, convenient for fending off the emptiness of wanting nothing. My desire for her was safe from the pressures of reality. It provided easy, complication-free meaning. It distracted from the bleak, looming questions of the inexhaustible suffering in the world and my seeming powerlessness to change any of it. It diverted me from my guilt at selfishly focusing on my own meager problems, instead of the larger ones gripping humanity.

My crush on her was a static thing. A luxury item in a store window that you had no plans on ever buying and knew would be out of place in your home, but that you nevertheless enjoyed looking at from the sidewalk.

Week after week, I looked at the schedule. I hoped to see myself scheduled with Hailey. I liked being around her even if I would never be with her.

Time passed. Little changed.

Josie and I talked about everyone we worked with, gossiping and spreading the news of all the salacious office drama. Yet I never once told her about my feelings for Hailey and she never once asked.

I'm sure that she knew. I'm sure that everyone did.

A couple months ago, during the second week of my astounding fifth year as a SmilePosts photographer, Josie and I were scheduled to work together. It was just the two of us. A rarity, especially in the early fall, when two veterans were seldom sent to the same school without any newbies to watch over.

The school, West Larrenville Elementary, was a special case. We were on the verge of losing the account after a disastrous spring picture day the previous March. That day there had been an accident on I-476 (aka The Blue Route). The first photographer to arrive had shown up forty-five minutes late. The second didn't show up at all because she was one of the people in the accident. (She was okay, with the exception of some aches and bruises, but her car was totaled.) It was a busy day on the schedule and George had no spare photographers to take her place. He rushed over to the school to help pose, but with only one camera to use, the day inevitably got out of hand and the school was furious.

Now in the fall, the big guns were brought out to keep the school from defecting to one of the local portrait companies, like Goldstein's or Portrait Heroes, our rivals who were always a threat because of their lower prices. Josie and I were handpicked for damage control. George and Dee said we were their two best photographers. The praise cut Josie deep. She sarcastically remarked to me that if she was the best they had, the others must "be really shitty." Her pride would not allow her to excel at "this dumb stupid job."

We were given a big speech the afternoon before going to West Larrenville by Vic, the salesperson responsible for the account. We were told the following: The secretaries there might treat us rudely, with pent up anger over the catastrophe that was the spring; Vic had to beg the principal to give us this chance to redeem ourselves, bribing him with two tickets to a Sunday afternoon Phillies game; we needed to walk on eggshells, carefully monitoring every word we spoke to every child and every teacher, not allowing so much as a slip of what could be conceived of as a fresh or inappropriate comment; we needed to arrive early, have our equipment set up in half the normal time, and as soon as we completed the last call for pictures, we needed to be broken down and out of there with record speed.

Also, we were being given gift certificates to Pizzeria Uno and if things with the school staff began to go sour, we were instructed to hand these out as a thank you for their patronage; however, if using these gift certificates did not prove necessary, we were supposed to return them to Vic at the office at the end of the day.

Josie and I walked into West Larrenville Elementary at seven-thirty A.M. the next morning, fifteen minutes before the scheduled arrival time of seven-forty-five. We fully expected to be greeted like Jewish bankers in Nazi Germany. Instead, the secretary was pleasant enough. In a line of work where schools have long memories and short fuses, the calm atmosphere was suspicious, as if Vic had given the front office a Men-in-Black memory wipe along with the principal's Phillies tickets. Josie and I did our best not to question the pleasantness.

As an unexpectedly positive side effect of the calamitous spring picture day, the school had created a relaxing schedule of thirty-five minutes per class, arriving two at a time to the gym. Josie and I needed no more than fifteen to twenty minutes tops for each class, even taking extra care with each child.

The spring photographer's failure was our reward. It looked to be an unanticipated good day.

Josie and I were both big readers. With seventeen-minute breaks between classes, we usually would have taken advantage of the time to put some pages in our rear-view mirrors. But that day, neither of us reached for the books in our backpacks.

We wanted to talk.

The conversation started out following the familiar entertaining beats. After the first classes, we talked about the movies and TV shows we had been watching. After the second classes, we dished, as per usual, about the antics of our co-workers. I was happy to hear that Rita was dating someone new and both of their politics were completely aligned. Josie was delighted to hear that Clint had recently asked me how to send an email attachment, an act he had somehow never performed before.

After the third classes, something interesting happened. Without any specifically intended pivot, the conversation veered into uncharted territory, away from the safe ground of co-worker gossip. We turned our spotlights inward.

"I'm happy for Rita," I said. "I know what it's like to want a relationship and have trouble finding one."

I'm not sure why I said it. Josie and I were alone. She had become a good friend. I wanted to unlock my mental safe of protected thoughts and share the contents with her. I wanted to honor her as a select individual worthy of hearing them.

I felt comfortable with her.

"Oh yeah?" she said. She was happy to listen, but she was tentative about pushing too far on the new path I had taken us. She wanted me to set the pace.

"I go on a lot of online dates," I said, "but nothing has stuck."

"Online dating is brutal. I'm lucky I don't have to do that," she said.

"You definitely are," I said. And then, after a brief hesitation... "It's so hard to find someone you really like. I had a girlfriend my senior year of college. First girlfriend I ever had. I was so happy. I couldn't believe that the thing I'd waited for forever was really happening. Problem was, I wouldn't let it be a normal relationship. I wanted a story. I wanted the movie moments. I wanted dramatic declarations and the high of culmination I felt when we got together, after years of waiting. I ruined it. I wouldn't let it be normal. At least, I think I ruined it. I don't know. Maybe she just didn't like me enough."

(I suppose the reader might wonder why I've failed to inform you about my ex-girlfriend up until now. The truth is, I felt closer to Josie than I do to you. Also, I didn't particularly feel like talking about it. If it weren't crucial to the context, I would have left any reference to Sarah out of this scene as well. Some memories you want to keep only for yourself.)

"Breakups are hard," said Josie. "I went through a couple rough ones before I met Nate."

"Oh yeah?"

"When my freshman year of high school boyfriend broke up with me, I cried for a month. It was stupid. He was an idiot. I saw on Instagram recently that he uses one of those ATV motorbikes as his primary vehicle now. I dodged a bullet."

I laughed. "I was stuck on Sarah until—" (I was close to mentioning Hailey, but I held back. Some lines needed to be drawn.) "I was stuck on her for a while."

"Anyway," said Josie, "I'm in a great relationship now and I'm still mostly miserable. So trust me, having a girlfriend won't fix everything. It might not fix anything."

"You're miserable?"

"Maybe that's unfair," she said. "It's definitely not fair to Nate."

"But is it true?"

"Maybe," she said. "Not because of Nate," she quickly added. "He's great. But having him doesn't fix the other issues."

"What other issues?"

She was about to answer when the fourth classes arrived. We pressed pause.

After the kids left, we sat back down and there was a moment of quiet, each of us silently allowing the other a conversational escape hatch. It was a chance to change the subject into something lighter or to reach into our backpack and grab our books before we resumed the frightening process of opening up.

Neither of us took the easy out. After a minute, I picked us up where we had left off.

"You were saying that you feel kind of miserable?" I said.

She took a deep breath.

"I feel stuck," she said. "I hate this job. Or no, that's not true. If I'm being honest, I like the job. The truest way to say it is that I hate that I like the job. I don't know what to do with my life. I love taking photos but I don't know how to make any money doing it in a way that feels fulfilling. And when I complain about it, I feel like a guilty spoiled brat, complaining about stupid white-people pointless shit when there are so many worse off people in the world. I want to help with the worse things, but I never do. I never volunteer, I never canvass voters. I think about it, but I never do it. I'm too lazy or too scared or I don't know what, but my guilt about not doing more doesn't make me do more, it just makes me feel more guilty. Or it makes me read articles online and get angry about politics and climate change deniers and religious zealots, but I don't actually confront any of them. I don't really think it would do any good if I did. Which is depressing. And speaking of climate change, it's like, I want to get married and have a kid or two, but am I being cruel by doing that? Is civilization going to be gone in a hundred years? Am I bringing a kid into a terrible future where they'll suffer under incredible heat and lack of water? Just because I selfishly want to create a little human, so I can feel better about myself? I don't know what I want. Or, I want a lot of things, but they contradict each other. I wish I knew how I was supposed to live my life."

Josie looked away from me as soon as she finished speaking, instantly vulnerable and afraid she had shared too much.

"I know what you mean," I said. "I have a lot of the same worries. I've been reading some self-help books lately."

"Really?" she said. "Do you, like, stand in the mirror and tell yourself that you're 'good enough, smart enough and doggone it, people like you?'"

I laughed at the ancient SNL reference. I sensed Josie trying to deflect us back into comedic territory to stave off further fragility. But I was glad she had told me what she did. I was glad we were having a serious talk.

"No, they're not like that," I said. "Not the books I connect with, anyway. What you said about wanting all these contradictory things, it makes me think of this Buddhist philosophy I've read about. The idea is that there's not really a self. At first, I didn't know what that meant. I probably still don't know what it means, but the more I've read about the way our brains work, and our psychology, it kind of makes sense. It's like, we have all of these different parts inside of us. There're all these different areas within the brain and different parts of it reflect different things we do, actions we take, thoughts we think. There's this part in the front of our brains, the prefrontal cortex, that's the center of our more rational, intentional thinking and planning, and it often contradicts the desires and judgments and cravings of our lower brain. I'm oversimplifying it, but the point is that we're not this contained whole, the way we think of ourselves. We're all these different pieces. And when you slow down and pay attention to your own thoughts, you see that all of this is happening, in some sense, without any control on your part at all. Your thoughts come and go, chronically and endlessly, and they constantly contradict each other and it's all happening on its own. There's no real central self."

"That's really interesting," said Josie. She processed my rudimentary lecture on neurology and its connections to secular Buddhism. "I don't know that any of it makes me feel any better though. The idea that we don't have free will, it's not exactly encouraging... Or maybe it is. At least it's not my fault that I'm doomed to work at SmilePosts. It's fated. I can't do anything about it... No, I changed my mind, that does make me feel worse."

"I don't think it's that simple," I said. "Free will or fate. I think they're two sides of the same coin. Neither is necessarily true. Fate implies that some force from on-high has laid out the future for us. Free will implies a central self that is in the driver's seat, making life decisions. Both imply a continuous, consistent identity and I'm not sure that exists. There's a sense in which choices are made, they're just not made by a unified person, like we perceive ourselves to be. They're made by parts of us, which conflict with other parts, and when one part wins out in a particular situation, a choice is made."

Josie was quiet for a moment, thinking it over.

"Okay," she said. "But even if what you say is scientifically accurate or whatever, I don't know that it makes any difference. My sense of self might be this emergent thing that comes from all of these little parts of me, but I still feel like I'm me. So when I feel sad or I feel like I don't have a future, it still hurts and I want to do something about it, regardless of how the decisions are made beneath the surface. Plus, the thing about what you're saying is that it's an easy excuse for doing nothing. You can say that you aren't helping to save the environment or fight tyranny because there is no 'you' that's in control of your actions. Even if it's the truth at some level, it's a scapegoat idea to prevent you from acting when it's not easy."

"Maybe," I said. "But to be honest, I'm not going to do any good in the world if I can't first deal with my own feelings of meaninglessness. That's the reality, at least for me. And when I acknowledge that most of my thoughts and feelings are out of my control, and that notions of good and bad are only ideas floating around in my brain, oddly enough, it makes me feel better. I can accept things as they are."

"Or you resign yourself so that things can't get any better," she said. "To me, there are some things that are good and worth fighting for."

"Maybe," I said, not necessarily willing to concede an objective morality to the world.

We were interrupted by the chatter of the fifth group of classes. They approached the gym doors. As we stood up, Josie turned to me.

"Are you unhappy, Blake?" she asked.

"I don't know. Sometimes," I said. "You?"

"Sometimes," she said.

We looked at each other.

It was one of those rare moments of true connection with another human being. The kind of connection you only feel a few times in your life, when the impenetrable boundaries of self are momentarily crossed and you feel seen.

Josie turned away first. She went over to her camera.

"First in line!" she called.

I photographed on autopilot. "Come in, stand on the feet, turn this way, tip your head, don't tip it that much, that's good, great big smile, great thanks you're all done, next student, come in, stand on the feet..." and so on.

As I made my way through the line of children, a far-away thought appeared like a distant train. At first, it was only a slow-moving speck on the remote rail of my perception, but as it came closer, it grew in size, speed, and sound.

Josie. Is this the girl I should be in love with, instead of Hailey?

The thought repeated. Louder. *Is she the girl I should be in love with?*

"Come in, stand on the feet, tip your head, great big smile..." *Is this the girl I should be in love with?* The thought chugged along.

We had an undeniable bond. She made so much more sense for me than Hailey. We liked similar things. We had a similar sense of humor. Longing for Hailey was all fantasy, but with Josie I could have something real. A true connection. I could acknowledge her as a real person, rife with complexities and flaws, but still capable of making me happy.

Of course, if you've been paying attention, you will be unsurprised to learn that my thoughts were not all on the same page. Accompanying the recurring question of my adjusted romantic focus was a significant resistance.

For one, there was the unbreachable fact of Josie's boyfriend. Though she didn't sound entirely happy with him.

Also, there was the terrifying notion of trying to pivot from friendship to a relationship with a co-worker at my long-term job, risking both the loss of an important friend and the destruction of any comfort I felt around others in the workplace. If I pursued this in any way, everyone else would catch wind of it before the second hand on the clock completed a full circle.

This was treacherous territory I was venturing into. No doubt. I could feel a mental security guard working hard to banish the new thoughts from my mind, protecting me from the steep consequences of falling for Josie.

Yet the thought repeated. *Is she the girl I should be in love with?*

We talked the rest of the day, during each long break. Our guard down, the conversation went in a number of intimate directions. We talked about the frustrating Catch-22 of applying for new jobs, butting against the axiom of being unable to get a job without experience, while being unable to get experience without a job. We talked about our families. I told her about my mom's neuroses and my dad's broken-record tendencies. Josie told me about her parents' divorce. She told me about her mom's upcoming wedding to some buffoon named Jacque. She told me about her drug-dealing brother and her dad's increasing alcoholism, worse every time she went to see him, which was less and less often. She told me that she had always wanted to be an adult, craving independence and responsibility, but now that she was an adult, she felt herself flailing. She said that she didn't feel like an adult and I said that I didn't either. I talked about my nostalgia for childhood, telling her about the strange experience of photographing at my elementary school. I told her that I missed being a kid, when the scale of life was smaller and easier to master. We both talked about how time speeds up the longer you live, each passing year a smaller part of the passing whole. We talked about evolution and science and history and politics.

And all the while, that new, perilous, exhilarating thought kept spinning around my mind. *Is this the girl I should be in love with?*

And then, more dangerous...

Am I in love with her already?

NINE
SUNDAY, MONDAY, TUESDAY

SUNDAY

On the day of her mom's wedding, Josie woke up with a massive headache.

Her hair a mess, the folds of her bedsheets imprinted on her face, she shuffled to the bathroom, popped open the medicine drawer, and took three Tylenols.

The noise of the crew in the backyard setting up for the event reverberated through both the house and Josie's pounding head. The morning sunlight peeking through the open blinds stung and she walked back to her bedroom with her eyes closed, thinking she knew the route by instinct.

She walked face-first into a wall, which, needless to say, did not help the headache.

The hired handymen were putting the finishing touches on the sukkah, under which Nicki and Jacque would be married that afternoon. A sukkah, which is a hut or archway made of natural materials for the Jewish holiday of Sukkot, was specifically requested by Josie's mom, despite the fact that neither she nor Jacque was Jewish. She had seen a photo in a magazine of a Jewish couple married under the vines of hanging grapes and decided that this was the exact aesthetic she needed to kick off her second marriage. This particular sukkah was covered in flowers, vines, and hanging fruit of all varieties – grapes, yes, but also apples, oranges, pineapples, mangoes, bananas, and kiwis. There was enough fruit to feed a small village in that marriage archway, which infuriated Josie. People could be eating that fruit.

Josie lay in bed that morning for as long as possible, waiting for her headache to lessen. It did not. She thought about the sukkah, which pissed her off, but in truth she viewed everything related to the wedding with disdain.

Shortly after ten, Josie's mom pranced into her room without knocking and dropped flower petals everywhere in a symbolic celebration of her flower-child happiness. Josie would have to clean them up later.

"Time to wake up my sweet girl," said Nicki. "You need to have your hair done!"

Having her hair done consisted of having dandelions woven in and out of unwashed waves. ("Should I wash my hair first?" said Josie. "Don't you dare!" said Nicki.)

Hours later, Josie was ready in her bridesmaid dress. She glanced in the mirror. She looked like an actress who had starred in a production of *A Midsummer Night's Dream*, ran from the theater still in costume, and then immediately become homeless for five years.

The guests trickled in: A mélange of hippies in one-piece frocks that looked like oversized pillowcases with sewed-on sequins, loud Frenchmen from Jacque's family who were either arguing or agreeing vehemently (it was impossible to tell), embarrassed conservative cousins trying to keep their heads down and not stare at anything too long or risk offending God, and hoodie wearing friends/customers of Landon's who had not received any invitations but who Landon had invited himself to drum up business. Landon could be spotted in various shadowy corners counting his cash and passing out small Ziploc bags of product.

Shortly before the ceremony, Josie's dad arrived. She knew her mom had invited him, most likely out of spite, but Josie hadn't thought he would take Nicki up on the invitation.

To his credit, he was the best dressed person there. On the other hand, he arrived already drunk, despite having driven himself to his former house.

"Dad, I'm surprised you came," said Josie.

"You look like a hobo," said Lou.

"I know," assented Josie, as Lou raided the locked liquor cabinet, having kept his copy of the key.

"Maybe you should slow down a bit," said Josie.

"I'm a grown man Josie."

"Are you okay dad? Why did you come? You don't need to see this shitshow."

"A man is not a man if he doesn't grin and bear it and watch his wife marry another man," he said.

"I think that's a somewhat unhealthy portrait of masculinity," she said.

"Where's the rum? I thought I had rum."

The guests kept coming. The backyard overflowed. A few stoned hippie guests ate the fruit in the sukkah before the ceremony, not realizing it was part of the décor.

Josie barricaded herself in her room for as long as she could, holding her throbbing head. She took two more Tylenol.

Finally, Nate arrived, straight from a twelve-hour shift that had turned into thirteen. He was exhausted but he was there to help Josie through this exasperating occasion. Clutching his suit in a cleaners bag, he closed her bedroom door behind him.

Josie could see he was tired. She knew in some rational part of her mind that it was generous of him to be there at all, overworked as he was, but lost in the thrum of her headache and the general madness of the day, all she felt was annoyance when he entered her room.

"I thought you were going to be here like an hour ago," she said.

"I tried. Work ran over," he said.

"I still don't understand why you couldn't request off. You knew this day was important to me."

"I told you why. I requested off this afternoon and tonight, so I couldn't request off this morning. The hospital is understaffed. And is this day important to you? You said you would skip it entirely if you could."

Overtired, he was more brusque than usual.

"I would. But I can't. And I need you here to help me get through it."

"I'm here," he said, testy. He didn't love the way he had been greeted, given that he could barely stand and had rushed over straight from the hospital to be supportive.

Then, in his Nate way, he took a deep breath and tried to alleviate the tension. He sat down next to her on the bed and put his hand on her knee.

"This is a look," he said, taking in her dress and hair.

"I look like the sixties took a shit," she said.

"You look beautiful. No amount of weeds in your hair could make you less beautiful."

"Don't think your sweet talk can get you out of trouble for being late."

"I was—" he was about to give a real excuse, but realized it was pointless trying to reason with her. He stood up. "Should I change into my suit, or should I just go outside and roll around in the garden?" he said.

"It doesn't matter. Whatever you want," she said roughly, unwilling to banter. She was enjoying taking out her frustrations on Nate for reasons she couldn't entirely pinpoint, and she wasn't ready to let up.

"Okay," he said, discouraged by the whole interaction, wanting only to lie on her bed and fall asleep. He changed into his suit.

The day weaved its way to the ceremony.

Josie stood next to her aunt, under the sukkah arch, waiting for the procession to bring Nicki down the aisle of folding chairs. A hanging apple was repeatedly knocked by the breeze into the back of Josie's head. She pulled the apple down violently and threw it into a nearby bush.

A musician friend of Jacque's played a shoddy rendition of "All You Need is Love" on acoustic guitar as Josie's mom walked across the grass slowly, pausing to take the hand of every person in the crowd who was close enough to reach. Josie was less focused on her mom than on the hired photographer, who was capturing her mom's procession from absolutely terrible angles. Josie spent the length of "All You Need is Love" thinking about how much better she would have photographed the event. Then she became furious with herself. She didn't want to care about wedding photography. She didn't want to possess her own arsenal of techniques. It was a terrible affront to her personhood that she now had wedding photography standards that elicited negative judgments when she saw them violated. She was so over this day. She wished she had another apple to throw and get out her frustration, but the next closest piece of fruit was a pear that was just out of reach, hanging on the other side of her aunt's head.

Josie saw Landon in the back of the crowd, passing out pills to a guy in a tank top. She saw her dad in a rear corner seat, drinking directly from a bottle of Tequila. And she saw Nate. Normally the sight of him calmed her down. Normally, she thought of him as the only consistent good in her life. But right now, his face made her angry. As her mom and Jacque said their absurd wedding vows, quoting Kahlil Gibran's *The Prophet*, Neil Diamond lyrics, and internet meme quotes like the saccharine and nonsensical "every day is the best day of your life," the real source of Josie's annoyance with Nate dawned on her. She was surprised to discover what it was.

The interminably long ceremony subsided. The local yoga instructor acting as officiant pronounced Nicki and Jacque as "woman and husband" and the folding chairs were cleared out to turn the lawn into a dance floor.

An inconsistent Bluetooth speaker played Jacque's personal playlist of international music. The hippie contingent let loose, dancing like they were possessed by summoned spirits.

Josie helped the caterers set up their all-vegetarian platters in the kitchen because she wanted to avoid the revelry. Nate approached her, looking to have a normal conversation and stay away from every other person there, but Josie shrugged him off.

"Not now, I'm busy," she told him, shuffling trays of tofu around the countertop.

She was not ready to say what she wanted to say.

Discouraged, confused, and practically falling asleep, Nate turned away, found a spare folding chair in the crowd, sat down, and closed his eyes.

Josie helped carry plates of food to the picnic blankets on the ground which served as tables at this event. She noticed that Nate had fallen asleep and she was grateful.

She felt less grateful for the behavior of her father. He was vomiting in the middle of the yard, sending hippies running away in terror during an Indian dance that was a little too culturally appropriated for Josie's tastes. At least he disrupted the dance.

Josie ran over to Lou.

"Are you okay?"

"Fine, fine," he said, thoroughly drunk. "I don't care that your mom's getting married. It doesn't break my heart. It doesn't make me sad."

"Oh Dad," said Josie.

Nicki entered their circle, disrupting the vomit scented moment of denial.

"How dare you! Why did you come here? All you wanted to do is ruin my wedding! You got puke all over Wilhelm's feet!" She indicated a nearby blonde bearded man who had been dancing barefoot. He cleaned vomit out from between his toes with a napkin.

"You invited me!" said Lou. "Clearly you wanted to get one last look at what you'd be missing!"

"I invited you because I wanted you to feel bad!" said Nicki.

"Well it worked! And I came because I wanted you to feel bad too!"

"Well I do!"

"Good!"

"I'm glad you feel bad!"

"I'm glad *you* feel bad!"

Just like old times, thought Josie.

Everyone had stopped what they were doing. They all watched the bickering exes in the middle of the backyard. Even Landon and his revolving assortment of customers had paused their exchange of cash and pills to watch the fight. Josie realized that she was caught in the crossfire of the crowd's stares. It was mortifying.

Nate's eyes were open. Hard to sleep amidst that commotion. He looked over at Josie with heartbreaking sympathy.

"I know you're gonna miss this!" said Josie's dad, as he pulled down his pants and flashed the entire crowd.

And... that was about enough for Josie. She stormed into the house, went to her bedroom, and locked the door behind her.

A knock followed shortly after.

"It's me," said Nate from the hall.

Josie forced herself up and unlocked the door. She pulled flowers from her filthy hair as he entered the room.

"You alright?" he asked.

"No," she said.

"This is a tough day for you," he said. "It's okay to feel angry. Or sad."

"When are we going to get married?" she said.

That took Nate by surprise.

"What?" he said, recalibrating, clearly afraid but trying not to let Josie see it.

"It's been like four years since you told me you wanted to marry me. Is it ever gonna happen?"

"I...," he searched for words very carefully. Josie stared at him, unblinking. She was in no mood for tiptoeing. She wanted this discussion to be direct.

He said, "I mean of course I want to, eventually, but... when did we...? What conversation are you referring to?"

"The conversation where I said, 'let's not have a wedding when we get married,' and you agreed. Which to me, implied that you wanted to marry me."

It was a surprise to Josie that this had been eating away at her in some unacknowledged place. But now that they were having it out, she felt tremendously freed. She waited patiently as the wheels in Nate's exhausted brain turned, trying to figure out the best way to respond.

"Of course I want to be with you forever," he said.

"Okay," she said. She waited for more.

"Josie, can we have this discussion later? I'm coming off a thirteen-hour shift..."

"It's a fairly simple question. Do you want to marry me or not?"

"Yes."

"Great, then let's get married."

"It's not that simple."

"Why not?"

"I want us to be able to save up. Buy a house."

"We're almost thirty!"

"We're twenty-eight."

"That's almost thirty."

"It's two years less."

"You've been saying the same thing for years," she said. "We need to save up money. You want us to buy a house. I need to get out of this goddamn house, don't you understand! And I can't afford my own fucking apartment, so guess what? – you have to pay up and move in with me somewhere. I don't really care if we get married right away. But we have to move in together. We have to. If you want to get married before we move in together like some fucking Norman Rockwell conservative painting shit then fine, but I have to get out of here. I need to get out of this fucking house. I can't stay here one more fucking moment!"

There was a moment of quiet. Before the conversation had a chance to resume, they were interrupted by the sound of police sirens.

Josie and Nate went to the window and opened the blinds to see the backyard. Two local officers marched into the middle of the grassy dance floor, towards Josie's parents who were flinging paella at each other and yelling obscenities, Lou's pants still on the ground. The policemen did their best to separate the fighting couple. Jacque stood nearby, eating the same paella Josie's parents were using as a weapon – a strong indication of her new stepdad's moral character. In the back of the yard, Landon and his customers leaped over the high hedges that marked the property's border, instinctively running from the cops, even if they weren't there for them.

The echoes of Josie's rant against Nate reverberated in her head, overlapping with the sound of her parents screaming at each other. The horrifying similarity filled her with fear. Was she no different than her parents were? Was her future with Nate destined to devolve into the same nightly screaming match?

There was an opposing viewpoint. Occasional arguments were supposedly a perfectly normal, often healthy aspect of a relationship. Josie could not remember a single real fight with Nate in the nearly eight years they had been together. On Nate's side, it was due to his understanding, diplomatic nature. But Josie was hardly as averse to opposition as her boyfriend. She avoided fights mostly because she didn't want to be like her parents. She stuffed her frustrations so far down inside herself that she didn't know they were there and now it was blowing up in her face.

She combusted with the realization that the one safe haven of her life was not as pure as she needed it to be. Her face fell into her hands.

Nate put his hand on her back. He closed the blinds.

"We shouldn't watch this," he said. "Look. Can we talk more about all this tomorrow? I'm not trying to deflect. I'm just tired. My mind isn't in the proper place to think this all out. I swear I'll be in a better mental spot to discuss it all tomorrow."

Josie was fraught. A fire of discouragement blazed.

"Fine," she said.

In the backyard, the policemen forced Josie's dad to put on his pants, then escorted him to their squad car.

MONDAY

The next day was Monday and Josie had to go to work.

She woke up at five A.M. and by five-fifty she was on the road towards Southwest Philly, a forgotten enclave of poverty, less remarked upon than the populated swells of North and West Philly, but even more destitute. Single standing row houses sprung up among empty lots at various corners of the streets like the few remaining teeth in a decayed elderly mouth.

She parked on the dirt plot that served as the parking lot for General Stark Elementary School. She loaded her cart and dragged it through the dried mud divots to the front door. The school had an enrollment of three hundred and twenty students. This was right beyond the three hundred student cut-off where SmilePosts usually sent two photographers instead of one. But too few students at Stark bought packages to justify sending more than one photographer. Even though the school had requested classroom group photos in addition to individual shots. Josie would be taking both.

She was instructed by the overwhelmed office secretary to set up in two different locations. The group photos would be taken in the basement on a thin stairway leading to the first floor. Upon seeing the stairs, Josie couldn't imagine fitting more than four students across a single step. The overcrowded classes of thirty-five students would be stretched into long vertical rectangles. Since the SmilePosts group photo template required landscape framing, most of the pictures would be taken up by the surrounding walls, with only a thin stretch of the class in the middle. She argued this point to the secretary and was told there were no other location options.

If Josie had realized where she was going to take individual pictures, she would have spent less time debating the group spot, saving her energy. The place they had picked for her was all the way up on the third floor, about a half-mile from the group location, in what was supposedly an "unused classroom."

Josie knew a storage closet when she saw one.

This so-called "room" was not even large enough for her main light to extend the proper distance from the camera. Josie made her case to the office. The secretary didn't much care. They had nowhere else to put her in the overcrowded and underfunded building. Josie insisted her photography station simply would not fit. The secretary insisted that Kay, the salesperson, had measured the spot when she had renewed their contract for the year. Josie said that she must not have measured it properly.

Josie called George to explain the issue, while the secretary called Kay. "I can't fit where they want me to," Josie told George. "It won't work. There's not enough space. I'll suffocate in here George. I'll be blinded by the main light which will be touching my face!"

George told her to hold because Kay was calling on the other line.

When he returned to the call he said, "Look Josie, we're gonna have to make it work today, maybe we can change it next year, maybe we can figure something else out, Kay will talk to them about next year, nothing we can do today, gotta make it work, can't lose the account."

Josie hung up and looked at the secretary, who was too tired to feel satisfied by her victory. "The first class will be arriving for group photos at seven-forty-five," she said.

"It's seven-fifteen now," said Josie.

"Yes," said the secretary.

"I'm supposed to start at eight-fifteen," said Josie.

"First individual pictures are at eight-fifteen," said the secretary. "Group pics start at seven-forty-five."

Josie called George again.

"George, I'm going to have to run four flights of stairs up and down on opposite sides of the building and I'm not going to have any time to set up my equipment, which won't fit anyway, and there's no way one person can possibly make this work."

"Okay, calm down. Take a breath," said George, in an odd reversal of the usual script. "Let me see if I can get you any help."

He called back five minutes later. Josie was already dripping with sweat from setting up her equipment as quickly as possible in an unventilated closet. "Josie I'm really sorry," he said, "but two people called out sick today and it's a crazy busy day and every single person is going to be on camera, even me, so you'll have to get through the day yourself, do your best."

Josie wasn't sure if she wanted to cry or punch someone. Maybe both. Though what she really wanted was to leave all of her equipment where it was, walk out of the school, and drive away, far away from everything, deep into the Appalachian Mountains and perhaps further, leaving it all behind, never to return.

But, of course, she didn't leave. She stayed. And it was the worst day she had experienced in seven years of working at SmilePosts.

By the end of the day, her legs ached from a dozen sprints up and down the four flights of stairs. The run across the building was extra hazardous during the lunch and recess stretch from eleven to two, when the halls overflowed with students completely uninterested in clearing a path for her. She weaved in and out of children's bodies, both small and strikingly large.

The classes were an average size of thirty-five students. When they arrived for their group pictures, chatting away, she had to scream at the top of her lungs to be acknowledged. The teachers, nearly comatose, were of little help.

After much struggle to arrange the children in height order on the staircase – physically having to grab their shoulders and force them into place because there was no time for patience, all her attempts at decorum quickly disintegrating on this hellish day, she eventually snapped a few terrible photos in which two thirds of the kids weren't smiling and the other third weren't looking at the camera. It was the best she was going to do. She then sprinted back up to the third floor to take individual photos of a different class, who were impatiently waiting in the hall.

She stuffed herself into the back of the closet, inviting in one child at a time for their picture. Many of them complained of the heat in the stuffy room, which was getting ever hotter from the overheated lights, with no place for the heat to escape. A majority of the pictures were tainted by beads of sweat glistening on the children's foreheads. Josie herself was drenched and stinking with sweat, but there was little she could do about it.

Around noon the secretary stopped by to tell her that she was a half hour behind schedule and needed to pick up the pace.

"I can't go any faster than I'm going," said Josie, with more attitude than she should have. Her patience reserves were depleted.

The secretary rolled her eyes and walked away.

Though she skipped taking a lunch, and was starving, and had to pee for about four hours before she finally broke down and ran to the bathroom, Josie only got further behind schedule. The classroom groups got all the more restless and impossible to gather after recess. Then, at one point, Josie arrived back on the third floor to find a first grader had stolen her box of combs from where it was tucked away in the storage closet. He threw the combs everywhere, much to the hilarity of his fellow students. He completely ignored his screaming teacher. It was chaos. It was *Apocalypse Now*. Josie could practically hear "The End" by The Doors playing faintly in the background.

The comb madness was nothing compared to the crushing events of her next trip to the basement.

She huffed and puffed down the stairs, her lungs collapsing in on themselves, only to find that her camera was missing. For time-saving necessity she had left the Nikon D300 used for group photos unguarded in the basement. Now it was gone.

"Where is it?" she screamed at the waiting fourth graders. They looked at her for a moment, then resumed talking.

She ran to the office. She told the secretary that someone had stolen her camera. Not only was it worth hundreds of dollars, but more importantly to Josie, it contained the memory card with all of the day's already taken group pictures. The thought of having to retake those photos was enough to make her run back up the stairs, climb onto the roof, and jump off.

The secretary seemed annoyed with Josie, as if it was her fault the camera had been stolen. She made a school wide announcement over the loudspeaker, demanding the camera be returned, threatening every student with no recess if it wasn't.

Josie ran back upstairs to take individual pictures. There was an ever-expanding hallway crowd of exasperated teachers and wild students. Josie tried, futilely, to make a dent in the line, while she waited for word on the group camera, rather hopeless of the prospects. Her energy turned to ash with every passing moment.

The secretary stopped by fifteen minutes later.

Miraculously, she held the Nikon D300.

"Here," she said, handing it to Josie. "You're an hour behind schedule. Kids get dismissed at three-fifteen." It was one-forty-three.

"Okay," said Josie.

(When she finally got back to the office that evening, George reviewed Josie's pictures and, alongside the group photos, found several images of a child's bare buttocks on the memory card.)

Josie left the school at four-thirty. She broke down all her equipment and carried it to the car, cripplingly exhausted, her muscles sore, having failed to photograph the final two classes on the schedule. She called George to tell him that she couldn't finish. He said, "it's okay, we'll go back." She said, "*I'm* not going back," and hung up without saying goodbye.

She stopped by the school's office on the way out. She told the secretary that SmilePosts would send someone to finish the final classes. She was handed a scorecard of one-star ratings, with comments like "terrible job, she didn't get to all the classes" and "photographer was rude."

"Thank you, have a good day," Josie said with a murderous smile. She got into her car and pulled into bumper-to-bumper rush hour traffic.

It would take her an hour and a half to get back to the SmilePosts office.

Josie had received a missed call and a follow up text from Nate at 4:05 and 4:07, respectively. She was breaking down her equipment when he called and had nearly answered, but decided she wasn't in the right frame of mind. She needed to emotionally settle first.

It had been a rough day and it was going to be an important talk.

Crawling at ten miles an hour, locked in traffic on the Schuylkill expressway, just rounding past the Philadelphia Art Museum despite having already been in the car for twenty minutes, the clock inching to five P.M., Josie decided that the day had left an irreducible impact. She knew she wasn't going to feel clear at any point until she went to sleep that night. She needed to push the talk with Nate until tomorrow.

She used Siri to text him back.

"In traffic, driving back to the office," she said, the phone transcribing her voice. "Sorry, long day. Talk tomorrow."

He didn't respond. He was strict about not texting her back while she was driving. He was probably mad at her for texting him from the road, even if she did use Siri.

When Josie slogged into the office at 6:07 as the sun began to set, filled with a thick haze of irritation, carrying her thin money bag with the day's few purchased packages, the building was almost empty.

The entire upstairs office was cleared out and the only people left in the photographer room were George and Dee, as expected, and unexpectedly, Rita.

"There she is," said Rita, speaking with way too much enthusiasm for someone who was in the SmilePosts office past six.

"We hear you had a rough one," said Dee. "Let us help with your paperwork."

"Thanks for hanging in there today," said George. "You're a trooper. I'll take your group pictures."

"Here, I can drop your money bag in the safe," said Rita.

Josie knew that George and Dee were assisting with the paperwork because they were desperate to go home themselves and couldn't leave until all of the day's jobs were complete. She was happy to let them do her work for her. Why Rita was still there was a total mystery.

She followed Rita to the safe.

"Why are you here?"

"Heard you had a tough day. Wanted to help," said Rita.

"That's not the reason. You're not that generous," said Josie.

"You're right. I stayed to get a taste of your trademark kindness and appreciation. Glad to say I'm not disappointed."

Josie was too tired for comedic banter.

"Rita," she said.

Rita dropped the money bag in the safe and turned to Josie.

"Look. Today's my last day," said Rita.

"What?"

"I got another job. At this art supply store in Dresher. Pays about the same as here but it's full time. And there's benefits. And I get a twenty percent discount which is nice. It'll save me money on painting supplies."

Josie didn't remember that Rita painted but she didn't want to admit that out loud. Her own failings as a friend would hurt her case of indignation.

"Just like that, you're leaving," said Josie.

"I wanted to stay and tell you. And say goodbye. Although we'll still definitely hang out. We'll have to get together more outside of work."

Josie felt deeply saddened by this news. So, of course, she expressed herself in anger.

"How long have you known about this?" she asked, a prosecutor out for blood.

"A couple of days," said Rita. "They wanted me to start right away and George was nice enough to let me go without two weeks' notice. I also didn't want to make a big deal 'cause I didn't want one of those goodbye parties we always throw for a leaving veteran. The last thing my body needs is to be eating a bunch of cake right now."

She waited for Josie to laugh. Or at least smile. She didn't.

"Anyway," continued Rita, "I don't like attention."

"Pretty fucking awful of you to do this. Leave with no warning," said Josie.

"Josie."

"So selfish of you."

Rita was hurt. She knew that her leaving couldn't possibly be the real source of Josie's nastiness, but it still sucked to have a friend talk to her that way.

"Why are you being like this?" said Rita. "I know you had a rough day, but Jesus."

"I'm not being like anything."

"You are. And you of all people. You want to leave this job more than anyone. Or at least you say you do."

"I do..." said Josie, disgusted by how little confidence she could inject into her assertion.

"So why can't you support me and be a friend?" said Rita.

"You're my best friend here. That's why I'm pissed at you."

"I thought Blake was."

"What?" said Josie.

"Isn't Blake your best work friend? You guys are always talking and texting."

"No. You are," said Josie, confused by the turn the conversation had taken.

"Okay. If you say so," said Rita.

Do people think there's something between me and Blake? Josie wondered. She pushed the thought aside.

Her phone rang. It was Nate again. She sent it to voicemail.

"Josie, what's the matter?" asked Rita.

Nate texted immediately. "Are you still at the office?" he said.

She wrote back, "Let's talk tomorrow."

"You're making me nervous," he responded.

"Are you okay?" said Rita.

Josie looked at Rita. She looked at her phone. She decided to ignore both. She couldn't deal with any of this right now.

She marched back towards George who was just coming across the butt photos on the memory card.

"Uh Josie?" he said.

"I have to go," said Josie.

She grabbed her paperwork for Tuesday and walked out the door, not bothering to complete her job from that day, leaving all the work for George, Dee, and perhaps Rita.

She'd had enough of that godforsaken Monday.

When Josie parked outside of her house, she saw that Nate's car was there waiting for her.

"Shit," she said.

Nate was in her room. Nicki had let him in.

"Hey. Sorry. We really need to talk," he said. "I don't want to let this fight fester."

"Yesterday you said you were too tired to talk and I listened to you. Why can't you listen to me today?" she said.

"I'm sorry, I can't let this go. There's something I need to say."

Nate dropped down to one knee. He reached into his pocket and pulled out an engagement ring.

"Will you marry me?"

Josie stared at him, processing. She put down her backpack.

"Are we going to move in together?" she said.

Nate, frozen on one knee, holding out the ring, was thrown off by the disconnect between Josie's cold reaction and the happy response he had imagined he would receive.

"Yeah, of course. Eventually," he said.

"Eventually," she parroted back to him.

"Yeah. We'll get married. We'll save up money. We'll buy a house. We'll move in together."

"You want to get married and not immediately move in together?"

"No. You're misunderstanding," he said, starting to feel awkward in his kneeling position. "When we get married, I want to move in together."

"Okay great, so let's move in together."

"But... I still want to save up money for a bit."

"So you don't want to get married?"

"Yes, I do. I'm proposing. Do you not see the ring?"

"You don't want to get married. You want to get engaged. It's not the same thing."

"I do want to get married. I just want to save up money to buy a house first."

"Didn't that ring cost a lot of money?"

"Not nearly as much as a house will," he said. "I was trying to meet you in the middle."

"Exactly what every girl wants to hear during her proposal."

Nate lowered his hand, put the ring back into his pocket, and stood up.

"Look. You said you were upset because I hadn't committed to marrying you. That's what I'm doing. I want to get married. I want to be with you for the rest of my life. I'm trying to make you happy by telling you I want to get married."

"I don't care about getting married!" said Josie.

Nate stepped back, hurt, confused. "You said—"

She continued. "What I care about is getting out of this fucking house!"

Nate was completely rattled. He desperately wanted to reign the moment back in. He had wanted this to be a happy memory in their lives and it was becoming anything but.

"Josie, I love you," he said.

"Jesus fucking Christ!" said Josie.

"Not the response I was looking for," said Nate.

They stood there in oppressive silence for an interminable stretch of time.

Josie sighed. She sat on the bed, her heated explosion at an end. On to anger's abandonment and the chill it leaves behind.

"I'm sorry," she said. "I'm really tired. I had a terrible day."

Normally, Nate would empathetically ask her what had happened, but he was not in the mood. He waited for her to resume.

"I'm not in the right mental place," she said. "Can we please talk more tomorrow?"

"Okay," he said, feeling the curve of the ring in his pocket with his index finger. "We'll talk tomorrow. Get some rest."

He turned and left.

Josie lay down on her bed and closed her eyes. It was her first moment of inaction in nearly fourteen hours. She could feel her system shutting down. Unfiltered thoughts flowed from the loosened grip on her consciousness.

There was an immersive dose of doubt, filling the room like rising water. It drowned her from contradictory directions. Fear that she had reacted inhumanely to Nate's proposal, an act of masochism as much as sadism, torturing them both for no good reason. Her conscience scolding her for saying no and defiling a special moment. Uncertainty rushing in from an opposing side about Nate and marriage and everything she had held true. A disconcerting relief at ignoring the proposal. She questioned her assumptions of happiness. Maybe she didn't want to get married to Nate. Maybe she didn't want to get married at all. All her fortifications crumbled, her axis spun on end.

How was she supposed to act when there was no way of being certain what she wanted?

While Josie was lying in bed at her mom's house, questioning her entire life, I was in my own bed, at my own parents' house, thinking about Josie.

She had been at the forefront of my mind for the previous two weeks, ever since our long day together. For a while, I expected my new feelings for her to fade as abruptly as they had appeared, but that expectation had lost all legitimacy a few hours earlier that Monday.

That afternoon I had looked at the schedule and seen that we were working together the next day.

I had felt a sheer rush of anticipatory exhilaration that was normally reserved for the sight of Hailey's name. And I knew that my feelings were real and were going nowhere.

All night I had been locked in an internal struggle. The thought of telling Josie how I felt and keeping it secret traded heavyweight blows. It was a true debate, unlike any I had ever had regarding my crush on Hailey, because I never thought Hailey was a legitimate choice for my future wife. Josie, on the other hand, seemed like someone I could be genuinely happy with. The threat of rejection and humiliation seemed like it might be worth taking for the potential reward. Even though Josie was in a long-term relationship and I would be kind of a homewrecker.

I thought a lot about *The Office*, the popular NBC sitcom I had watched multiple times on Netflix. I mused over the great love story of Jim and Pam. Pam had a fiancé when the show began (who was, admittedly, a jerk) and Jim dated Karen for a while (who was very nice) but these other relationships never eclipsed the fact that Jim and Pam were the ideal match. I couldn't help but egotistically equate my own situation with the narrative that *The Office* writers had whipped up. Maybe Josie was my Pam. I aligned my new crush on Josie with the show's storylines and wondered whether us ending up together was what the writers had intended all along, though it was real life and there were no writers and I didn't believe in destiny.

As I lay in bed that Monday night, I rehearsed a revelation speech to Josie with unconscious effort. It was the kind of monologue that Billy Crystal shouted at Meg Ryan in *When Harry Met Sally...* as Auld Lang Syne rang in the new year, romantically declaring that "when you realize you want to spend the rest of your life with somebody, you want the rest of your life to start as soon as possible." My speech included various poetic verses on the qualities of Josie's character and sappy lines about my heart melting in her presence. Spinning through my head, the speech went through various incarnations, from too much to too little and back again, all while I felt absolutely no confidence that I would be brave enough to deliver it.

And then Tuesday came.

TUESDAY

"Morning," said Josie, seeming rather drained, as we stepped out of our cars.

We were at Martin Van Buren Middle School in Kennett Square, an area in far Southeastern PA near the border of Delaware, known nationally for growing half of the United States' supply of mushrooms and known locally for the pervasive smell of gym socks that the mushrooms give off. It truly is an inescapable odor anywhere in Kennett Square. It's hard to imagine why anyone not directly making money from the mushrooms would choose to live there. Each time you pull into Kennett, the pungent stank pushes its way past your preemptively closed windows, overpowering the thin glass to entrench itself in your car seats for at least a week after you've been there. It's an awful smell. It's the unavoidable bully in the halls of Van Buren Middle School. You cannot escape the nasal taunts no matter where you hide.

"God it smells terrible," I said to Josie. "You never get used to it."

Josie nodded in assent, but said nothing. There was definitely something off with her. She was unusually quiet. I felt crushed that she didn't want to talk to me. My romantic speech plans were already plummeting in a tailspin.

We were greeted by the other SmilePosts co-workers photographing at the high-enrollment school that day. Bonnie was there, as well as newbies Mike, Quame, and Jade.

"Smells like shit," said Mike. "What the hell is that?"

Now there was the proper reaction.

We set up in the gym, trapped in an olfactory cocktail of mushroom aromas and pubescent body odor. Mike gagged as he unfurled his background.

"Look at Mike," I said to Josie, hoping to join together in mockery of his retching.

"Yeah," said Josie. It was unclear if she knew what she was agreeing with. She was trapped in her own thoughts.

She was standing right next to me and I missed her.

Josie, for her part, didn't realize that she was ignoring me. She was thinking about Nate. And her life. She was so awash in stifling, saddening doubt that she didn't particularly notice the terrible smell of the mushrooms. Well, maybe a little bit. It was impossible to not notice that smell at all.

She went through the motions of setting up her equipment and later taking the photos, barely present. Her lack of mindfulness hardly affected the quality of the pictures. At this point, the portrait process was automatic and needed little assistance from her conscious mind. On autopilot,

GREAT BIG SMILE 395

she told each child to stand on the feet and tip their head and smile, while her mind focused on the more pressing issue of her hopeless future.

A couple of hours into the day, I approached her during a short break.

"Hey, are you okay?" I asked.

"Yeah, I'm fine," she said reflexively.

"I'm here if you need to talk about anything," I said.

She stopped. She looked at me, thoughtfully.

"Thanks Blake," she said.

I didn't know it, but inside she was wondering whether I was the only person she really liked at the present. And wondering further what exactly that meant.

That was when we first heard the alarm.

It was an unusual, grating sound, scary before we even knew what it indicated.

A full class of students who had just entered the gym all froze. Terror seized their faces. They knew what the alarm meant, while we didn't.

"Okay, don't panic," their teacher Mrs. Hartley said, looking panicked herself but trying to remain calm.

The decibel level in the gym increased a hundred-fold. The shrieks of frightened thirteen-year-olds pinpricked our ears.

A second class, scheduled to arrive at the same time slot, ran into the gym from the hall, increasing the fear and noise further.

Josie and I looked at each other. Something was obviously very wrong.

Mrs. Hartley shouted several times over the alarm and the screaming. "Everyone listen. Everyone listen! EVERYONE LISTEN! PLEASE!"

Finally, enough children quieted down that she could be heard. We SmilePosts photographers listened eagerly along with the students, all tense, all scared.

"Everyone listen please," said Mrs. Hartley, attempting to project authority, while talking quickly and anxiously. "This is a lockdown procedure. Please everyone gather on the far wall of the gym. Miss Unwager,

Mr. Levin, and I will guard the doors," she said, indicating the second class's trembling young teacher, who was holding back tears, and the elderly gym teacher, who was busy locking all points of entry to the gym.

"Everyone remember our procedures," said Mrs. Hartley. "We are to remain quiet and in place until the lockdown is over. We don't know exactly what's happening right now—"

She was interrupted by a break in the alarm over the loudspeaker system.

"Attention everyone," someone, presumably the principal, said over the loudspeaker. "Lockdown with intruder. I repeat, lockdown with intruder. This is not a drill. Remain in place. Lock all windows and doors. Remain in classrooms at this time." Then the alarm resumed.

The kids started screaming and chattering again, the nervous energy boiling over.

"Everyone please!" shouted Mrs. Hartley several more times until she was able to regain some semblance of control. "Miss Unwager and I need to take role call as procedure." She began with her own class, since Miss Unwager was unable to pull herself together to talk.

In the tentative quiet, we all listened for a sound that we hoped not to hear. A terrifying bang that would eclipse the roll call and the clanging alarm. Praying the sound would never come, we waited on edge for a gunshot. We couldn't help it. There had been so many horrifying news stories over the years of school shootings. Far too many. And now we were in lockdown in Kennett Square and we feared for our lives, remembering all of the tragic television coverage, all of the clips of survivors crying, retelling the stories of their classmates' untimely deaths at the hands of disturbed peers.

We stood there, petrified, wanting to run, bolt, sprint, escape in some way, our survival instincts kicking into high gear, but more scared of leaving the contained gym for whatever was happening in the halls, thinking that the lockdown procedure must exist for a reason, must be based on some predication of safety and survival, we hoped. I thought about conversations I'd had with co-workers in the past, joking and debating about which parts of our equipment would work as weapons in case of such an emergency. Generally, the consensus was that the metal poles which screwed together to construct the monopod would be optimum. But right then, unscrewing the monopod to acquire a weapon never entered my mind. I was frozen in place with everyone else. I saw Bonnie crying, talking to someone on her cell phone, probably her husband or one of her kids, maybe telling them she loved them in case she never saw them again.

I looked down. Josie was holding my hand. Gripping it. I was so scared that I hadn't felt her fingers clasp around my own. We looked at each other, not turning our eyes away. Both shaking. Both unsure what to do or say.

Finally, she broke the silence between us. "I bet it's some kid who couldn't take one more day of this fucking awful smell," she said.

I smiled through trembling lips.

"It really does smell like shit," I said. And then I added, "I'm in love with you."

She gripped my hand harder. She looked at me. I continued.

"I don't know what's gonna happen. I wanted to say it. Josie, I think you're the most wonderful, smart, funny, compassionate person I've ever met. There's no one I'm happier to be around. If we get through this, I feel like we could make each other happy for the rest of our lives. You're the person I want to wake up next to every morning. You're the one I want to grow old with. Josie... I know you have a boyfriend. But I think if you consider the possibility—"

"Shut up," she said.

I got quiet.

"You had me at 'smells like shit.' You had me at 'smells like shit.'"

She pulled me in close and she kissed me.

TEN
THE MIDDLE

OKAY. I ADMIT IT. That never happened.

The previous chapter, like much of what I've written, was a mixture of true hearsay, patchwork half-memory, inflated fact, re-sculpted reality, and outright fiction.

There was no dramatic school lockdown. No climactic romantic dialogue that borrowed heavily from *Jerry Maguire*. No kiss.

Josie wasn't even in Kennett Square with me the last time I photographed there. The mushrooms, however, do smell as bad as described.

I felt grimy exploiting the tragedy and terror of school shootings for the sake of making my narrative more exciting, but it's what my college professors would have wanted.

My screenwriting teachers always taught me to "raise the stakes." Expand conflict and maximize the unexpected, they preached. Keep a person in the audience on their toes. Inflate the drama, put the protagonist in maximum peril, make disparate solutions all seem impossible, until at the very last moment, with a sigh of relief, everything works out in a satisfying culmination. Avoid boredom and tell a good story, by any means necessary. As long as those means fall within the confines of the tried and true three-act movie structure, which we were told to follow unquestioningly in every script we ever wrote. "This is what the audience wants," the professors said.

Real life rarely unfolds in a three-act structure.

I have tried to capture some true essence of my life and the lives around me in these pages, but much of what I have written is speculation, at best.

I knew that Linda was divorced but I possessed no knowledge of her ex-husband or her personal life. I made it all up, including her infertility. It served the story.

I knew that Ed had a wife and two boys, but I invented their personalities and family dynamics. Josie and I used to think we detected a flirtation between Ed and Linda, but we could have been imagining things. Maybe they were just friends.

Ethan and Dana did really date for a while, but I don't know what went on between them in their private hours or why they broke up.

The story of Ethan getting Linda pregnant was a bit of "raising the stakes," that was purely fictional. I added it for the sake of drama.

A couple of years ago, Josie saw on Facebook that Linda was pregnant. She was long gone from SmilePosts at that point. Presumably, the father was the guy who had his arm around her in the photo.

Ethan was, in all truth, fired from SmilePosts because of his terrible pictures and lack of effort. He was also, in reality, kind of an asshole. Yet most of us enjoyed his company, despite his selfishness and ego. Mostly because he was funny.

I like to think that I know Josie better than the others, having gleaned more of the facts of her life from our conversations over the years. We've been close friends. That's real.

Even so, the chapters from her perspective were largely conjecture. My descriptions of her life went far beyond the boundaries of my knowledge. It was guesswork and invention, it's true, but also an honest attempt to explore the viewpoint of a person I care about.

The human mind has an automatic tendency to fill in gaps of information. This is true on a perceptual level and a narrative one. We look at an optical illusion and we might see a shape or color that's not actually there, our brain formulating a non-existent pattern. A similar thing happens with our interpretation of people. You meet someone and you form an impression of who they are based on the limited information you have. Then, as you spend more time with them and learn more, your impression expands and changes, but it always feels complete. You always feel like you know who they are, when, in truth, you know nothing of the sort.

Our brains provide answers. Sometimes these answers are wrong, and they're almost always incomplete, but the mind absolutely cannot abide gaps.

We don't do well with ambiguity. Which is most of life.

I'm sure that many of the thoughts I put into the minds of my coworkers reflected my own worries and ideas more than their own. And I know that several scenes I placed others in were remixes of experiences from my own life. I was filling in the gaps.

But despite it all, I tried my best to portray these people in an accurate way, taking the scientific sampling of my interactions with them and expanding it to reflect the truth of their personalities, as best I could.

It's possible I got them completely wrong.

I like to think my portrayals are similar to the school portraits I've been taking for years. They are crucially limited in their depictions of the people they feature. The posture is forced, the smile unnatural to some. They are manipulated and imperfect, but still a record of a person as they were in that moment. Change is inevitable and swift, misinterpretation expected. But some truth always remains.

📷

Josie and I really did have the long day of conversation I described in chapter seven. And I did start to question whether I should love her instead of Hailey.

But my determination to say something was rather slower in developing than I portrayed it. The fall season came to an end and the question lingered in my mind. I thought about Josie in a new way every time we talked. She told me about her mom's wedding, which she said had "sucked," but she did not elaborate on the specifics of the suckage. She certainly didn't mention any conflict with Nate. I made up their relationship struggles to justify a conclusion in which Josie and I ended up together.

This past winter break, submitting to the nagging texts of my college friend Stu who had recently moved out to L.A., I took my first ever trip to Hollywood. As the flight approached, I got excited. I thought that perhaps this was a turning point. I would fall in love with the city and decide to move there, taking the necessary steps to begin my future in earnest, finally moving on from the odd life layover of my career at SmilePosts.

In the air, passing across the continental United States, I watched a Jason Segel comedy, I read a few chapters of *The Unbearable Lightness of Being*, and I thought about Josie. Daydreaming about Josie was crucially different from daydreaming about Hailey. My crush on Hailey was an anxious experience, interspersed with highs born of uncertainty. It was the thrill of skating on thin ice as the cracks spread below, knowing if you stood too long in one place you would plummet into the icy waters. The risk was often the source of the thrill. Thinking about Josie, in contrast, was a comfort. It was the warm fireplace you lay in front of, wrapped in a soft blanket, relaxing after a cold day outdoors. (For the record, I've never had a fireplace, nor do I know how to ice skate.)

I touched down at LAX and Stu picked me up in his 1998 Ford Taurus. I spent four days exploring the City of Angels, taking in the warm weather, the crowded hiking trails in the hills of Griffith Park, and the surprising grime of Hollywood Boulevard. All the while, my emotional fortification imploded inside me with a dynamite blast of panic and a cool down period of depression.

There was something in the reality of Los Angeles that was crushing. This dream factory of my imagination, this place that had produced *The Godfather* and *It's a Wonderful Life* and *Back to the Future*, classic films that existed in an aura of golden light in my mind, was a real place, where real people lived, grinding away at living, buying groceries and filling cars with gas like anywhere else, except there the gas was over four dollars a gallon. I pictured myself out in L.A., struggling to survive, struggling to stand out amongst the thousands of people with similar dreams. Floundering in that sun-dappled desert with its expensive arboreal makeover. At SmilePosts, I could at least feel like a top-quality employee, whereas in L.A. I would be another schmo dreaming of a glory that I would probably never find. I felt a rush of irrational homesickness as if I'd already been gone for years. The thought of leaving my family and my hometown, the only place I had ever known, elicited a wave of sadness I could not contain. All I wanted was to go home and lie down in my own bed and forget the world.

On the flight back to Philly, I thought again about Josie. I imagined her in my arms. This time, the dream was less theoretical. I wanted to take action. I wanted to set my life onto at least one positive path. In that moment of so much uncertainty, she was the only thing I felt sure I wanted.

We returned for spring training. Josie and I joked and laughed as we learned the new spring program. This year's setup included a fake windowsill that the children leaned their chins against, looking out from the façade of a Cape Cod living room, a box of faux flowers hanging below the window. It was a tableau that would seem casually classist when we took it to inner city Philadelphia.

Every day I felt closer to telling Josie how I felt, shocked by my own burgeoning certainty that I would say something, surprised I wasn't more petrified by the possibility.

On the last afternoon of training, I found myself alone with Josie in the parking lot, each of us loading our cars with the equipment we had left in the office over winter break. There were a couple of fall picture days that had been rescheduled for spring due to snow day cancellations. We both had jobs the next day.

As I loaded the cases into my car, I felt an eruption coming. Just like that, I was going to tell her how I felt, consequences be damned. Just like that, a crucial moment in my life was going to occur. I wasn't in control. The speech dictated itself. The words impelled my mouth to speak, refusing to linger inside any longer.

"Josie," I said.

"Yeah?" she said.

And then I said... well I don't remember the exact words, to be honest. All dialogue of recollection is an act of paraphrasing, of course. Any conversations I've attempted to recreate are my own version of what was spoken. It's not like I walk around with a tape recorder.

I said...

I said...

Hmmm. I find myself not wanting to share what I said. Not even a paraphrased version. It's embarrassing. I tried to orate with a romantic speech, the kind of monologue you would hear in a movie's third act. But it felt fake and forced from the start. Josie was unpleasantly surprised by the revelation of my feelings for her. The distaste was plain in her expression from my first words. I kept talking on and on because it was scarier to stop talking and hear the rejection I knew was coming. As I spoke on, my testament to our undeniable match withered, losing all steam and conviction as it went. Nervously I prattled on, not knowing how to hit the brakes. In the grip of that terrible expanding awkwardness, I started thinking about Hailey, started longing for Hailey, my crush on her snapped back into its place of out-of-reach surety, and all I wanted was for this interminable mistaken moment to end so that I could run back into the building and catch a glimpse of Hailey's pretty freckled face before she went home.

When I finally silenced myself, Josie was quiet and short in her response.

She said, as kindly as she could, that she didn't feel the same way about me. She said she was sorry, though she didn't seem sorry. Mostly she seemed uncomfortable, eager to get as far away from me as possible.

I didn't blame her.

Josie and I haven't talked since.

The next day, while photographing at Upper Wissahocken Elementary, I ran into the bathroom and cried. I had lost a friendship and I had lost my hope for fulfilled love.

I got home that day and I started writing all of this, thinking that expressing myself on paper might help me feel better.

Maybe it has. I don't know.

We all view our lives through a narrative framing that doesn't truly exist. I'm probably more literal about it than most people. I've watched too many movies.

I remember a moment with my college girlfriend, shortly after our first kiss, when we held each other in that uncomfortable dormitory bed and stopped talking, content in the quiet sound of each other's breath. I looked out the window, at the tree branches beyond the glass, and from another room somewhere in the building I heard the faint sound of Mariah Carey's "Always Be My Baby." And I thought, "roll the credits." End it right here, don't make me go on to another moment. This is the moment. This is the moment that the movie would end.

And then it occurred to me, for the first time, about the falseness of endings. In stories, a character comes to some point of fulfillment or tragedy or hope, and the screen cuts to black or the final page is turned. The writer leaves you at a moment of maximum impact. Even unsatisfactory endings are false because they are able to call the narrative quits when there's nowhere good to take it. Everything comes to a halt and the story is over.

Real life does not feature such endings. Because life is not a story.

Life does not contain a story's balanced rhythms or its organized brackets, which limit the scope and scale, funneling the content into something conceivable.

I am not a character in a story. I am not graced with dramatic climactic kisses that cut to the end credits, while a quirky song or a wistful composition plays as the names of contributors scroll by.

Even if Josie had wanted to leave Nate and date me following my histrionic speech, we couldn't have immediately suspended our existence, leaving us eternally in this moment of culmination and happiness. We would have moved on from that special moment and dealt with the reality of a relationship. Its joys, but also its drawbacks and conflicts. Maybe in the long run (or the short run), our coupling would have fallen apart and we would have broken up, retroactively sullying the purity of that moment when she leaned in to kiss me for the first time.

Real life is not gracious enough to end after an exceptional experience.

Real life is a perpetual middle.

No one remembers life's beginning. No one remembers being conceived, popping into genetic existence as their father's most vigorous sperm burrows into their mother's anxiously waiting egg. No one recalls sliding down the birth canal, vacuumed out of their comforting watery womb, crashing into the unpleasant air.

I don't know if anyone experiences life's end. I have no way of confirming if victims of various violent deaths or slow sufferers of deadly diseases or the excessively elderly expiring from natural causes feel a sonic boom of departure or a slow ethereal fade. Maybe death is like falling asleep. You always remember waiting to fall asleep, on the brink of unconsciousness, but you never experience that key moment of transition. Death looms at the end, but without any certainty or substantiality, a known mystery at best, a blank void at worst.

All that we ever know is middle.

At any point in my life, I'm always hovering between where things began and where they might conclude. Always waiting for something to come and wishing something hadn't left. Occasionally I find moments of purity, moments I would be happy to remain in, only to watch those moments fade away, refusing to linger, refusing to cut to the credits.

Always in the middle. Unable to escape the middle.
Because life is not a story.
Still.
A book is a story.
And a story needs an ending.

VI.
BLAKE
(CONTINUED)

BLAKE SITS on the child-sized toilet at Upper Wissahocken Elementary, wiping the tears away from his eyes with the base of his palm, steadily ignoring a first grader's increasingly incensed accusation of "are you pooping in there?" on the other side of the stall door.

"I deserve her," Blake had said out loud to himself before the poop police interrupted his privacy. He thinks back on this statement of romantic injustice which has poured out of him, almost unconsciously, along with the tears.

He's not sure who particularly the "her" referred to.

Did he mean Josie? Hailey?

Did he mean Sarah, his college ex-girlfriend who he rarely spoke of to anyone, but who he thought about almost every day?

Maybe "her" did not refer to any girl in particular. Maybe it was a more ambiguous pronoun, the encapsulation of twenty-eight years of unfulfilled wanting. "Her" was the impossible symbol of the perfect match he dreamed of – a woman so obviously meant for him that there could be no denial of their united destiny.

He craves love so badly and it hurts so much being unable to find it. For all of his dreams of creative success and adulation, he thinks that love is the only thing he has ever really wanted.

Blake pulls himself together, stands up and exits the stall to the shocked revelation of the first grader, who had not realized he was taunting an adult with his poop interrogation. The first grader's mouth hangs open. He is speechless and scared.

"Hi," says Blake, as friendly as he can muster in his current state.

Too late, Blake realizes that he has to pee. He can't return to the stall or use a urinal now. Not with the slack-jawed first grader standing in front of him. It's too awkward. Besides, he's already late for the next class waiting impatiently at his camera station. There's nothing to do but hold the urine inside, along with his tears.

A few hours later, Blake returns to the SmilePosts office.

The newbie co-workers he photographed with at Upper Wissahocken Elementary said nothing about his demeanor. He thinks he has effectively disguised his gloom. Until he plops down his paperwork and catches Clint's stricken stare from the candy jar at George's desk.

"Bro, are you okay? You look like shit," says Clint, with graceless sympathy, as he unwraps a bubble gum flavored Dum-Dum.

"I'm fine," Blake says, but everyone at the office is now looking at him.

Everyone, that is, except Josie. Her eyes are completely focused on her own day's paperwork.

Blake wonders if the whole office knows about the failed declaration of love he made to Josie on the previous afternoon. He can't imagine she would have told them and he sees no other way they could have found out. This logic hardly reassures him. He feels under glass, scrutinized by the others like an exotic specimen.

Clint walks up close to Blake and whispers, as if they could have any privacy after Clint's spurt of attention. "Bro, if you need anything, I'm here for you," he says. Annoyed as Blake is with Clint, he still recognizes it as a good-hearted offer from the most inexplicably consistent person in his life.

"Thanks Clint," he says appreciatively. "I'm okay," he lies.

The weeks pass. Blake and Josie see each other around the office, but they don't say a word to each other. Perhaps the others notice, perhaps they don't. No one asks Blake directly about their rift and he has no plans to raise the subject on his own.

He feels incredibly sad whenever he sees Josie and can't talk to her, but it's not the stillborn romance he mourns. It's their friendship.

He misses having a cohort to share absurd anecdotes with and distract from the cold, dark winter afternoons with laughter.

He's angry at himself for botching a pure, true bond through a foolish grasp for love, but he sees no way to repair the situation. There is no turning back the clock.

Over the years he has snapped thousands of photographs, momentarily freezing children in place, trapping them in a brief oasis from time's forward arrow. It's a feint.

Photos present the illusion of stillness. The real thing is nowhere to be found.

He said what he said to Josie. It's too late to take it back. It's too late for their friendship to be what it once was.

A month passes. Two months.

The tension between Blake and Josie is still solid but there are intermittent signs of a thaw.

She stands with Bonnie, making fun of a returned retake portrait of a blonde boy in a sombrero, an offensive image in a number of ways. Blake laughs unintentionally, immediately regretting his violation of their shared silence. Josie looks at him and smiles for a split second, forgetting herself, pleased by the familiar sound of his laughter. She quickly turns her attention back to Bonnie.

About a week later, Blake issues a passionate defense of *Mad Men* when someone at the office calls the show "boring." Normally, he forces himself to be subdued on debates of cultural opinion, but his affection for the prestige drama is so strong he can't stand idly by and listen to its disparagement. He praises the show's subtle thematic framework, perfectly constructed episodes, and rich character development.

"Blake's right," Josie says from across the office. "*Mad Men* fucking rules."

She gives him a brief nod, as if to say this was too important an issue to remain on the sidelines. He appreciates the united front. Then they look away, each privately embarrassed by each other's gaze.

Several days after that, at a weekly Wednesday meeting, George performs a SmilePosts-themed rap he has written. Ostensibly this is done to raise morale, but Blake suspects that George wrote the rap in his free time and wanted to share it for his own satisfaction, hoping to be met with adulation for his rhymes. It's a surreal, borderline-offensive moment.

"SmilePosts captured that memory successfully / By asking them to pose for us respectfully..." George raps, waving his hands around like a crazy person.

Everyone in the office cringes. Dee looks desperate for a way to pull the plug on the performance, but she is not brave enough to interject.

At once, from opposite sides of the room, Blake and Josie catch each other's eyes. They shake their heads in disbelief. No amount of awkwardness is large enough to prevent them from sharing this unfathomable, once in a lifetime moment. Josie sarcastically bobs her head along to the rap. Blake lamely flashes a peace sign. Josie laughs. They turn back towards George who is now dropping the lyrics, "Middle schoolers making faces with frivolity / But no matter, I'll respond with civility."

It's really not a bad rap, Blake thinks. He looks back towards Josie, but he is unable to get her attention. The moment has passed.

On a Monday in mid-March, Blake walks into the office at the end of a long day and finds a huddle of female co-workers in the middle of the room. There's Bonnie, Dee, Shayla, several newbies, and the seven dwarf customer service ladies from upstairs.

Josie stands in the middle of this horde, holding out her hand, showing off an engagement ring.

Apparently, Nate has finally popped the question.

Josie has never been the type to care about jewelry or diamonds. She would be the last person to ask another woman to see her engagement ring, declaring the whole tradition to be stupid and materialistic. "It's just a dumb little rock," Blake remembered her saying in their second year when a shortly tenured newbie had come into the office, newly engaged, showing off her ring to an excited crowd.

Josie has disregarded her deeply held beliefs in regard to her own ring. She looks at the admiring others and she looks down at her finger and her face glows with pride. Blake knows that it's not the ring itself that gives her so much joy. It's the commitment it represents. She truly loves Nate. He knows that. He has always known that.

He pops his head into the circle.

"Congratulations Josie," he says, casually, but undeniably genuine.

She looks at him. He walks away before she has a chance to respond.

About an hour later, as Blake walks to his car, Josie runs up to him.

She has lingered in the building, talking to the others, walking on air today and eager to share her happiness as people pass through the office.

"Blake," she says.

"Yeah?" he says, taken by surprise.

She hesitates. It seems she has made the impulsive decision to break down the walls between them but has not thought through her conversational plan of attack.

"How are you?" she says.

"I'm good," he says. "How about you?"

"I'm good," she says, far more convincingly than he did.

They are quiet for a moment. He's glad this conversation is happening, but it also makes him nervous.

"I'm really happy for you," he says.

"Thanks," she says. "I miss you," she adds. "I miss my friend."

Blake takes in her sincere, direct olive-branch.

"I miss my friend too," he says, emphasizing "friend" to make it clear his previously declared romantic feelings don't matter. The friendship is the important thing. He really means it.

"Are we good?" she says.

"Yeah. We're good," he says.

She nods her head, approving the motion of returning their friendship back to normal.

He thinks about making a joke of some sort. He doesn't.

"Alright then," she says. "I got to get the hell out of here."

He presumes her meaning is that she has to peel herself away from the office on this particular day. Though she might mean "get the hell out of here" in a larger sense. She might mean that she needs to leave Smile-Posts and move on with her life.

It's impossible to be sure. He has no way of knowing what's going on in her head.

She walks back into the office.

He opens his car door, throws the next day's paperwork into the passenger seat, and heads home. Another day gone. Another one approaching swiftly on its heels.

Blake wakes up the next morning feeling as content as he has in a long time. Patching things up with Josie has relieved a great pressure he wasn't fully aware of until it was gone.

He can smell the earliest inklings of spring squeezing in through his bedroom window. It's the first day on the calendar in which March has shown signs of transitioning from lion to lamb. Still only forty-nine degrees at five-thirty A.M. but he can feel the potential of the rising warmth. The birds outside chirp happily for what seems like the first time in months. The temperature is supposed to get to sixty-five on this day. A blessed sixty-five.

To Blake, there is no more blissful feeling than the first taste of spring weather after a long, cold winter. Relief, he thinks, is an underrated emotion.

He does his morning routine, eats breakfast, checks the internet, makes his lunch, puts on his SmilePosts uniform.

He gets in the car at six-fifteen and hits the road. He needs to be at a middle school that's forty-five minutes away by seven-fifteen, leaving fifteen minutes of spare time for unexpected traffic.

Blake cracks his windows. The early morning air is unconstrained. Soft, cool, undaunted by the sun. He has a realization – over the years he has come to enjoy his early morning drives to work. The empty highways, the sleepy suburbs, the rising city, the isolated buildings in a vast sea of cornfields. He loves to watch the landscape on the side of the highway slowly emerge from the shadows. He enjoys the fog drifting off the fields and the mild orange of the sidelong sun glinting off the blades of grass. Too many of his co-workers combat the mornings harshly, fighting the early hours with coffee, screaming radio DJs, and bitter moods. To them, the air is acrid and unwelcoming. Dawn senses the disposition of those who travel under its gaze, giddy and hospitable to those who embrace it, striking and wary of those who do not. Blake has become in sync with the early morning air. He breathes it in deep and holds it in his lungs.

He arrives at the school along with the sun. It is six-fifty-eight A.M.

He pulls into a visitor's spot and rolls his window all the way down. He pays his respects to the silence that the morning warrants, as the unseen in the surrounding neighborhood awake in their quiet houses. In the early hours before the bustle, the chaos, and the thrum of a typical human day, Blake can detect the forgotten balance of the past. The time when we were a part of the world, instead of its masters.

His mind feels rested and clear. As he waits for his co-workers to arrive and the clock to strike seven-fifteen, he thinks.

He is twenty-eight years old. He has been working at SmilePosts for five years that have passed in the blink of an eye. Often, he has felt that this half-decade has gotten away from him, perhaps completely been wasted. Not this morning. This morning it feels like time well spent.

Blake knows there is a tendency for current feelings to alter one's larger perspective. He feels contented this morning. This present emotion is, in great part, responsible for his positive view of the recent years.

He also knows it's too simple to boil any life path down to a black and white judgment. Working at SmilePosts has contained good and bad aspects, like anything else. This is life, a confusing swirl of pleasure and pain, joy and suffering, peace and stress, boredom and excitement, stillness and motion. All mixed up and existing simultaneously.

Even moments of longing can be satisfyingly beautiful, he thinks as a gentle breeze passes through the open window. He feels blissfully overcome by all that he wants and the crisp, reassuring rewards of all that he has.

Blake is abruptly and surprisingly certain that whenever he leaves SmilePosts – and he will eventually leave – he is going to miss it. In whatever future profession he finds himself, he will look back at this period fondly, possibly regretful that he had to move on.

He'll miss the summers off collecting unemployment, certainly, but he'll also miss the rhythms of the days, the quiet echoes of empty auditoriums, and the tranquil repetition of assembling his equipment, which doubles as satisfying morning exercise. He'll miss the adorable five and six-year-olds smiling at him every day, telling him their private indecipherable stories, all these cute little humans flashing their teeth in cherubic grins. There's something to be said for a profession where people smile at you all day long.

Most of all, he'll miss his co-workers and the camaraderie that exists between them. He'll miss the humorous lunchtime chats, sitting on gym floors, hoping the gym teacher isn't overhearing the wildly inappropriate content of your conversation. He'll miss the retake review sessions, laughing about the ineptitude of quickly fired newbies. He'll miss returning to the office at the end of each day and being greeted as a crucial member of the tribe, appreciated both for his work and for who he is as a person. He'll miss the people there waiting for him.

His fellow picture people. The faces of whom will be long forgotten by the students, though their unheralded work will live on for decades in family photo albums, on the walls of staircases, and in nostalgic social media posts uploaded onto the internet long after the pictures were first taken.

He will remember them, these picture people who come from all around the territory's wide range. All with their own histories and memories. The young, still maintaining hopes and dreams of greatness. The no longer young, successfully settled into contentment, occasionally wondering what happened to the life they once imagined. Like any group, some are happy and some are depressed. There are those to whom life has gifted a lack of substantial problems and those for whom the days provide nothing but struggle. There are those who live in the present – perhaps out of effort, perhaps out of necessity – focusing on the task at hand, doing each day simply what they know they must. They are like any group of co-workers thrown together for any length of time. They complain about the annoying situations that the job presents and they complain about the co-workers they don't like. They form new bonds of friendship and laugh about the hilarious things the children say. They mostly keep their inner worlds to themselves, shielding their true sadness and avoiding discussion of the world's tragedies whenever possible, favoring amusing anecdotes they saw on the internet. A few of them fall for each other and start secret relationships that are nonetheless common knowledge immediately. Some occasionally wonder what's really going on in the minds and private lives of the others they work with, craving a dig beneath the surface. But mostly, they stick to appropriate small talk and try to get through each day as smoothly as possible. They are all inescapably human, making a living by telling others to smile when sometimes it's the last thing they'd like to do.

There is no doubt that the portraits they photograph tell a created story. One of eternal smiles and pastel-colored backgrounds and brand-new outfits from Target. But in a sense, all photographs are creations.

Transpositions of the real world into unrealistic freeze frames that never fully grasp the constantly changing entity that is reality. Why do we pose in any pictures? Why do we smile in them? It's an attempt to capture the best of us. We photograph ourselves as we would like to be and how we hope we are. The picture day people sometimes feel cynical, caught up in personal dramas of which the children are unaware. They might judge the portraits they take as patently ridiculous in their open schmaltz. It doesn't matter. Despite a heap of personal doubt and a cloudiness of fortitude, when the picture day people snap their photographs, they are playing a small part in the battle against the harshness of life itself and coming down firmly on the side of optimism.

"Smile," they say. Please do as they ask. The world could always use more smiles.

ABOUT THE AUTHOR

Jeremy Dorfman is a graduate of New York University's Tisch School of the Arts. Before moving to Los Angeles and working as a TV producer on shows for networks including ABC, NBC, and Netflix, he was employed for many years as a school portrait photographer in the Philadelphia area. He still finds plastic combs in his car. He is the author of the novels *All That Remains* and *Swampy Goes to Prom*, as well as the short story collection *Perfect*.

jdorfman.com

Made in the USA
Las Vegas, NV
20 August 2022